Ripples And Repercussions

A D'Accio Investigations Novel

R. D. Chapman

Copyright © 2026 by Reneé D. Chapman
ISBN: 978-1-968068-08-0

Editor: Ray Rhamey
Cover Design by Seton Ra

Shades of Fall Publishing
www.ShadesOfFall.com

Ripples And Repercussions

D'Accio Investigations #2

Chapter 1

The conversation appeared to be devolving, but the two arguing at the corner table were too far away and the bar's music too loud for me to hear what was being said. I assumed the two guys leaning against the wall behind them were the man's bodyguards as they were razor-focused on the woman. And the way their eyes were narrowing? Things were approaching volatile. One was even fingering that fancy sidearm he was prominently displaying. Smart, considering just how dangerous the female feline shifter snarling at their boss could be.

The woman slammed her fist on the table and spat something the man probably deserved but didn't appreciate. Dodging his arm grab, she pushed up and away. I tried to follow her out the door, but was delayed by three drunks doing some kind of line dance. Finally reaching the sidewalk, I caught a quick glimpse of her as she turned into a dark alley at the end of the block.

I ran, instinct telling me she was heading for Jenson Park, one block away. Naturally, her shifter ears heard my pounding feet behind her and she bolted straight for the greenery at the end of the service lane. I was gaining fast, but she disappeared down a well-worn path between bushes. I plowed to a stop at the park's edge. No way was I following her in. Jenson Park had over a hundred and twenty acres and no nighttime lighting whatsoever.

"Mandy?" I called out on the chance she was eyeballing me through a bush. "I just want to—*son of a pig!*"

My reflexes flattened me to the ground as a snarling tiger sailed through the air above me. I didn't waste time getting up, simply pulled my gun from its holster as I rolled over and aimed square at the cat's right eye as it whirled to face me.

The tiger froze in mid-crouch.

"Mandy Reese? Or should I say, Amanda Rivas?" Her whiskers twitched. "Name's Curt D'Accio. I'm a private investigator. I want to ask a few questions."

I rose carefully to my feet as she apparently gave me some thought. After a few low growls, the tiger morphed back to human. I kept my gun trained on her, even as the woman rose to her feet a minute or so later. I politely kept my gaze above her collarbone.

"You're not one of Tallon's goons?" she asked, suspicion filling both voice and blue eyes.

"That who you were arguing with back at the bar?"

"Yeah, the lying, belly-crawling loan shark. Questions?" she said, folding her arms across her chest.

At least her breasts were covered now. "Which fence did you give the statue to?" Legit pawn shops wouldn't touch something of that high-value, knowing it had to be stolen.

"Statue?"

"The Rearing Stallion. The one you stole from Mr. Androsh."

Her chin jutted out. "Can either of you prove that?"

"Actually, he can," I told her. "He's prepared to give the police your name, er, alias, if he has to go to them—which he doesn't want to do. If he gets it back, he'll forget all about you."

Four seconds of glaring later, her shoulders sagged. "No fence," she replied. "It was a contract job."

Well, crap. "Who for?" No response. "And you're still going to a loan shark?" That statue was worth forty-five thousand—no telling how much on the black market. She should have gotten a fat fee.

"The legal weasel I hired to do an appeal is damn expensive," she finally said, scowling.

"For the brother currently doing life in prison?"

I had run a full background on her after digging out her real name from the alias she'd given my client, then did likewise for her only sibling, a First-Gen tiger. They both had juvenile petty-theft arrests/convictions against them, while Mandy had an additional charges-dropped arrest for assault. Then nothing for either until Aaron Rivas was convicted of murder a couple of years ago. Now his sister was following him into the big time with this theft.

Her eyes flashed and she took a step forward as her tiger released a low growl. "Aaron didn't kill anyone," Mandy snarled. "I'm not going to let him spend his life in prison for something he didn't do. I'll get the money however I can."

"Being argumentative and insulting might make it a tad hard to get a loan," I told her, my tone amused.

"He wanted me to do another job. I didn't like his new terms."

Interesting. "Getting arrested and convicted of grand theft won't help your brother either," I told her. I didn't holster my gun, but I let it drop to my side.

Her chin jutted out again. "You going to turn me in?"

"You haven't given Mr. Androsh much choice." I spotted two wolves trotting into the alley. "Tallon's?" I asked, flicking my gaze over her shoulder.

"No, his are all Zeros," Mandy replied, after giving them a quick glance. She darted past me into the park.

Ah, that explained why she'd taken me for one of his gang members. I holstered my gun. A couple of distinct snaps as bones realigned told me Mandy was putting her fur coat back on. Considering she wouldn't have had time to undress before shifting earlier, that would be the least scandalous way to travel. With Jenson Park being the largest natural area inside the city, it gave shifters a place to run and stretch both limbs and libido. Bagging shredded clothing was part of the job for park employees.

Mandy reappeared as the wolves reached us. She managed a polite *chuff*, despite the purse in her mouth, and they gave a polite *yip* back. They gave me a disdainful sniff before they headed off on their Sunday-night romp in the park. Mandy's tail-flip as she turned to leave was a rude parting gesture. I took a wary step backwards, but she padded away without spraying me with a Gen's ultimate insult.

***

Entering my office the next morning, I stopped dead in front of the coffeepots. Plural. I cast an inquiring look at my secretary.

"I got tired of your grumbling," Diana said a bit primly. "The black pot is your sludge; the white one is safe for the rest of us."

Discreet and efficient, Diana Kylman has been with me since I opened D'Accio Investigations six years ago. She handles everything from office work to hysterical clients in a professional and composed manner, including that incident with a client's knife-wielding husband who was furious with my "meddling." He unwisely turned his back on her. After calmly and expertly applying the baseball bat kept under her desk, she called my lawyer, police, and paramedics. In that order.

"Hallelujah," I said, grinning. No more carting in the occasional thermos of my infamous four-heaping-scoops of coffee to work. Grabbing a large cup, I filled it nearly to the brim and inhaled the rich aroma. Sipping, I turned…and nearly spit it out on a laugh. Diana had her nose pinched.

"Anything else new?" I asked, grinning.

"Office expenses are going up," she returned, mock-serious.

"Worth it. Would you get Sam Androsh on the phone, please?" I asked before heading into my private office. Draped my jacket on my chair and stripped off my holster, placing it and its resident in a drawer. I didn't carry my .357 Ruger all the time. Fortunately, I'd heeded my common sense last night and taken it with me. Stretched, scratched, then headed over to feed Gertie. The thirty-five-gallon fish tank was tucked in the corner between a large bookshelf and an even larger triple-pane window, one of the selling points for leasing this office. I had my computer booted up and logged into by the time Diana signaled Androsh was on the line.

"Morning, Mr. Androsh. I'm afraid I have bad news for you. Your Rearing Stallion statue is probably sitting in a collector's private museum."

"W-what?" he sputtered.

"It was a contract job, not a crime of opportunity. I tracked the thief down last night. According to her, your statue was specifically targeted, undoubtedly for said collector."

"Well, then. If you know that, go get it," Androsh demanded.

"It's not that simple," I told him patiently. "The underground market works on anonymity."

"Well, she handed it to someone. You can damn well *make* her tell you who. Then make them tell you who has my statue."

"If you want to go wrangle with a Second-Gen Siberian tiger, be my guest."

Silence. "Second-Gen…*tiger*?" It was a stunned whisper.

Mandy obviously hadn't told him she was a shifter. Like me, Sam Androsh was a Zero and wouldn't have been able to tell by scent. Apparently, he was uncomfortable at the thought of fangs and claws close to his jugular. Or privates.

Zeros were the humans before Mother Nature started to mix things up. Somewhere along our evolutionary history, children were born with claws, fangs, and increased senses, abilities matching the predators around them. First Generation, the scientists of today labeled them. Then children that could also shift fully into their animal form began appearing around twenty thousand years ago. The Second Generation. The first recorded Third Generation shifter, a wolf and her wereform, was slightly over six hundred years ago. The massive blending of human and animal was still rare and gave everyone else—Zero and Gen alike—the willies. I had never met a were-shifter personally and not sure I wanted to, either.

"As I was saying, anonymity. The only thing not fake in the whole transaction would be the cash changing hands. You'll need to file a theft report with the police to take this any further or file an insurance claim."

"No!" he screeched. "What do I tell them?"

"I'm sure you'll think of something," I said dryly. He'd hired me to avoid involving the authorities. He didn't want it coming out that he'd been 'entertaining' a young woman while his wife and kids were on vacation in the Bahamas. Mandy had gotten access to the whole house, not just the master bedroom. She and the statue had disappeared while he was in the bathroom.

In a tone I'd call spiteful arrogance, he said, "Since you've failed to find and retrieve what I hired you for, I expect a full refund.

And you can count on me informing others about your incompetence."

A year or so ago, I would have responded with a similar arrogance. But events in the past two years had mellowed me as well as putting silver threads in my otherwise dark brown hair.

"I'll refund what's left on your retainer and send it along with your report," I replied, keeping my tone mild. "As for the latter, that will result in a defamation lawsuit, of which confidential details will undoubtedly be exposed to verify—" The line went dead.

Two hours later, I shoved all my notes into a folder. Wandered out to get another cup of coffee. I handed the folder to Diana and told her Mr. Androsh's report and expense list was in her computer's Review directory.

"He'll probably need a refund," I told her, taking a sip. *Ummm*.

Diana would proofread the report, correct any typos, calculate total expenses, and file a paper copy along with all my notes for posterity and computer crashes. To further offset the latter, our Closed directory files were backed up nightly by Alliance Storage Service.

Wandering back to my desk, I rotated my chair to the left and stared unseeing out the window. Wondered what story Sam Androsh would spin…at least for his wife. Falsifying a police report would get him in legal trouble. Wouldn't make his insurance company happy, either. Regardless, I'm sure they'd draw their own conclusions on how a young, good-looking woman had gained access to the house. I took another sip as my thoughts turned to Mandy. Part of me felt sorry for her, believing as she did in her brother's innocence. No one wanted to believe a family member was a murderer, but that certainly did not excuse the stealing. Even for 'good' intentions.

Gave myself a mental shake and moved on to current work. Like tracking down any witnesses to Carol Manning's fender-bender on 42nd Street. She insisted the other driver was the one at fault, though she'd been the one getting a ticket and fined. Now she was being sued by the driver—one Josh Rickman—for whiplash and other physical trauma.

I logged off my computer, donned my jacket, and grabbed my gun and notes. Passing Diana's desk, I told her I was going to go prowl the streets.

I grimaced at her response of "Try to avoid the sewer."

Two weeks ago, I had tracked a runaway First-Gen mastiff teenager to his hideout in an old sewer drainage channel. There were times I still seemed to smell it, even though I'd tossed everything I'd been wearing that day, including a practically new pair of boots. Almost everything, I amended thoughtfully, eyeing my weapon as I tucked it in the top drawer of the cabinet. I made a mental note to give my holster and its leather harness a deep cleaning.

Our filing cabinet was actually a safe. Last year had been a volatile one, my office and filing cabinet getting ransacked. After the third days-long rebuild of paper files, I had purchased a heavy-duty, four-drawer, steel upright safe with a combination lock. The salesman proudly informed me the identical safe was used by the military to store their classified documents.

Hadn't had a problem since.

***

I trudged back into the office at a quarter to five, tired, wet, and a bit out of sorts. The last was from both the late-season thunderstorm that had blown up with little warning and a dearth of witnesses.

Diana stepped out of the small bathroom, a clean coffeepot in each hand. "Sorry, I didn't think you'd be back today."

Bummer. "That's okay," I said, peeling off my jacket. At least my shirt was dry. "Go ahead, I'll lock up."

"You might want to consider using our stash and change," she said, taking in my dripping clothes.

That wasn't a bad idea and headed toward our supply closet.

We kept a selection of sweatpants and T-shirts in various sizes on the bottom shelf. My report on a previous client's husband's shenanigans had caused the Second-Gen cougar to shift in a snit fit, shredding both her clothes and my client chair. Fur-traveling at night was widely accepted but, while not forbidden, it was frowned on during the day. I'd loaned the embarrassed woman my coat and office until a friend showed up with clothes. Diana added the cost of a new chair to her bill.

"By the way," she continued, turning from the coffee bar, "the signed contract from Georgia came in earlier. A second file with Henry Bartel's pertinent information is attached to the email. Both files are printed and on your desk."

Miss Angela Bruhn, the Atlanta-based Pohlman Security Company's HR representative, had called on Friday, requesting a full background and reference investigation for a potential hire that had grown up in the Omaha area. Flattered at the way-out-of-town job, I asked the youngish-sounding woman who had referred me. *"Nobody,"* she'd admitted cheerfully. She'd picked my agency out of the phone book listing *"because I liked your name."*

My ego had taken that as 'whatever works.'

"You'll also find Mr. Androsh's report on your desk," Diana finished.

I grunted out a "thanks," selecting a pair of dark gray pants and a lighter gray T-shirt from the stack. Grabbing a pair of socks, I squished my way into my office and closed the door. Stripping, I dropped everything in a bundle on the floor by the door. Redressed, I left my shoes off, hoping their insides would be somewhat air-dried by the time I needed to leave.

I didn't give Androsh's report more than a cursory scan. Attached my signature at the bottom of the expense sheet to authorize the refund amount then tossed it in my out-basket.

Picking up the Atlanta contract, I scanned it to refresh myself on what I'd agreed to. I grimaced, still not happy with the two-week deadline it specified, as I might have to track down people who'd moved or gone out of business. Miss Bruhn had insisted she couldn't keep Mr. Bartel dangling for longer than that. Pohlman Security was in an expansion phase and needed to quickly fill positions on several new contracts.

The second printout was two pages of names, addresses, past employments, and dates. The company had the candidate list practically everything from birth to now. At least the man hadn't bounced around the country. It appeared he'd gone from the Midwest straight to Atlanta. I only needed to check those that were in our local area, but she'd provided all of it in case I found a link. I was impressed and made a mental note to remember their company for any future need.

I pulled out an empty folder, labeled it, and then inserted the printouts. I'd do my best, especially in light of that huge fee they were paying. But, in two weeks, Miss Bruhn would get whatever I got. I was good, not a miracle worker.

Diana gave a light knock and popped her head in, wishing me good-night. "Oh, tell Angie that recipe she gave me for baked chicken breast turned out great."

"Will do," I replied, waving her off.

Angie was my primary source of street information and a good friend. Back in March, I had spent two weeks sleeping on her couch, hiding from the media storm caused by my meddling, secret father-in-law who'd leaked the news about my brief marriage to Tabitha Chandler. I hadn't announced it, believing the Foundations she'd established were the best places for her estate's wealth. The fantastically good meals Angie had whipped up while I was there had been an unexpected bonus. Whenever she's ready to leave the sex-trade behind, I'll happily back any kind of food-industry endeavor.

Chapter 2

Halfway home, my cell phone rang. It was my brother-in-law's all-around assistant, Brent Carlton, telling me that Russell was in the ICU at Nebraska-Creighton Medical Center. I did a U-turn in the next intersection. While Russell and I weren't exactly friends, we did understand and respect each other. Russell Chandler was a tough Second-Generation wolf. It would take a lot to put him in Intensive Care.

I found a pale-faced Brent sitting in the ICU waiting room. Dried blood colored his jacket and pants. "Brent," I said, alarmed, "shouldn't you be getting attended to?"

He looked blank for a moment, then glanced down. "It's not mine."

My alarm jumped a couple of notches. "What the frigging hell happened?"

"Lightening. Can you believe that?" Brent said with a shaky laugh.

"How bad?"

"Compound fracture on his right arm and I don't know what else. The doctor was to update me after Russell got out of surgery but," he waved a hand in the general direction of the nurses' station, "that's not happened yet."

My jaw set. The nurse looked up as I approached the counter. I identified myself and added, "I'm Mr. Chandler's brother-in-law. Can you provide any information on his condition?"

The nurse gave me a polite smile. "Doctor Brookstein will be out as soon as his patients can spare him."

No telling how long that could be, I thought grumpily, taking the seat next to Brent. "What happened?" I asked again.

"We were at the warehouse on Abbot Drive. Russell had called a meeting with the workers to discuss the new quality control measures being planned. They were quite pleased to learn some of those were recommendations they'd made at a meeting last month," he said with a smile that slowly faded. "Then he and Mr. Browning, the foreman, stepped out on the loading dock for a private chat. It wasn't a direct strike—thank God. More like a sideswipe. The bolt hit a nearby truck waiting to be unloaded. Lit it up like a second sun. And the boom?" Brent shook his head. "Caved in part of the dock wall after blowing Russell and Browning through it. Plenty of blown out windows and ruptured eardrums."

"Yours?" I asked, concerned.

"Right ear; clean perforation. Should heal in time. Mr. Browning is also here," Brent said, nodding toward the ward doors. "He was in even worse shape than the boss." He leaned his head back against the wall and sighed. "At least I'm sure it's not the Chandlers this time," he muttered.

Yeah? Before I could ask for clarification, a man in a doctor's uniform stepped through the ward's double doors. Totally bald and on the short side, five-nine tops, I automatically assessed as we stood. Pale brown eyes regarded us tiredly out of a face lined either from age or regrets. Maybe both.

"I'm Doctor Brookstein. You're both here for Mr. Chandler? Then you'll be happy to know his overall prognosis is good. Plenty of superficial cuts but only a few required stitches. We've set the broken arm, mesh-binding the bone since he's a shifter. The Lichtenberg lines and muscular spasms are transitory and should clear up within a few days. His ruptured eardrums will heal but pose the most significant long-term issue, especially his left ear. It sustained significant damage to the ossicles—the three inner bones. Audiometry tests after he's healed will assess the level of any hearing loss."

I breathed out a sigh of relief. Russell's wolf wouldn't be happy, but partial deafness was livable and would probably still be better than a Zero's. "Can we see him?"

Brookstein shook his head. "He's currently in a Gen's rapid-repair cycle. It'll probably be several days before he's conscious."

Rapid repair had been Mother Nature's boon in a savage world.

The more serious a shifter's injury, the more likely it would kick in, repairing the worst of the cellular damage and replacing blood at an accelerated rate. The downside was vulnerability: the individual often unconscious during it as the body redirected its energy. Then, at some undetermined milestone known only to itself, it switched off and regular healing took over. It had very little effect on bones. However, depending on the shifter and the break's location, careful shifting over several days could heal them. Usually. Would it work on those tiny inner ear ones?

The doctor must have been thinking along the same lines.

"Shifting is out until I'm certain the arm has healed enough to not cause more damage," Brookstein said firmly.

That's why he'd used mesh instead of pins. The latter would

interfere with a Gen's shift. I had seen pictures of unfortunates that had tried it. The glued netting would eventually dissolve, absorbed either naturally or spontaneously during a shift.

"Then you'd best tell him that as soon as his eyes open," Brent replied dryly.

"I'll do that. The other lightning-strike patient that came in with him. You know him?"

"Yes," Brent confirmed. "Mr. Browning is a company employee. How is he doing?"

"I'm sorry. We lost him about a half hour ago," Brookstein said. "He went into cardiac arrest and we couldn't reverse it. Does he have family?"

Brent's mouth opened, closed. His throat bobbed from a hard swallow. "An ex-wife; no kids. Parents. I-I'll contact…someone."

"If you'll have them call the hospital's Administration Office, they can help with the procedures for releasing the body."

It was said so matter-of-factly, I started to snap at him. Until I noticed that the lines around his mouth were a little bit deeper. Another regret added to his list. "We'll do that," I told him instead. "Thank you."

Giving us a brief nod, Dr. Brookstein disappeared back inside his domain.

I took a dazed Brent by the arm and ushered him down the hallway and into an elevator. We were stopped several times by concerned staff on seeing his bloody clothes, but we finally made it out to the parking lot.

"Sorry," Brent said, leaning against my car. "This is so unreal. I mean, we were all talking, discussing business a few hours ago. Now? Russell is in ICU and Mr. Browning is dead."

"It can knock you off your feet," I agreed, then winced at the bad choice of words. "I'll drive you home."

"Thanks, but to the warehouse instead? My car's there since I rode to the hospital with Russell." He sighed. "And there are things there I need to take care of anyway."

"By the way, what was that comment about the Chandlers?" I asked, going around to the driver's side.

"Oh. Nothing. Forget it," he said, waving a hand before plopping down in the passenger's seat.

"Uh-uh. Give," I said, sliding under the steering wheel.

Brent stared out the side window. "Just something that happened a few weeks ago," he said.

"Like what?" By now, intrigue and a bit of worry had joined curiosity. When nothing was forthcoming, I crossed my arms. "This car is not moving until I get an answer." After a couple of seconds, Brent's gaze turned back to me.

"Russell was on a night run through Jenson Park and was ambushed by three Gens in their animal forms: two wolves and a panther."

My eyes narrowed. "Panther?" I repeated. The Chandler family had a strong leaning toward that form.

"Russell said he didn't recognize any of them and, no, the cat didn't have a Chandler family scent. Fortunately, a couple of bear siblings were nearby, saw the attack and waded in to help beat them off. No idea of the who or why." He glanced sideways. "But we did wonder."

"What's Russell's issue with the Chandlers?"

He shrugged. "The same it's been for years. They believe Chandler Import should belong to a *true* Chandler, not some upstart whose mother *connived* their way into the family."

Russell had been eight when Stephen Chandler married Cynthia

Greenbaum and legally adopted him, much to the dismay of his uptight family. From all I'd heard, the man had treated Russell as if he was his natural son. His mother had fought off several of her in-laws' attempts to take over the company after Stephen died in a skiing accident. Evidently those frigging assholes were at it again.

"They've been demanding seats—plural—on the board," Brent continued, "and high-placed positions in the company itself. I wasn't supposed to say anything," he said, chagrin lacing his words. "Russell didn't want to get you involved."

"Why the hell not?"

Brett shrugged. "There's no proof the Chandlers were behind the attack, and, truthfully, it's hard to believe they'd go that far. I could see them trying to intimidate Russell, but the damn cat almost severed his jugular," Brett bit out harshly.

Unfortunately, Russell and I were both aware of the extremes a person could go to. "Was there a police report filed?"

"Yes, but he insisted on keeping it out of the news. He also paid the bears' doctor bill. The sister was a First-Gen and her wounds were worse than her Second-Gen brother's."

Fuming, I cranked the engine, wishing I hadn't left my weapon back in the office safe. "If the Chandlers are involved, who do you suspect the most?"

Without hesitation, he told me "Darrell Chandler, Stephen's oldest brother. He's a conniving, cold-hearted rattler. Except he doesn't give a warning before striking."

The drive to the warehouse was made in silence. Dropping Brent off with a "thanks and keep me posted" admonition, I headed home. Russell didn't want me involved? Because of our stilted relationship? Well, too bad, I was. I even called the Greenbaums, his biological grandparents in Lincoln, and relayed Dr. Brookstein's upbeat prognosis. They thanked me profusely and asked to be kept informed.

<u>Chapter 3</u>

The next morning was busy. After hammering out a report for a case I'd finished last Thursday, I opened Stephen Reynald's file. He was a lawyer from next door. Claybourn, Wieberg, Blacksmith and Associates provided a semi-steady flow of income, with requests that were generally quick background checks. I gave them a flat rate, which they reciprocated for minor legal actions I might require, like notices to delinquent ex-clients. If the needs of either party went outside the usual, discounted rates were applied. A quick scan confirmed I could pound out his task in a couple of hours.

I was almost done when Diana stuck her head in my doorway.

"I'm heading off for lunch," she announced. "I'll stop by Omaha Police Department on my way back and pick up Russell Chandler's assault report."

OPD wouldn't share anything on their investigation, which would still be open, but the assault report was public record. A quick check showed it was 11:05 and my stomach rumbled its desire.

"Would you mind picking up a couple of mushroom burgers and fries from Runza on your way back? Mr. Reynalds put a rush on this background check."

"Will do. You have a one o'clock appointment with a Mr. Victor Thoreen," she said, "and Mr. and Mrs. Kurt—with a 'K'—Filbrandt at two-thirty. Good luck with that one."

I was still scowling when the bell tinkle over the outer door signaled her exit. When both spouses showed up, it usually meant their issue was sensitive, emotional, or messy. Quite often, a combination of any or all three.

Reynald's report and my lunch were both finished shortly before Mr. Thoreen arrived. My potential client appeared to be in his mid-fifties with shrewd eyes and a shock of white-blond hair against pale skin. He was also a canid shifter of some sort.

I can tell if someone is a shifter—I call it my Generation radar: Gen-dar for short. I know their species and sometimes their actual form, though not their Gen-level. Wolves are the easiest to spot, which is probably due to their natural aggressiveness. However, there was one annoying individual my internal radar stubbornly remained silent about on both species and form. I couldn't look up his vital stats, either. If I tried, I'd be getting a visit from a stern-faced person asking why as soon as they saw the flag in the database log. Police were among those that required special permissions to view their data. Not that I blamed them, understanding the reasons.

"What can I do for you, Mr. Thoreen?"

"I'm Russell Chandler's attorney."

My back stiffened. Surely, I'd have heard if Russell had taken a turn for the worst. Not to mention… "Did you replace Marlee Heiser?" That's the name on the documents Russell kept sending me.

"No. She handles his corporate business. I handle all his personal business, and, before your knuckles get any whiter, Mr. Chandler is on the mend. His blood pressure and blood count have stabilized and Doctor Bullard expects him to exit rapid repair sometime tomorrow."

I relaxed. "Thank you for that. I don't understand why you're here, then. Mine and Russell's personal lives are totally separate."

"Too much so, in my opinion," he replied forthrightly. "However, Mr. Chandler has designated you as both Guardian and Conservator in the event he is incapacitated in some manner. Unconscious in ICU meets that criterion," he added dryly.

"I'm flattered," I managed. Surprised, actually. "But you'd be more qualified to handle his affairs than me."

"Mr. Chandler has a deep respect for you and your ethics. In light of your history, I have to agree with his assessment. I will, of course, advise and monitor as needed. He has also appointed you as his proxy for all things relating to business. I've so informed Miss Heiser. She's expecting you in her office at Chandler Import Headquarters at seven o'clock this evening."

I had moved past surprised to stunned. "What? Why?"

"She'll provide a full summary on the company later. Tonight, you'll need a quick briefing on the issues coming before the board when it meets at eight."

I slumped back in my chair and gave him a horrified look. "Tonight?"

"Tonight," he echoed, amused. He reached into his briefcase and pulled out a legal-sized envelope. "This contains a copy of both the conservatorship and proxy appointments. I recommend you take it with you to the meeting."

I ran a hand across my face. "Mr. Thoreen. I appreciate this, really, but it's completely out of my area of expertise. I haven't even been to a board meeting in months."

Mr. Thoreen stood. "You can take that up with Miss Heiser.

Have you ever met her? No?" His eyes suddenly twinkled. "My advice? Don't start off your association by being late."

I escorted him out into the main office and headed for coffee as soon as he was out the door. Wishing I had something even stronger to add to it, I poured a full cup. Turning, I found Diana giving me a quizzical look.

"New client?" she asked.

"Nope." Leaning against her desk, I told her about my new obligations. Expecting the same surprise I'd felt, she merely nodded and said, "Makes sense." A bit miffed, I returned to my desk and used the time before my next appointment to read Russell's police report.

The Filbrandts' problem did indeed meet all three of my usual assessments. Kurt Filbrandt was partner and half-owner of Maddox & Filbrandt Accounting Services on the ninth floor of the Woodworkers Union Tower. Five months ago, he entered Omaha's mayoral race. The Filbrandts believed he was being set-up for a smear campaign.

About two weeks ago, according to Filbrandt, he was having lunch at *Midtown Café* when a young woman plopped down at his table without an invite. She introduced herself as Rosalie Sayer and said she represented a group interested in hearing his views on several key issues. He'd politely answered her questions— reasonable questions, he admitted. As she went to leave, she'd leaned over and placed a hand on his arm, smiling, and thanking him for his time while apologizing for interrupting his lunch.

Then, last night, he was approached by the same woman in the Tower's underground parking lot after another late night of political plotting with his campaign manager. She spoke briefly with him, asking how his campaign was running. Then she appeared to stumble and he automatically reached out to steady her. She immediately pressed herself up against him and kissed him soundly on the lips.

His anger on a tight leash, Filbrandt said, "Shocked surprise held me for a couple of seconds before I pushed her away. She smiled and said, 'Hope your golf game is better', then patted me on the cheek and sauntered away. *Smiled* at me over her shoulder. That's when I saw the photographer half hidden several rows over. He climbed into a dark blue vehicle and took off. This, this Rosalie Sayer left just as fast—a brown car. Since she was the same woman from the luncheon, I'll bet there's photos of that, too."

I'd lay money on it. Looking up from my notepad, I asked, "And you've never met this young lady—" Mrs. Filbrandt went from Zero to Gen in one breath. Her lower face elongated slightly and she jabbed a claw in my direction.

"Doo naw caw 'hat 'ramp laady," she managed around a mouth full of fangs.

Her husband reached over and clasped a paw. "Remember your promise," he admonished her. "My wife's First-Gen tendency is to shift when her emotions run high," he explained, as her features morphed back to human. The fire that had blazed in her golden fox eyes still burned in her human brown ones.

"I'm working on it, but I refuse to apologize in this instance," she said, her tone brusque.

"I can't blame you," I said. "The most obvious reason, of course, is one of your opponents or an overly exuberant member of their staff. Or a family member. However," I cautioned, "we can't rule out old-fashioned blackmail by enterprising con artists taking advantage of your political endeavors or an unscrupulous competitor."

Mr. Filbrandt's expression turned even more sour.

Mrs. Filbrandt leaned forward, practically vibrating in her chair. "We need you to find stone-solid proof he was deliberately targeted with manipulated lies. Proof both the newspapers and our lawyers can validate to squash any future whispers."

At least she hadn't shifted.

"It's not just about my campaign," Kurt said heavily. "It will impact my personal and business reputations. Whispers, the sideways glances my family and business associates will have to endure."

"Understood," I said, nodding. "I'll start by researching the other mayoral candidates and staff. And Rosalie Sayer. It's probably an alias but it's a starting point. Contact me immediately when you're contacted by the extortionists," I added, jotting down my personal number on a business card.

"You don't believe they'll release them to the public first?" Mr. Filbrandt asked shrewdly.

"No. Whether it's about knocking you out of the race or a straight blackmail attempt, they'll wait to see if you'll withdraw or pay up. Or request both." One enterprising way to fund a political campaign if that was what's behind it.

I went over the contract details, accepted their retainer check, and escorted them out. Back in my chair, I leaned my head back and stared unseeing at the ceiling. Russell, I'd keep an eye on. Then there's Bartel, Thoreen, Heiser, an awkward board meeting, and now a politically hot case. And it was only Tuesday.

Not to mention, I still had Carol Manning's fender-bender case to squeeze in somewhere. The clock got a quick glance. Great. I had gotten the complainant's address from the DMV and wanted to surveil him for a bit. Josh Rickman lived in a nice suburb, so my two-seater sports car shouldn't stand out too much.

***

I arrived promptly at Miss Heiser's office at six fifty-five in a nice suit, sans Ruger. I'd left it at home as coming armed probably wouldn't make the right impression. She gave me a quick rundown of the six board members and the items currently under discussion. *"Things you would know if you had bothered to attend meetings,"* she had growled at me. Yep, she was most definitely a wolf. And, yes, maybe I should have. I'd inherited twenty-five percent of the company from Tabitha's estate.

The news of our marriage had thrown it back into probation and the Chandler family into shock. By the time everything was settled, I had a life-long stipend as well as the shares, but had managed to keep everything else pretty much how Tabitha wanted.

Miss Heiser also had the time to throw in a couple of company contracts for review. There were sentences, whole paragraphs she'd have to explain and—honestly—I'm still not sure I understood everything. I just signed where indicated and hoped Russell didn't beat me over the head with them later.

We walked into the boardroom with five minutes to spare and found two extra people. Recognizing them, I wished I had brought a weapon.

"What are you two doing here?" Miss Heiser demanded.

"They're trying to cancel the meeting," a slim, middle-aged woman said, scowling.

"We *are* canceling it," Darrell Chandler said arrogantly. "With my nephew incapacitated for the foreseeable future, I'm assuming control of Chandler Import."

Really? When the assholes usually refused to recognize Russell as family? Or had done anything to help build the company?

"You two pompous assholes don't have that authority," Heiser told him coldly.

Good for you, Miss Heiser.

Malice flashed in both men's eyes. Trace Chandler took a step forward, but his father pulled him back. With a nasty smile spreading across his face, Darrell pulled a folded-up paper from his inner pocket. Tossed it on the table. "This is to serve notice from my lawyers. They are drawing up papers to appoint me as conservator of all Russell's assets until such time as he is deemed able to resume his responsibilities."

A condition I bet they hoped never happened.

"Unenforceable and unnecessary," Heiser said, meeting his nasty smile with one of her own. "Mr. D'Accio is filling that position."

All eyes zipped to me.

"Unacceptable," Darrell sneered. "He's not even a member of the family."

I tossed Mr. Thoreen's envelope on the table next to Darrell's paper. Stanford Dawson grabbed it and pulled out its contents. Those on both sides of him leaned over to read it, too.

"I've been appointed as Russell's guardian, conservator, *and* proxy," I said flatly. "Despite your narrow and selective interpretation of *family*, I am Russell's brother-in-law. I'm also part owner of Chandler Import."

"These papers were filed six months ago," Dawson said, his expression as neutral as his voice. So was the quick look he shot at Darrell, whose expression definitely wasn't. Poleaxed would be a good description.

"Mr. Chandler was being proactive," Miss Heiser confirmed. "After his mother's death, he took steps to ensure the company—all his assets—would be protected in the event something happened to him. Mr. D'Accio's roles are currently temporary but will become permanent if the worst happens."

I kept my dismay hidden. Mr. Thoreen hadn't mentioned that.

"That, that's not right," Trace sputtered as his father's face turned a deep red. "That effectively gives him one hundred percent ownership of Chandler Import."

"Temporary *control*, not ownership," I stressed. "The doctor is confident Russell will make a full recovery."

"You've held up this meeting long enough. Leave," Miss Heiser said brusquely. "I can call Security for an escort if you prefer."

In two breaths, Darrell's expression went from near apoplexy to a cold promise of future retaliation. Shooting an unreadable look at Dawson, he stomped out. Glaring at me through vicious slits, it was obvious Trace hadn't slithered far from the nest. He stalked out after his father.

Instinct told me we'd be brawling in the future.

"Watch your back," Heiser said bluntly as she motioned me forward.

I took the seat at the head of the table. She sat to my right. Stanford Dawson slowly folded up the sheets of paper, placed them back into the envelope, and then slid it down to me.

Clearing my throat, I glanced around the table. "Okay, this meeting is now open." There was a muffled snort. "In session." Whatever. "You all know me, Curt D'Accio. Let's start by introducing yourselves." I had recognized Stanford Dawson because Russell had dated his daughter up until last summer. Considering the exchange I'd just witnessed, he has apparently now aligned himself with Darrell.

Introductions over, I gave them an hour to have their say on whatever subject was firing them up and then called it done. I also declared the next meeting on hold until further notice, which would be after I talked with Russell. They weren't happy. Excellent. Neither was I.

Chapter 4

I was in the office bright and early, needing to get as much done on the Atlanta job as possible before the Filbrandt case went hot. Which it would. The blackmailers-slash-extortionists wouldn't wait long to make their demands.

"This is a surprise." Diana stood in my office doorway, hands on hips.

"Got a lot to do," I told her, glancing up.

I hadn't beaten her by much, just long enough to get coffee started and make a couple of phone calls. According to the ward nurse, Russell Chandler was still unconscious but stable. As I feared, the *Midtown Café* deleted their security videos after seven days. No help there, but I knew that my next phone call would be. Woodworkers Security kept their video files archived for six months, permanently for issues like my ambush last year by a Second-Gen tiger in full fur. It had helped support my claim of self-defense. Fake Rosalie and her camera partner had to have staked the parking area out multiple nights, waiting to catch Mr. Filbrandt alone.

Diana set a cup down on my desk as I hung up with Security Chief Tomason. I pulled it to me gratefully. "Diana, no new appointments this week, please. I'm maxed out and chances are I'll be out more than in."

"Good. I can catch up on admin work," she said, head dipping in a nod.

After several revitalizing sips, I started pounding out my report for Carol Manning. Unable to find any witnesses to contest the accident, she was stuck with the fine. At least the pictures I'd taken of Josh Rickman and his two sons playing soccer in their backyard would get the lawsuit tossed. After handing everything off to Diana, I gave Miss Manning a call to update her. Promised her both report and pictures would be in her email later today.

I settled in and started my usual background checks for Mr. Bartel.

The modern age had helped simplify that process with a lot of public databases. *Too many*, Grandpa D'Accio often grumbled. Citizens could fill out the ubiquitous government forms for the requested information. Law enforcement was able to log directly into them using their name and badge number. Several years ago, Nebraska had become one of the few states that extended that courtesy to private investigators with active licenses, but only for its local and state databases. Getting Federal and another state's information still required forms.

According to vital statistics, Henry Bartel was thirty-two, a First-Gen jackal, with no marriage or kids listed in local records. Found nothing of real interest, although he did have a police and court record. I doubt the teenaged speeding ticket and fender-bender would be held against him. After updating my notes, both paper and digital, I pulled out Mr. Bartel's reference list and started making calls. If I was lucky, I could interview at least half of them by phone.

***

Luck was not on my side. By midafternoon I'd worked my way down the list and only had about a fourth of them checked off. One person had relocated to somewhere in the Dakota Territory, according to her ex-husband. The current manager of one of Bartel's previous places of employment had no clue where the previous manager had disappeared to.

"Disappeared?" I'd asked, curious at the man's turn of phrase.

"Yep, and that's all I'll say," the man said before hanging up.

Hmmm. The note I made beside Mr. Cassell's name was to check police and court records. My next call was to Merle Smith. I offered to buy her dinner if she would give me a rundown on the mayoral candidates. I wanted more information about Filbrandt's competitors than their PR verbiage.

"What kind of case are you working on?" she asked, unable to hide her interest.

Merle was a reporter for the Omaha-Herald. Marge Lockewild, my childhood friend and all-but-blood sister, used to be my journalist contact. She was murdered last year by a narcissistic sociopath. Merle had taken over both Marge's position at the paper and as one of my resources.

"Now, Merle, you know I can't divulge that."

"No, you can't tell me about your client. I asked what kind of case it was."

"It touches on the mayoral race, which is all I'll say and why I'd like to know more about it."

"You'll give me the info when the case is closed?" I hesitated and she crooned, "*Ooooo*, that tells me it's a sensitive one. Hinky shenanigans at the campaign office?"

I never have learned who nicknamed her 'Marshmallow Merle.' Talk about a misnomer. The woman was sharp and as tenacious as a badger digging its dinner out of the hole said meal had fled into.

"It will be up to the client and how the case turns out to determine what's releasable," I told her firmly. "Dinner?"

"Deal. Meet you at *Cajun Louie's* at six."

Good choice. My mouth was already watering at the thought of *Louie's* specials.

I shrugged into my jacket and gathered up my notes, planning to stop by Woodworkers Tower's security office first. I'd requested copies of the last three weeks of video recordings in their underground parking lot, and they should be ready by now.

I was barely in my car when Diana called me. Amanda Rivas was on the office line. She refused to make an appointment, refused to come to the office, yet claimed it was important that she speak with me. My initial reaction was surprise, followed by curiosity, so I told Diana to get a rendezvous spot and I'd meet her there.

Twenty-five minutes later, I was parked outside of *JoJo's Place*. On the one-to-ten scale for bars on Nineteenth Avenue, *JoJo's* was a five…ish. At this time of day, I was reasonably sure my car and tires would still be here when I came back out. Inside, the tables were sparsely populated. Still, there were enough hard stares to make my shoulders twitch.

No sign of Amanda, so I walked up to the bar and ordered a beer from the hard-eyed woman that gave off the vibe of a large feline. JoJo? She plopped it down in front of me.

"You the PI suit meeting someone?"

Interesting. No names. "Yes."

She gave a head jerk to the left. "Second door past the johns."

Tossing a bill down for the drink, I wandered down the hallway. Eyed the indicated door for a moment, finally deciding this wasn't the right place for a setup or ambush. Still, I pushed the door completely open before stepping into what was, surprisingly, a small conference room. A rectangular table with eight chairs took up most of the room, with an extra chair in each corner.

Amanda sat in one of the chairs facing the door. In her early-thirties, her average-sized frame was dressed conservatively in a long-sleeved sweater and black slacks. Her dark brown hair brushed her shoulders.

I took a seat at one end, which kept the door in my viewing range, too. "Must be some interesting meetings held in here."

"*JoJo's* is neutral territory." Her long fingers picked at the label on her beer bottle. "People can meet, exchange information or hash out a solution to issues between them." She paused. "Keeps the body count down."

Bet the corner seats were for bodyguards then. "Does it? Out of curiosity, how can that be guaranteed? I mean, tempers flare, things don't go the way someone wants and, presto, instant brawl."

Amanda's smile didn't reach her eyes. "The one and only time that happened, it didn't go well for both parties," she said without elaborating.

Something to keep in mind, then. "What can I do for you, Miss Rivas?"

After a moment of hesitation, she said, "I've asked around about you. You've got a reputation."

I do?

"Word is, you're good at what you do," she continued, "that you play straight and fair. And you're rich," she added with a touch of defiance.

"You want me to *pro bono* something?"

"No," she said forcefully. "I intend to pay your bill, just not all at once. You can afford to take installments."

I had a sudden inkling of where this was going.

"I want to hire you to prove my brother did not murder that old woman."

Yep, thought so. I eyed her for several seconds. "It's hard to believe something like that of a family member. What makes you so sure that he didn't?"

Her chin came up. "Dad died in an accident, then Mom took sick with cancer. I've basically raised my younger brother since I was fourteen." Her fist slammed into her chest. "I *know* him. I *know* he's not lying. My brother may be a thief, but he's not a murderer."

The wariness, the nerves had disappeared. Conviction filled her voice and fire blazed in those dark blue eyes. Amanda was still looking after her brother.

"What happened to your lawyer?"

She scowled. "That piranha? I fired him. He wanted more money and had nothing to show for what I had already paid him."

"Before I decide anything," I crossed my arms, "tell me about Aaron."

"Health services barely covered Mom's medicine and doctor visits. We had to come up with ways to earn money for food and such. Aaron," she sighed, "turned out to be a natural thief."

I nodded, having seen their police records. "There wasn't anyone else who could help?"

Amanda snorted derisively. "Our only other relative was an alcoholic that lived in the bottle. Died there, too. After I turned seventeen and started working as a street prostitute, he hit me up for a, quote-unquote, loan."

Street walker was the lowest ranking in the sex trade, but the easiest to get into. The license only required one to be of legal age and maintain regular health checkups.

"We did okay for a few years." She paused. "Mom managed to hang on long enough to see Aaron graduate. I was twenty. We stumbled along for a couple of months then, suddenly, it was Aaron's seventeenth birthday. We had a long discussion about robbery penalties as an adult versus as a juvenile. He went to a trade school and became a mechanic—a damn good one," Amanda said proudly.

"And still stealing," I added, and gave her a pointed look that said, "*and you.*"

Her cheeks flushed a mild pink. "That was my first theft in years and I told you why," she replied defensively. "But, yes, Aaron would occasionally pad his income with, uh, extracurricular jobs."

The guy had to have been good. I'd found no arrests since he hit legal age.

"I'd finally, *finally* talked Aaron in to stopping. Too risky. Given his age and history, a judge would probably give him the max sentence if caught. Then…" her jaw tightened, "Tallon offered him a very large sum to steal the Rembrandt. Aaron swore to me he'd only taken the job to fund opening his own repair shop."

"So, Tallon is a broker as well as a loan shark?"

"Maybe," she hedged. "Or he tried using my brother to fill a posting himself. I do know Tallon's been running his own theft ring for several years now. He must immediately pawn or sell the stuff on the black market because they've never been caught with the goods."

After a moment's debate, I pulled my notebook out. "What's Tallon's full name?"

"Clayton. Clayton Tallon. His middle one is probably *bastard.*"

"Okay, now tell me about the theft-murder."

"The Rembrandt was different from all the others. I think it was the first time Tallon had specifically targeted a theft for the black market or that high-value. For a collector, no doubt, which is why he contacted my brother. He was counting on Aaron's reputation to get it for him."

Amanda sighed, took a long swallow of beer. I let the silence stretch and waited.

Finally, fingers laced together around the bottle, she continued. "Aaron spent a week checking out the house and grounds. Spotted a flaw in their security and spent several mornings in a tree with binoculars. Because the security panel was viewable from that angle," she said when both of my eyebrows went north. "He'd watch the two staff females inputting the security code. It took that long to get the correct numbers and sequence since one of them would sometimes be blocking his, uh, sight.

"Long story short, Aaron disabled the alarm and pried open the den window. He had just taken the Rembrandt off the wall when the lights suddenly flicked on. Old lady Agatha herself stood in the doorway. Aaron bolted for the window, figuring he'd get away before she woke the house with screaming. Except things got crazy. She didn't scream; *she* attacked Aaron."

Startled, I looked up from my notepad. "She went clawed?"

"Hell, no. She grabbed a statue off a small table and started in on him. So, he's dodging around the room, trying to get to the window. He took several blows on his arms because he was protecting the painting. Which, oddly enough, Aaron said she didn't seem too worried about. At that point, Aaron said to hell with the job, dropped it, wrestled the statue away from the crazy woman, and shoved her away from him. *Shoved*," she repeated forcefully.

Leaning forward, Amanda looked me in the eye. "He swears, on our mother's grave, that he *never…never* once hit that old woman with that statue, and she was alive when he dove out the window."

"That was the murder weapon?" She nodded. "Is it possible that he did and, maybe, doesn't remember?" I asked, trying to be neutral. Her returning glare sure wasn't.

"No," she said, her eyes turning the gold of her cat. "But if he had clipped her with it," she added, her tone vindictive, "the old goat would have deserved it since she was doing her best to brain him."

"Okay," I agreed warily. Pissing her tiger off would not be a good idea. "Were there other people in the house?"

"Yes, several relatives." Amanda's eyes returned to normal. "As she never screamed, they weren't alerted in any way as far as Aaron could tell."

Huh. Why didn't she? "So, you believe someone else—someone in the house—killed Mrs. Mulligan after your brother fled and it was blamed on the robber. When and who found her body?"

"She was found next morning by the house staff who'd arrived as usual. Which means anyone in the house could have come down after Aaron, seen what had happened and taken advantage of it, undoubtedly for greedy reasons. Mrs. Mulligan was rich."

Only way to afford a Rembrandt. "How did the police link your brother to the crime?" A professional thief would have worn gloves and taken other precautions.

"Long fingernails."

I winced. Been there, felt that.

"She ripped his shirt, scratching Aaron when he wrestled the statue away. Then there were his arms; she'd whacked him good a couple of times."

DNA retrieved from under her nails would have been on file from his younger days. That history, plus the bruises, would have equaled an open-and-shut case as far as the authorities were concerned.

"Due to that, Aaron wasn't too surprised when he was arrested. He figured the worst would be a breaking-and-entering charge since he didn't actually steal the painting. Maybe an assault charge he could argue down to self-defense. But murder?" Amanda shook her head. "One day. His trial lasted one day and his public defender was basically useless. Will you help us?"

The silence stretched as I debated. If all she'd told me was true, including knowing when her brother lied, Aaron had gotten a bad deal. I saw resignation in her eyes and suddenly realized I was her next-to-last option. If I turned her down, which I'm pretty sure she more-or-less expected, she'd go back to Tallon. Amanda would press on, risking her own freedom to fight for her brother's. Something deep inside me resonated with that determination.

"I will take your case, Amanda, but it will be contingent on three things."

She straightened. Hope replaced resignation.

"First, never lie to me—you or your brother. This case will be hard enough without having to fight that."

"I promise, for both of us," she swore. "And call me Mandy."

"Second, I'll only work on the murder charge. The breaking and entering stands."

Mandy shrugged. "That charge was dropped."

I frowned. "That doesn't make sense. The B&E is what leads to the murder."

"Oh, they brought it up," Mandy scoffed, "but only in passing. Why bother with a few years when a murder conviction will get life? Third?"

That did make sense. "I'll take payments, but they'll be honest money," I told her firmly. "No stealing."

She scowled. "You don't have to worry about that. If I had decided to go that route, I'd be at *Burton's Hangout* sitting across from Tallon instead of here with you. However, about those payments? There might be," she cleared her throat, "a gap between them."

Uh-huh. Meaning Mr. Androsh had filed that police report and there was a warrant out. Explained why she wouldn't come to my office. I wasn't surprised to find Mandy's contact information was a CC, a cheap cash-and-carry phone easily disposed of. I did give her the side-eye when told I could also leave a message with JoJo.

"Mandy. You need to understand something," I cautioned, using my most serious tone. "Given the circumstances, it may be impossible to prove your brother didn't kill Mrs. Mulligan. Our best scenario might be finding evidence that indicates one or more other people also had opportunity and motive. Even then, there's still no guarantee the district attorney will set a new trial or overturn Aaron's conviction."

"Unless you can prove conclusively that he didn't do it and who did," she responded eagerly.

I flashed her a smile. "I appreciate the confidence. I'll do my best."

Back in my undisturbed car, I added a few notes and to-do items into my notebook. Checked the time, then the addresses on Mr. Bartel's reference list. Great, two of them were between me and *Cajun Louie's*. I could knock them out before my meeting with Merle. And I still needed to stop by Woodworkers Tower for copies of their security videos.

***

I exited the elevator on my floor, unlocked and entered my apartment, my mind already focusing on the upcoming video fest.

Bolting the door, I turned and nearly jumped out of my skin. Raynor Silverstone. Sitting in my recliner, drinking my scotch. "What are you doing here?" I blurted out.

"It's our anniversary." That earned him a blank look. "It's been a year since we last talked, shared your excellent scotch. Remember?"

"You knew what coming to me could entail."

"I want justice."

Yeah, and a strong drink sounded good. Dumping my briefcase and the box of disks on the kitchen table, I collapsed onto the couch opposite him. He poured a second glass from the bottle on the coffee table and handed it to me. Took a healthy sip. Sighing, I leaned back and let the day's frustrations melt away.

We sipped quietly, neither of us apparently needing to talk. My mind wandered, reflecting on the past year's events. Was he, too? After all, he'd caused a lot of it. And there was this *one* tiny thing I had been wondering about.

Clearing my throat, I asked, "Why an accident?"

Last February, Cynthia Chandler's car had careened down a steep incline in the Loess Hills. Icy roads and bad luck were the assumed culprits, as she ended up dying from blunt force trauma after being thrown out of the car. Officially.

"I, uh, sort of expected more along the line of a bullet through the head." Or finding her ripped into pieces.

Raynor's voice turned hard. "I wanted her to see my face. I wanted her to die at my hands. I took great satisfaction in slamming her head against that rock. Not as satisfying as ripping it off would have been, but less problematic. Cynthia's wolf could be a hell of a fighter when she chose, and it would have been a bloody battle."

Which would have left his DNA all over the place.

"Are you in town on business?" Crap. I couldn't believe I asked that. *It had to have been the scotch*, I swore silently, scowling down at my half empty glass.

"No. In fact," Ray polished off his drink, "I've decided to retire. Return to my roots here in Omaha. We can do this more often," he added nonchalantly.

Let's not. I emptied my glass in two swallows.

He suddenly grinned. "No response? Lynx got your tongue?"

I shrugged. "Not really much I can or should say."

"That's one of the things I like about you—your honesty," he replied, rising.

I politely walked him to the door.

"Darrell and Trace Chandler are determined to take over Chandler Import. At least one of the board members is working with them," Ray warned before stepping through.

He was keeping tabs on me?

I watched him walk to the elevators with the graceful fluidity of his cat. He was a Second-Gen Lynx. He was Wolfbane. The name whispered with respect and fear, if at all, among the denizens of the streets and bars. Few knew the real identity of the deadliest of assassins. Even fewer knew he was my father-in-law. Tabitha's mother had gone to great and bloody lengths to keep her tryst with Raynor Silverstone hidden.

I put the bottle in the cabinet, the glasses in the sink, opened the box on the table, and pulled out the first disk.

Chapter 5

Mid-morning, I dragged myself into the kitchen. Got a pot of coffee going before collapsing into a chair. I'd spent most of last night reviewing the security tapes after Ray left. I was right in that they'd staked out the garage, starting on day six of my copies.

Most nights, Mr. Filbrandt came down with a varying number of coworkers. Laughing, talking, waving goodbye to each other. Except twice. The first time, 'Rosalie' had started toward Filbrandt, who was unlocking his car. When several other late-night workers exited the elevator, she pivoted back to a plain brown Honda. Three nights later, no one popped out of the elevator to save him.

The actual video of that night was missing. The file labeled "October14" was actually a copy of the previous day's video. Security Chief Tomason would not be happy when I informed him of that. After reviewing the videos again, I had two pages of notes and was comfortably certain of four things.

One, the photographer was a man, based on body movements and build. He'd left his car when 'Rosalie' started toward Filbrandt. Starting to swing around it to get in position for his shots—with a very professional looking camera—he scrambled back to the driver's side when they had to abort. Regrettably, black clothing covered him head to foot, including a hood hiding most of his face. They'd been very aware of the cameras.

Two, he was about five-ten or -eleven, comparing his height against his car: a dark blue Ford sedan. Three, they always parked in the same spots as they waited. Both of which, not surprisingly, were empty in the day-after video. That meant the spaces had been leased through the Woodworkers Security office. Bet my unopened bottle of MacEverson scotch that all the information they'd provided to Security was bogus, but it was more points for me to track down.

Come on coffee, drip faster.

Fourth, and the most disquieting, what was really at stake here? Would someone have planned this thoroughly, this neatly, to win a simple mayoral race? Was there something else in play and the campaign a conveniently useful coincidence? Either way, I had a sinking feeling there would be additional damning 'evidence' presented that Mr. Filbrandt was unaware of. The exploiter's next move would be telling.

Two cups of invigorating coffee, a shower, and a can of ravioli seasoned with Grandpa's special spice blend later, I was ready to tackle the day.

Arriving at my office, I surprised Diana in the middle of repotting Charrise. Marge had presented me with the potted ivy— boldly labeled for its clingy namesake from a previous, uh, encounter. Originally twined around two posts, it had grown to needing four. We pruned it to keep it in check or it would be all over the place. Sort of like the real Charrise's hands had been.

Letting Diana know Thomas Tall Elk would be stopping by, I hurried on to my desk. I needed to get my notes typed up. I had called my old mentor and partner at Halligan Investigative Services last night, simply telling him I was maxed out and had two hot cases. Could he help? He'd agreed to work on the Atlanta-Bartel B&R job, even finishing it depending on how other things went. Between the digging I expected on both Filbrandt's and Mandy's cases, I had a feeling he would.

Thinking of Mandy, I pulled out a new client folder and filled it out as much as I could, making a mental note to pull a copy of both Rivas siblings' background information from Sam Androsh's file. Copies of the police reports and court transcripts would have plenty of other information on the case, including a list of everyone in the house at the time of the murder. It had to be one of them if it really wasn't Aaron Rivas. Despite his sister's adamancy, I wasn't totally closing that gate. No telling what could happen during a blind panic. With the case closed, I shouldn't have any trouble getting the information I needed.

I asked Diana to put in the requests and to start an invoice file for our new client and handed her the twenty-dollar bill Mandy had given me before we parted.

My unflappable secretary didn't bat an eye at the unusually low retainer. "Any other arrangements?" she asked calmly.

"Um…we'll track expenses. She'll pay in installments," I said, escaping back to my desk. Pretty sure that lip twitch of hers hid a smile.

I made a quick call to the Woodworkers Tower's security office about the missing video. The guttural-growly tone Chief Tomason's voice acquired told me just how unhappy he was. The overwriting of one file with another could have been an accident. Considering what that video would have shown, neither of us believed it. Someone in his department had been compromised. He assured me he would handle it personally. He also promised to email the parking information for the two persons of interest in the videos.

Tackling my notes on the Atlanta-Bartel case, I had just finished assembling them into some semblance of order when a First-Gen bear lumbered through my doorway. I stood to shake his hand. Standing six-five with broad shoulders to match, his hand swallowed mine.

"Good to see you," I told Thomas Tall Elk, grinning broadly.

"Good to see you, too," he returned, settling in my client chair. "So, things are getting dicey, Dice," he said, a twinkle in his dark eyes.

I rolled mine. Tom was one of the few who used my nickname. "You wouldn't believe the week I've had."

He sobered instantly. "I heard about Russell Chandler. How's he doing?"

Crap. I hadn't called today yet to check. "He's in ICU right now. His doctor expects Russell to fully recover, although there may be some long-term issues."

"No doubt. You don't come away unscathed from a strike like that. So, the Atlanta job?"

I gave him a run-down of Miss Bruhn's requirements. His forehead crinkled at the two-week time limit. "Yeah, I know. She'll have to settle for what we can get." I pushed the folder toward him. "Basic background check is done—hit the usual public resources. I've got about a third of the referrals done, but they were the quick and easy ones. Sorry."

He flipped the folder open and scanned its contents. "Think this Mr. Cassell is in jail?" he asked, evidently reaching that particular note.

"No, I think he's on the run from something that'll put him there."

"Hmmm. A lot of footwork, then. I'll leave him for last," he said, closing the folder.

I nodded in agreement, noting he hadn't commented about the Dakota Territory entry. But then, being a Ameri-Tribe member from there himself, he could find her faster than me. He'd know which Elder or Council member to speak with.

"I'll keep in touch, let you know how it's going," Thomas told me as I walked him out, feeling like a kid next to his bulk. "Let me know if there's anything else I can help with."

"Thanks, partner," I replied warmly, shaking his hand.

I wandered over to the coffee pot after he left. *Partner*. I hadn't called him that in over six years. Not even when he helped out last year as I recovered from a concussion. It felt good. If my business kept growing, I might need one here soon. I tucked that thought away.

I returned to my desk with a full cup, braced for the coming dig for information. Rosalie Sayer had to be an alias, but I still ran a standard background check. Nada. Zilch. As expected, the name didn't exist in anywhere. On the chance she'd only falsified her last name, a not uncommon tactic, I went back to the usually most helpful database. Searching Nebraska's Driver Licenses by first name, approximate age, and description netted me fifty-two responses. Well, not too bad. Taking a fortifying gulp of coffee, I began scanning their photos, the kind of drudge work that made up so many of my days.

I finished them up by lunchtime and had two possibilities: Rosalie Applegate and Rosalie Hendrix. Both women's photos bore a strong resemblance to the woman in the security videos. Diving back into databases, I found nursing and marriage licenses for Rosalie Totusek Hendrix. Only found a small misdemeanor fine for a teenaged Rosalie Applegate in court records and nothing else. That made her the more likely of the two. Still… If Applegate was my suspect, I would've expected a longer court record. A budding criminal normally had a history of gradually escalating offenses. On the other hand, she could have been enticed by a large payout.

Either way, paying a visit to both of them went on my to-do list. Probably late afternoon or early evening would be the best time to catch them at home. In the meantime, I'd pay a visit to the *Midtown Café*. Maybe one of the staff remembered Mr. Filbrandt and his 'guest' that day.

I was halfway through my deli sandwich when an email came in from Merle Smith. She'd sent the list of campaign staff for all three candidates, which I'd asked for to mask which was my client. That…was a lot more names than I expected. Then I groaned at her note saying those were the full and temp hires. It did not include the transitory volunteers, only there for a week or so. A copy went into the Filbrandt folder. I could feel the clock ticking. There wasn't enough time to research and/or interview all of them. My best bet was tracking down either the woman or the photographer.

Headed out to do my running, I told Diana I'd probably be gone for the rest of the day.

Her "Don't forget, you've got court tomorrow morning" stopped me dead in my tracks.

I hung my head. Crap.

"You did."

I totally had, her tone making me feel like I'd been caught sneaking out the bedroom window. I was a prosecution witness in an insurance arson fraud case I investigated earlier this year. Heaving a sigh, I thanked her for the reminder.

"Have a good afternoon," she said.

I didn't. The blackmailers struck even sooner than I expected.

***

The *Midtown Café* was a dead end. Most of the staff recognized Mr. Filbrandt as he was a regular. One said the woman's picture looked familiar, but none of them could place the two together on any particular day.

I was headed to Papillion to interview Rosalie Hendrix when I got a phone call from Kurt Filbrandt. They had received a large manila envelope in the mail with the blackmail photos. At the next major intersection, I turned north.

Their house was located in an established neighborhood on a tree-lined street. It was a modest, middle-class home, especially for someone whose income had to be in a higher bracket. My opinion of the unpretentious Filbrandts went up. Mrs. Filbrandt met me at the door, pissed but still human.

"I know they came through the mail, but could you get any specific scent off them?" I asked, as she closed the door behind me. It was a long shot, but her fox half might have caught something.

She shook her head. "The outside was covered in too many scents," she said, leading me down a short hallway. "The pictures themselves are nearly scent free."

We entered a large open space containing both kitchen and dining area. Mr. Filbrandt was seated at the table, scowling down at pictures spread out in front of him. He didn't say a word, just swept his arm out with a here-they-are-have-a-frigging-look glare.

The first two photos were of that lunchtime 'meeting' he'd mentioned. It showed them sitting at a table, conversing and eating lunch. The unknown photographer had gotten them at just the right angle to make it look intimate, especially that smiling, hand-on-arm farewell gesture. The next set were of that 'hot' kiss and 'smiling exit' in the underground parking lot.

"I assure you," he said coldly, "that kiss was not consensual."

My response of "That's obvious" surprised him.

"When you deliberately pull someone toward you," I explained, "an elbow's natural move is downward as the forearm comes forward. You grabbed Cece's arms to steady her when she pretended to stumble. When she unexpectedly pushed herself into your chest, both of your arms were shoved *sideways* out of the way," I tapped the photo, "as can be plainly seen."

Mr. Filbrandt stared for a moment, then pushed the remaining pictures to me. A quick scan had my eyes narrowing. These were the 'extras' I had been dreading. I looked up and across at him.

"Yes, that's my car parked in front of a seedy motel," he said, his words holding a restrained anger. "No, I didn't drive it there. It was stolen last month as I attended a political luncheon and was recovered in a rural area south of Kanesville three days later. Sitting on cinder blocks. At the time, I counted myself lucky at only having to replace four tires. Now?" He pointed at the five pictures.

One was taken from somewhere behind the car, showing the identifiable tag as well as the front of a motel room that a man, matching Mr. Filbrandt from the back, was opening. The next two pictures were shot through the room's window. Dirty shears blurred the two people inside, but they were definitely having sex. Another picture showed a skimpily clad Rosalie Sayer lounging in the open doorway, exposed in more ways than one by Filbrandt's car's headlights, as she smiled and waved at it. The last one had a sideview of the car as it pulled away, the driver in silhouette.

From an outsider's perspective, all this would appear damning. Very damning.

The gossip circuit would go wild.

"This came with it." His wife handed me a slip of paper.

It was a demand for ten thousand dollars. Naturally, failure to meet the demand would have the pictures released to the news services. And he had ten days to do it.

I studied the money-drop instructions.

"If the only goal was to discredit your husband by one of your contenders, the pictures would have been sent straight to the newspapers," I said. "Unfortunately, this doesn't rule out someone from their circle. The money could simply be a bonus."

"Meaning, they'll collect the money and then gleefully 'expose' me afterwards," Mr. Filbrandt said, his jaw flexing.

Yep, that. "While an opportunist con artist is still possible, this whole scheme is too well planned—too extensive." Like the missing security video. "Is there any other reason—maybe a business competitor—that could be behind this?" I got a very firm *no*. "Then your blackmailer is most likely someone whose ambitious plans hinge on their candidate being elected."

I rubbed the back of my neck. "Mrs. Filbrandt. You said the pictures were *nearly* scent free. What did you get?"

"A hint? The impression of a male? It's hard to explain to a non-shifter."

"Zero? Shifter?" She shook her head. Bummer. That would have helped eliminate some suspects. The guy had to have used gloves in a well-ventilated area.

"How about where she rubbed up against your husband?" And that's not an awkward question.

"Too many scents overlapping," she said. "Co-workers, campaign workers, Mrs. Cartwright."

"A client that wears a lot of perfume," Mr. Filbrandt explained, grimacing. "I usually take a shower first thing when I get home to save Trish's nose, but, well, we got sidetracked with this." He ran a hand through his hair. "Can you do this? In ten days? I don't want to quit the race, but I do not want to subject my family to malicious, spiteful gossip."

"I'll do my best," I promised honestly. "But you and your wife need to decide what course to take. Just in case."

Mr. Filbrandt reached over and curled his hand around his wife's. Meeting his gaze, her head dipped once in a silent expression of commitment and support that tugged at my heart. Reiterating my promise, I left them there. I took the incriminating material with me as I let myself out.

I sat in my car, the motor running, and stared at the house for several minutes. I finally identified the heavy feeling in my chest: loss. An emptiness that reached down to my soul. I'd briefly had what the Filbrandts did until it was brutally torn away. They didn't deserve this. I resolved to do more than my best. *Look out assholes, I'm coming for you.*

Back at my office, I made copies of the photos, placing the originals safely in my filing cabinet. I adjusted my copies by cutting out Mr. Filbrandt in the luncheon pictures and his car in the motel ones. That protected his identity and focused attention on the main subject. Then I headed out.

"Definitely gone this time," I told Diana as I breezed past her desk.

∗ ∗ ∗

It was well after midnight when I parked in front of my apartment building and trudged wearily inside. Hours of footwork had produced mostly negative results.

Like the *Midtown Café,* both Rosalies were also dead ends.

The address on Rosalie Applegate's license belonged to her

parents. She had enlisted in the Army, currently stationed in Arizona, and was using their address to keep it active. Rosalie Hendrix worked in a small private clinic in West Omaha. She and another nurse were currently attending a week-long medical seminar in Denver. That ruled out her ambushing Mr. Filbrandt in the underground parking lot on Monday. Not to mention, nursing staff don't usually get a two-hour lunch break, which she would've needed to thread traffic across town to have a photo-lunch with him in East Omaha and get back to work on time.

After that, I walked the streets. Literally. Angie took Thursdays off to rest up for her busy weekends. However, there were plenty of other street workers who probably knew every motel, seedy or otherwise, in the area. I was hoping one would recognize the one in the pictures despite the lack of specific details. One woman thought it might be a motel in the Boondocks. Another one thought, maybe, down in Plattsmouth. I also got a lot of variations on "they all look alike after a while, honey."

Just when I was about to give up, I got lucky. Information, not sex.

A male prostitute took one look and said, "Southside Motel in Kanesville, in the low-rent district." When I pressed him for verification, he replied "Been there several times. I recognize those dirty shears they call curtains. The night motel manager gets his kicks watching through them."

Only one older worker recognized the false-Rosalie, which had been my second hope. Although it was a short lived one. *"One of the smoothest pickpockets I'd ever seen,"* Betty said. *"I saw her work a bar one night. Pants, purses, even got the bartender's tip jar when he turned his back. Name? Not a clue."*

Which made me just as clueless.

Chapter 6

I managed to get a decent night's sleep. Showered and put on one of my better suits. Called the hospital and found there'd been no change: Russell was still unconscious, although he was determined to have exited rapid repair. Southside Motel was on my evening schedule when the night voyeur would be on duty. A quick call to the DA's office revealed that I wouldn't be needed until the afternoon session.

Excellent. I had another police report to read.

Stored my gun in the top cabinet drawer as I wasn't about to take it to court. I didn't want to drive all the way back home to get it, especially since my evening plans were east, across the river. I'd barely settled behind my desk when Diana informed me that Mr. Thoreen was on the phone. Darrell Chandler was filing to have my conservatorship tossed and replaced with him. Grounds were lack of experience and any real interest in Chandler Import. Mr. Thoreen said he even specified the number of times—three—I'd attended board meetings since acquiring part ownership.

I pinched my nose bridge. Should have asked Ray what he'd heard about the Chandlers when I had the chance.

Keeping my anger tightly controlled, I said, "No, I don't have corporate expertise, Mr. Thoreen, which is why I left the day-to-day running in Russell's hands. As for board meetings? I'm a PI. My hours are irregular and can change on a phone call or the turn of a clue. I also accommodate people for the best time to interview them. There's often a limited window in which they are able, or willing, to talk with me. As a matter of fact, I'm interviewing someone tonight across the river.

"Not to mention," I added hotly, my control slipping. "Russell appointed *me*. Not his uncle. Not his frigging cousin. He obviously felt that Chandler Import would fare better with me than those—" I broke off and took a calming breath. "I can muddle along just fine with you, Miss Heiser, the board, and whoever else providing input and steering my ass in whatever direction it needs to go."

Thoreen laughed heartily. "Very salient points, Mr. D'Accio, which, reworded, I'll use to counterargue. Plus, most judges will hesitate to overturn a person's wishes without good cause."

Giving myself a few seconds to settle afterwards—silently cursing the two Chandlers helped—I picked up the police report of Filbrandt's car theft I'd asked Diana to get. It didn't have much more than what Mr. Filbrandt had told me. Stolen from a parking lot in Omaha, recovered without tires in a wooded area halfway between Kanesville and Glenwood.

Hmmm. Were the blackmailers working out of Iowa? Using places they were familiar with? I made a note to that affect and expanded my evening plans to include showing the luncheon picture of Rosy—my nickname for the elusive woman—to the street workers across the river.

Chief Tomason's email came in, and I wasn't surprised by its contents. Ten days before the night in question, Rosalie Sayer had claimed to be a temp hire for the Filbrandt campaign, who was using one of the company's conference rooms as his HQ. She hadn't been the first, so his office didn't think anything about it, or paying cash for only a month's lease in the underground parking area. Two days later, Frank Ayers, the name given by the photographer, did the same. That would match up when I started seeing them in the videos, eight days prior to the kissing event.

The Chief had been pissed enough to do my work for me, checking their information. Both cars were rentals, both by Rosy, but their tags belonged to different local agencies. The Iowa driver's license she'd listed had been fake. An addendum said he was still looking into the missing video.

I fretted for a few minutes afterwards. With court coming up, I was kind of limited in what I could do. After a moment, I pulled out my notes on the mayoral candidates Merle had regaled me with over *Louie's* Jambalaya and gumbo specialty.

Melissa Brower. Mid-forties, a Zero native of Omaha with a degree from Nebraska University at Omaha in Legal Studies. Specialized as a real estate lawyer after passing the bar. Full partner at Stanosheck Realty and Escrow Services. Divorced, one kid: a son following in his mother's footsteps as he was enrolled in Legal Studies at NUO. Merle had described Brower as a mercurial woman, nearly wolf-aggressive in her attitude and for obtaining any set goals, and with a campaign that was as flamboyant as she was. Qualities, Merle claimed, that had a lot of voters shying away and put her in the 'least likely' category to win.

Okay, I could see her going for an opponent's throat with everything she could find. But would she generate it in an all-out bid to win? I gave it a moment's consideration, then moved on to the next candidate.

Jerry Louderback. Late fifties, a First-Gen coyote originally from Kansas City. His Marketing and Finance degrees had been earned at Kansas State College. He'd interned at Wellington Wolf Boots HQ, eventually moving into a full-time position. He'd relocated to Omaha six years ago for a Chief Finance Officer position with Marlin Marketing Corporation. Never married, no kids on record. Merle described him as Melissa Brower's opposite: a staid, deliberate planner who had been his college chess champion three years in a row. The expected personality type for someone in his professional field.

Aannnnd that made him an excellent candidate for Mr. Filbrandt's blackmailer. But would he risk it? By nature and profession, he'd be very risk aversive.

Last candidate was my client, Kurt Filbrandt. Her quick review rounded out what I already knew of him. Early forties, a Zero Omaha native, accounting degree from NUO…co-partnered with Neal Maddox seven years ago…married with two children… *lawsuit?* Oh, against Neal Maddox five years ago for breach of contract. Plaintiff lost and had to pay Maddox's legal expenses. Ouch.

According to Merle, Kurt Filbrandt currently appeared to be the favorite over the two challengers. He offered a steady, out-going, middle ground for the voters, she had said with a distinctly approving tone. Bet I knew who she would be voting for.

I watched Gertie swimming and chewed over their information. Both of my client's opponents' personalities made them suspect as the blackmailer. *But were they?* I stretched the fingers of my left hand as far back as they'd go, then slowly rolled my fingers closed into a fist, one finger at a time. Stretch, close.

Would either one of them risk it?

Stretch, close. Thought some more.

Deciding to tackle the campaign workers, I logged into Omaha's public court records and started down the list. When I'd finished checking the last one, I'd found eleven misdemeanors, two civil lawsuits, two DUIs, various moving violations, and one very intriguing manslaughter arrest. Charges were dropped due to lack of evidence and the primary witness missing. Despite the dubious conclusion, Merle's list indicated that Lillian Strom was currently Melissa Brower's senior campaign advisor.

That definitely piqued my interest, so I ran a couple of other checks on the woman. Lillian Strom was aged forty-eight and had one marriage, one divorce, no children. First-Gen cougar. White Ford Impala with no points on her driver's license. A degree from Nebraska University at Omaha in Psychology. Except for that one arrest, Lillian Strom's background was otherwise unremarkable.

Still, public perception was paramount for any political animal. Even if Miss Brower believed Strom was innocent, she ran the risk of alienating support and votes from others who weren't so sure. She should have at least had Lillian Strom in some behind-the-scenes position, not front and center.

A glance at the clock said anything further would have to wait. I had witness duty.

***

It was almost four o'clock before I got back to the office from the trial. Defense tried to get my testimony tossed under an improper search challenge. *"I just canvassed area storage facilities with a list of possible names, based on the 'keep it simple' rule."* As soon as I had found the unit rented under Mrs. Culvert's deceased grand-mother's name, I informed my client at Eggers and Klinger Insurance and they contacted police, who took it from there with a legal search warrant.

Today's trial had reminded me I hadn't applied the same simplicity rule to the fake Rosalie. There might be a reason why Applegate and Hendrix appeared similar to her. Retrieving my weapon and holster, I donned them at my desk. Shrugging my jacket back on, I picked up the Filbrandt folder, wished Diana a good weekend, and started my evening rounds.

First, I headed to Bellview, just south of Omaha. Showing the Applegates Rosy's luncheon picture produced only headshakes. They didn't know her or anyone else familiar. From there, I took the bridge across the river to Glenwood and turned north. I wanted to look over Filbrandt's car recovery spot, though it was doubtful there was anything to find after all this time. When I did locate the overgrown farmstead, after passing the turn-in several times and finally getting directions from a local, it only strengthened the Iowa connection. If it hadn't been for an anonymous tip, probably from one of the blackmailers, it could've been years before it was found. Couldn't have that; they needed it for their setup.

It was getting dark as I pulled into the Southside Motel's cracked and pitted parking lot. The office was set between two wings stretching to either side of it. A small overhang protected the office front and the recessed alcove on its left that held the requisite ice, drink, and condom machines. The exterior paint was several years past redo, and the number to room three was hanging upside down. Several cars were parked in front of various rooms, light shining through thin curtains matching the same flimsy material in the blackmail pictures.

Yep, this was the place. Just to be sure, I walked over and compared the visual of Room 2 with its picture. Double yep. As I entered the office, I wondered how many times 'John Jones' had registered in the past week.

The woman reading a book behind the desk was in her fifties or was a hard-worn forty something. She stood as I entered, her suspicious gaze running down my suit.

"Miss Olson," I started after a quick glance at her name tag, "my name is—"

"You a police detective?"

"Uh, no. Private detective, name of—"

"Fif—seventy-five bucks to see the register," she said, eyeing me again.

I pulled out my wallet and paid before the price rose higher. Register viewing must be fairly regular here. She pulled out a large tome from under the counter, plopped it down in front of me, and went back to her book.

A ruler served as a place-holder for today's date. Leaving it in place, I leafed the pages backward to the dates I'd gotten off the police report. There, September twenty-fifth. The night after Filbrandt's car had been stolen. R Sayer, Room 2, 9:17 PM. Keeping the same alias made tracking her movements easier. Which might be deliberate, I thought, scowling down at the page. Leaving behind the 'proof' for anyone attempting to verify or disprove the pictures.

Adding the room information in my notebook, I succumbed to curiosity and did another search. The answer to the J-J question? Eight in the past week. Twice last Monday.

I closed the register. "When does the night manager come on duty?"

"Seven," she answered without looking up.

I wasn't sitting out front for an hour. Getting back into my car, I drove into Kanesville for a bite to eat.

***

If there was a particular image for a voyeur, the motel's night manager was it. Lanky, greasy hair brushing his collar, twitchy eyes that wouldn't meet mine for more than three seconds, and a whiny voice that set my teeth on edge. Paul Millton was also about the poorest excuse for a wolf shifter I'd ever met. It took a hundred dollars for him to 'remember' the night of September twenty-fifth and the activity around Room 2. I should have changed into raggedly jeans after court.

"I assumed they were making a video for their own use, private or commercial." His shoulders did a nervous jog. "We get that once in a while."

That posed a number of questions I didn't want answered. I laid a twenty on the counter. "Did you see the photographer?"

He licked his lips. "Average height, kind of chubby, bald. Camera was professional grade, bulky, with an extended lens."

That matched the camera in the security video. "Zero or Gen?"

"Never got close enough to sniff."

I added another twenty. "Did you see his car?"

"Well…"

Another twenty joined the pile.

"Truck," he promptly said. "Black with matching topper; diesel engine, brush guard and chrome roll bars."

I blinked. Yeah, bet that had stood out. "Ever seen that truck again?"

"Nope."

Added one of my cards to the stack and pushed it over. "Call me if you do or remember anything else about that night."

Turning on my car's interior light, I updated my notes. I'd check with the photography groups. If the man was or had been a professional photographer, there should be a record of him somewhere. After that, I spent several hours showing Rosy's picture around Kanesville's streets and bars.

I dragged myself back to my car a little after one. Frustrated, irritated, exasperated, irked—I could probably find a few more descriptors if I had the energy. I'd come up with exactly nothing for the countless showings of her picture. Unlocking the driver's door, it occurred to me that Rosy could be an out-of-towner that'd been imported for this particular con. I made a mental note to ask Mr. Filbrandt if he remembered her having an accent of any kind as I slid under the wheel.

Chapter 7

An early Saturday morning phone call to Mrs. Hendrix had netted me a between-one-and-two window to visit. She lived out in West Omaha, not too far from where she worked. I made good time to her home. The house was a bit more upscale than I was expecting, with a large yard and a front porch nearly buried in flower pots. I was greeted with warmth and curiosity. I explained I just needed her to look at a picture and see if she recognized the person in it.

Oh, boy. Did she.

Rosalie's eyes turned gold, her jaw elongated, and her hand morphed into a paw with the short claws of a canid. That didn't keep them from punching a couple of holes where it held the picture.

"Wha' 'as my frigging sis'er done now?" she growled.

Hallelujah. Keeping my tone somber, I said, "Blackmail and extortion, I'm sorry to say." I rescued the picture. "Can you—" I got a give-me-a-minute paw wave. Rosalie stomped down a hallway. I followed, assuming that was why she'd left the door open, and we ended up in a kitchen. By then, she'd regained her human form and headed straight for the fridge. She yanked out a beer; I declined the offer of one.

Leaning against the counter, Rosalie ripped the beer's top off and took several swallows. "Dammit. We thought that piece of family embarrassment had left town for good."

"What all has she done?"

Rosalie snorted. "What hasn't she done. She's either not caught, people won't press charges, or she skates the system."

"You wouldn't happen to have an address for her?"

"If we did, the family would've made sure she was inside when we burned it down."

Oookay. "Do you know where she went when she left," I asked, breaking out my notepad.

"Iowa, I heard. Don't know where, don't care as long as—wait." Rosalie straightened. "She's here? She used *my* name?"

"Just the first. Introduced herself to my client as Rosalie Sayer."

The Rosalie in front of me gave a very unpleasant laugh. "The earthquake you feel tonight will be Mom. Sayer is my maternal grandmother's family name."

"Your sister's full name?"

"Cece Dawn Totusek."

I asked her to spell the last name. "Is she a Gen, too?"

"No."

"Do you know where she liked to hang out when she was here? Any known associates?"

"She liked nights at the *Dead End Bar*. I see you know it," Rosalie added when I made a face.

Yeah, the place was that in more ways than name. It sat on a dead-end street on the border of the area known as the Boondocks, the southeast portion of Omaha that was the site of the city's original docks. The area had flourished, 'booming' from both the trade going through it and the residential growth that grew up around it. But times changed. Larger barges and modernization at newer docks upstream had been its death knell. 'Boondocks' became a misnomer. Then a sneer as the area gradually deteriorated over the years. It was now at the bottom of the social and job strata. Many of its hard-working residents eked out an existence in the low-income, hard and/or dirty jobs that most people curled their noses at. Making a bad reputation worse, many of them were also involved in various illegal activities.

Which meant the majority of the *Dead End Bar's* clientele scraped the bottom of the social and moral barrels or were those who liked swimming in the sewer. It took a brave, well-armed outsider to stick his nose in there and he still ran the risk of being carried out—possibly in a coroner's wagon. Even cops preferred visiting it as a threesome. Which is why I'd kept my two previous visits there short, during daylight, and with my Ruger loose in its holster.

I closed my notebook and dug out a card. Handing it to her, I said, "Thank you for your help, Mrs. Hendrix. If you happen to hear from her," I waited out the cussing, "or hear of her, please give me a call."

"When you catch that mangy excuse for a human, do us all a favor?"

The venom in her voice caught me off-guard.

She angled forward and, enunciating each word with knife-edge precision, said, "Brick up her cell."

Not animosity: hate. Cece Totusek hadn't just burned her family's bridges, she'd detonated them, pylons and all. Heading for my apartment and its home office, I felt buoyed, the opposite from last night. I had a name now. One I didn't think finding information on would be hard. And the case for an Iowa connection just got stronger.

Yep, I found plenty.

Yep, she'd definitely skated through the system.

Miss Cece Totusek started her dubious career at the ripe old age of eleven, when she was arrested for shoplifting. The first of many that I found in the Omaha Police Department's public database. By fourteen, she'd added petty theft, vandalism, trespassing, battery, and resisting arrest. For most of them, due to her age, she was either fined or sentenced to community service. And that was for the charges that weren't outright dismissed.

Then, at fifteen, she was expelled from school for slicing up a boy. The parents pressed criminal assault charges but the jury returned a not-guilty verdict. What? I dug out the court transcript on it. Her lawyer's winning argument was that, as a Zero, she had the right to defend herself against a First-Gen with claws. Most of the witnesses admitted they weren't sure of the sequence of things because it happened so fast. However, one witness stated that it was the boy's claws coming out in self-defense after Cece attacked him. Based on the impression I was developing of Cece Totusek, I was willing to bet the lone witness had been right.

The school had still refused to reinstate her and I didn't blame them. How much had the family covered up? And what? Something had caused that level of hate I saw in Rosalie Hendrix's face.

OPD records for Cece only went another three years. A few minor charges, like trespassing for which she was fined and a couple of heavier ones: arson and robbery. The arson charge was dropped due to conflicting evidence. The robbery was reduced to possession of stolen goods for which she served three months in the county jail, did two months' probation, then disappeared. Guess that's when she moved to Iowa.

I logged out of the OPD database, pondering while I wandered toward the kitchen. The dearth of charges those last years was probably due more to her not getting caught than not doing them. I made a mental note to be on guard whenever I was around her. Cece Totusek was just plain bad.

Thomas Tall Elk showed up to give me an update as I finished my beef and broccoli. He waved away my apology for not having anything non-alcoholic to offer him. My offer to make coffee was quickly declined.

"My refrigerator and cabinets would match yours if my daughter didn't show up every other week and restock both."

A decade-plus older than me, Tom had lost his wife to cancer a little over a year ago.

"How are you and Lisa doing?" I inquired.

"Adapting," he replied. His eyes lost focus for a moment, then he bounced back. He pulled the Atlanta folder out of his briefcase. "I've got about another third done, so far."

"That's great, Tom. I really appreciate this."

"No, I appreciate you asking. Gets me out of the divorce jobs that have recently swamped the agency."

Ouch. It wasn't unusual for our reports and/or testimony to be used in divorce cases. Especially when the parents were fighting for custody. I hated it when kids were used as pawns between battling parents.

"My condolences. Mike doesn't mind you subbing out to me?" Mike Halligan was owner of Halligan Investigative Services, where I'd launched my PI career under Tom's mentorship.

Tom chuckled. "Mike wanted to know if you had anything *he* could help with and for the same reason."

After a good laugh, we started going over the file. He'd even made contact with Bernedette 'Bernie' Mitchell. The Ogallala Sioux had moved back to the Territory to work on her parents' buffalo ranch. Finished with the files, we hashed old times and cases over glasses of water.

"So, how's your other hot case coming?" Tom asked. "What you can say."

I gave him a high-level outline without naming which of the mayoral candidates was my client. As a fellow PI, I trusted his discretion, and bouncing things off him might generate new ideas.

"I've identified the woman. Cece Totusek is one of those that are born bad. She's been in trouble of some sort since eleven years old."

"Eleven?" Tom echoed. "That is bad. Violent?"

"Not for the most part, although there are a couple of instances. According to her sister, Cece left Omaha about six years ago, right after finishing up her possession sentence. The fact that she's back in town, working a major con, says she hasn't changed. Assuming her social habits haven't changed either, her sister gave me a lead on where I might be able to find her. I plan on visiting it tomorrow night as nighttime appears to be her preference."

"Where is that?"

"A bar, naturally," I said, trying to pass it off as inconsequential. I shouldn't have bothered.

Tom eyed me suspiciously. "What bar?"

I cleared my throat. "*Dead End.*"

He spit out a curse. "Who's your backup?"

"I'll be armed." It came out a bit weaker than I intended.

Silence. "Are you frigging crazy? Are you aware that the number of corpses Patrol has been picking up down there has more than doubled in the last three months?"

My jaw dropped. "What! That hasn't been in the news."

He snorted. "Of course not. It's the Boondocks. Nobody important there. I've overheard the phrase 'good riddance' more than once."

"I wasn't actually planning on going inside," I hedged. "Just… sort of…" Tom's arms crossed and his scowl deepened, "hang around outside and approach her if she showed up," I finished in a slightly apologetic voice.

"And this paragon of lawful obedience is going to stand there and have a nice chit-chat with you?"

Uh, oh. I recognized that deceptively calm tone. Mount Vesuvius was primed to erupt. "Okay, okay. Dumb idea," I admitted waving my hands. "I've only had a few hours to work with this information. You taught me to think through all possibilities," Tom's eyebrow quirked upward, "then toss the really stupid ones," I said with a sheepish grin.

"Uh-huh. Consider that one tossed. I'm your backup. What time?"

Chapter 8

I sauntered down Derby Avenue. Old jeans, faded flannel shirt under an old jacket, and scuffed boots completed my—hopefully—not-a-threat-ignore-me attire. The locals would be alert for any potential problems and there was no way to hide from a shifter's nose and hearing.

My car was prudently parked at an all-night convenience store several blocks to the west. The buildings slowly grew more worn, less maintained, as I drew closer to my destination. Only a few of the streetlights I passed were still working, and they'd be needing new bulbs soon. A few homes had at least made an effort with mowed and uncluttered yards. Peeling paint, a missing porch support, and taped-up windows, however, told their own story. It wouldn't be too many more years, I thought sadly, before the Boondocks epitaph was extended to these blocks.

Reaching my destination, I leaned up against the side of a boarded-up ice cream store. The street continued on past me, curving to the right where it ended at a rusted-out playground with its feeble streetlight. I had an unrestricted view of the *Dead End Bar* at the end of the block. It had an old-fashioned, saloon-type overhang and boardwalk across the entire front with a light burning on each end. More light splashed out of the single window next to the centered door. I eyed the smattering of cars in its parking lot, knowing they only represented a portion of the body count inside. There'd be walkers, some of them arriving by the beaten path that disappeared down one side of the bar.

Tom should be—I nearly jumped out of my boots when he suddenly appeared next to me, dressed similarly. "Dammit, Tom, you nearly gave me a heart attack." I'd forgotten how silently the big man could move.

"You need to settle," he said, propping up the building beside me. "You're too tense and shifters will pick up on it. Like I did a block away."

Aarrrgh. I was taking several deep breaths when a guy walked past, his gaze cutting sharply to us. "—and I told the asshole there was no frigging way that was going to happen," Tom said nonchalantly.

That's right. We're just two guys, hanging out, talking. "Did he see it your way?" I ad-libbed in return.

"Uh-uh. We continued our conversation outside," Tom replied as the man continued on down the sidewalk.

"A Zero," I murmured when he was out of earshot. Tom nodded, probably knowing by scent. We watched him cross the street into the parking lot and then into the bar.

"How long do you want to give her?" Tom asked.

I shrugged. "According to her sister, Cece liked beer and hustling pool, using the latter to pay for the first." Tom's grin was white in the dim light. "If she's not here by ten…I've got a copy of her picture I can flash around inside." The grin disappeared but his exasperated sigh was audible.

Since it was a little before eight, we settled comfortably as possible against the wall. Surveillance, staking out, whatever you called the boring event, PIs did a lot of it.

Time passed slowly. Cars left; cars pulled in. Walkers arrived; none left. The ones coming up that side path would be Boondockers.

My thoughts wandered from worrying about Russell's continued unconsciousness, to irritation at his Chandler relatives, to whether or not to renew the lease on my current apartment. Ever since my social and financial status had been catapulted upward, not a week went by that someone didn't show up at my door with varying proposals: financial, social, or romantic. Diana filtered out most of those that arrive at the office, though a few have managed to get past her.

I was mentally reviewing Mandy's story when another person came up the path. I squinted as a female figure crossed under the light and pulled open the door. Straightened.

"That's her?" Tom asked.

"Think so. Timing is right, too," I said, giving my watch a quick glance. 9:34.

A battered pickup passed us, pulling into the parking lot and disgorging bodies from both the cab and truck bed. Eight guys, laughing and slugging each other on the shoulders as they made their way inside.

"I'm going to go stick my head in and take a peek. Make sure it is Cece."

"Then what?" Tom asked. "You start something in there and they'll finish it. We can't fight the whole bar. By the way, those eight guys from the truck are all wolves."

Frigging great. They'd been too far away for my inner radar to flag them. Another advantage of working with Tom and his shifter senses. I stared thoughtfully at the building, formulating and rejecting several ideas. Ah, hah. That would do it.

"Remember that big drug bust they did in the warehouse district a couple of weeks back?" I asked.

"And?"

I pushed away from the wall. "What's the one thing guaranteed to alienate everyone in there?"

Tom swore softly. "You're crazy." That didn't keep him from falling into step beside me.

I gave him my best maniacal smile right before I yanked the door open. I stepped to the side to let Tom enter and ran my gaze around the room. The music was at a comfortable level to accommodate both Zeros and shifters. Ditto for the soft lighting, which made it easy to spot my quarry. Yep, it was Cece. She was chalking a cue stick over in the game section. Ignoring all the side glances and sniffs, I stalked toward her.

One of the men around the pool table said something because she turned in my direction. Frowned.

"You!" I declared loudly, stopping several feet away. "Did you think you could get away with it?"

"I don't know what you're talking about," she said, eyes narrowed.

Bet she thought I was talking about the blackmail scheme. Or anything else she might be involved in. My peripheral vision caught a brute on my left starting to rise out of his chair. The guy's butt reversed direction when I added, "How long have you been an informer? Or did you rat out Victor because he dumped your ass?" I continued to pretend-rant.

Cece's jaw was hanging open.

"How. Else. Did the police find the warehouse *and* know when

Vic would be there?" I said derisively, jabbing my finger at her. My acting coach would be proud.

Victor Gleeson, a suspected but previously unproven drug distributer, had been arrested as he oversaw the breakdown of drug-filled bags into saleable packets. The news had reported an anonymous 'tip' led police to it and I was now capitalizing on it.

"It wasn't me," Cece yelled, her gaze darting around the room.

No, that had been me. One of Angie's associates had her 'date' cut short when the customer got a phone call to report for work. Knowing we were friends, she'd gone to Angie with what she'd overheard with her wolf hearing. Angie had called me, asking me to report it so a male voice would protect her friend. I had made the call from a public payphone, stressing to the Narcotics detective I spoke with that "you need to haul butt as it's happening now."

The stares that had been boring into my back were now aimed at Cece. She paled as a mixture of growls and snarls rumbled throughout the room.

Oops. Don't need this to get out of hand. "You're not going to get away with it," I said, taking a step toward her. I ducked, the pool cue swishing above my head. Tom caught it, yanked it out of her hands. Grabbing balls off the table, she proved to have excellent aim—*oowww*—as the 7-ball smacked me solidly in the sternum. Dodging a couple others himself, Tom collided with me and we both went down.

Cece bolted past us and was out the door before we regained our feet.

We dashed after her. Tom stopped at the edge of the boardwalk. I could see his nostrils flexing as he tested the air before taking off down the pathway, me hard on his heels. I appreciated Tom's unsurpassable sense of smell as much as he did my summer stock experience. Unless she got in a vehicle or somehow diffused her scent, Tom would easily track her down.

Her hideout was 2631 Amhurst Lane, about a fifteen-minute walk from *Dead End*. A third-hand sedan minus a rear bumper was parked in front of the small, dilapidated house. We treaded carefully through the junk-filled yard. Tom made a circling motion with his index finger and disappeared around the corner as I braved the three steps up to the porch. Two were so rotted I was surprised they held my weight, and the top step was missing entirely. I eyed the boards in front of me before gingerly stepping over the hole and moving to the door.

Knowing Tom would be positioned by the back door by now, I drew my gun and tested the doorknob. Not locked. She must have been in a big hurry as that was a big no-no in this neighborhood. Standing to the side, I pushed the door wide open. No gun blast. No shifter pouncing.

I peeked around the doorjamb.

A shadeless lamp lit one end of a lopsided couch that was the only piece of furniture in the room that spanned the whole front of the house. Wynvard or 'stacked' houses had been popular eighty, ninety years ago. The rooms were linear, one behind the other, with a living room and kitchen anchoring the two ends. Everything else would open off the hallway that, for this house, was in the righthand corner. I slowly toed my way across to carefully peer down it. There were only two doorways between me and the kitchen. So, one bedroom, one bathroom.

The hall was dark except for the light streaming out of the first doorway. I sidled up to it. Cece, her back to me, was hastily shoving clothes from a pile on the bed into a suitcase. Unless they were hiding under the bed, she was alone. Nor did I see any nearby pool paraphernalia or substitutes she could lob at me.

I leaned against the doorframe and crossed my arms. "Going on a trip?" I inquired nonchalantly.

She whipped around. "You!" The sight of the Ruger propped on my right bicep stopped her for a moment. Then, "Who the hell are you?"

"Curt D'Accio."

"Yes, Curt D'Accio," she said, voice heavy on the sarcasm, "I'm leaving town as fast as I can. You've put a bullseye on my back." Fists clenched, she took a step forward. "I didn't rat anyone out. I don't know Victor Whoever so he couldn't have dumped me. Why, asshole? Tell me why."

"Easiest way to get you out of there with minimal ruckus. So we could talk."

"So we could *talk*?" she repeated in disbelief. "About what?"

"About blackmail and extortion, Miss Totusek. Or should I say, Rosalie Sayer." Her eyes widened. "Are you part of it or just hired for those pictures?"

"Pictures?"

"Where you had luncheon with Mr. Filbrandt. Where you supposedly shared a passionate kiss in the Woodworkers underground parking lot. Where you simulate a rendezvous at the Southside Motel."

She gaped at me for several seconds. "How do you know all that?" she demanded.

"I'm a PI. Tracing all aspects of those pictures was fairly simple. Based on what Mr. Filbrandt told me—" Her hand flew up, halting me.

"Wait. The mark already has the pictures?"

"Uh-huh. With a ten-thousand-dollar demand."

I waited until she ran out of breath. "Talk to me, Cece. The sooner you tell me what I want to know, the sooner you can find a rock to hide under before the police get involved."

"Freddy hired me," she said, shooting me a dirty look, "both for the pictures and because I knew this area."

"Who's Freddy? Real or alias?"

"Alfred Duninger, the guy with a fancy camera. Said he had taken a job here in Omaha. Paid me a thousand dollars up front, promised four more when we were done." She spread her arms out. "Obviously I've not gotten it or I'd be out of this dump."

"Uh-huh. Where's Freddy now?"

"Who the hell knows," she snapped. "I haven't seen him all week. And now I know why he's not answering his phone. Ten thousand frigging dollars, the rat!"

"So, the con artist has been conned," I said bluntly. Her jaw flexed. "He not only left you behind, but you are the only one tied to those pictures and the motel register. And it's your word that he's the photographer." Not counting the motel manager who might get amnesia.

This time her string of profanity included a few words I hadn't heard before.

"Did Freddy ever tell you who hired him?"

"No, and I didn't want to know."

"Not even a pronoun? He? She?"

"No."

I blew out an exasperated breath. "Did he say anything? Even odd or unrelated comments?"

Her tone sarcastic, she said, "He did say he was glad he wasn't in politics. That they were the biggest con artists around. The pictures were supposed to be released about a month before the election to ruin the target's election chances."

Yep, that put it squarely into a political motive. Freddy probably couldn't resist taking advantage and making some bucks in the meantime. Straightening, I holstered my gun. Her shoulders relaxed a little bit.

"Who was impersonating Filbrandt at the motel?"

She shrugged. "Some guy Freddy hired. He thought he was taking part in a porno film." Her teeth flashed in a wide grin. "He was good."

I rolled my eyes. "Freddy's description?"

"Average height and brown everything. Skin, hair, eyes."

"What's his phone number?"

She shook her head. "Wouldn't matter. It's a CC phone."

Crap. The cheap cash-and-carry had probably already been chucked.

"If that's all, I need to get out of here before a bunch of drunks show up wanting pieces of my *non*-informant ass." Giving me a final glare, she turned back to her packing.

Thinking of Rosalie Hendrix and her family, I said, "Stay out of Nebraska."

Her acknowledgement was a backhanded finger flip and a "piss-on" snarl, a Zero's rude equivalent of a shifter's tail flip and spray.

Rejoining Tom out front, I told him what all I'd learned.

"Going to let her go?" he asked.

"She's a minor player in this con," I replied absently while copying down the number on the Iowa license plate duck taped to the truck lid. "The authorities can deal with her after Filbrandt goes—*crap*," I muttered under my breath. I'd slipped back into our comfortable partnership of the past over the past hours.

Tom's cheek twitched. "You'll have to tell me about your client someday." He studied the house for a moment. "Especially if this turns ugly," he told me.

Tom said he was parked at a gas station southwest of here. We agreed to meet at our favorite Denny's for a late supper, the one we'd sit in and compare notes back when we had worked together. My treat; he'd earned it. Told him I'd meet him there after Cece pulled out. She might be a criminal and a con artist, but I didn't like the idea of her injured or worse because of my theatrics. It ended up with both of us watching until she drove away.

What did our consideration for her welfare get us? Another rude finger minus the verbal spray.

Chapter 9

Monday morning saw me at my desk, filling out government forms requesting Iowa's information on Alfred Duninger: vital statistics, driver's license, and police/court records. Here's hoping Cece was right and it was his real name, I thought, filling out the form for the Federal National Criminal Database. I logged into the Nebraska's Department of Motor Vehicles database. Just because he didn't know the Omaha area didn't mean he wasn't familiar with another part of our state.

Got the "Zero Records Found" response. Same for my Nebraska vital statistics searches. Definitely not from here. No guarantee he was a native Iowan, either. Hopefully, the FNCD will have something on him.

A quick on-line search gave me a list of Iowa Professional Photography Association websites. My twelfth call, to the one in Davenport, provided the first concrete evidence that Alfred Duninger did indeed exist. He'd been a member with them up until seven years ago, when he was dropped for unspecified 'unprofessional conduct.' I mentally rubbed my hands together in anticipation of the information from all those forms I filled out.

I called Mr. Filbrandt, updating him that I had identified the woman, had a lead on the photographer, and that the primary motive definitely appeared to be political, with one of the scam engineers apparently getting greedy.

"Thank you, Mr. D'Accio. My wife and I have made a decision. If you can't resolve this in the time left, we will go to the press ourselves. Neither of us will stand for political or personal extortion," he said in a firm, matter-of-fact voice.

"Some may believe it's real. That you got caught, and now you're trying to bluff your way out of it," I warned.

"So be it," he replied in the same tone. "At that point, I imagine the police will take over the case?"

I nodded, even though he couldn't see it. "I'll be happy to hand over all my notes to them. The police will be able to access information outside the state better than I can. Which might be what's needed to break this open." I couldn't help being impressed as we hung up. If I lived in Omaha, he'd definitely get my vote.

My call to the hospital produced mixed news this time. Russell's vital signs had improved and were stable, but he still remained unconscious. The ward nurse felt confident he would probably be moved from ICU to a private room later today after his physician's assessment.

Diana stuck her head in the door. "Are you taking appointments this week? And Mr. Koelzer from next door needs a quick background check on a witness."

Filbrandt's case's end date was coming up, whether I resolved it or not. It'd be a day or two before I got anything back on Alfred Duninger, if at all. Come to think of it…

"Diana? Those records for Aaron Rivas come in yet?"

"No. I'll call over and check on them."

I wanted to see them before going any further. Might as well keep busy. "Go ahead. Start appointments on Wednesday and get Mr. Koelzer's information."

I had Joel Koelzer's report typed and ready to go by lunchtime and passed it off to Diana for her admin stuff. He wasn't going to be happy. Koelzer's witness had a longer RAP sheet than Cece Totusek. No felonies, though, and his longest stint behind bars was six months. Still, I hoped this guy wasn't supposed to be a character witness.

The news from the courthouse was irritating: someone had dropped the ball on Aaron's records. The individual Diana spoke with apologized and said we should receive the requested documents by tomorrow.

I was unwrapping my deli order when an email came in from Angela Bruhn in Atlanta wanting to know the status of my research into her potential hire. I politely replied that I couldn't guarantee 100 percent completion by next week, but most of the list should be done. The reply that popped into my email box almost immediately?

"One hundred percent is the preferable goal."

Really? I kept my fingers off the keyboard, figuring not replying was the wisest action.

Taking a large bite of my sandwich, I chewed and brooded. I was at a standstill. Part of me wanted to go interview Lillian Strom, but there was nothing to indicate she was behind the blackmail. I methodically worked my way through lunch while trying to figure out the biggest question in this case. Why? Why go to the length and effort that was put into it?

When Merle called wanting to know if I'd like to take a walk in the park, I declined.

"It's a nice day for late October. Sunny. Just a bit nippy. Might get you out of that grumpy mood. Never know who you might run into," she said, nearly purring. Which was pretty good for a Zero.

I reconsidered. Getting out of the office did sound good. I was also curious about that last comment, which was probably the real reason for her calling. "Who, Merle?"

"Miss Melissa Brower. She'll be doing a meet-and-greet throughout Jenson Park. 'Letting the people get to know her' was the phrase her publicist used. I thought since you've shown recent political *interest*, you might want to accompany me and the camera man."

Uh-huh. She was still trying to figure out who I was focusing on. But it would give me a chance to observe Miss Brower and her entourage. Maybe ask a few innocent questions and get the wheels turning.

"I don't know," I said, pretending to hedge. "After all, meeting with me would be wasted. I don't live in Omaha and therefore can't vote for any of them." I grinned at an unladylike sound. "As you said, it is a nice day, and Diana probably would appreciate me getting out of the office for a while. Where and when do you want to meet?"

***

Melissa Brower's meet-and-greet lasted several hours. She shook hands and listened—really listened—to those who had questions. Her replies had been straightforward and succinct, no dodging or hedging as politicians were known to do. I had to admit, I was impressed. Then I nearly ruined it. I had sidled up to one of her campaign followers, and nonchalantly asked if there'd been any ethic complaints. That perked up Merle's ears and had Lillian Strom whipping around. Oops. Forgot about her shifter hearing.

Strom immediately demanded to know what I was talking

about, what I had heard. I managed to placate the outraged woman by telling her it was just something I heard in the gym. *"You know, just guys bouncing balls and ideas around, wondering how far a politician would go."* She assured me in glacial tones that, as a lawyer, Melissa Brower knew exactly where the lines were and would not cross them for any reason.

Merle, however, knew me better. She kept pestering me all the way back to the parking lot. My patience snapped and I told her, yes, someone had come to me with a frigging complaint. No, I wasn't going to tell her any frigging thing else. Merle was muttering and her camera man snickering when they drove off.

Alone at last, I leaned against my car, watching the last rays of light slowly fade into twilight. For some reason, I'd always favored this part of the day. Something inside me would go…quiet. Perhaps some genetic memory remanent of a time when our ancestors settled in for the night? I sighed. The nights of today's modern world were almost as busy as the daylight hours.

I climbed into my car, firing it up and cranking the heater on full. The temperature had dropped as fast as the sun. I headed home. I'd go through my notes and the pictures. Again. Maybe see something I'd missed the first couple of times. Check email for any returns on my Alfred Duninger requests. Unfortunately, that information would be about as helpful in finding him as a kid's sandbox shovel in a hog pen. Still, I could take a decent DMV photo around to all the motels and hope to get a positive hit.

That'd take time, something the Filbrandts and I were running out of.

Chapter 10

Two police detectives bustled into the office shortly after nine o'clock. "I'm Detective Macron," one woman said, producing her badge. "My partner, Detective Ellerbeck."

My Gen-dar said Macron was a feline, her partner a Zero. Escorting them to my client chairs, I wondered who or what had brought the detectives to me.

"How can I help you?" I asked.

"You recently ran a number of inquiries on Alfred Duninger," Detective Macron said. "Why?"

All database searches were logged, showing who requested what on whom. The fact they were asking was a bad sign. "He's a person of interest in a case I'm working," I replied warily. "Your interest?"

"His body was pulled from the Missouri River last night."

I slumped back in my chair. "Well, crap. There goes my only solid lead." Then added, "Sorry. That was an insensitive response. You're Homicide?"

"Yes. What were you investigating Mr. Duninger for, and how does it pertain to your case?"

I sat silent for a moment. "My case involves an issue that is both sensitive and *non-violent*," I stressed, treading carefully. "Therefore, all aspects of it remain confidential until his death can somehow be linked to either my case or my client."

I got identical pursed-lips expressions from them. They asked more questions, made the usual threats when I didn't answer to their satisfaction, and finally stomped out. They'd either get a warrant or not. Felt like stomping myself as I made my way to the coffee counter. Whatever information about Duninger I received now would be useless.

"That Detective Macron is very haute couture," Diana remarked, sorting through the morning mail.

"A what?"

"High fashion," she said, glancing up. "She was wearing at least six thousand dollars' worth of clothes."

I blinked. "You're sure?"

"Regina coats start at twenty-one hundred, and hers wasn't from the bottom line. Boots—probably also Regina—would be about six, seven hundred. Couldn't tell much about the pants and blouse, but I doubt they and her undies came from Woolworth's. Want to know how much high-end brassieres cost?"

I shook my head vigorously.

Grinning, she handed me a couple of envelopes. "And those were real diamond studs in her earlobes."

I didn't know a darn thing about women's clothes, but I did have an idea of what a police detective made. "Then she either has another source of income or spends every penny of her salary on clothes. Which seems stupid either way, considering some of the scrapes and rough takedowns they get into."

Disgruntled, I returned to my desk. Tossing the mail aside, I placed a call to Kurt Filbrandt and explained the unexpected turn of events.

"Whether or not his death is tied into your problem, it does bring my investigation to a screeching halt," I told him honestly. "He was the single lead I had to whoever is behind the blackmail attempt. Since you and your wife have decided to fight this, I recommend you go to the police, not the press, and tell them everything. That way, if the pictures are released, you can announce that the *fraud* is already under investigation by the authorities."

After a pronounced sigh, Mr. Filbrandt said, "I concur. The police will want to contact you."

"They will. With your permission, I'll provide them with the pictures and copies of all my notes." Saving them the trouble of getting a subpoena should keep the hostility factor down.

"Granted. Thank you, Mr. D'Accio, for your efforts. Please forward me your bill."

I spent the next hour typing up a final report for Mr. Filbrandt and turned it over to Diana. Then made copies of everything. The picture copies went into my case file along with my original notes. The original pictures and my note copies were stuck into a blank folder for the police. I'd add a copy of my report to it after Diana proofed it.

After wallowing in frustration and regret for a few minutes, I opened up my email. Might as well see what I'd received on the late Alfred Duninger.

His DMV license had been renewed three years ago with an address in Des Moines. His photo revealed an unmemorable face, one easily ignored and quickly forgotten. An asset, undoubtedly, for blending into surroundings while stalking and taking clandestine pictures. Duninger's RAP sheet wasn't nearly as long as Cece's and had only minor infractions, up until the last entry. It was an extortion conviction seven years ago that earned him three years in prison, which explained his expulsion from Professional Photography.

I frowned in thought. He'd evidently moved to Des Moines right after he got out. How had he supported himself? No further entries meant he'd either kept his activities legal or underground. Considering his last job, I'd go with the underground market. I didn't bother with his vital statistics, as they were irrelevant now. All of the information was. Well, it wasn't my problem anymore. Still, I moved the emails over to a storage directory instead of deleting them.

I called the hospital midafternoon to check on Russell. The word 'comatose' was used for the first time.

***

As expected, the police showed up at my office the next morning. I recognized her, as we'd crossed paths before. Detective Sheila Chizek, the Robbery/Fraud Unit's senior detective. I wasn't surprised that she'd been given Mr. Filbrandt's case. She was dedicated, smart, meticulous, and as tenacious and stubborn as a badger. Had the personality of one, too, despite being a First-Gen cougar. Probably why she had a different junior officer every time I saw her. Although, she was apparently working solo at the moment.

I led her into my office. Picked up the prepared file off my desk and handed it to Chizek. "This has copies of all my notes, my final summary report, and the blackmail pictures received by the Filbrandts." My hope that she'd take it and leave were dashed when the detective made herself comfortable in a client chair. I mentally prepared myself for a grilling.

"If this is going to take more than an hour, I'll need to have my secretary reschedule my ten o'clock appointment."

"That might be best," Chizek replied absently, pulling out my report summary.

Almost two hours later, I was at the well-done stage. Chizek wanted clarification of every note I'd made, of every step I'd taken and why. Even wanted my suspicions and guesses, which was a pleasant surprise. Most police detectives brushed off a PI's opinion.

"Alfred Duninger," Detective Chizek said, finally closing the file and leaning back in her chair. "Do you believe his murder is tied to this?"

"I honestly can't say for sure, since there's no telling what else he was involved in," I told her. "However, it does seem a bit coincidental. Especially since his associate in generating the blackmail material, Cece Totusek, told me the photos weren't supposed to be released until a month before the election."

"It would have hit like a bombshell."

"Uh-huh. I'm guessing here, but Duninger may have gambled Filbrandt would quietly pay up and his employer would never know."

"Except Mr. Filbrandt didn't. What's more, he did something unexpected: he proactively hired you. You started digging and something alerted said employer. Who was obviously not pleased at having his-or-her plans ruined and made their displeasure known."

"Well, you can dig harder and deeper than I can," I told her honestly as she stood to leave. "Perhaps you can find a link to that employer. Clayton Tallon," I suddenly blurted. "Have you heard of him?"

"Clayton Sanford Tallon?" Detective Chizek enounced carefully, her tone ominous.

"Uh, I don't know his middle name," I said, regretting my impulse. "Loan shark?"

"Is he involved in this?" Her voice would chill a polar bear.

"No, but I've heard some…things about him."

"Like what?" she said, leaning over my desk.

"Rumors. Nothing that would stand in court," I cautiously replied.

Her gaze bored into mine. "If you learn anything that will, Mr. D'Accio, you will let me know. Immediately. And if I find you are withholding that information in the name of 'client confidentiality,' you will regret it. Very much so. Understand?"

"Yes, ma'am," I replied promptly. Tallon, for whatever reason, was a personal thorn in Detective Chizek's paw. She had just learned I might have a set of pliers. *Good going, Dice.*

Diana brought me a cup of coffee after they'd left. "Thanks," I told her and sighed with gratitude. "I feel like I've been beat up one side and down the other."

"Detective Chizek did sound a bit demanding," Diana agreed. "Your nine o'clock rescheduled for two-thirty tomorrow. The copies of Aaron Rivas's court records have finally come in, and Miss Heiser called. She needs you at Chandler Import HQ to go over a number of documents."

I grimaced, having already gotten a taste of what that would mean. "Call her back; tell Miss Heiser I'll be by first thing in the morning." With my afternoon free, Aaron's case took precedence.

I spent the rest of the day going over the trial documents. The more I read, the more certain I became that Aaron had, more or less, been railroaded. It'd been a heinous crime splashed on the front pages and the authorities had wanted to resolve it as quickly as possible. Unfortunately, the official police reports and crime scene photos were missing. There was a note explaining that those copies had been delayed due to an equipment glitch. Technology at its finest, I mused.

***

At a quarter to eight, I stood at the mouth of an alley between two towering warehouses. Nebraska's capricious weather had blown in a heavy cloud cover and the cold wind ruffled my hair. Beside me, Nate stared uneasily into the pitch-black opening. Not a shred of light from the streetlights behind us penetrated it. I had called Angie, asking her to meet me tonight. Mandy's comments and Detective Chizek's reaction had aggravated my itch. I needed to scratch it, even if Clayton Tallon was on the periphery of my investigation.

"I can see why it's a shifter bar," Nate said sourly. "They're the only ones who could find it. I know for a fact a shifter's dark vision isn't one of your pluses."

Doctor Nathanial Gordon had done his internship in the emergency rooms of Chicago, Albuquerque, and Charlotte before moving to Omaha. I doubted there was an injury he hadn't seen or treated. Not only was he my personal physician, he was the best kind of friend: the one that would stand beside you when others turned away.

I'd swung by his apartment after getting a worried call from Myra Elsome, Nate's receptionist. She had told me he'd handled a bad ER case on Sunday, wasn't answering his phone, and asked me to check on him. Finding the same hollow-eyed, glazed stare he had been wearing when we'd first met, I basically dragged him here. He needed out of that apartment. Out of his head even more.

Grinning, I pulled a compact flashlight from my jacket and flicked it on. "Which is why I have this. Come on; Angie's waiting." I strode in confidently, Nate trailing behind me.

We were almost at the mid-point when Nate skidded to the right as an opening yawned on our left. There was no railing to keep the unwary from falling in. Unmarked, unlit steps led down into an equally pitch-black stairwell.

"Dammit, we could have fallen and broken our necks!" Nate sputtered.

"Does occasionally happen," I confirmed nonchalantly, starting down the steps. "I'm told they ensure the body is found at the bottom of steps elsewhere or a fire escape."

"That was a joke, right?"

"Nope." I held the flashlight out and pointing down to illuminate the steps for him.

A couple of low-voiced swear words later, Nate asked how I'd found this place.

"Marge brought me." For the next several moments I wasn't leading Nate down the steps, I was following Marge down them.

"We call ourselves Despos. *It's a place for castoffs and the downtrodden. It's a safe haven to lick wounds, to rebuild oneself and find the courage to face tomorrow. It's a refuge from the full-throttle world, a quiet place to simply relax and just let go. Some only come for the time they need it, others become regulars."*

I swallowed, missing her all over again.

Several steps in at the bottom, I turned the flashlight off. Nate bumped into me. "Give it a couple of seconds," I assured him, turning him to the right. The dim outline of a recessed door became visible as our sight adjusted to the dark.

"Uh, Dice? Maybe I should wait back at your car."

"Chicken?" I replied, reaching for the door handle.

"Cluck, cluck."

I was still laughing when we entered a dimly lit room that ran the full width of the warehouse above us. The lighting, what there was of it, was mostly over the bar and along the walls. A few of the room's support pilings also had softly lit sconces, the sections of the room between them shadowed. Tables scattered around the room were placed further apart than normally found in bars to give the occupants a semblance of privacy. Booths were randomly tucked against two walls and spaced apart like the tables for the same reason.

I confidently wove my way to the bar that ran almost the full length of the left wall. After two years, I was a regular and got the occasional nod in passing. Nate was getting more than a few discreet inhales as we crossed the room. Not only was I bringing a stranger, he was another Zero.

Reaching the counter, I pulled out my wallet. I had not yet reached that highly coveted and elusive run-a-tab status. "Hey, Boris. It's been a heck of a day. I'll take a MacEverson. Nate?"

"White Top beer. Please?"

I hid my grin. Boris was a lot to take in on first glance. He was a huge bear of a man, literally as well as figuratively. I'd spotted Angie in a booth along the back wall and headed that way after paying for our drinks. She scooted over so I could sit beside her. Her full breasts were barely covered by a low-cut whisp of a shirt that said she was in working mode. Her hand curled around a beer bottle.

Angie eyed my glass. "That kind of day, huh?"

"You wouldn't believe it," I said with feeling. Marge's death had sent me reeling into near alcoholism. My friends knew I had been limiting my scotch intake since then.

"Angie, this is Nate Gordon. Nate, meet Angie. You've both heard me talk about the other." Custom was to only give a prostitute's first or working name. It was up to them if and when to provide the rest. I hadn't learned Angie's last name myself until hiding at her place.

"I've heard good things about you, Dr. Gordon. I'm thinking of switching my six-week checkups to your clinic."

His gaze dropped to his beer. His tone neutral, he said, "My receptionist can set up the appointment."

She looked questioningly at me. I shook my head, telling her to let it pass. I'd deal with him after we finished. "What do you know about a loan shark named Clayton Sanford Tallon?"

"Enough to know to stay away from him. He's a bigoted jerk with a corn cob stuck up his ass." I nearly snorted scotch. "Runs his loan sharking and gang out of a bar called *Burton's Hangout* in the Hansen area. They're all bitter Zeros, jealous of anyone born with Gen traits. Double that if they have siblings that do. What's your interest in him?"

Yeah, our fickle genetics could lead to all sorts of family problems, from resentment to down-and-nasty fights.

"I came across his name in a recent investigation. When I happened to ask an Omaha robbery detective about him, she nearly climbed across my desk. Threatened me if I withheld any information about him."

"Huh. Rumor mill does have him linked to a few thefts."

"According to a client, he's branched into black market acquisitions."

"Huh," Angie repeated. Drank some beer. "Hadn't heard that. Not like that'd be bantered around—those guys are ruthless."

"Anyway…I was hoping you could do a bit of snooping? Maybe?"

She gave me a hard look. "Why? Is he part of what you're investigating?"

"Not directly. Honestly?" I waved my glass. "I've heard enough that, well…I don't like it. Or him." *Lame, Dice, lame.*

"I admit, a lot of people would be overjoyed if he was taken off the streets. Money lenders aren't nice people, and Tallon is the worst by far. He's a ghoul, feeding off of people's desperation." Angie's eyes glowed the golden hue of her cougar. "Especially shifters."

Mandy's experience had certainly proved that.

"I'll take whatever you can learn, rumor or otherwise. Just…be careful. Yes, I know," I admitted when she rolled her eyes, "you can take care of yourself. Humor me, Angie. Take extra care."

She nodded. "Will do. Did that cop give you any specifics? No? That figures," she said derisively. "I need to go. Got a nine-thirty appointment across town." She finished her beer in a couple of gulps then grabbed the jacket lying next to her. I stood to let her out.

"See you in a couple of weeks, Dr. Gordon. My next checkup?" she added when he gave her a puzzled look.

"Oh. Right. See you then," Nate said.

Angie shot me a sideways glance before leaving. I slid back into the booth. It was time to deal with his problem. Seeing Nate's bottle was empty, I signaled the waitress and paid for another one.

"So," he said, clearing his throat. "Unusual bar. It's…quiet."

I nodded slowly. It didn't have the usual bar accoutrements of TV screen, dart board, or pool table. "It's meant to be a place to heal and to regroup. Fighting will get you a three-month ban, which Boris will happily enforce." Nate snorted. "There's music, but it's kept shifter low. If you concentrate hard, you might be able to pick up strains of it."

Nate's face scrunched up briefly. "Yeah, I think I do. Marge brought you?"

"Originally it was to meet Angie and for information back when I was hunting Tabitha's killer. Later…I needed it," I told him. "It also helped me get through losing Marge."

We paused as the waitress deposited Nate's fresh beer and scooped up the two empties.

"Aren't you worried that word may get back to this Tallon fellow that the two of you are investigating him?" Nate asked.

I reached down and absently tapped the side of my seat. "Sound suppression system, both sides. Set for a shifter's audio range." Nate leaned over to inspect them. Keeping my voice gentle, I said, "Nate, you knew what going back into ER medicine would mean."

The hand around his beer tightened. "You know? Yeah, you do. That's why you came by my apartment."

I nodded. "Myra called. She's really worried about you."

"Did she tell you why?" he said harshly.

"No, just that it was bad enough you had her reschedule your entire week's appointments."

For several heartbeats, nothing. Then the dam broke.

"I spent hours—*hours*—stitching up her wounds. Slashes across her entire torso, her arms as she'd tried to protect herself. Her face? Almost in ribbons, both eyes and one ear gone. Who does that, Dice?" His hand around the beer bottle trembled. "Who does that to an eight-year-old child?"

Shock froze me for a moment. I pulled his beer away and shoved my glass at him. He emptied it in one gulp and spent the next minute coughing. Then he was crying. I sat silent, letting him get it out. Truth was, my eyes were a bit damp, too.

My friend cared, truly cared, about his patients. About people. He'd quit Emergency Medicine after years of repairing the damage inflicted upon them by others. The final straw had been having to tell a young woman—savaged by a boyfriend—she'd not only lost the child she was carrying, but any future ones. The uterus had been too badly damaged to save. I had been surprised when he went back, even part time.

And this…this not only brought it all back, it was even worse.

It was a good ten minutes before Nate ran dry. One of the waitresses plopped a dry towel on the table in passing. Tears, I guess, weren't unknown here.

Nate ran it across his face, then gave me a sheepish smile. "Thanks, I needed that."

A corner of my lips kicked up. "That's what friends are for. Nate," my tone turned serious. "If you can't find some way to handle—constructively—the really bad things…"

Nate's head was slowly bobbing. "I know, I know." He fell silent for a minute, then started chuckling. "I suppose I could go howl at the sky like Bernard does."

"Howling might work. Bernard?"

"My wolf neighbor. Does it at least once a week. Said it keeps him sane and his teenage son alive." Paused. "I'm pretty sure he was kidding about his son."

"I don't know about that," I said, sporting a wicked grin. "I drove my dad up a tree once. Literally. He didn't come down for over an hour." A Second-Gen cougar, my dad's growls had rumbled through the backyard until mom had threatened to shift and knock him off his limb. As a Second-Gen panther herself, she could do it.

It felt good to hear his laugh. "Why don't you give howling a try next time, Nate? Can't hurt. Ready to go?"

"Yeah."

My flashlight got us up the stairwell and into the alley. I tucked it back into my jacket as we neared its entrance. We could make do with the streetlights.

"Hey, Dice? It's over a dozen steps down. Why isn't it called the Cave?"

I snorted, having had the exact same thought on my first visit. "Fifteen to be exact. Its full name is the *Desperation Depot*," I told him, zipping my jacket closed. We stepped onto the sidewalk where a strong gust nearly blew me into Nate. Wow. The wind had really picked up while we were inside, and those gusts were howlers. I exchanged nods with a grizzled old-timer I recognized as he passed us on his way into the alley. "Named by a previous owner that—" My ears registered the shot even as the bullet slammed into my chest. Everything went black.

Chapter 11

Nate's head jerked up and he forced his eyes wide as he blinked away the sleep that had tried to sneak up on him. He hadn't been this tired in a long time. He'd been up for over twenty-four hours on top of not sleeping well the last few nights. A two-handed face massage banished the last of the drowsiness. Pushing himself up out of the chair, he moved over to his friend's bedside and examined all the equipment readings.

Nate grimaced at the blood pressure reading. Still way too low. The heartbeat was steady if weak, though, which was a very good sign. He stared at the figure lying so still in the bed, bandages encasing the left half of his chest, his pallor that of the corpse he'd almost become. *Dead*, he'd thought at first, when his friend dropped to the pavement with blood streaming from both sides.

He should have known Curt D'Accio was too stubborn to die.

He'd ripped off the bottom of Curt's shirt and stuffed it into the chest wound. The man who'd passed them seconds ago used a claw to rip apart Curt's jacket, wading and shoving its shreds into the exit wound on his back to staunch the bleeding as much as possible. The amount of blood soaking their hands spoke of arterial damage.

Another man hunkered down beside them, telling them the police and ambulance were on their way.

Hang in there, Dice, hang in there, he'd repeated over and over as the ambulance raced to the nearest hospital. By sheer luck, that was the Saint Benedictine Hospital, three blocks away. It had a well-earned reputation for handling severe trauma cases, mostly due to its close proximity to the Boondocks. Then hours in the OR to repair the damage. They'd finally wheeled Dice into the recovery room almost an hour ago.

The door *swished* open behind him. Expecting one of the nurses doing a check, it was, instead, the head of OPD's Homicide Division.

"He's not dead yet," Nate yelped.

Lieutenant Sinclair came to an immediate halt. "Yet? Is that still a possibility?"

"No, he's stable," Nate mumbled, embarrassed at his gaffe. He ran a hand across his face. Boy, he really needed sleep.

"How is he?" Sinclair asked, coming up to the bed.

"His left clavicle was shattered. Bone shards nicked his left carotid artery and the medial cord in the brachial plexus nerve bundle that goes through the shoulder. The exit wound in his shoulder was relatively tight, so I'm guessing a high-caliber round that simply drilled through."

"It was," Sinclair confirmed. "Bullet was found in the building directly behind him. Unfortunately, it had smashed into a steel rib. We'll not be able to get a ballistic reading off of it."

Nate didn't have the energy for the cussing that deserved. "The next twenty-four hours are critical," he said instead, nodding toward his unconscious friend. "Infection, a missed bleeder…anything that'll require going back in. I'll stay with Curt until he's moved to

ICU. They'll take over the watch there. If no issues arise, he'll be moved to a regular room when he's deemed stable. All in all," Nate finished, blowing out a breath, "he was lucky."

"Definitely, since the combination of dark and adverse weather conditions likely fouled the sniper's shot."

Nate nodded, having already concluded that. He locked his attention on the lieutenant. "Don't take this the wrong way, but why are you here?"

Sinclair stared down at the silent figure for several moments, then stuck his hands in his pockets. "Not sure myself. I read the reports and, considering his injury rate last year, I thought I would…check on him."

Huh. How about that. There had initially been a fair amount of animosity between the two men when they were hunting a killer last year. Toward the end, the lieutenant had lost some of his "stiff-necked marbleness," as Curt had put it. Evidently, Sinclair now found himself liking Curt D'Accio and didn't know what to do about it.

Nate kept his grin hidden. "I'm sure Dice will appreciate it," he said, getting a swift side-eye glance from the man. "I'll let him know you stopped by."

Sinclair's chin dipped once, either in acknowledgement or goodbye, since he turned and left without another word.

Nate had settled back into the uncomfortable chair when an angry Doctor Patel strong-armed the door open. He stared, shocked, as it slammed against the wall. *Gen-strength* his hindbrain warned as he scrambled back to his feet.

"What the hell are you thinking?" Dr. Patel demanded as she stalked toward him.

"I have no idea what—"

"Do you see that?" she snapped, pointing at a low blood pressure reading. "Have you bothered to check his latest tests results? Seen his abysmal red blood count? His organs are not getting the oxygen they need. He needs blood," she snarled, "and you haven't ordered any."

"He doesn't need it," Nate said, steeling himself for the argument coming. There was no way around this. Curt had needed blood during surgery to keep him stable as the two of them had worked on him. Now he'd have to explain why it was no longer necessary.

"He most certainly does, *Doctor* Gordon," she replied sarcastically. "You might be his personal physician but here, in this hospital, I'm responsible for his well-being. I'm ordering blood."

"And you'd be responsible for endangering that well-being," Nate returned calmly. "As said personal physician, don't you think I would know his system? Run an erythropoietin screening."

"He's a Zero," she returned hotly.

"He's a Zero-Plus," Nate corrected, mentally apologizing to his friend.

Surprise crossed her face. "A what? Seriously?"

Although he was a non-shifting Zero, Curt had inherited several of what were considered shifter-only traits, including the rapid repair ability. By now, his kidneys would be flooding his bloodstream with that specific hormone, forcing a significant increase in blood production.

Giving her a wan smile, Nate said, "Run the EPO test, Dr. Patel, as you would for a shifter."

***

Thirty-five minutes later, Dr. Patel reentered in a less hostile manner.

Nate straightened up, but conserved what little energy he had left by not standing. Her expression confirmed what he knew she'd find. "The count was high."

She looked from him, to Curt, and back to him. "I've never heard of a Zero going through rapid repair. It's…it's unheard of. Startling."

He shrugged. "I'm sure those who saw their first shifter in a Third-Gen wereform felt the same." While probably taking several steps back. "Mother Nature has been messing with our evolution for millennium. Dice—Curt, is probably one of the first in this aspect. Besides rapid repair, his reflexes are better than normal for a Zero and his hearing, strength, and instincts are near or comparable to First-Gen levels."

She tapped her chin. Her tone thoughtful, she asked, "How did you learn about it?"

"Dealing with the injuries Curt has acquired in his profession as a private investigator." A yawn snuck out before Nate could stop it. "Sorry. His family doctor learned it when Curt was badly injured in the car accident that killed his parents. He's also the one that labeled him a Zero-Plus."

"And he didn't publish the information?" she said in disbelief.

"The doctor felt it would be an invasion of Curt's medical privacy, especially while he was grieving and healing."

"He could have done so later, after Mr. D'Accio was healed," she insisted.

"Why?" Nate demanded. "We know what rapid repair is. We know what it does and how it functions. Yes, it's normally a shifter trait of which Curt D'Accio is not. Being an anomaly, however, does not give the medical profession—or anyone—the right to poke and pry into his and his family's lives."

He glared up at her. "Because that's exactly what will happen. What factors might have influenced the inheritance? What are his family's demographics? Another Zero relative to pester? Did Curt inherit anything else? Kind of hard to run a business dodging requests for interviews and blood samples. My friend is a person, not somebody's stepping-stone to medical fame and research grants."

"I understand, but the medical community needs to be made aware of the possibility that there could be—*is* a new strain," she returned. She eyed him for a minute then asked, "How long have you been up, Dr. Gordon?"

"Too long," Nate muttered.

"You need to go home. We'll be moving him to ICU shortly," she added when he started to object. "I'll stay with him till then. Do you have someone who can come get you?"

Checking the equipment again, he saw that both the systolic and diastolic numbers of Curt's blood pressure had gone up a few points. His friend was on the mend. Nate pushed himself up.

"I'll call a taxi. You have my number if anything comes up."

Chapter 12

Consciousness came slowly, along with an awareness of pain. I felt the bed under me, heard the soft sounds of machinery, and smelled the unmistaken odors that told me I was in a hospital. Again. Brain woke a bit more. Right. I'd been shot. Again. Bleary-eyed, my gaze wandered around the dimly lit room. Didn't look like ICU, so guess I'm going to live.

Suddenly my brain came fully awake. Sniper. *Nate*! Was he okay?

Beeeeep! Beep, beep, beep!

A young man came hurrying through the door. "You're awake. That's good, but I need you to calm down, Mr. D'Accio." He moved over to the equipment. "No need to stress; you're going to pull through this just fine."

"Did another man come in with me?" I demanded. "Was he shot?"

"Doctor Gordon came in with you—*beeeeeep*—no, no! He wasn't shot. I understand he's the reason you made it here alive. He treated you in transit and worked on your surgery."

I heaved a sigh of relief. "Where's here?"

"Saint Benedictine Hospital. Can I get you some water? How would you describe your pain level?"

"Water sounds good; pain's a throbbing seven or eight."

I checked out the rest of me while the nurse was gone. There was an IV attached to my right wrist and a huge bandage on my chest, across my left shoulder and a lump down against my shoulder blade. My left arm was strapped to my side. The dim lighting said the ward was on night mode. The nurse returned with a cup, straw, and syringe. I asked what day it was.

"It's Saturday morning, roughly three AM. Dr. Gordon authorized pain medication when you needed it." He injected the clear fluid into the second port tied to my IV line. "I'm going to raise your head up a bit. Let me know if you get dizzy or anything else."

Saturday. I'd lost two days. Several sips of water later, I was already exhausted. Nurse Roddy, according to his nametag, nodded when I mentioned it.

"You lost a lot of blood on top of the trauma of being shot, then surgery. Your body has a lot of recuperating to do." He eyed me curiously for several seconds. "Doctor Gordon is your physician of record, but Dr. Patel will also be checking on you. Anything else? Then I'll let you get some rest. Would you like to lay flat again? Then, simply press the call button if you need anything." He scanned the equipment around me before saying "Good-night."

Roddy walked over to a computer situated on a built-in shelf. I closed my eyes and tried to think of the shooter possibilities. I didn't bother opening them when the door *swooshed* open.

"How's things in here, Roddy?" a low female voice asked.

"Just inputting his latest stats," Roddy replied in an identical manner. "All in normal ranges. The morphine I injected in his IV a few minutes ago should be taking effect"

Yep, I thought drowsily.

"Have you seen his EPO test results?" Roddy continued softly.

"Uh-huh. Remarkable."

Hope that's a good thing was my last thought before drifting off.

***

The room was full of light when I woke again. My bladder was pretty full, too. Pressing the call button got me a nurse, thankfully male. My bathroom request was nixed in favor of a plastic container with a handle, which he expertly held for me. Pretty sure I failed to match his nonchalance. Business as usual for him was embarrassment for me.

"Lunch is in about an hour," he said, returning from the bathroom dump. "Missing breakfast as you did, I can get you something a bit early if you want."

My stomach's loud grumble answered that question.

I was still working my way through soft-cooked eggs, sausage patties, and unbelievably weak coffee when Nate walked in. I gave him a sour look. "Have you ever tried to eat with one hand? Especially when it's not your primary one?"

"Can't say I've had that experience," Nate said with a grin.

"Well, you're in a frigging good mood."

The grin vanished. "I am. Because my best friend is grumbling about having to eat one-handed instead of being fitted for a casket."

I immediately felt bad. "Sorry. You're right. I hear you're the reason I'm not."

"It was touch-and-go there for a bit," Nate admitted. "How much have you been told?"

"I've lost two days and had surgery." He was eyeing the equipment attached to me.

"Right." Nate pulled the visitor's chair over next to the bed. "Your stats are all good. What's your pain level?"

"Not too bad. I got another injection of that good stuff through the IV."

"Good. How are you feeling otherwise?"

"Grumpy."

Nate flashed a smile. "Sorry, no medications for that."

I glanced down at the bandages. "How bad, Nate? In layman terms, please."

"Your left collarbone was shattered when the bullet drilled a hole through you, which I rebuilt with pins. Bone shards nicked, among other things, an artery and a major nerve bundle in your shoulder. Your left arm is strapped to prevent any inadvertent movement by you or the med staff that might undo my work. I rate the nerve damage as mild as the medial cord wasn't severed and should heal without any issues."

"Should?"

"Nerves heal in their own way and at their own rate," Nate said. "Let me know if you experience more than a mild pain or any numbness in your arm or hand."

I stared off unseeing for several moments as I absorbed all he'd said, and what he hadn't. Nicked aorta? How close to dead had I come?

"Anything else, Doc?" I finally asked in a lame attempt at humor.

"Your secret is leaking."

"Huh?"

Nate rubbed the side of his nose. "You needed a blood transfusion while on the table. The in-house doctor working with me got rather demanding about starting another one after you were moved to Recovery. I had to insist on Dr. Patel running a screening for erythropoietin before she'd believe me. That's the hormone that controls red blood cell production," he clarified at my blank expression.

"And my levels were high." I sighed, resigned.

"Rapid-repair high," Nate agreed. "And yes, I had to have the EPO test done. Staying quiet and letting them hook up a bag or two would've been bad. Additional blood on top of what your body was mass producing would have been a system overload with blood clots at the top of the risk list. With you being a Zero, you can expect curiosity, perhaps even a bit of grilling, from the staff here."

EPO, huh? Then it had already started, if my scrap of memory from last night was accurate. I pushed the roller table away. "It was bound to come out sooner or later, Nate, especially with the way I keep getting hurt," I grumbled good-naturedly.

"There is that," he agreed.

Nate called in a nurse who helped him remove my bandages. He examined my chest wound closely, then asked me to lean forward. After examining the one back there, he asked me to wiggle my fingers. I did. On my right hand. Nate rolled his eyes and the female nurse shot me a grin.

"Very funny," Nate said. "Left hand, smart ass. That's good. Now shift your arm sideways—*no*! Do not try lifting it. That's it, just a little bit."

"Feels a bit stiff, a little tingling, but no pain," I told him.

"Won't be any as long as you're getting morphine," Nate said, eyeing my arm. "If you would, please, nurse," he said, motioning toward me. "Keep the arm immobilized for at least another day, then we'll see about a sling. Also, normal pain killers should suffice from here on out."

"No more good stuff?" I mock-groaned as the nurse pulled a wound dressing kit from a drawer and started rewrapping me.

"Be glad," Nate said dryly. "If you need it, then you have a problem. As it is, both wounds look good—no redness or excessive weeping. I think you're safely past any infection, so we'll discontinue the antibiotics after today. I'll order up an X-ray to check how your collarbone is healing."

Nate and I chatted for a bit, learning he'd left my Ruger and keys with Diana. I asked about my phone. He obligingly dug it out of my bagged personal items that were stored in the room's small cabinet. Dead battery, of course. Nate said he'd get it charged up; he'd also pick up clean clothes for when I was released. By the time I was wrapped and tucked, my eyelids kept dropping. He patted my good shoulder.

"Rest, Dice. You need that most of all right now."

***

Rest. Right. I snagged naps between getting X-rays, reviewing them with Nate, having a nurse remove my I-V, and enduring a not-short-enough discussion with a Dr. Patel about being a Zero-Plus. Then any idea of rest evaporated after getting a call from my mom's parents on the hospital phone next to my bed. Papaw and Mamaw Moser lived out west in Tryon, in the middle of farming country. After assuring them I was going to be okay, Mamaw told me Papaw was also 'laid up.' He'd been helping a neighbor load a tractor on a trailer last week, when it toppled off onto him, breaking both his legs.

"Why didn't you call—let me know sooner?" I blurted out.

"How often do we hear about your injuries?" she replied tartly. "At least, the ones we don't read about in the news."

"Well…well…that's different," I sputtered lamely.

Then Papaw got on the phone. Hearing his rumbling laughter and "I'm doing just fine, pup" untied the knot in my stomach, although it didn't completely erase my worry. We talked for several minutes and I promised to call once I was out of the hospital.

Chapter 13

With worry about Papaw on top of a growing shoulder throb, I was in a sour mood when two policemen showed up. I nearly growled at them, but managed to dig up enough self-restraint to answer their questions tactfully.

"Detective Mead, OPD Assault Division," Mead said brusquely. "Detective Tyree," waving toward his younger partner. "So. What'd you do to get shot?"

Or not. I locked my hard gaze with his. Held it without answering, waiting for a non-asinine question.

Police officers have a tendency to eye private investigators with wary suspicion, equating us with case interference and/or the use of questionable methods. While, admittingly, some of my peers do that, I try to avoid either. I'm used to their arrogant or disdainful attitudes, but Mead was downright hostile. It glared at me from his eyes.

The other detective cleared his throat. "Do you have any idea who would have a reason for shooting you?" Tyree asked.

At least he'd been polite. "Suspects? Sure," I said tartly. "Darrell and Trace Chandler."

Mead's snort was derisive. "You're accusing two of Omaha's most respected businessmen?"

"Two of Omaha's snakes," I snapped, noting that only the younger one made an entry in his notebook. "They want control of Chandler Import and were extremely unhappy with me being appointed as Conservator when Russell Chandler was injured." I made a mental note to find out what Russell's status was.

"Have you learned anything?" I asked, addressing the polite detective.

"Shot came from the second floor of the Thompson and Sons Industrial Warehouse. Two shifters coming up the sidewalk—opposite side of the street—dropped when the shot sounded. Both are combat veterans. By the time they had pinpointed where it came from and got there, a dark blue or gray sedan was barreling down the street. Too far and dark to get the license plate. The room and stairwell he used were skunked."

Skunk bombs were favored by both criminals and pranksters. A few drops of skunk-oil added to smoke bombs not only produced the unpleasant eye-and-nose results, painfully so for shifters, but they ruined any scent evidence. It had taken days to 'de-scent' my office when it got hit with one.

"They went after the guy?" I said, amazed. Nate had told me about the shifters that'd helped him at the scene. Now these two.

"Said they knew you and that you were, quote, 'a frigging alright guy'," he replied, an amused light in his eyes.

"Yeah, yeah. You're a good guy. What about your PI cases?" Mead said, checking his notebook. "Your history shows a propensity toward cases of, or resulting in, violence. Most recent was back in July."

The name and the reason for his hostility suddenly clicked.

That was when Phyllis Gustin had hired me in a mixture of fear, desperation, and anger. She was being prosecuted for aggravated assault. Miss Gustin and her at-the-time boyfriend had a heated argument, which ended when she belted the son-of-a pig and stomped off. But she swore on her grandmother's grave she didn't go back later and beat him with a thick tree limb. The man was unable to positively identify his attacker as the first hard blow had been from behind and rendered him senseless.

Detective Mead had been the investigating officer. Evidently the earlier and very public argument, coupled with Phyllis Gustin's First-Gen jaguar muscles, job as a park employee, and no alibi, had been evidence enough for him and he'd arrested her. He hadn't bothered to check if there was anyone else that had a reason to beat the guy nearly to death, leaving him with numerous broken bones and a nasty concussion.

I did. I found her ex-boyfriend liked to play cards in the backroom of a bar on Thirtieth Street. Six days before the beating, he'd won over five thousand dollars from another player. According to two others at that same game, the poor loser had screamed 'cheater' and lunged across the table. It'd taken several of them to pull the loser off the winner and eject him from the bar.

Turns out Mr. Loser had a volatile temper. When I questioned the very muscular dock worker, I ended up in a brawl that nearly took my head off. If the police hadn't shown up, courtesy of a concerned neighbor, he might have since I didn't have my weapon with me. Further investigation found two witnesses: one that saw him rummaging through some recent tree trimmings which matched the type used in the beating, and the other—a preteen on skates— who dodged around him and his "fat stick" two streets over from said beating scene.

Mr. Loser—aka Donny McGill—was arrested and Phyllis Gustin's case was dismissed.

I gave up any pretense of cooperation. "Maybe because I'm not afraid to tackle issues that are overlooked, waved off, or mishandled by others." Mead's face went as red as his hair while his partner's face blanked. "None of my cases—current or recent—involve violence."

"Bullshit," Mead snapped, earning a glare from Tyree. "There's Alfred Duninger, the murdered photographer involved with your blackmail case."

"Duninger was a criminal involved in who-knows-what. There's no frigging evidence that his demise is linked to Filbrandt's case."

"I say it is," Mead said, jaw jutted out in defiance.

"That's not your call," an unexpected voice said.

Both detectives spun around. Lieutenant Sinclair stood in the doorway. The tension in the room jumped ten-fold. Wow. You'd think their two departments would be on good terms, related as they were. Evidently not.

"Not your case, not your department," Sinclair continued, walking to the foot of my bed.

"You taking over Macron's case?" Mead practically sneered.

I gave Mead the side-eye. Could that be considered insubordination?

"No." Sinclair's voice was as cold as his icy-blue eyes.

"Then what are you doing here?"

"Also not your concern."

Whatever Detective Mead started to say, he thought better of it and snapped his notebook shut. Telling me "We'll talk later," he stomped out. Sinclair pivoted slowly, his attention focused on them.

I found it interesting that a large who-knows-what Gen wouldn't turn his back on them.

I still had no idea of what Sinclair's shifter form was. In fact, my Gen-dar refused to even give me his species. Instinct, however, said it was big, meaning either a tiger or large bear. His human form was at least six-seven in height and he didn't dress those shoulders off a rack. I was willing to bet he shopped at 'Bare Essentials.' It was a shifter retail store owned by bears, pun intended, that catered to the larger-sized person.

"I guess he didn't like me upending his case last summer," I grunted. My finger jabbed the call button on the control thingy beside me.

"Neither did the Assistant District Attorney," Sinclair said.

The door *whooshed* open. Sinclair spun, his body tensing, and I caught a glimpse of claw tips. It only lasted a moment, then he was back to being his usual impassive self. Looking back over her shoulder at someone speaking as she entered, the nurse missed the show.

"Yes, Mr. D'Accio?"

"My shoulder is starting to hurt. Could I have something for it?"

"Of course. Doctor Gordon left a couple of prescriptions for you. I'll be right back."

As soon as she was out of the room, I shot Sinclair a suspicious look. "What's going on? You watched Mead like a vulture and he was being insubordinate. Then you went into defensive mode when you thought he might be coming back in behind you."

"The ADA had to dismiss that case as it was built on faulty, incomplete evidence due to the arresting officer not investigating all possible avenues of inquiry. He ensured that his unhappiness rolled downhill, starting with the Police Commissioner's Office.

Lieutenant Whitcomb, head of the Assault Division, made sure Detective Mead was made aware of that in a stellar ass-chewing that was just short of an official reprimand."

The corner of his upper lip lifted in what probably was his version of a smile. Then he continued with, "It didn't help when an internal review of his past six-months' of cases found two others with holes that the reviewer believed should have been plugged. Fortunately for all of us, follow-up revealed that the additional information wouldn't have made a difference in the legal cases' resolution. Mead is being scrutinized closely. One more screw-up and he'll be back on patrol duty."

No wonder he'd about popped an eyeball at my poke. My eyes narrowed. "The man is on thin ice and has anger management issues. Has he made threats?"

The nurse's return forestalled Sinclair's reply. I washed down the two pills she handed me with my water bottle.

"Well?" I asked after the door closed behind her.

"Not directly but, as you said, he has anger issues," he said, shrugging it off. "Your shooting tells us a couple of things. First, there must have been a compelling reason to take you out as soon as possible. Otherwise, given the poor conditions, he would have waited until a better shot presented itself. The strong, gusty wind undoubtedly nudged the bullet sufficiently off-track to ruin the kill shot. And it's not like you hole up in your office or apartment," he added.

"Serenading the pack here," I told him sourly. Yes, I'd been lucky.

"The bullet was recovered but it's too mangled for a match if a suspect weapon shows up. However, the sniper should have used a different caliber, one that would have blown a larger exit hole. If the shot didn't kill you, the blood loss would have. To me, that indicates assassination isn't his main line of employment and was using a weapon he's familiar with."

I'm alive because someone went the cheap route?

"Be sure to pass that on to Detective Mead," I said darkly. "I doubt he'll care."

"Regardless, the investigation of such had better be in his reports," Sinclair replied. "What are you currently working on?"

I hesitated; he wasn't going to like it. "I've been hired by someone who believes a family member was improperly convicted of murder. They think the police investigation was botched."

His eyes sharpened. "Was it?"

"Still investigating. I promise to let you know what I find," I hastily added.

"Do so. Nothing else?"

I shook my head. "Not witnessing for a nasty court case, either."

He contemplated me for several moments. "With your accelerated healing, you should be released Monday or Tuesday."

Sinclair knew about my rapid repair. "And?" I said warily.

"It'll be interesting to see what happens." Without further ado or comment, he was gone.

I fumed as the door slowly closed behind the stiff-necked… whatever. Interesting, huh? Expecting a repeat? The sniper failed and is unlikely to try again with the police involved. *You hope,* drifted up from my hindbrain.

I then spent several minutes trying to picture his claws. I finally gave up; it had been too little, too fast to identify them. The fact that he had gone defensive so fast was a bit worrisome. Was he still having issues at OPD? The lieutenant had faced a lot of antagonism when he transferred in from Denver to take over Omaha's homicide department. I shook my head, remembering the almost claws-out brawl I'd witnessed in his office.

Finally, I turned to a more worrisome puzzle. My fingers stretched and rolled as I pondered. What warranted my killing?

I was still pondering when supper was served. Fortunately, the peas came with mashed potatoes. Mixing the two together made eating easier and kept me from having squishy bed partners. I was forking up the last bite of meatloaf when Mr. Thoreen walked in. According to the wall clock, I still had thirty-five minutes of peace and quiet before the onslaught of visitors.

"I told them I was your lawyer," he said, catching my glance. "Which I can legally claim through the Conservatorship."

"That's fine. How's Russell? I can't get anyone to tell me." I rolled the tabletop away.

"That's because he's on an informational blackout, per my authority. Russell is still unconscious, still stable. Doctor Bullard isn't worried yet, because Russell's brain is still recovering from the shock—literally—that it experienced. Says he won't worry unless it lasts another two weeks."

"Let's hope not," I murmured.

"Agreed. Darrell Chandler tried to circumvent the Conservatorship again once word of your shooting became public."

"Yeah," I growled. "How much do you want to bet he was behind this?"

"Zip, I'd say," Thoreen replied as he carefully laid his briefcase next to my legs. "Regardless of our personal opinion of him, he's not an idiot. He knows how it would appear in regard to control over Chandler Import and that he'd be thoroughly investigated. No telling what they might find if that happened," he added, his tone amused.

"What about his son, Trace?" I replied, too mulish to let it go.

Thoreen got a thoughtful look on his face. "If he did, it would be his first independent act. His father keeps an iron foot on his throat. Interesting conjecture, though." He popped the briefcase latches. "Miss Heiser needs your attention and subsequent approval on a few items."

Darn, I missed our appointment. I looked down at my bound arm, then cocked an eyebrow at him.

"Right. You're a lefty. Verbal approval will be sufficient under the circumstances. I'll annotate any comments, questions, or changes for you." Mr. Thoreen then pulled out a thick wad of documents clipped together.

That was a few? Turned out not too bad. Unlike Miss Heiser, he skipped all the legalese sections and just read over the main points and annotated my responses in his notes. "Last one," he said, handing me a single-page document.

"Customs?" I said, after a quick scan.

"A new Quality Control office is being created. Chandler Import brings in bulk orders from Europe, Africa, the Dakota Territory—worldwide, basically," Mr. Thoreen said, waving his hand. "Currently, unless there is visual damage, the cargo is distributed unopened to the wholesalers that ordered it. There's been an increase in complaints about damaged goods since the first of the year. The retailers blame the wholesalers who point at Chandler Import, and everyone demands reimbursement."

"How do we know it wasn't the wholesaler or one of the local transport shippers that caused the damage?" I challenged.

"We don't," he said, nodding, "and precisely why CI has refused to pay those demands. By instituting an inspection of all incoming cargo, any damage will be ascertained before it leaves Chandler Import's warehouse. Unfortunately, the issue has already cost CI a long-term client and several others are muttering about it."

Sounds like an excellent idea to stop further business losses.

"Said inspection," Thoreen continued, "means Chandler Import employees will be breaking open other governments' customs seals on boxes and containers that they aren't the end recipient of. Which means we need the authority to do so. Otherwise, that would be a fast vacation to a federal penitentiary."

I grimaced. Those were not nice places.

"This will have to wait," Thoreen said, taking the paper from me. "This authorization has to be signed and on file before Miss Heiser can submit the required paperwork and make staffing plans. Mr. Chandler had hoped to have everything in place by late-November. Retailers are wanting to get their shelves stocked in time for Christmas shoppers and several large shipments are expected over the next month."

"My arm is immobilized only to stabilize the main shoulder wound. Doctor Gordon plans to unwrap me in a day or two. Then give me another couple of days to work out the stiffness. Will that keep everything on schedule?"

"Hmmm…more or less. I'll brief Miss Heiser to have everything prepped to go." He began stacking everything back into his briefcase. "Give me a call when you're ready." Snapping it shut, he held out his hand and we shook. "Best wishes on your recovery." Grinning, he added, "I really don't want to work with Mr. Chandler's relatives-in-law."

Considering what that would imply about my health status, neither did I.

I didn't have long to mull over either Sinclair's or Thoreen's visits. Thomas Tall Elk was the next one in. He assured me the Atlanta job was as done as it was going to get.

"It would take a badger to dig that missing ex-boss out of whatever hole he's buried himself in," Tom told me in a slightly disgusted voice.

"Know any?" I asked, half in jest.

'Yeah, but you wouldn't believe what he charges per hour," he replied.

"Wait. You know one?" While not as rare as Wolverines, the only other member of their specie family, they weren't all that common either.

Turned out he knew two, both Ameri-Tribe. One lived up in the Dakota Territory. The other was his wife's cousin, who was a director at a local senior retirement community. Before I could ask about her, Diana arrived.

She assured me my Ruger was filed in the office safe, then added, "Your car is in your building's parking lot." I chuckled at her smug expression. She'd been pestering me for a chance to drive it since I bought the blue Crossfire sports car several years ago.

Merle Smith brought a small portfolio of articles concerning my shooting "for my files," while not-so subtly probing for any new info. *Sheesh. Reporters.* Even Angie popped in for a visit before heading off to work. Nate showed up with a bag of clothes and my fully charged phone plus its charger from my apartment. A couple of fellow *Despos* surprised me by stopping in briefly. We'd only exchanged a few words and head-nods at the bar, yet they'd come to check on me. I almost keeled over when they told me Boris had promised 'first drink on the house' when I made it back.

I'd lost most of my old, long-term friends back when I was suspected of murder. Only Nate had stood by me as the others drifted away. Finding I had acquired more friends than I knew of—or at least friendlies—in the past year had a warm glow filling me.

Conversation was flowing amicably when a six-foot-three woman with broad shoulders and silver hair pushed her way through the door.

"Grandma!" My grin got bigger the closer she came until, finally, I was enveloped in a careful, one-armed hug.

"Everyone, this is Grandma D'Accio and…" I glanced at the door, "Grandpa?"

"Back on the ranch," she said, tucking the covers tighter around me. "Several things need finishing before winter blows in. I'm here to help out till you're up and moving on your own. The person I spoke with didn't say anything about your arm," she added, taking in my bandages.

"Arm's fine, ma'am," Nate said. "Just a temporary precaution for now. I'm Doctor Nate Gordon," he finished, identifying himself.

I introduced the others and the next hour sped past as we talked and laughed. The tiredness I'd been ignoring finally washed over me. Eagle-eyed Grandma noticed it.

"Let's call it a night folks, as it's getting late and Curt looks done for."

Diana and Tom waved goodbye and headed out. Nate said he'd be back tomorrow to check on me. I sighed, leaned my head back, and gave my grandmother a tired smile.

"I'm glad you're here, Grandma, even if it isn't the best of circumstances."

She frowned down at me. "Have they made any progress on finding the SOP who did this?" I shook my head. Her eyes narrowed. "Any idea, yourself, of who or why?"

"No. I have a couple of things going on at the moment, but nothing that—I don't think—would warrant this." I patted my chest.

"I don't like it. You should have a guard on your door," she said.

"It's highly unlikely anyone would try something in the hospital. It'd be hard to get a gun past several floors of shifter noses." Gun oil has a distinctive odor.

Grandma snorted. "I can think of three other methods of killing, not counting claws. Right now, you're as helpless as a week-old cub."

My mind instantly flashed to Russell, who was even more helpless. If it was one of the Chandlers…

"Maybe I should have them roll a cot in here for me," she continued, thoughtfully.

Grandma D'Accio wasn't just big, she was a First-Gen polar bear that could move as fast as wolf. I still remembered her taking down a rogue boar that had made the fatal choice to charge at ten-year-old me and my friends. With her shifter senses and claws, no one would get past her.

"Thanks, Grandma, but that's not necessary. You had a long drive to get here. Go on, make yourself at home and get some sleep." Nate had given her my apartment keys. "Ah, first? Could you help me into the bathroom?" I asked, flushing. Getting up and down gave me the most trouble, not to mention pain. At least I didn't need help once inside.

Tucked back in bed, I got a final shoulder pat and kiss on my forehead. In the quiet that settled in after she left, I found my thoughts wandering in the past. Happy memories replayed like videos of my parents and grandparents. Of my spirit-sister and my wife. *Only my grandparents remained now*, I thought somberly. If not for luck and Nate, I, too, would only be a memory.

Chapter 14

As predicted, I was released into my grandmother's tender care on Monday. Thanks to the rapid repair, my bullet wound was healing quite well. My collarbone was mending also, according to the X-rays Nate spent an inordinately long time studying. When he'd freed my arm, he'd refused my request for a simple arm sling, like I used the last time I'd been shot. Instead, I was wearing a clavicle brace. The figure-eight contraption around my shoulders was stiff and uncomfortable.

Grandma's Chevy Conestoga was a work truck masquerading as a car. Front and back rows were easy-to-clean bench seating that would accommodate three hefty guys or a squished medium-sized foursome. The large rear area had hauled everything from bunkhouse groceries to sacks of grain to a calf needing special vet services. I highly doubt, though, that its namesakes of yesteryear were a bright cherry-red. Grandma had insisted on something easy to spot if 'Connie' broke down on the prairie or in a snowstorm.

It also had a high clearance with, fortunately, pull-up handles to assist getting in. Teeth clenched in preparation, I started to lift myself up. Hands suddenly gripped my waist and gently hoisted me onto the seat. I was too relieved to be embarrassed and scooted all the way in.

"Thanks, Grandma."

She stretched the seatbelt out. "Can you get it latched?"

I nodded, carefully managing it mostly by feel. It's amazing how many muscles, front and back, are used even in the tiniest movements. And while the brace might keep my collarbone safely immobilized, it didn't stop the painful "tugs" on my shoulder.

I was surprised to see Tall Elk leaning against my car when we pulled up next to it. Using the handle, I gently slid to the ground. "Hi, Tom. Didn't expect to find you waiting."

He straightened. "Filed my report with your secretary. Thought you might have questions about it."

His eyes weren't on me, instead they were flicking around the parking lot. "Don't think anyone would try again here, or so soon," I said quietly.

Arms filled with my hospital bags, Grandma came around to stand next to Tom. "I wouldn't stake your life on that," she said. "You were shot for a reason; we need to assume that reason still exists."

"That if-at-first-you-don't-succeed thing?" I said, remembering Sinclair's comment.

"Uh-huh. Let's get you into your apartment."

By the time I was settled in my living room chair, I was in need of the pills we'd picked up at the hospital pharmacy.

"Your Atlanta client has called about her report," Tom said. "Your secretary told her it and the expense report would be emailed by close of business. She's emailed copies to your home computer for review…when you're up to it that is," he added, eyeing me with concern.

Thought I had hidden it better.

We talked, exchanging case stories for about an hour, giving me time to rest and for the pills to kick in. When we finally got around to the reports, they were as Tom-concise as I expected. The summary included Mr. Cassell's status as unknown, which would disappoint Miss Bruhn. But it would take an intense search, and a lot longer than two weeks, to track him down. I sent the okay back to Diana to email everything to Atlanta. I also added a note for her to cut a check to Tom for the majority of our fee. He'd earned it. I thanked him heartily as he took his leave. He made me promise to call if I needed any further help. Of *any* kind, he had stressed.

I spent the next hour and a half in near agony. From drooling, that is. My apartment was filled with the exquisite odor of Grandma's three-years-running State-Fair-blue-ribbon corn chowder. After my umpteenth, "Is it ready, yet?", I was finally chowing down a large bowl of goodness.

Nate showed up in time to get a bowlful himself.

"Ma'am, that was excellent," Nate said, pushing back from the table.

"More left," she replied, ladling up another bite.

"Thank you, no. Those two bowls were more than enough."

"Curt's working on his fourth one," Grandma said, amused.

"Three and a half," I muttered, not wanting to sound like a complete pig.

Nate got that thoughtful 'working something out' look of his I recognized. "Your body is rebuilding. Replenishing," he said in a noncommittal tone.

Hmmm. That was undoubtedly true. Yet, the way Nate was studying me had my hindbrain waving a caution flag.

Nate led me into the bedroom after Grandma refused his help

with the dishes. He checked all my bandages, then had me do a series of arm stretches and hand squeezes.

"Any numbness, stinging, or just plain weird feeling in the arm or hand?" Nate asked.

"Just a kind of tingly sensation when I stretched my arm out."

"Excellent. You'll need some amount of physical therapy.

"I'm still a member of Pappio Heights Gym." I had used them to get back into shape after an extended convalesce. "I dropped my membership back to standard, so I don't have the option of a private trainer anymore. I can re-upgrade."

"Only if they have an orthopedic physical therapist on staff," Nate said, scowling. "You need a therapist, not a drill sergeant; someone who knows how to work with musculoskeletal injuries, not exacerbate them. If they don't, let me know and I'll get you a referral. Either way, give yourself a week, doing simple arm exercises to keep it from stiffening up."

"Got it. Now, what's cooking in that brain of yours?"

Nate blinked. "What?"

"You were acting kind of weird there at the table."

Another blank look, and then, "Oh, that. I'm correlating your healing progress as matched to that of a Gen's. The fact you have rapid repair, alone, is fascinating. Doctor Patel practically chased me out of ICU with questions a couple of times."

"Yeah, she paid me another visit this morning before checkout. I agreed to let her write up my case as long as there was nothing in it that would let someone guess my identity."

Nate's smile lit up his face. "That's great. She's wanting to change protocols, do the EPO test for everyone so no one is inadvertently endangered. The medical profession *needs* to be put on alert, Dice," he said, his voice turning somber. "Not for just this situation, but for any other changes. Who knows what the next evolutionary phase will be? How do we test for it?"

Dedication, thy flagbearer was Nathanial Gordon. It was what made him such a great doctor. Its downside?

"Nate," I asked softly, "how are you? About what happened in ER?"

Pain flickered in his eyes. "I'm dealing. I can't stop it from happening again…to someone." A deep, burning anger suddenly filled them. "But I can do my best to ensure they survive and the ones responsible pay as dearly as possible."

"Amen," I replied.

Nate left shortly after that and I attended to work-related housekeeping. Slogged through almost a week's worth of emails. *Whew!* Let Mr. Thoreen know I had been sprung and got an update on Russell's status. No change. By the time the late evening news finished, so was I.

"Been awhile since I helped you get ready for bed," Grandma said, her tone ruminative.

"Do I get a bedtime story?" I teased as she unsnapped the two top straps from the brace's back center piece. She carefully pulled it away from my shoulder bandages.

"Hmmm. Maybe. You did eat all your supper."

The good-natured banter continued as she helped me into a T-shirt and then re-strapped me into the frigging thing. Thank God I could do the pants myself in the bathroom. Positioned on the bed, I grasped her strong hands as she gently lowered me down. Safely flat, I let out a sigh.

Getting up or down was the worst, as it required using the shoulders and everything in between. Besides being painful, too much stress on the collarbone could cause it to break again. Nate would not be pleased.

"Any particular time you want up?" Grandma asked as she pulled the covers over me. I shook my head. "Then give a yell when you want up. I'll hear you."

I chuckled as the light clicked off. She'd hear me if I farted.

***

Grandma got me vertical, practically lifting me straight up out of bed come morning. Since I wasn't planning on going anywhere and my night clothes were clean, I threw a flannel shirt over everything and called it good. Grandma's country breakfast was waiting for me. Bacon, sausage patties, pan-fried potatoes with onions, eggs, toast, and the perfect cup of coffee. Dad's parents were where I'd gotten my strong coffee preference.

Again, I found myself eating almost twice what I normally would. If this kept up, I was going to need new pants.

After breakfast, I went through the pile of mail Grandma had collected from my box. Bills and a couple of donation requests from charities I supported were stacked off to one side. I'd deal with them later. The remainder I asked Grandma to trash for me.

"You don't go to Halloween parties?" she asked, studying two invites. "You could probably handle a couple of hours at one of them."

"Those are society wingdings, Grandma. The conversations are boring, the food bite-sized, and hands roam. Yeah, laugh it up," I said, mock-scowling at her wide grin. "And there'll be at least two that'll try to attach themselves to me."

"So? A fling might be good for you."

Dumbfounded, I sputtered, "I'm not ready."

"It's been over two years, Curt," Grandma replied gently. "I never got to meet the wonderful woman you married, but from your stories about her, I know her. I know Tabitha would want you to get on with your life. Fully."

My head was slowly shaking by the time she finished. "I have gotten on with my life, Grandma, just not…that way. Not yet."

I got a shoulder squeeze before she walked away. It took a couple of minutes before the kaleidoscope of memories faded away, ending as they often did: *Remember me*. Her final words a bloody whisper. Maybe someday, when it was more ache than hurt…

A mental shake followed by several deep breaths and I was ready to face the day. I had a slew of phone calls to make. An hour later, I sat back and sipped on the coffee Grandma had set at my elbow, mentally checking my to-do list.

Diana and the office? Check. Everything good there. Mr. Thoreen? He'd be by tomorrow morning with the customs paperwork, along with a few others Miss Heiser had added. Russell? Not only stable but showing signs of approaching consciousness. Left voice messages for both Lieutenant Sinclair and Angie, letting them know I was at home. Mr. Filbrandt? I'd assured him, as I had during their Sunday visit, my attack had nothing to do with their case, and, despite it now being in police hands, to let me know if there was anything I could do for them.

I scheduled an appointment at Pappio Heights for next Monday after learning they did, indeed, have a fully licensed Ortho PT staff member. Expressing surprise, the manager admitted it was to assist those members recovering from injuries, whether caused externally, like mine, or internally by overzealous workouts. There were several individuals I had seen there that may have ended up needing the PT's services.

I tried all afternoon, unsuccessfully, to get in touch with Mandy. Finally, on a hunch, I logged into OPD's public database. Yep, her luck had run out on Friday: she was sitting in jail on a grand theft charge. That was unlucky for me as well.

I wanted to talk with her brother, personally, getting a first-hand, detailed description of Aaron's movements that night. I had planned to take Mandy with me. I had a fairly good BS meter, but I figured he'd be less inclined to test it if she was there.

I made another call to the office, asking Diana to schedule me for a visit with Aaron Rivas at the Nebraska State Penitentiary. As soon as possible, preferably. My PI credentials usually got me in without too much trouble.

By suppertime I was dragging. Diana had couriered Aaron's records and the tardy crime scene photos to the apartment. I'd spent the afternoon re-reading the trial transcripts and scrutinizing the crime scene photos. Mandy hadn't been kidding about the bludgeoning: the woman was unrecognizable from the neck up. Blood was splattered all around her, including on the Rembrandt propped against a chair several feet away. Couldn't help wincing, wondering if it was ruined or if portrait experts could clean it up. Aaron's public lawyer had tried his best, but the prosecutor's rebuttals had overwhelmed him.

No fingerprints? Not needed when you had DNA under the victim's fingernails.

No prior history of violence? He panicked, and there's a first time for everything.

No blood tells? There was plenty of time to discard all clothing and bathe elsewhere.

That lack of any blood residue anywhere in his car or apartment had been the lawyer's best defense argument. But there was no defense against the time gap between crime and arrest. There were no witnesses to him fleeing the scene, bloodied or not.

Grandma's excellent chili perked me up long enough to deal with a bandage change before tucking me into bed. I'd had the same energy drain recouping from a previous gun shot, too. Nate had called. He'd set me up with a four o'clock appointment tomorrow for a general checkup and X-rays. I intended to walk out of his office wearing a sling instead of the shoulder corset.

***

Next day's document marathon didn't take too long and we were finished by mid-morning. Either Miss Heiser had hit bottom for now, or Mr. Thoreen had wisely curtailed them. I fully expected more to materialize, especially since the one-page customs form had birthed two more pages. Once everything was finalized, the inspector position would be posted for applicants.

Midafternoon, I walked out of Nate's clinic a free man. At least, free of the frigging figure-eight harness. Surprisingly, he hadn't given me any argument about switching to a sling. Still, I used the handle to pull myself up and into Connie.

"We could have taken my car," I grumbled, buckling up.

Grandma gave me a bemused look. "I'm not about to try and wedge us both in that small blue excuse for a car."

"Really?" I replied, pretending to be affronted. "At least it doesn't smell," I made a show of turning my head and taking several deep sniffs, "like cow patty."

She shot me a sideways glare. "No, it doesn't. We put a tarp down."

"Uh-huh. How high up the sides?" I asked, grinning. There's a reason one doesn't tailgate an open-slat cattle car or dawdle when passing it.

Her lips twitched. "Are you implying your sniffer is better than mine?"

132

"No ma'am, wouldn't dream of it," I replied, automatically checking traffic along with Grandma as she pulled out of the parking lot.

"Hmmm, maybe you're right." She inhaled deeply. "Maybe I do catch a whiff of something. Since you can pinpoint it better than me, you'll have to do the honors."

"Honors?"

"Scrubbing Connie's insides until *we* can't smell it anymore."

I pointed at my sling. "Invalid."

"You've still got one good arm and the rest seems to be healing just fine," she said. "I thought for sure Dr. Gordon would leave you in the brace until at least the weekend."

I managed a one-shoulder shrug. "He said my X-rays were good."

Stopped at a red light, Grandma pointed a raised eyebrow at me. "I believe the word he used was *exceptional*."

"Yeah, well, my body's had a fair amount of practice these last few years," I replied, a bit uncomfortable. "Not to mention having rapid repair. A doctor at the hospital is going to write up a case study."

"Oh?" she said sharply.

"It's getting kind of hard to hide that I'm not a normal Zero, Grandma. I did get her promise to keep any identifying information out of it."

She snorted out a *harrumph* and we finished the rest of the ride home in silence. Letting us into my apartment, I was halfway across the living room before I realized Grandma was still stuck at the door. Sniffing.

"Grandma?"

"You know of a lynx with access to your place?" she asked.

I stiffened. "Lynx?"

"Uh-huh. I've scented him a time or two out in the hallway; assumed it was one of your neighbors."

I rotated slowly, searching the room. There. A rectangular box. On the side table next to the chair he likes to sit in. I was reaching for it when a clawed white paw pushed my hand away.

"Don't touch it," she snap-growled.

I shook my head. "It's okay, Grandma. This particular lynx won't hurt me."

"And if it's not him? Someone who *would*?"

"Not likely," I said after a brief pause. Ray Silverstone was the only one who'd made it through my locks. Still, I lifted the lid gingerly.

MacEverson Scotch. The silver label had my eyes widening.

"Most *acquaintances* don't leave six-hundred-dollar gifts," Grandma said dryly, her hands reverting to human. "You being courted?"

"No. He's just, uh, an acquaintance."

Her expression was skeptical. "What's the note say?"

Note? Oh. I gently slid it out from under the bottle. Opened it. Cleared my throat before quoting, "Glad you survived. The shooter won't." Then winced at Grandma's piercing gaze.

"So, you've an *acquaintance* that leaves expensive gifts *in* your apartment…knows how to track down a sniper…and has no qualms about taking them out? Interesting acquaintances you have." She swiveled on her heel and headed toward the kitchen. "Got some leftover chili we can finish up, or would you rather have something different for supper?"

I licked dry lips. "Chili is fine." How do I explain Ray?

I was saved by the ringing phone. I spent the next hour fielding calls from well-wishers. Made one myself to Tryon to check on Papaw. We commiserated together about being at the mercy of bossy women. Mamaw must be slowing down, because Papaw's "ow" was a full second behind my head-bop.

The rest of the evening went smoothly. I spent the hours between supper and bedtime studying the crime photos. Neither of us brought up the subject of an aggressive lynx.

Chapter 15

Merle interrupted breakfast, fuming about me not giving her the blackmail story. *Today's StoryLine,* a bottom-feeding tabloid, had announced it with a prominent display of the alleged adulterous pictures of Mr. Filbrandt on this morning's front page. Reminding her I couldn't discuss my case at the time, I gave her a quick rundown on the facts. "Besides, no one with any common sense believes what that gossip rag prints," I scoffed.

"They have *pictures,*" she snapped. "The kind that linger in one's mind. The article is sensational enough to potentially, *potentially,* affect the election's outcome."

I pinched the bridge of my nose. She was right.

"Okay," I drawled out, thinking fast. "This has to be messing with OPD's investigation. Get with Detective Chizek—she's the lead. Offer them a chance to shine in an exclusive interview *and* with a credible news source—you. About how they are already investigating a *proven* bogus blackmail attempt and the photos were leaked as threatened in obvious punishment for not paying it."

"Yes. Yes! Need to do it quick; the noon report. We'll do it live. Thanks, got to run." *Click.*

I finished breakfast with a grin, figuring things were about to get exciting. I wasn't wrong.

A furious Detective Chizek called. I assured her that if I had been the blabber, the article's contents would have been different and with me as the hero for debunking it. Merle called again, wanting to add me to the interview. I declined. Chizek had all my information and I wanted my name kept out of it. Unfortunately, whoever leaked the photos also leaked my name to the sleazeball that authored that *StoryLine* article. Said sleazeball called, wanting my 'perspective.' Grandma yanked the phone away, telling him exactly what her perspective of him and his paper was, then hung up on him. But not before informing him, in her bear's deep growly voice, what *might* happen if they slandered my name.

The hospital called, informing me that Russell was conscious. Visiting was not yet encouraged as the doctors would be performing tests, both cognitive and physical. I passed that happy info on to Mr. and Mrs. Greenbaum.

I watched Merle's noon interview. You couldn't tell it had been put together in a rush. Detective Chizek laid out how the still unknown blackmailer had generated the pictures. How the photographer—now deceased—and his accomplice had turned innocent encounters into an implied relationship. Even going so far as to pay a now ex-security employee a thousand dollars to overwrite a security video file because the recording would show how flagrantly deceptive it was.

While bribery was what I'd expected, I hadn't known they'd found him. The interview's whole theme was one of vindictive punishment for failure to pay up. Both of his challengers were on hand to express their outrage at the blackmail attempt and their admiration of Kurt Filbrandt for standing up to it despite the threat.

"While I hope to beat Mr. Filbrandt next May, I intend to do it honestly," Melissa Brower had told the crowd. Jerry Louderback had echoed the same.

Still, there was bound to be skepticism due to the attempt's extreme setup.

Police Commissioner Franklin managed to get himself in front of the camera, eloquently expressing his outrage for a full two minutes. He closed the interview by assuring us that he and all his officers would work tirelessly to bring the perpetrators to justice.

Grandma and I both rolled our eyes at the grandstanding. After all, he was running for reelection on May's ballot.

We headed west shortly afterwards. The Nebraska State Penitentiary was located halfway between Lincoln and Omaha and north of both in what appeared to be the middle of nothing. The three formed a rather nice isosceles triangle. My visit with Aaron Rivas was scheduled for two-thirty and I would only be allowed an hour with him.

The guards at the main gate weren't sure about what to do with Grandma, since Diana hadn't put her on the visitor list. To be fair, it hadn't occurred to her since this was the first time I hadn't driven here myself. Evidently all parties, even those remaining in the vehicle, had to be on the list just to get past the gate. It's probably in the frigging fine print. After a brief consultation with Warden Jefferies, my sling and Grandma's growl got us in.

***

The evening was spent doing several bouts of arm stretches and going back over Aaron's case. After our talk, I had a detailed description of his movements that night. He admitted to being unnerved by Agatha Mulligan's silence and *"the crazy look in her eyes."* He still swore he never once hit her with that statue, insisting

"I just wanted to get away from her." The most interesting additional information, not found anywhere in the trial transcripts, was of him taking a quick look back after diving through the window. He was adamant about seeing the woman picking herself up off the floor and she was nowhere near the Rembrandt.

Aaron also blamed himself for his sister's situation. *"If I hadn't listened to Tallon, none of this would be happening."*

My BS meter stayed silent for the entire meeting.

With all that fresh in mind, I gave the photos another close scrutiny. Then I called Sinclair's office and left a voice message asking him to stop by my office tomorrow. The lieutenant was not going to be happy. In my professional opinion, Aaron Rivas was innocent of murder.

<u>Chapter 16</u>

It was a little past ten o'clock when I leaned back and let out a contented sigh. It felt good to be here, back in my office. In my chair. Doing simple background checks. I refused to let an achy shoulder ruin my mood, although I did slide my arm into the sling to give it a rest.

I checked my coffee cup. Empty. I was too relaxed to get up for a refill.

Diana materialized in the doorway. "*Zeeb's* opens in ten minutes. Order in or go out?"

"In," I said lazily, as I didn't have a car. Grandma still insisted on chauffeuring me around. "My usual, please. I have one of Miss Blacksmith's requests in Review and ready for your admin magic." I'd hold off on the other background check until after lunch.

"Will do. Lieutenant Sinclair called a few minutes ago. I let him know your afternoon was open. Good thing those new larger client chairs came in this week," she added, before disappearing back around the corner.

I glanced down at the briefcase sitting beside my desk. Taking a deep breath, I let it out slowly. Aaron's future rode on this meeting.

***

I motioned to the photos spread out across my desktop. "As you can see, Lieutenant, it was a very bloody crime. The autopsy," I patted the pile of documents next to me, "reports her skull and neck were literally crushed at multiple points. Someone not only wanted her dead, they wanted to obliterate her. That level of damage points to an intense emotion, either hate or a towering rage."

"Or desperation to get away," Sinclair added, giving me his patented marble stare.

I ignored that and went into my argument. "Aaron Rivas felt neither—he was trying to extricate himself from what had become a dangerous situation. He needed to get out of there before someone came in to help. He *defended* himself from Agatha Mulligan's aggressive statue attack, wrestled it away from her, *shoved* her down, and bolted out the window. Aaron swears he physically saw her getting up off the floor *and* across the room from where he'd dropped the painting during their brawl."

Sinclair crossed his arms. "I would expect one in his situation to say that."

Playing devil's advocate? "The prosecution's theory was that Aaron Rivas was surprised in the act of theft, beat the old woman to death, then fled, leaving the priceless painting behind in his panic. In that all-important time gap before being arrested, he cleaned up, somewhere, and got rid of anything bloody."

"It's a well-known fact that panic short-circuits the brain. Can I assume you have a different theory?" he said.

"Someone took advantage of the situation after Aaron fled," I replied, keeping rein on my temper. *One knot head proof coming up.* "Maybe they argued first, or maybe they just grabbed the statue. Either way, they came up behind Agatha Mulligan as she went to retrieve the Rembrandt, beating her brutally." I tapped the picture showing the victim's remains and proximity to the painting. "This unknown person then walked over to the window, leaving a small blood trail." I tapped the appropriate photos showing the progression across the floor. Sinclair leaned forward to get a better view them.

"Reaching the window, they leaned against it. Maybe wiggled a bit to ensure it was properly smeared. Then they stripped, dropping their clothes on the floor." I pointed to a close-up photo of an oddly shaped large blood splat under the window. "Their last act was to smear the window a bit more and do a quick shake of clothing out it, thereby splattering blood tell as further misdirection that the killer went out that way." I indicated the two pictures showing the ground around the window, which included close ups of a single set of in-and-out footprints.

The lieutenant leaned back. "Granted, that story may be as plausible as the DA's, but it doesn't negate Rivas's culpability," he said, his tone holding an unmistakable challenge.

Giving the devil's advocate my best return-to-hell smile, I laid out my evidence. "Aaron wore gloves, preventing fingerprints. Yet, there were fingerprints on the statue's base, which the prosecutor glossed over as they were too smeared to be useable. If Aaron had raced across the floor in a panic to get away before anyone else came in, the blood trail would have been more like irregular splats than neat drips."

Sinclair's eyes narrowed and he leaned forward to study the photos again. Nothing told a story better than pictures. I drew his attention to several that showed the room's general layout.

"Notice that of the four small tables scattered around the room, the one in arm's reach of the window is the only one without a covering. Why? The killer used it to clean off and wrap up their clothes to keep from dripping back to their room. The killer couldn't physically leave a blood trail out the window without also leaving a second set of prints because the ground was still soft from the day's rain. Which is why," I added, readying what I considered the most telling, "there is no blood splatter found outside a three-foot diameter around said window despite his supposedly blood-covered condition when fleeing the scene."

His head came up sharply. "None?"

"Not a drop, according to the forensic team's report, which included several experienced shifter sniffers. Nor was blood scented anywhere in his car or in his apartment. Detective Macron's report," I pulled it out of the file, "lists seven other people in the house. There is no indication of questioning them, of searching the house for possible blood tell, or investigating any of them for possible motive. No indication of canvassing for witnesses. No indication of any thought given to the crime scene other than the most obvious. It appears the detective simply walked in and accepted everything and everyone at face value. No investigation necessary," I said in a scathing tone.

That was a major failure of protocol. As the primary lead, Detective Macron should have had her team doing all the above, if for no other reason than that of eliminating those in residence as suspects or accessories. Finding trace evidence under Agatha's fingernails was no excuse for sloppiness. Any other evidence was long gone now.

The lieutenant's jaw set. He held out his hand and I handed over the report.

"I'm surprised you let her get away with…" I trailed off warily. That was a frigging hot glare I was getting.

"I did not review this case," he said, enunciating each word with great precision. "According to the date, this happened while I was transitioning into the department. Since my installment, Detective Macron's work has been faultless."

Understanding dawned. "Lieutenant Olsen didn't see it. He left it for you to review as the incoming and it fell between the cracks." Or was shoved there. One of those nursing a resentful snit-fit at Sinclair's appointment could have filed Macron's report without the benefit of the Lieutenant's review out of pettiness.

Silently, I waited as he read the report.

Macron couldn't have been that sloppy an investigator or she wouldn't have made detective. And she had been 'faultless' since? Why had this case been so mishandled? Had she simply taken the lazy, easy way for some reason, or had she been influenced in some manner by the house members? At minimum, she was due an ass-reaming. Suspended or fired could also be in her future. Either way, she deserved it. The detective's lack of any real investigating or analysis of the crime scene had already cost Aaron over two years of his life.

One had to wonder what other cases Detective Macron may have mishandled, hopefully less egregious than this one. Would Alfred Duninger's case be getting the same poor treatment? I sneaked a peek at the lieutenant. Bet that thundercloud expression meant he was wondering exactly that. Wondering how many cases were going to have to be reviewed. Just like Detective Mead's had been. Not only was OPD going to end up with another black eye, they needed to seriously look at whatever complacency was developing among their officers.

Sinclair tossed the report down on top of the photos. Glared at the political mess strewn across my desktop. "One of the seven family members is the actual killer." It wasn't a question.

"Uh-huh. Unless you want to postulate a second intruder entering after Aaron and doing the deed? Right. The DA can re-open the…" I trailed off when he switched the glare to me.

"*No*" rumbled out from somewhere deep in his chest.

"No? Why the hell not?" I demanded.

"Because neither District Attorney Peterson, Commissioner Franklin, or Chief Constantine are going to risk their already muddled reputations on anything that's not 100 percent conclusive," he replied in a harsh, tightly controlled voice. "Conclusive in that Aaron Rivas absolutely could *not* have committed the crime he has been tried, convicted, and sentenced for. Because," his voice dropped into the growly zone, "all you have is a different *interpretation* of the existing facts."

My mouth opened, closed. Resisting the urge to curse, I fumed silently along with the deep chest-rumbling from the other side of my desk. If this had been brought up during the trial, enough reasonable doubt would have set Aaron free. Hell, if it'd been properly investigated, he wouldn't have even been charged with murder, just burglary. But Sinclair was right. A second legal embarrassment, in months of each other, could cost them their political careers. Especially Commissioner Franklin, with his upcoming re-election bid. I found the attitude unacceptable and made a mental note to donate to his opponent's campaign, even if I couldn't vote.

"Well, then," I said sharply, "I'll have to find new facts that prove Aaron Rivas did not kill Mrs. Mulligan and/or that someone else could have just as likely done it."

Chapter 17

Lieutenant Sinclair carefully kept his expression impassive as Detective Macron took a seat in front of his desk. The emotions that had roiled through him all night were now locked tight under a glacial calm. Learning she was on duty today, he made it a point to get in early to catch her at her desk.

Macron's face was unreadable, but her posture was one of wariness. Was it due to his Gen nature? As a Gen herself, she'd be able to scent what he was. Or was it because of being called into his office when he hadn't been scheduled to work this Saturday? Maybe a bit of both?

Coldly, bluntly, he opened with, "Detective Macron, your record has been exemplary. Mostly."

"Mostly?" she echoed cautiously.

"Agatha Mulligan murder case, two years ago, April 2004." She stiffened. "A private investigator has requested copies of those records. I've been informed that he has been hired to prove Aaron Rivas, the man convicted of her murder, is innocent."

"Not an unusual occurrence, sir," she said. "People look for the tiniest loophole to get out of their conviction."

"In this case, he stands a good chance of succeeding due to your botched investigation." A flush moved up her neck. "I've seen the file myself, read all the reports, examined the crime scene photos. You screwed up worse than a first-year trainee," he said coldly.

Macron's entire face was red now, her jaw clenched.

"You will review the case in its entirety. Monday morning, you will present yourself along with a list of everything you did wrong and an explanation of why you were so derelict in your duty. Am I clear, Detective Macron?"

Her jaw unlocked. "Yes, sir."

"Dismissed."

He waited until the door closed behind her before heaving out a sigh. His transfer from Denver to Omaha hadn't been all that unusual; his assuming command of the Police Department's homicide division had been. Questions were raised up and down the command chain on why the position hadn't been filled locally. Why Lieutenant Olsen's last act before retiring had been to heavily endorse him as his replacement. The antagonism and resentfulness he'd encountered had gradually, grudgingly given way to acceptance. Even Brinkman, who'd nearly gone claws-out with him last year, fully accepted him now.

This mess with Macron would undoubtedly bring some of that back. There'd be those that, even while acknowledging her poor performance, would still feel he was being too harsh with her. His thoughts turned back to Denver, to that last argument with his precinct captain.

"Detective Arnold is young. She made a mistake," Captain Merriday had said.

"That wasn't a mistake, it was negligence," he'd argued back.

"Nonsense. You're over-reacting."

"And you're overly protective of her. There are damn few cases she hasn't made a mistake on. You keep brushing it off, which is going to bite the whole department sooner or later. My reprimand stands."

"No, it doesn't. I have removed it from her file. I won't let—" Merriday shrank back in her chair.

Sinclair remembered it all, including the shame of how he had nearly lost control. His claws had shot out and the sudden sharpening of vision said his eyes had turned the black of his Gen form. It had only lasted a few seconds, but the damage was irreversible. He'd regained control, turned, and left the office. Left the building and its smell of fear. Two weeks later, he'd been called into Captain Merriday's office and told of the upcoming position in Omaha and why. He'd applied for it with his captain expediting the request. None of his co-workers had asked him to stay.

Regardless of whether or not D'Accio could prove his case, Detective Macron would be getting a reprimand. He just hoped that her explanation, whatever it was, didn't give the department an even worse black eye.

Chapter 18

My weekend was fairly quiet. I spent it doing arm exercises, visiting Russell, convincing Grandma I could manage being on my own by rolling carefully out of bed both mornings, and working on a plan to find a killer. Fortunately, databases don't have union hours and I pulled all the information I could get on the seven individuals named in the documents: two grandkids, Agatha's sister and brother-in-law, a niece, and the niece's husband and son.

I had also enlisted Merle's help, having learned that lone-wolfing had its limits. She was on board as soon as I explained Aaron's situation. Merle promised to go through the paper's archives for anything interesting about the families, as well as speaking with a few of her peers.

Russell was getting stronger every day. Physically. He still had trouble processing speech or remembering things. Doctor Bullard said his brain was still healing and would improve in time. When I asked "How much?" he was honest enough to admit that it was all up to Russell's body. In the meantime, I was still stuck as conservator.

The only other interesting thing that happened was Chandler

Import's main warehouse burned down Sunday night. Several inches of new snow and a fast fire department response had kept it from spreading to adjacent buildings.

****

"That doctor friend will keep check of your bandages? Change them as needed?" Grandma asked, putting her last suitcase in Connie's back end. She'd refused to let me help carry one. She was heading home, albeit reluctantly.

"Yes, Grandma. I'm seeing him later this morning."

It was barely past sunrise, though the sun was struggling to make its presence known through the gloomy-gray overcast. With a projected snow front moving in and a long drive ahead, she needed to be on the road. As it was, she'd be running ahead of the worst of it. As an expert driver in a formidable vehicle, she stood better odds of getting home safely than most. But nothing was 100 percent. The pileup that involved my family's car was testament to that.

Hands on hips, forehead furrowed, she said, "You're sure you'll be okay?"

"Yes, Grandma. Promise. I'll keep my eyes and ears on alert," I said, giving her my best trust-me grin. I got back a narrow-eyed squint.

"Uh-huh. How about taking risks?"

"That kind of goes with the job," I replied blandly.

"You're a PI, not a cop," she retorted. "At least keep the stupid ones to a minimum." Stepping forward, she enveloped me in a bear hug. "Take care."

Hugging her back, I nodded. "Call when you get home…or if there's any problems."

Climbing under the wheel, she cranked the motor. The heavy-duty, 440-engine woke with a deep rumble. We both automatically

150

listened for a couple of seconds, but heard nothing amiss. Perfect.

Grandma closed the door and I gave her a final wave. The engine's rumble settled into a smooth purr as she shifted into gear. Starting to roll forward, she braked and rolled the window down partway.

"Say hello to *that lynx* for me," she said. With a wink and the press of the accelerator, she was gone.

Shaking my head, I returned to my apartment. She had never asked about or even mentioned *that lynx* again after that night, probably believing he was one of my street contacts. I mentally ran over my day's agenda as I showered and dressed. The normalcy of the routine perked me up, even if it did take a bit longer than usual.

First up was Nate. He wanted to give me another once-over. Arriving promptly at nine, the first thing he did was send me off with his nurse to take another X-ray. Returning to the exam room, Nate changed my bandages as we waited. I admitted my shoulder still being somewhat stiff and sore, and only experiencing a bit of pain in my arm when I used it for something and stretched too far.

"Understandable. I want to do another x-ray next week to check it."

"Nate," I said, buttoning up my shirt. "I know you're concerned, and I appreciate the attention, but I'm not having any problems. I can even roll myself in and out of bed," I said, grinning. My grin faded when Nate just sat on his stool, gazing at me all serious like.

"Nate?"

"The pain…is it accompanied by any numbness, tingling, or sharp jabs?"

"There's been one or two sharp jabs—here and there and then gone," I replied slowly. Something was wrong. "No numbness, but an occasional…itch. What's going on, Nate? What aren't you telling me?"

"The sensations in your arm are normal, to be expected as the plexus nerve bundle heals. Your clavicle?" He hesitated. "It's not healing normally."

A nurse entered and handed Nate the large envelope that held my X-ray. She gave me a smile before exiting. He arranged it on the wall viewer and backlit it.

He studied it Frowned. Studied it some more. Finally, gut clinched, I had to ask, "What's wrong with it?"

He motioned me over. The pin was obvious, centered in the new bone growth around it. My brow furrowed as I studied it. I might not be a doctor, but I couldn't see anything that screamed *wrong*. I glanced sideways and said exactly that.

"That's because there isn't anything medically wrong with it," Nate replied.

"You said—"

"An adult clavicle takes six to twelve weeks to heal. Normally," he tapped the X-ray, "you shouldn't have this level of bone regeneration for at least four weeks. Yet, you've reached that stage in only a week and a half, undoubtedly fueled by that expanded appetite of yours. The bone is beginning to harden," he ran a finger across the bone on both sides of the pin, "and I estimate it'll be fully healed in another week to ten days."

Stared at the image for a minute, my brain whirling. "Rapid repair," I said slowly, "doesn't do bones. And I've completed it."

"Yes, and no."

I gave him a sharp look.

"Your EPO levels are normal, which means the rapid repair cycle *that we know of* has completed. This is something else. It's…"

Nate rubbed his neck, "it's different. It has to be a new type of rapid repair. Or maybe," he gave my X-ray a thoughtful look, "it's simply a new extension of the current one."

"I sure as hell didn't have it when I was eighteen!" I exploded. "Do you know how long it took me to heal from all those broken bones?"

He held up a placating hand. "I know, I know. And five years ago, your broken toe healed at the expected rate. But something has changed, Curt. Something that has laid dormant within you has woken up. Was it triggered by all those injuries over the last two, three years? Or by reaching your physical prime? Both? Hell, maybe one of those particles physicists are always coming up with zapped a couple of your chromosomes in passing. I just don't know."

Nate shook his head, frustration in his expression as well as voice.

"That's what you were watching in my earlier X-rays."

He nodded glumly, staring at the illuminated image. "I didn't want to say anything until I was sure."

"So, I'm a Zero-Plus-Plus now?" I said sourly.

Nate blinked, then chuckled. "We'll have to wait and see what happens with your next bone break."

***

I sat in the parking lot outside my office, staring unseeing at the solid mass of clouds hanging low over the city. Questions ran around in my head like rabid squirrels. Was this new bone rapid repair an extension of the normal one or a new, separate repair altogether? Was it now a permanent feature or a one-time anomaly? Was there anything else hidden, just waiting to smack me between the legs?

After some mental teeter-tottering and a small bout of panic, I let loose a sigh that came up from my toes. Nothing I could do but roll with it. "What's one more plus?" I muttered to the steering wheel. Especially when the only downside I could see was a higher grocery bill for a few weeks. I finally climbed out and headed in. I had a meeting with Merle at ten. My database searches had provided plenty of basic facts about my suspects, but I wanted whatever information and gossip she'd scrounged to round them out.

I'd barely gotten situated behind my desk when Diana escorted Merle in. "Coffee, Miss Smith?" she asked. "Don't worry, it'll be from the good pot," she added when Merle's nose curled.

My efficient secretary not only brought Merle a cup of coffee, but also the black pot and refilled mine as well. I took a deep inhale of the goodness steaming out of my cup as both women curled their noses.

"How do you stand that?" Merle asked Diana.

"I close his door," Diana replied, straight-faced. "I'm also thinking of having an exhaust fan installed over the coffee bar." She pivoted on her heel.

Nonplussed, I watched her close said door, not sure if she was joking or not. Returning my attention to Merle, I found a grin almost wider than her face.

"Ha, ha. If you're through dissing my coffee, can we get down to business?"

Still grinning, she opened the portfolio she'd brought and pulled out a large bundle of paper. Plopped it down on my desk. I stared at it, dismayed. It was at least two inches thick. Maybe three.

"I printed out anything pertinent to the Mulligan family for the past two decades," Merle stated. "You can read through them at your leisure, but I can summarize the highlights."

"Please do," I said, relieved. We both pulled out notebooks. "How about I lay out the basic family stats and then you humanize them?"

Merle nodded and reached for her cup.

"Mrs. Agatha Bellmont Mulligan: the victim. A native Omaha Zero, she was sixty-eight at time of death. One marriage. Widowed at fifty-five when Otto Mulligan, her First-Gen coyote husband, died from a massive heart attack. Two children, both deceased. Frank Mulligan: Second-Gen coyote, no marriages or children, died of a drug overdose at twenty-one. Jennifer Mulligan Huntington: A Zero, one marriage, one divorce, two children, died at thirty-three from a hit-and-run."

I looked up. "Never solved, by the way. Agatha got custody of Jennifer's twelve-year old twins. I have almost nothing on the father, Montgomery Huntington; he's just a name in the appropriate databases. Do you have anything on him?"

Merle patted her notebook. "Covered."

"Good." I paused to swallow some coffee. "The Huntington kids are fraternal twins, age twenty, no marriages or children on record for either. Different gender, different Gen. Gail is a First-Gen coyote; Corwin is a Second-Gen fox.

"The other side of the tree is Kathy Bellmont Bristol. Age seventy-one, First-Gen wolf. One marriage: Jonathan Bristol, age seventy-one, also First-Gen wolf. One child: Jadine Bristol Decker, age forty-six, a Second-Gen wolf. Jadine has one marriage: Warren Decker, age fifty-one, a First-Gen wolf. They have one child: Terrence Decker, age eighteen." I couldn't stop the grin. "And the family odd-ball as a Second-Gen bobcat in a mostly canid family. Think they were expecting another wolf?"

"Maybe. With that many in his direct line, but we don't get to pick our genes."

I should know. My parents and both sets of grandparents were shifters of some kind, while I'm a Zero. *Plus-Plus.*

"Anything else before I bring out the good stuff?" Merle asked.

I tossed my notepad onto the desktop. "Your turn."

Smirking, Merle opened her notebook. "Besides the opus I printed out, I spent an interesting evening with Millie Velradsky, who works the Omaha-Herald's social desk. She filled me in over fajitas and margaritas, including what didn't make it into print."

Her expression said this was going to be good.

"According to Millie, Mrs. Agatha Bellmont Mulligan was a snobby, old-fashioned elitist, and an all-around bitch. Yes, that's a quote," she added seeing my expression. "Agatha's attitude ranged from condescending to rude depending on how far down the social ladder she considered you. She was tyrannical to her family members, especially the twins. If anyone cried at her funeral, they were croc tears. She was worth over sixty million dollars at the time of death, not counting her share of the family's Bellmont Trust."

Wow. "I knew we had some wealthy families here, but… really?"

She gave me an enigmatic look. "Have you checked your and your brother-in-law's balances lately?"

I shrugged. "Mine's nowhere near that, and I have no clue what Russell's is." Her *harrumph*-with-a-stare response before returning to her notes made me uncomfortable.

"Mrs. Mulligan's will had a few disbursements, but most of her personal assets were in a separate trust with the twins as the only beneficiaries. If she had included them in the Bellmont family trust, then, potentially, Kathy's descendants would also benefit."

I thought that over for a moment. "The Bellmont Trust payouts follow down a family line?"

"Yep."

I opened my mouth; Merle raised a finger.

"Don't get ahead of me. Jennifer Huntington, Agatha's daughter, was a free-spirited party animal in just about every way and indulgence you can imagine. Except drugs. I have it on good authority she wouldn't touch them due to the nature of her brother's death. When she met Montgomery Huntington, sparks and underwear flew, followed by a short-notice wedding. Three months after that, she's pregnant. She was twenty. He was thirty-six, a Zero, and some kind of minor Baron back in England."

"Didn't last," I grunted.

"Nope, because Jennifer couldn't, wouldn't, stop the partying. Montgomery put up with it until the twins were about eighteen months old. Then he suddenly divorced her and went back to England."

She looked up, a twinkle in her eyes. "It's never been confirmed, but Millie says the rumors are that it was due to finding out the twins weren't his."

My eyebrows shot up. "The Gen tests?"

Genetic science had developed rapidly over the last sixty or so years. Nowadays, analysis of one's genome was pretty straightforward and accurate. It had become routine for parents to have their children tested between their first and second birthdays. Young shifters came into their animal form usually around three years of age, which made trouble controlling their tempers and instincts a bit more problematic than for Zero toddlers. Knowing ahead of time what to expect, parents with non-Zero children would be better prepared and kept the number of lawsuits to a minimum.

There could also be unexpected consequences. When hunting for my wife's killer, we'd uncovered a Gen test that revealed Tabitha Chandler wasn't Steven Chandler's biological child. That, coupled with other information we had uncovered, was the linchpin that identified the killer. Her own mother.

"That's mine and Millie's guess. Being a Zero, he wouldn't have been able to scent if she'd been with anyone. Afterwards, the party rolled on until someone rolled over her with a dump truck."

"A *dump* truck?" I echoed in disbelief. I hadn't checked her death's details.

"Stolen, of course. It was a real mess."

"I'll bet."

"Other than *that*," she said, her nose wrinkling. "Agatha Mulligan all but accused her niece's husband of being responsible, despite Warren Decker having an iron-clad alibi—he was advising ex-mayor Bennington on how to set up a scholastic fund for his grandchildren. Like you said, Jennifer's death was never solved and things continued to simmer between Agatha and Kathy's family for years. Sometimes quite publicly."

"Why was she so dead set against him?" I asked, as she took a quick sip of coffee.

"Later. Before we switch to the other side of the tree, let me finish with the twins."

Muttering "Where is it?" she flipped a few note pages. "Ah. Found it. According to Millie and that opus, both Gail and Corwin Huntington are stuck-up, conceited snobs—chips off their grandmother's block. Freshman at NUO, they dropped out after Agatha's murder in favor of partying, loafing, and enjoying life. They're both allergic to doing anything that requires work or responsibility. Regular chips off their mother's block in that respect.

"Gail's immediate circle is a revolving opera of snit fits, cat fights, and dramatic exits—preferably with a camera nearby. It's basically a drama-queen club, with each one feeding off the others for attention."

"She likes notoriety."

"Uh-huh. Corwin Huntington is not quite the party animal his sister is," Merle continued, "resulting in far fewer headlines and drama. However, Millie says there's an undercurrent around him that makes her think he's keeping his drama better hidden than his sister." She paused. "I have to agree with her. There's been a time or two when it feels like there's two conversations going on around me: one with their mouths and another one with their eyes."

"As in I-know-something-but-no-way-in-hell-will-tell-you?"

"Exactly. Corwin also differs from his sister in that he has several stable male friendships. They gravitate mostly toward hunting and sports."

I studied my desktop for a moment. "So, their motivation in Agatha's murder would be to get rid of a domineering spoilsport, full access to two trust funds, and freedom to do as they want."

"Assuming it was one of them," Merle said. "They would have been eighteen at the time."

"Wouldn't have mattered," I said, pulling my notebook toward me. "They sound like sociopaths—borderline or full. Age would be irrelevant." Which brought up an interesting thought. "How do they stay out of trouble?"

"Alex Griffin," she replied succinctly.

My lips flattened in disgust. The man's reputation as a legal shark was unsurpassed. He was the man to hire if you needed to beat a rap, especially if you had actually done the deed.

"He keeps them out of trouble by whatever method works, same as he did for their mother. Like the drug possession charges against Corwin last year that were dropped suddenly and without reason by the prosecuting attorney. Griffin has a PI firm, Allread and Gledhill

Consulting, on retainer that will use any means, go to any length to dig out information. Rumor has it that some of it has been…" she paused, "questionable."

My jaw tightened. I had heard of them and their *questionable* ethics. They, and others like them, were a big reason law authorities didn't like private investigators.

I was still updating my notes with Merle's information when Diana came in carrying two bags from *Zeeb*'s Deli. I was surprised to see it was a few minutes past eleven.

"I knew we'd be at this for a while," Merle explained, "so I left a pre-order of your usual and a turkey sub for me with Diana. Perfect break point, too," she added, peeking into one bag.

Diana returned a minute later, both coffee pots in hand. We thanked her and dug in, with me teasing Merle about her coffee choice. Hard-nosed reporters and wimpy coffee just didn't seem to go together, I told her.

Chapter 19

Stretched out on the corner of a snowy rooftop, the sniper was partially hidden by an elevator's mechanical housing. He'd donned a white coverall before stepping out, and the current light snowfall also helped to hide him. Sighting through the rifle scope, he found the triple pane of windows.

Found his target.

He mentally grumbled at the lousy angle. It'd have to do, since he'd roll off the building if he scooted over another inch. The guy was having lunch, currently waving a couple of French Fries at the woman seated across from him. They were both laughing.

As last meals went, not bad, he thought, centering the scope's crosshairs on the target's head, just above the left ear.

The deep-chest rumble of a big cat sounded behind him.

Chapter 20

After lunch, a bathroom break, and another coffee refill, we were ready to resume. As soon as Merle found the right place in her notes.

"Here we go. Kathy Bristol, Agatha's older sister. She was active in a number of charities until last year, when she and her husband retired to California. The woman doesn't have her sister's prejudices and has no trouble associating with anyone. Millie says she is well liked and considered to be the epitome of an old fashioned, dignified lady—except when her sister got her goat. Then Kathy's wolf came out."

"Like Agatha's accusation against her son-in-law? Do I get to hear why now?"

"Agatha Mulligan hated her nephew-in-law because…" Merle drew it out, "…he was from the Boondocks."

That was unexpected. "Bet that made for a lot of tension, considering Agatha Mulligan's personality."

"Oh, yeah. Agatha attended the wedding—we're assuming social pressure—but not the reception."

"Can't associate with all those inferior types," I snarked.

"You'll see a lot of that tension in the printouts. Comments, snide remarks, etcetera. Then Agatha managed to sink Warren Decker's chance for a partnership at Rudolf Matlock and Associates, an investment firm. That kerfuffle they managed to keep quiet. Mostly. Millie was covering one of the firm's to-dos that was supposed to include a partnership announcement, except that portion of the evening's agenda was skipped without comment. Later, she was heading down a hallway toward the kitchen—had questions for the chef about some of the menu items. Never made it. Turned a corner in time to see Warren Decker punch a hole in the wall. A couple of men were with him, trying to calm him down. One of them hustled her out with a warning about printing anything about it. Warren took a position with his current firm about six weeks later. Ah…" she turned a page, "Monjaraz, Glandt and Associates. Another investment firm."

"Sounds like he had good reason to hate her." I jotted down a quick note.

"Not just him. Three months before the murder, Agatha tried—discreetly—to keep Terrance out of her husband's old college fraternity. The fur flew. Both Warren and Jadine made no bones, privately or publicly, about their feelings toward Agatha Mulligan and her manipulations. And yes, I realize that does make them prime suspects."

My brow scrunched as I did the math. "Wait. Terrance would've been fifteen or sixteen. He was in college?"

Merle flashed a smile. "The boy is a genius, or near so. He had entered NUO's Engineering program that fall. There's a couple of nice articles," her pencil pointed at the pile on my desk, "about him. He's majoring in mechanical engineering, and is projected to be graduating one year early. Terrance Decker is quiet, studious—the polar opposite of his cousins. He either shuns the spotlight or his parents keep it off him. I can't see him killing his not-so-great aunt."

Me neither. "Could Kathy have had enough of her sister?"

Merle frowned. "I don't see it. Even their public fur-fights were only verbal. The claws on both sides were kept figurative."

I sighed, made a note. "That leaves Agatha's niece, Jadine Decker. What's the gossip on her?"

"Intelligent, socially active, sits on the board of several charities, and highly irritated by her aunt. Millie says she's heard a few off-the-record accounts that indicate that, when crossed, Jadine Decker can be an extremely cold bitch herself. Not averse to pushing people out of the way or even toppling whole boards to get something done the way she wants it."

"How irritated? Any mention of temper or violence?" I asked, fingers drumming on my desktop.

"Temper, yes. Violence, no. At least, not since a number of minor fights during high school. She has excellent control over her wolf and squashes her adversaries in a very civilized manner."

Hmmm. "Think she could kill her aunt?"

"Wouldn't rule it out. Especially if Agatha was messing with her family again."

"Okay. Give me a minute." I turned to a fresh page and made a list. "Based on what we've discussed, we have four viable suspects. In order of possibility: Warren Decker, Jadine Decker, Corwin Huntington, and Gail Huntington. Beneath them, as in least probable, are Terrence Decker, Kathy Bristol, and Jonathan Bristol. You agree?"

"Yes. Except you can drop Jonathan Bristol completely."

"Why?" I asked, ignoring the growing ache in my shoulder.

"The Bristol and Decker families were residing at Agatha's at the time of the murder because the Bristol home was undergoing renovation. Kathy Bristol had flat refused to rent elsewhere when the Bellmont family home had plenty of room. I understand they simply showed up one day with a moving van. Agatha wasn't given any notice or allowed a say in the matter."

I had wondered about that, given the level of animosity between them.

"Oh, my," I snarked. "A Boondocker under her roof. It's a wonder Agatha didn't go through it." I shook my head. "That house was a powder keg."

"Which finally blew. Anyway, the renovations were changes needed to accommodate Jonathan. A recent stroke had paralyzed his right side. He's confined to a wheelchair, and he wasn't a lefty at the time, but is now."

"Meaning he shouldn't have been able to beat Agatha Mulligan's head into pulp." People could surprise you, if given enough motivation.

Merle made a face. "Thanks for that lovely picture. Anything else?" she asked.

"Not at the moment, no."

Rising, she stashed her notebook into her portfolio. Watched as I took the sling out of my desk drawer. "You appear to be healing pretty good. Any word on whoever shot you?"

"Nope. Still don't even know why." Standing, I slid my left arm into it. Muscles I hadn't realized were tense relaxed as it took the weight.

She draped her purse strap across her shoulder. "Really?"

"Really," I echoed, walking her out.

***

I had scheduled my gym session for late afternoon. Based on previous experience, I didn't expect I'd be up for anything but a

165

soothing hot shower and a chair afterwards. Nope. Not even close. My physical therapist was a well-toned female named Maisy Jansson that spent the first twenty minutes asking questions about my injury and the medical treatment of it. When I left, an hour-plus later, my shoulder still ached but no more than what I'd arrived with.

Still, that hot shower and comfy chair sounded good. Knowing Grandma had arrived home safely made things even better. Pulling out of the gym parking lot, I decided a glass of scotch would bump the evening's rating even higher and help get me through that stack of reading.

<u>Chapter 21</u>

I didn't even get to finish my first cup of coffee next morning before my phone rang. The caller ID had me grimacing.

"Morning, Miss Heiser, what can I do for you?... No, I'm not planning on coming into the office…Miss Heiser…" I pinched my nose bridge. At the two-minute mark I'd had enough.

"Miss Heiser!" I interrupted. "Did the manager and his staff go up with the warehouse? Then I'm sure all of you, working together, can fill out forms, answer questions, do whatever needs done post-fire. I'll come by *if* something requires my specific attention or signature, or you can have one of the interns hunt me down. Otherwise, send a copy of any pertinent documents and emails to my business email. If I disapprove of something, I'll let you know."

I didn't need this right now, I thought irritably as she went on about space and inbound cargo. "Just rent something while the manager searches for a permanent—what? ... Hell, no. We are not nursemaids. If he can't make frigging decisions that fall under his frigging job description on his frigging own, then fire his ass and promote whoever's actually been doing his job for the past whatever. Anything else for me *specifically*? Great. Then you can go do your job, too."

I disconnected and gulped down coffee. Russell, in the name of every god out there, heal faster.

Two hours later, I was making my way carefully past busy snowplows to Monjaraz, Glandt and Associates on North 120th street. I'd set up an appointment with Warren Decker, my prime suspect.

I'd spent the wait reading the last of Merle's stack of articles. They had given not only a more rounded perspective of each person but added a few nuances to the relationships between them. The Huntington twins now occupied the two spots below Warren, with Gail nudging her brother out by a snotty smidgen.

My phone rang as I turned into MG&A's parking lot. It had gone to voice mail by the time I pulled into a spot and cut the engine. Found it came from the office when I checked the caller ID.

"Curt, A Detective Brinkman made a two o'clock appointment. He also wanted to know what your schedule was yesterday."

Brinkman…Brinkman…oh, right. He's the detective that almost got into the office brawl with Lieutenant Sinclair. A Second-Gen bear if I remembered right. I couldn't think what—oh! Had to be about Alfred Duninger. Brinkman must have taken over the case from Detective Macron, who might be in trouble from that Mulligan case. He probably wanted to go over my notes with me personally. Double-checking Macron—which I sure would, given her history. What did yesterday's schedule have to do with it though?

Shaking my head, I headed into the office building.

MG&A's office wasn't hard to find and surprised me. I had unconsciously expected a conservative, stodgy décor. Instead, it was modern sophistication. The honey-toned paneling provided a warm backdrop to jewel-toned chairs set in two small groupings. Two large prairie-themed pictures hung on the walls above them. I had only a minute of two to admire my surroundings before the friendly receptionist led me back to Mr. Decker's office.

"Come in, Mr. D'Accio, come in," Warren Decker said, standing to shake hands as the woman closed the door. "I appreciate you coming to us, especially as I realize your primary finances are managed through the Chandler Foundation in Nassau. I had assumed that, locally, you had followed whatever financial direction Mr. Chandler had provided you with."

"Why would he, or I, do that?" I said, curious.

His eyebrow matched mine. "To put it bluntly, you didn't have a whole lot of capital to invest prior to last year. Please accept my belated condolences on the loss of your wife."

I thanked him as I took a seat across from him.

He placed folded hands on his desktop. "Here at MG&A, we will work hard to meet all of your investment and financial goals, both long and short term. I can—"

I held up a hand to stop him. "Thank you, but there's been a misunderstanding. My business here today is not financial."

"You're a private investigator," he said, after a brief pause. "You have to know we don't give out any information on our clients."

"I'm not here about a client. My questions are for you."

Surprise flashed across his face as he cautiously asked, "What questions?"

I pulled out my notebook. "I've been hired to look into the murder of Mrs. Agatha Mulligan."

He blinked. "Why?"

"There is doubt surfacing that the man convicted of it, Aaron Rivas, is actually guilty of it." That stunned him for about five seconds.

His eyes narrowed. "If it wasn't him, then you believe it was one of us in the house?"

Sharp. I put my cards on the table. "I've seen the crime scene photos, Mr. Decker. Read the abysmal police report. I fully believe Aaron Rivas did not do it. Unless you want to believe there was a *second* intruder, then yes, that is the most likely scenario."

Decker's wolf rose to stare at me out of his eyes.

"And, naturally, you believe it to be me because of my background." His voice acquired guttural undertones.

I briefly wondered how often he'd had to endure the prejudice of his wife's social circle.

"No, sir," I said, meeting his gaze squarely. "However, you are heavily suspect due to the very public antagonism that existed between Mrs. Mulligan and you. Among other things, she tanked your partnership at your previous firm. You were physically seen punching a hole in the wall due to it. I'm sure her prejudice against your son rankled, too."

His wolf withdrew, mollified at my reasoning. "I despised the woman. There wasn't a more bigoted, vindictive person on this Earth. She was even planning on 'tanking' my position again."

Wow. Even after two years, his voice still resonated with loathing. "Here?"

"Yes. Mr. Monjaraz, our senior partner, happened to mention in passing a month or so afterwards that she'd scheduled an appointment through his secretary while he was on vacation. He was curious if I knew what for." Warren bared his teeth. "Naturally, I said I didn't, but there was only one reason that blight on humanity would have done so."

I made the logical leap. "She was trying to ruin your job

prospectives, same as with your last company."

"When her well-deserved justice finally happened, all I could think of was 'good riddance.' If Agatha Mulligan *had* lived long enough to make that meeting and was successful, I could have—quite happily—ripped her throat out. For my family's sake, it's a good thing I didn't have to face that temptation."

"Your family was undoubtedly grateful too."

"I've never told them. Mainly because of Kathy and Jadine. Memories were bad enough as it was, no sense in making them worse. Have to admit, I felt sorry that the guy who'd done us such a huge favor would be punished for it. And now you're saying he didn't do it?" Decker shook his head. "That had to be a real blow, especially over a fake."

"A what?" I said, startled.

"The Rembrandt on the wall turned out to be a fake," he said, chuckling. "Excuse, me, a reproduction. We found the real one later in the basement vault. The twins immediately wanted to sell it, of course," he said disdainfully. "Agatha probably knew they would and had it listed as a Bellmont Trust asset instead of in her Mulligan Trust. Mrs. Bristol refused to release it."

I stared, nonplussed. That explained Agatha's lack of concern about it during the skirmish, but… "Then why didn't she just let the thief take it?"

He shrugged. "It was still worth a decent amount, though nowhere near the real Rembrandt. I found the contract for it in Mrs. Mulligan's files. She had commissioned the reproduction about a year earlier, shortly after she bought the original. It even included an extra twenty thousand to the artist to not speak about it. My guess? It was meant as a theft decoy. Which, obviously, it was."

None of which was in the detective's report, which was

acquiring more stink the more I dug into this case. Jaw set, I jotted all that down.

"The morning of the murder. What do you remember of it?"

He grimaced. "All of it. I don't think I'll ever forget."

Understandable. "Could you walk me through it?" I asked. He stared at me for a second, then his gaze shifted to some spot over my shoulder.

"I had just come out of the bathroom in our suite—I wasn't feeling well—when I heard screaming. I raced downstairs. Gail was just ahead of me. We found the house staff inside the doorway of Agatha's den. I looked in…it was terrible. As much as I hated her, Mr. D'Accio, dying like that…" He paused. "Then I heard Gail say 'Grandmother's been murdered' and realized my wife and son were approaching. I pulled Abigail and Louise—they're the servants— out into the hall and slammed the door shut before they would see…would see. I simply stated Agatha was dead and we needed to call the police. I stood in front of the den's door until they arrived, then joined the rest of the family in the drawing room. Fact is, we spent most of the morning there."

I scribbled as he spoke. "What was the overall atmosphere?"

"Upset—shocked, of course."

His hurried correction went into my notes. "Did anything unusual happen in the days preceding the murder?"

"Unusual is a relative term," he said wryly. "Cold shoulders, hot words, and yelling were the norm in that house, especially during our stay. Agatha hated us being there and took it out on everyone, including the servants. I'm surprised they didn't quit en masse."

"Do you recall hearing anything that night? Footsteps in the hall? Anything?"

"No, but then I wouldn't have. The twins slept on the second floor. We were on the third."

"You think one of them could have done it?" I asked, noting he hadn't mentioned his son.

"Had to be, if it really wasn't the thief. They both hated their grandmother. She kept a tight rein on them and a choke hold on their allowance. They were only in college because Agatha made it a condition for receiving it. When she died, they both dropped out. Gail did so immediately; Corwin at least finished out the semester. Come to think of it," he gave me a sly grin, "Gail had a vicious row with Agatha the night before the murder when she refused to allow the twins to attend a party on the upcoming Friday."

I kept my politely interested expression. Trying to angle suspicion away from his family was no surprise.

"Jadine had to step in to keep them from going to that party," he continued, giving vent to a contemptuous snort. "It was her warning that partying two nights after their grandmother's murder wouldn't sit well with their social peers that kept them home. Fuming like a smokestack, in Gail's case."

"Who else was on the second floor? The third?" I asked.

He gave me a hard look. "My son Terrance also had a room on the second and as far away from the twins as he could get. Kathy and Justin had the other suite next to us."

I paused. "Mr. and Mrs. Bristol were on third? Wasn't he partially paralyzed?"

"On the right side," Decker said, nodding. "Agatha had installed a small personal elevator that went directly to the third floor. Her rooms took up one whole side of the hallway."

"Rooms?"

"A very large master suite with an adjoining sitting room.

Agatha's father converted the obsolete servant quarters into that and two guest suites across the hall."

I was scribbling furiously. "Naturally, you wouldn't admit to it if your wife or her parents took a late-night stroll?" I said, receiving a very wolfish smile.

"No, I wouldn't, and no, they didn't. I would have heard them."

I closed my notebook and stood. "Thank you for your honesty. I'll see myself out." Stopping at the door, I paused and looked back. "From all appearances, you're on track for a partnership here. I hope you get it."

As I left MG&A's offices, instinct told me Warren Decker probably wasn't my murderer. Of course, my guts had been wrong before. Checking the time, I figured I needed a nice lunch before heading to the office and a grilling from Brinkman.

***

Happily stuffed with shrimp alfredo, I arrived at my office with plenty of time to prep for my meeting with Brinkman.

"Did Detective Brinkman happen to call back and cancel?" I asked Diana.

"No."

So much for that hope. Passing her desk, I stopped dead in the doorway to my office. Stared at the chairs arranged in a semi-circle in front of my desk: my two client chairs plus two chairs from the outer office. Pivoted to Diana.

"Detective Brinkman did call, but it was to let us know to expect four, including Lieutenants Sinclair and Larson."

Huh. Larson must be from the blackmail side of the precinct. Brinkman had to have dug up something interesting on the Duninger case if the heads of both departments were sitting in. I was about to plop my butt behind my desk when the bell over the door tinkled.

"I want to speak with D'Accio. Now," a woman's voice demanded.

I walked out, already disliking whoever belonged to that voice. A tall woman in an expensive pantsuit and an aggressive stance was in front of Diana's desk. The expression on her face mirrored the arrogance she'd spoken with. Despite her display of wolf attributes, my inner radar said she was a Zero.

"Senior Agent Sutherland, DEA," she said, flipping open a leather wallet to display her badge as I approached her. Flipped it closed. "I'm here to impound your files pursuant to an active investigation."

Crap. Wait. "Files?" I said as the plural form registered.

"Everything you've worked on for the past two years."

Two years?

"And I want the actual files so that nothing is *inadvertently* left out," came the imperious order.

She'd just insulted my integrity. "No," I snapped, shock giving way to anger. She took a step forward, her finger nearly poking me in the chest.

"I am a federal agent and you will provide me with those files."

"No," I repeated furiously, despite the legal minefield I was stepping into. "You cannot just waltz in here and make that kind of demand."

"Then I'm arresting you on charges of obstruction and—"

"EXCUSE ME!" said an unexpected male voice loudly.

I looked around for its owner. Where? Then I spotted Diana sitting primly behind her desk, phone off the hook.

"My name is Ralph Jetter. I am Mr. D'Accio's legal representative and there'll be no arresting anyone just yet."

I almost laughed out loud. Diana had called him and then

activated the speaker.

"From what I can discern from the heated conversation, the rather vocal female wants full access to your files. Is that correct Mr. D'Accio?"

"Yes, and I've told her—"

"I am Senior Agent Sutherland, DEA, and I have every right to seize those files. They pertain to an ongoing Federal investigation."

"She wants everything for the last two years," I snapped out.

"*How* long? Are you investigating my client and/or his business practices?"

Agent Sutherland's lips pressed tight. "I'm not at liberty to discuss an open investigation."

"No, but you would be *obligated* to inform him if he was a person of interest in said investigation," Mr. Jetter said, his tone scathing. "Has she made any such claim, Mr. D'Accio?"

"No."

"Then there's no reason for such an extensive request and, the last time I checked, judges weren't issuing fishing licenses."

I crossed my arms and smirked.

"My client and I will comply when you present a *properly* executed warrant with *properly* defined parameters that are relevant to your *properly* identified investigation."

I made a mental note to make sure the backups were up-to-date.

"In the meantime," Mr. Jetter continued, "I will be filing a complaint with the local Drug Enforcement Agency office on the *improper* and *unprofessional* actions by one of their agents. 'Sutherland' you said?"

Agent Sutherland spat an unprofessional word and stormed out, sideswiping one of the lawyers from next door in the hallway.

Stephen Reynald stuck his head in the door. "Need a lawyer?"

he asked, grinning.

"Got it covered, thanks," I replied, waving him off. Shut the door and turned.

"Mr. Jetter would like to speak with you on your personal line," Diana informed me, hanging up her phone.

I laughed, gave her a thumbs up, and headed into my office. The man had represented me for everything from trespassing to a murder. Thankfully the latter had been dismissed.

"I have no clue what that was about," I said as soon as I picked up my phone.

"She's looking for something. Any cases you can recall that might have aspects that would interest the DEA?"

I ran a quick search through memory. "Not that I can think of. At least, nothing in the last two years. If she's fishing, something or someone must tie in, but two-years' worth? Think Agent Sutherland will get her warrant?"

"Not unless she's more forthcoming with the judge. She'll need to be a bit more precise on information and timeframe."

The line was quiet for several moments.

"Tread carefully," Mr. Jetter finally said. "DEA agents carry a lot of weight and they're not afraid to throw it. Let me know if or when you hear from them again."

I sighed as I hung up. Thank goodness my meeting this afternoon only concerned blackmail and murder.

***

It didn't. Warning bells went off when Larson was introduced as head of OPD's Narcotics division. I eyed my guests as Diana handed cups of coffee around. In front of me were Lieutenant Sinclair, Detective Brinkman, Detective Addison, and Lieutenant Larson.

"This isn't about the Duninger case, is it?"

"No, and I hear that it's pretty much stalled," Brinkman replied.

I leaned back in my chair and adjusted my sling, not that I really need it. However, it gave me an air of infirmity—*hah!*—and hid my advanced healing. Catching Sinclair's gaze, I quipped, "Okay, Lieutenant, let's have it."

"Yesterday, at approximately three-thirty, an anonymous male called OPD's desk and said to check the rooftop of the Donovan Office Complex," Sinclair said.

"That's next door." That explained the police vehicles I'd spotted when leaving yesterday.

"Patrol officers were dispatched; Brinkman and Addison responded to the subsequent call-in of a dead body."

Death obviously hadn't been due to hypothermia. "Alright. How does it involve me?"

"We recovered a rifle that was lying next to and partially under him," Brinkman said.

"Shooting position," Sinclair interjected quietly.

"Ballistics has verified that the weapon contained bullets that matched in weight and caliber to the bullet fired in your attempted assassination on the evening of October 25th."

I processed that for a moment, along with their contemplative stares. "Was he on the side facing my building?" I asked Brinkman. He nodded. "Line of sight to my office?" Addison nodded. "Think he was about to take another shot at me?" All four nodded. This was just getting better and better. "How did he die?"

"Someone blew most of his head off," Brinkman stated matter-of-factly.

I shrugged. "Wasn't me." That explained the schedule request.

"You happen to have a guardian angel?" Lieutenant Larson asked neutrally.

"Not that I know off," I said, keeping my body language relaxed. *Guardian demon, maybe.* The silence and dubious expressions lasted for another couple of seconds.

Brinkman pulled out his notebook. "According to your secretary, yesterday you had a nine o'clock appointment with Dr. Nathanial Gordon, followed by one at ten with Miss Merle Smith, a reporter with the Omaha-Herald. The two of you were in conference until shortly after two o'clock. Lunch was delivered from *Zeeb's Deli*, which you both ate in here. After Miss Smith left, you worked at your desk until leaving at approximately four-thirty for Pappio Heights Gym."

I nodded in confirmation. "Had my first PT session with Maisy Jansson—you can verify. Went straight home afterwards."

Brinkman exchanged an unreadable look with Sinclair, then went back to his notes. "The deceased had been there awhile—he was partially covered by new snow. That and the cold temperature has made time of death iffy, but we're guessing between ten and two o'clock."

"Footstep impressions in the older snow could still be made out," Brinkman continued. "The assassin—the live one—walked up behind the would-be sniper, shot him in the back of the head, turned and walked back to the stairwell." He looked up. "We're assuming he's the one that called later."

"Don't know why he bothered waiting," Addison grumbled. "Not like our shifters could track his scent. He'd worn Who-do."

"Who do *what*?" I sputtered, not sure if I should laugh or not.

"It's a new product on the underground market," Brinkman said sourly. "As in 'who-do-you-think-I-am,' which is exactly how someone with a warped sense of humor is advertising it. It's a condensed spray composed of the spray and/or urine from several different species, making it impossible to tell which scent belongs to the one wearing it."

Crinkled my nose at the thought of someone willingly wearing that.

"Fortunately for us," Lieutenant Sinclair added, "it's expensive. Most run-of-the-mill criminals won't be using it—skunking is cheaper."

Brinkman pulled a photograph from the folder in his lap. Handed it to me. "Do you recognize him?"

I studied what appeared to be a standard mug shot. The man in it was nondescript in every way. Medium brown hair, gray eyes, plain round face with no scars, moles, or other identifying marks. The perfect camouflage. I handed it back with a firm "No."

Brinkman flipped a page. "The deceased has been identified as Thomas Besset, aged fifty-one. A Zero with no marriages or kids. Did one stint in juvie for assault, followed by a couple of drug possession busts in his twenties. Nothing since. He lived quietly in a modest home, worked at Millard Gardening and Lumber Supplies. Didn't interact with neighbors, throw parties, or run his television loudly. Neighbors and co-workers alike were stunned to hear of his death, though the details have been kept quiet."

"He's not known to be a professional assassin," Sinclair said, taking up the narrative. "He's not linked to any known radical or fringe groups. In fact, there's not a lot known about him at all, except that paperwork found in his home shows he's got a very healthy bank account in the Cayman Islands. Our best guess is that he's on a private payroll."

Silence, not counting the crackle of tension in it. I kept my gaze locked on the lieutenant. My gut said we'd arrived at the main focus of this meeting. "You know it wasn't me that killed him. Can we get to the purpose of this meeting?"

"In our evidence locker," Sinclair drawled, "we have six other bullets, collected over the course of four years, that ballistics has confirmed were fired from that rifle. All of the deceased were tied into the drug trade in one form or another, including an undercover cop murdered five months ago."

And there it was. The DEA connection.

"One of mine," Lieutenant Larson said, an angry glint in her eyes. "Naturally, Mr. D'Accio, we can't help but wonder how and why you fit into that select group."

I heaved out a deep sigh. "This would explain the visit I had earlier today from Senior Agent Sutherland. She's—"

"DEA," Larson interjected with a scowl, then embellished it with an expletive. "What did she want?"

"All my case files for the past two years."

Larson's surprise changed to a thoughtful stare. I let the silence hang. Hopefully they'd scoot right past the 'he must be involved' theory to the more likely one.

"Sounds like a you-know-something-you-don't-realize scenario and they're trying to take you out before you do," Brinkman said.

Yep, that one.

"DEA must have had a flag set," Larson said, exchanging a look with Sinclair. "They would have received notification as soon as the ballistics report was filed."

Sinclair nodded. "And it wouldn't have taken long for them to discover D'Accio's had a number of cases over the years that have resulted in the apprehension and breakup of several drug operations. Add that to the two attempts…" He frowned. "But why go back so far? The knowledge has to be fairly recent or they'd have already eliminated him.”

“Something happened that made them realize it was hanging out there?” Addison offered.

“Victor Gleeson’s bust maybe?” Brinkman contributed.

“Possibly,” Larson said thoughtfully. “Taking out a major distributor would have definitely shaken up a few things. Make them re-evaluate, re-examine. They’re undoubtedly turning everything upside down trying to find that anonymous tipster.”

“And eliminating anyone who could potentially have incriminating information,” Sinclair added.

They were back to staring at me. Thoughtfully at least, this time. “Honestly, I have no knowledge about Gleeson, his people, or his operation,” I said, holding up my hands. Technically, I had merely passed on the info about him.

“That you know of,” Brinkman tacked on. “To attempt a shot in bad weather conditions—both times—there had to be a compelling reason to remove you so quickly.”

Yeah, yeah. Old news. I leaned back in my seat and crossed my arms. Giving Sinclair an irritated glare, I said, “Why don’t you tell me what you have on this group. Maybe something will ring a bell.”

“At this point, he has the right, in fact, the need to know,” Sinclair told Larson. “We all do.”

Larson nodded. We waited while she paused, as if to gather her thoughts.

“A major drug supplier has been operating in the US for over a decade. We’ve never gotten more than rumors, here and there, because it’s a tight, ruthless organization that doesn’t hesitate to terminate problems—actual, possible, or just-in-case. We don’t even know who the main players are or how the sons-of-pigs are bringing the product in from South America.” Frustration briefly leaked into her voice. "Even their name, Mashazan Cartel, was derived from their special blend of poison and was assigned by someone in DEA since 'Bastards' was too universal for their breed.

"They are the single source of 'masha.' Its main ingredients are cocaine and mashaza, which is a plant that grows all through the Andes at high altitudes. It's an odorless powder that is slightly sweet on the tongue and tasteless if added to food or drink. It's not as addictive as pure cocaine, but its damage to the cardiovascular system is far worse."

She stopped to take a breath, and I'm sure that was a flicker of pain in her eyes.

"Officer Erin Plummer had been working undercover for a small-time dealer named Ajax for almost a year, trying to learn his distributor, which we'd hoped in turn would lead us to the cartel. Frustrating didn't begin to describe it, as drugs and cash were exchanged anonymously through various drop points. A male using a public or CC phone would call Ajax with the drop location and amount due. Ajax would immediately collect the drugs and leave the cash. The lack of any advance notification left Erin unable to alert us and to set up an intercept.

"We were slowly piecing the bits and pieces together. Identified another couple of dealers—left them alone as we didn't want to scare off or alert the local distributor. Then Erin contacted me, saying Ajax was expecting a drop within the next four or five weeks. Masha production has to be complex because there's not a steady flow of it like straight cocaine."

"Dependent on the plant harvest, most likely," I said. Did they use greenhouses?

"Agreed. Anyway, I made the call to bring in DEA," her jaw set, "only to learn they already had one of their top agents in the area, undercover and as part of a parallel investigation."

"Typical," Brinkman snorted. "Feds and their one-way street."

"Opinions aside, we combined resources. Erin and Agent Damian Lopez struck up a 'relationship' as a cover. We put out feelers and as many eyes on the street as possible. We hoped to either catch the product as it came in or intercept Ajax's drop. Either one would put us one step closer to Mashazan."

Larson's voice went hard. "Then Erin was shot dead walking out of her apartment. Agent Lopez vanished that same night and his body has still not been found. Ajax was eliminated the next night in a still unsolved homicide-mugging. Both of his underbosses had fatal 'accidents' within days. Everything we had been building, us and DEA, fell apart."

That went way past ruthless and into psychotic. "What about Victor Gleeson? Is he cooperating…or afraid of an 'accident'?"

"Victor Gleeson is a dead end—no pun intended—as he was passing on the same treatment he received to Ajax," Larson said, disgusted. "Gleeson was the distributor for this regional area, which included Omaha and Kanesville. He received his own anonymous no-notice call of where to pick up his shipment and the amount owed. He would then haul it to his warehouse and break it down for distribution. His method of payment differed from Ajax's due to the significantly higher dollar amount. Gleeson would transfer the funds to the Caribbean account that was provided with each shipment, which was then closed shortly afterwards and the money re-transferred elsewhere. Again, pickup points varied as did the off-shore bank used."

"Whoever is running this outfit is a tactical whiz," I said in grudging admiration. "Do you think they'll shut down the Omaha connection as too risky now?"

"I doubt it, at least not permanently," Larson replied. "The amount of product we seized—both masha and straight cocaine—from Gleeson's operation says Omaha is a major revenue source for Mashazan. The organization will have to make new arrangements and line up a new distributor for this region."

"Meaning you're starting over from scratch." My grimace shifted into a frown. "Do you have any idea how Erin and Damina were made?" What missteps to avoid?

"Yes, which brings us to the second reason for this meeting," Sinclair said.

"We want to use your office as the central hub of our investigation," Larson said.

"And that very stout safe of yours to store notes, correspondence, whatever," Sinclair added.

Only one reason they'd ask that. "OPD has a leak," I said flatly. And why they'd arranged the meeting here.

"Or the DEA," Larson said. "Which I favor. There's no way the Mashazan Cartel has been operating virtually invisible for a decade without inside information. *High-level* info specific to drug enforcement movement and/or plans."

"That's actually one of the reasons for my transfer from Denver," Sinclair said, instantly becoming the center of attention. "This has to remain between us," he added firmly. After getting our verbal agreement, he continued. "Lieutenant Olsen had been secretly tracking an OPD problem for almost a year. He didn't know who to trust because the leaked information didn't seem tied to just one department. Was it an officer or a detective? Was their knowledge firsthand or from chatting up their buddies in the breakroom? Was it coming from someone in the Commissioner's office?"

"Why wasn't Internal Affairs alerted?" Larson said, outraged.

"Because the individual or individuals are very careful. They don't leak everything, especially for what would be a relatively minor bust. Also, one department isn't always cognizant of what's going on in other departments, or the informer could be off-duty or maybe on vacation. And for the record, at least one piece of leaked data came from Internal Affairs." He ignored Larson's gasp. "But again, at what level did the leak occur? Too many unknowns."

"That's why he went outside the police department," I said, drumming my fingers on my leg. Yeah, his options would have been limited.

"Olsen contacted my Denver captain—they're distant cousins—and explained his situation. The lieutenant wasn't looking for his own replacement but planned to work with whoever Captain Merriday felt could be trusted and was willing to transfer. Captain told him it would be risky, as the traitor would be highly suspicious of anyone suddenly coming in.

"However," Sinclair said neutrally, "the captain happened to have an individual that was currently out of favor and would have a valid reason for transferring if-when the traitor did a check. Olsen agreed."

Was it something he did? Or refused to do? The lieutenant's body language said it still bothered him.

"That's why he threw in his early retirement papers," Brinkman said crossly. "I liked him."

"Yes, both his retirement and my transfer were unpopular actions," Sinclair said calmly. "Naturally, there would be distrust and antagonism at my appointment, but the level of hostility from some did exceed my expectations."

Brinkman had the grace to flush.

"So, you came in knowing there was a major problem and—what? Two and a half years later the problem is still here?" Larson said, glaring at Sinclair.

I immediately went to his defense. "Pretty frigging hard for him to do anything when his every move, every order is going to be scrutinized, argued, protested, or foot-dragged. Which still seems to be an issue, Lieutenant Larson."

An uncomfortable silence filled the room. Sinclair gave me an almost imperceptible nod.

"Sorry," Larson said gruffly. "So, it's safe to assume a leak from both OPD and DEA."

"Great. Just what we need," Addison muttered.

"I have all of his notes and Lieutenant Olson visits occasionally, supposedly to check on his old department. We're still not sure where the leaks are, but we've determined a few areas where they aren't. Which is why your office is a safe third-party."

I mentally echoed Addison's gripe. "Yeah, go ahead and drop me whatever you get," I told them, running a hand through my hair. "If I'm not here, Miss Kylman is completely trustworthy and can store it in the safe."

Sinclair leaned forward slightly. "Detectives Brinkman and Addison will continue their investigation into Besset's death, with the suspected motive—officially—tied to your professional or personal life. We'll keep all information about drugs or a DEA connection limited to us four with your office as our central point. That way nothing is on our desks or in our computers."

"And the traitor?" Addison asked, a canid growl reverberating under his words.

"Lieutenant Larson and I will handle that. Everyone keep a close watch but, otherwise, proceed as you normally would. If the person or persons suspect we suspect, they will pull back. Or run. I do not want them to run," he enunciated with a half growl.

Something the others agreed with, from the ensuing comments. Especially from Lieutenant Larson. Wow.

"I take it we're not going to share our reports with the Fed?" Brinkman said.

"We'll be as forthcoming as DEA and Agent Sutherland are," Sinclair replied without a hint of sarcasm.

"Anything else?" I asked, scanning my visitors. Got head shakes. "I'll do a thorough review of my records, starting with the most recent. Assuming, that is, I get to keep them. Think Agent Sutherland will get her warrant?" I gave them a rundown of our encounter. Got several chuckles this time.

Lieutenant Larson snorted. "Fishing license—I like that. Your lawyer is right. She'd need stone-solid justification for that length of time. You can count on that question being at the top of my list when I pay Agent Sutherland a visit. Because," her soft drawl belied the hard glint in her eyes, "it appears that DEA still has an active investigation, which they've not provided my department any information about. Or who took over in place of Agent Lopez."

"If I find anything of interest—even remotely—I'll give both of you LTs a call. I'll also be on guard and hope they don't bring in another sniper. Kind of hard to dodge them."

"Speaking of which, any thoughts on our killer's killer?" Larson asked as we all rose.

"If the ones in charge were worried about the mounting ballistic evidence, it would have been simpler to get rid of the gun instead of their pet sniper," Brinkman said, buttoning his coat.

"Maybe a competitor?" I suggested, ignoring his sideways glance. It was possible. But given the circumstances, my assassin father-in-law was the most likely.

"We don't need a drug war, thank you," Larson said as everyone, even Sinclair, grimaced.

Sinclair stayed behind long enough to hand me a folder and thumb-drive that held all of their notes and both his and Olsen's private phone numbers. I felt so honored.

Chapter 22

I started Wednesday with a hangover. I went home last night with a briefcase full of files and a headache. I'd been targeted before and had the scars to prove it. But those had been individual, one-off attempts. An organized campaign to eliminate me was an unwelcome first. I had figured I was entitled to a glass of scotch.

One led to another and…well…

The empty bottle sitting on the kitchen counter got a guilty glance. Shaking my head in remorse proved to be a very bad move. Grabbed a couple of aspirins, which I upgraded to three and downed them with water. The pile of folders strewn on the kitchen table would have to be gone over again, as everything after the second glass was fuzzy. I set the coffee pot to brew my usual morning allotment of two cups before heading to shower and dress.

A half hour later, I sipped coffee and contemplated the gun lying next to my briefcase. I had brought it home with me after yesterday's revelations. Trouble was, I couldn't wear the holster yet, as the left strap irritated my bandages. I could stuff it in my waistband or coat pocket, but fat lot of good that would do me, I groused. The problem was my arm. Any fast movement, much less the twist-and-grab to pull a weapon, was still currently beyond it. Even with my so-called extra healing.

That was unacceptable. Possibly even fatal.

My next appointment with Maisy was this afternoon. We were scheduled for three days a week for the next two weeks. I'd change that to daily. I'd even take a drill sergeant on the days she wasn't available.

Nate would be by afterwards to change my bandages. The current ones were mostly large, waterproof Band-Aids with enough stick-um to keep them on. Good thing I didn't have a lot of chest hair.

I swallowed another aspirin before heading out for the office. I had things to do, people to see, a case to solve. I wasn't about to sit around in my apartment, waiting and wondering. Part of me almost hoped there'd be another attempt. I wouldn't be surprised if I had shadows also hoping the same thing.

***

"Huntington residence," a female voice stated over the intercom. I was sitting in the small turn-in allocated for vehicles in front of the house gates.

"Curt D'Accio to see Abigail and Louise Burnsworth. I'm investigating the murder of your former employer, Agatha Mulligan, and would like to ask you both some questions."

I had called the house this morning to set up an appointment with the twins. On learning they were out of town, I decided to pay the staff an unannounced visit. Detective Macron had at least managed to record the names of the cook and housekeeper wife-team that had found the body. It would also give me a chance to view the house and its physical arrangement.

"What's to investigate?" came the puzzled response. "The

murderer is in prison."

"His guilt of that crime is now being questioned."

There was a long pause. Then, "The Huntingtons are not in residence. It would be better if you asked them your questions after they return."

"I intend to," I informed her, keeping my tone firm but polite. "I also have questions for you and your wife and would prefer to ask them without the twins hovering nearby." Then added, "You might also."

Another long pause. I figured they were discussing it. Arguing maybe.

"We don't have to speak with you," said a different, harder voice.

Definitely argued. "Look, I could return with the police and a warrant, but I'm trying to keep this *unofficial* for now." I knew my bluff had succeeded when there was a click after a couple of seconds and the gate began opening.

"Drive up to the front entrance," the voice snapped.

Driving slowly up the long driveway, lined with winter-baren trees, gave me a chance to examine the three-story Victorian-style house.

Located on North 90th Street, it was one in a long line of gated estates that had sprung up back when this was a rural area on the city's outer fringe. Dark-brown trim complimented the tan brick walls and large-paned windows. A wide covered porch ran the full length of the front and a bay window protruded off the first floor's right exterior. Thick, evergreen windbreaks framed both sides of the house and probably had a matching one linking them somewhere behind it. I stopped at the front as instructed as the driveway continued on, doing both a loop back on itself and splitting off around the house's left corner. Low stone and brick rings bordering what would probably be filled with seasonal flowers jutted up through snow in front of the porch and in the center of the loop.

Graceful ironwork bracketed the four steps leading upward, and I'd barely made it to the top when one half of the double-door entrance swung open. Bet the woman in the doorway glaring at me belonged to the second voice. She stepped back to allow me entrance.

I found myself in an old-fashioned two-story foyer lined with walnut-toned paneling. Pocket doors to the right and left hid whatever rooms were behind them. A two-tiered chandelier hung above us with—

"Is that the original ceiling rose?" I asked, awed. It was beautiful; its intricate design spread at least two feet around the light's base.

"Of course," the woman replied a bit haughtily, closing the door behind me.

She was my height, with shoulder-length hair a mixture of silver and brown. Her skin tone was from a Middle Eastern ancestor. Her eyes were like green emeralds, which matched the current hardness of her gaze. She wore black slacks and a flannel shirt.

A second woman about the same height hovered in the hallway leading toward the rear of the house. Her completely silver hair hung in one long braid over her shoulder. Gray eyes held worry and—was that a trace of fear? She also wore black slacks, but paired with a medium-gray blouse. Both women appeared to be in their mid-fifties and were Zeros, according to my inner radar.

Flashing a pleasant smile, I said, "We can do the interview in the kitchen, if that will make you more comfortable." The laidback approach semi-worked, as the hostile one's shoulders relaxed but didn't soften the glare by much.

We passed several closed doors and a richly carved staircase before reaching the kitchen. The hall took a 90-degree turn to the left at that point and I could see a closed door about ten feet down it. The kitchen was very un-Victorian. A snug, built-in dining nook was opposite modern appliances and counters where a dishwasher swished quietly. Beside it was a door that appeared to open into a butler's pantry. Another door at the far end probably led outside.

"As stated, I'm Curt D'Accio and I'm investigating Agatha Mulligan's murder. Which of you is which?" I asked politely. Abigal was the cook, Louise the housekeeper.

"I'm Abigail Burnsworth," said the green-eyed glarer.

"Louise," said the other woman. "Would you care for something to drink?" she added a bit hesitantly.

"Thank you, no," I replied, sliding into the nook. I took out my notebook as the two of them settled opposite me. Continuing to keep my tone professional but friendly, I opened with "May I call you Abigail and Louise? Thank you," I said, when they nodded. "I've read over the arrest and trial documents. If the police investigation had been done properly, the most Aaron Rivas could have been convicted of was breaking and entering. Which," I finished blandly, "sort of narrows the suspect field, doesn't it?" As with Warren Decker, there was no way to dance around the obvious.

"You're implying it was one of the family?" Abigail said, looking at me with suspicion.

"The window was wide open. Someone else could have…" Louise's timid voice trailed off.

My expression might have had something to do with it. Flipped my notebook open and reviewed the few good notes I'd gleaned from Macron's police report. "Louise, you were the first one to discover the body?”

She swallowed. “Yes. I had started my rounds. I opened the door and…I still see her sometimes…in nightmares. I screamed. Abigail came running.”

According to Aaron, Agatha had left the door open when she attacked him and it still was when he went out the window. Another telling detail.

“Her scream brought everyone running,” Abigail said, clasping Louise’s hand. “Mr. Decker from the third floor was only a couple of steps behind Miss Huntington.”

“And the others? When did they arrive?” I asked. The sequence of who-showed-when could be important, along with any discrepancies between stories.

“Not far behind,” Louise said. “Mr. Decker was shoving us back into the hall as his wife and son approached. Mr. Huntington was right behind them,” Abigail’s eyes rolled. “Mrs. Bristol merely leaned over the banister. Mr. Decker slammed the door closed and told me to call the police. I admit I should have already done that, but…I froze.”

“*We* froze,” Abigail corrected, squeezing her hand.

I gave them both a wry smile. “I can’t blame you for freezing; it wasn’t a pretty sight. What was your average daily schedule like?”

“We arrived around five-thirty and I started breakfast,” Abigail said. “Nowadays, it varies, depending on who and how many are present.”

“I usually made a quick pass through the first floor for any cleanup—*normal* cleanup that might be needed,” Louise said, a hitch in her voice. “Still do.”

“Cleanup?”

“Unless there were evening plans, we’d leave around eight.

There was often some snacking or drinking after that—usually in the front drawing room or Mrs. Mulligan's den."

It was too much effort to find a trashcan or the kitchen sink? "Had there been signs of drinking that night?"

"Oh, yes," Louise said. "I'd cleaned up the front room by the time everyone dressed and gathered back downstairs."

"Weren't you told to not touch anything by police dispatch?"

Louise's eyes widened. "Well, yes, but I assumed that was just for the, the den. The police detective didn't ask about the front room."

I shook my head. Another black mark against Detective Macron. "You wouldn't happen to remember who drank what?" It wouldn't be the first alcohol-fueled rage-killing.

Louise's forehead scrunched, then she shook her head. "I'm sorry. I don't…except for the three beer bottles. Those were Mr. Decker's. I remember them because I was quite surprised. He doesn't usually have that many at one sitting."

Abigail snorted. "His wife would have had to use Mrs. Mulligan's elevator to get him upstairs. Black Mountain," she added on seeing my curious look. "No one else in the house will touch it."

Black Mountain was the high-octane of beers. Three had the average shifter sliding out of their chairs and would give a Zero alcohol poisoning. Four would take out the larger ones—mostly bears and tigers—while five would risk alcohol poisoning even for shifters. I don't think I'd ever heard of someone going that far.

Warren Decker hadn't lied specifically, but his omissions and leading assumptions amounted to the same thing. That was annoying but not surprising.

As a First-Gen wolf, he wouldn't have heard an elephant tromping through the third-floor hallway after three BMs. His wife was probably lucky he stayed on his feet long enough for her to manhandle him upstairs before he collapsed. And once he went down, that would have been it, unless he had the constitution of said elephant. The odds of him getting up a few hours later, going back downstairs to commit murder and meticulously frame another were zero. Maybe negative. No wonder he didn't 'feel well' the next morning.

"When they came downstairs, initially, how were they dressed, or undressed?" Back to sequence.

Abigail shrugged. "Nightgowns or pajamas—only the bottom half for Mr. Huntington. Except Mr. Decker. He was wearing the same but badly wrinkled clothes from the previous night."

Louise snickered. "Apparently Mrs. Decker had not only left him dressed, she'd dumped him in the other bedroom. Couldn't blame her. Besides having to change out all the bed linens, I had to air the beer-sweat out of the room, too."

I looked up from my hastily scribed notes. "Other bedroom? You mean, in the other guest suite?" The one the Bristols were in?

"No. The other one in their suite."

What? I asked her to describe the guest suite. Turned out, each one had a sitting room sandwiched between two bedrooms, each with their own bathroom. I kept my anger tamped down as I entered all of that in my notes. Another lie by omission by Warren, as this meant neither spouse could alibi the other. Not only that, it was information that should have been in the police report.

"Thinking back," I managed in a level voice, "how did the family members seem to react?"

The two women exchanged an undecipherable look.

"They were somewhat shocked at what had happened, yes. But," Louise cleared her throat, "the only one that was truly upset that Mrs. Mulligan was dead was her sister, Mrs. Bristol."

"Definitely," Abigail agreed. "Originally, she'd only heard Mr. Decker's announcement that her sister was dead. She didn't learn it wasn't by age-related means until after coming downstairs with her husband. She went positively white and might have fallen if Mr. Bristol hadn't pulled her down onto his lap. You were in the kitchen," she added when Louise glanced at her.

I tapped my notepad thoughtfully. That sounded too extreme a reaction to be fake. "Is there a reason you rolled your eyes on Corwin Huntington's arrival?" I asked Abigail.

She snorted. "People screaming, yelling, and he saunters down like it's any other morning."

Interesting. "Is he always that calm?"

"*Controlled* might be a better description," Louise said, frowning, "the opposite of his sister." Abigail nodded in agreement. "The boy has always been self-contained, keeping his thoughts and feelings close, if you know what I mean."

I did. "Did anything happen that stands out in the day or two before the murder?"

The two women shared an eye roll. Louise admitted there had been a lot of tension among the family members.

"From what I've learned, *antagonism* would be a better description," I said mildly.

Abigail did one of those elbow-and-head combo nudges at her wife.

"There was a big argument the day before," Louise admitted reluctantly. "That wasn't unusual in itself, but…well…this time, the twins were literally screaming at Mrs. Mulligan. Miss Huntington, especially; she even threw her water glass at her grandmother before storming out of the dining room."

At least Warren Decker had gotten that right. I next asked about the sleeping arrangements at the time of the murder. Again, their information matched Deckers's, with the additional detail of Terrance Decker and twins on opposite ends of the hall.

"Was there any additional house help? Nights? Weekends?" They'd be familiar with the house contents and floorplan.

"Two women came in mid-morning during the week to help with the house cleaning as needed. Still do. One of them, Cynthia Kudlow, will sometimes stay to help Abigail if she needs an extra hand in the kitchen for a dinner party. For large events—a formal yard party or such—they hire the extras from a temp agency."

Curiosity had me asking about the current arrangements, since it was a big house for two twenty-somethings. The twins had moved to the third floor, with Gail claiming the master suite. The second floor—and sometimes the third—had become an impromptu hotel, as people in the twins' social circles had a tendency to 'drop in' for a night or two, Abigail informed me unhappily. I was willing to bet it was a full house after one of their parties and explained her earlier comment about breakfast.

I asked to see the den where the murder took place.

After a pursed-lip minute, Abigail agreed, overriding Louise's small protest. She led me back out to the hall and opened a door. "This was Mrs. Mulligan's preferred room," she said. "It was a combination office, library, and family conference room."

The large room looked vastly different from the crime photos. Gone were the solid, heavy, comfortable furnishings. Modern pieces were scattered around the room, which had been upgraded into a trendy hangout, complete with a pool table in one corner and a wet bar in another. The built-in shelving lining one wall held bric-a-brac and not a single book. Where the Rembrandt had hung was a mounted display of two crossed baseball bats. Souvenirs?

"Did you know the Rembrandt hanging in here was a reproduction?" I asked. Both women shook their heads. "Did anyone?" Again, two head shakes.

"We were all quite shocked when the restoration service Mrs. Bristol took it to informed her so," Abigail said. "Mrs. Mulligan had to have swapped them one night after we left. The real one was in the vault, which we had to wait for the lawyer to open. He was the only other one with the combination."

Why all the secrecy, even from long-time servants? Why fight over a fake?

"I know," Louise said, evidently reading my expression. "Two lives ruined. Which could have been avoided if Mrs. Mulligan had let it be known the real Rembrandt was in the vault."

"Or let him take it," her wife muttered.

Stepping back out, I studied the hall's layout. The den's door was the only one on the right side of the hall, about halfway between the staircase and the kitchen. I asked about the other doors. On the opposite wall was the coat-closet-turned-elevator access. Another one was a what-not room that had once been Mr. Mulligan's study. Agatha's books had ended up there, according to Louise. A large formal dining room was behind the closed door in the short hallway around the corner. It ran along the backside of the study and connected to a room behind one of the closed-off pocket doors.

I studied the wall again, visually measuring it. The den had been large. Still…and this was a Victorian…

"Is there another set of stairs?" I asked. My peripheral vision caught Louise stiffening.

"There's an old servant set," Abigail confirmed, "Just off the kitchen."

"Show me."

Abigail moved to the kitchen entrance and pressed a decorative plate beside the doorframe. A two-foot section of the hall wall popped open a couple of inches. I finished pulling it open.

"Didn't give them much room, did they?" I commented, staring at the narrow steps. No signs of dust.

"In those days, servants were expected to be grateful they had a job," Abigail informed me dryly.

I stepped inside. "This goes all the way up?"

"Yes. It opens at one end of the hallway on each floor. The twins occasionally use it as a shortcut to the kitchen."

"At the time of the murder, whose rooms were the closest to these stairs?" I asked.

Abigail thought for a moment. "That would have been Mr. Huntington's on the second and the Decker suite on third."

I turned to Louise. "Would you like to let us in on your secret?"

"S-s-secret?"

Abigail gave her a sharp look.

"The reason why you're biting your lip. Why you look like you're about to pass out." It was the first time I'd seen anyone actually wringing their hands.

Her gaze darted between me and Abigail. "They said they'd caught the murderer. I-I didn't think I needed to say anything. It-it could have been anything."

"What could have?" Abigail asked, forehead wrinkling.

"The stairwell cleaning is usually done every other week. It wasn't due again yet but," she swallowed, "I needed to keep myself busy after…after Mrs. Mulligan's death. I found…there were… several treads had brown spots." She burst into tears. "I'm sorry, Abby. I should have told you."

Abigail drew Louise into a big hug. "*Ssshh*. It's alright. Like you said," she shot me a dark look, "it could have been anything. The twins aren't the neatest."

Yes, it could have. It could also have been dried blood stains. A Gen would have known after a quick sniff-test—which Detective Macron was. Still, being an experienced housekeeper, Louise must have suspected what they were. There's no frigging way to prove anything now, I thought, disgusted.

"They said…" Louise gulped, "the murderer was *caught*, Abby. And, and, and there weren't any more…s-spots. Anywhere. So, I, I didn't think it mattered. If he's right, Abby, that poor boy…" Louise buried her head in Abigail's shoulder.

"If it's any comfort," I said, resigned as Louise wound down to sniffles, "it probably wouldn't have made a difference. The detective in charge had already made up her mind, especially—as you said—there weren't any other 'spots' to back it up. Do you remember which treads had them? How far up?" I asked, hoping to eliminate a few suspects.

"Not exactly, but they were…" *sniff*, "between the first and ground floors." *Sniff, sniff.*

Crushed that hope. Thanking them for their time, I asked about the twins. Gail Huntington was skiing out west and should be back on Saturday. Maybe. Seems she had a habit of changing her schedule on a whim. Corwin Huntington was on a jaunt in Brazil with friends. He wasn't due back for at least another two weeks. I left them with one of my cards and the request to let Miss Huntington know I'd like to schedule an interview with her.

I drove away from the house silently cursing Detective Macron up one side of her designer pants and down the other. If those brown spots had been blood, and fresh, and Agatha's, and Macron had done her job properly, it could have completely redirected the investigation.

***

My PT session got off to a rocky start. Maisy did not approve of back-to-back sessions.

"Rest is an important part of recovery, Curt. It allows your body to adjust, to acclimate to the new demands on it." Maisy shook her head. "You're not just rebuilding muscles, but also ligaments, cartilage—everything that was damaged in your shoulder area. Overstress those new tissues and you could end up tearing them. Not only will it set you back, possibly permanently, it could also cause collateral damage in your arm."

After a flippant comment about using a drill sergeant on her off days, I had gotten a response that nearly froze parts of my anatomy.

"Maisy, I need my arm back in full working order as fast as possible. I've already survived two attempts on my life. No telling if or when or where there'll be another one."

It took a minute or two of internal argument, based on her expressive features, but... "Fine," Maisy finally agreed, albeit grumpily. "We'll intersperse your regular sessions with *short* sessions and *only* during the week. With this intense of a schedule, you will *have* to give your body time to 'settle in'," she did the air quotes, "over the weekend."

I counted that as a win and meekly followed her directions for the rest of the session.

Chapter 23

The next evening found me nursing a large glass of water and a sore shoulder in the *Despo's* corner booth and waiting for Angie. The day had been one frustration after another, culminating in getting chewed out by Maisy for overstretching my arm in our first short session. Hopefully, Angie's info would be the bright spot in an otherwise miserable day.

She slid in opposite me about a half hour later with a beer, grinning at my glass. "Must have been another bad—" The grin vanished; she leaned forward and sniffed. Cocked her head at me.

"I, um, kind of overdid it the other night," I admitted. Boris hadn't even blinked when I requested it. Simply said it didn't count as my 'first drink.'

"How's your brother-in-law?" she asked, giving a brief nod and settling back.

"Memory and speech are doing better, but the doctor won't release him yet." Russell was even more frustrated than me and, while Doctor Bullard might not have appreciated it, I took his slightly profane but clearly enunciated response as a good sign. "His Greenbaum grandparents have visited him a couple of times."

"At least he's improving," she replied, an undecipherable undertone making my ears prick up. "I've worked the past week in the Hansen area," Angie continued, "which is Tallon's primary turf. In a nutshell, Clayton Tallon is an *asshole* of megalomaniac proportions."

I couldn't contain my snort. That made it unanimous.

"I tried chatting up the other street workers casual-like—you know, trying to get a feel for the neighborhood. Didn't get a whole lot, especially about the local movers and shakers. Then I was chatting with Dixie when Tallon and a couple of his guards happened to come walking down the sidewalk. She immediately broke off in the middle of a sentence, turned, and went in the opposite direction. I trailed along, waiting until we turned a corner before asking what was going on. She stonewalled me, saying she just remembered an appointment. It took two more days before she finally trusted enough to confide in me."

She took a swallow of beer and her eyes dropped to slits.

"People go to Tallon for a loan because they have no other options and he's exploiting them." Her voice was steel-hard. "He often has them steal something, from where they work or elsewhere, by threatening their percentage rate or beatings. Others might get offered the money in exchange for specific information or *assistance* they can provide. Dixie's brother, Dave, worked at Callahan's Electronic Warehouse. Tallon's demand was the building's security routines and codes. Two weeks later, they had a major break-in."

I rubbed my chin thoughtfully. "I remember that. It was last spring. They lost hundreds of thousands of dollars-worth of inventory. Inside collusion was suspected." This matched Mandy's information about his theft ring.

"Uh-huh, and when they narrowed it down to two people, Dave confessed," Angie said. "He's currently sitting in prison for his part in it."

"Regardless of why or how bad he needed money, he did make himself an accessory," I said, not without sympathy. "Why isn't Tallon in the next cell?"

Angie took a *really* large swig of beer before answering.

"Because they can't pin anything on him. It's his word—as a *standup-citizen*," I could've cut the sarcasm with a knife, "against an arrested thief and the fact he's never been caught with any stolen property. He maintains that people stealing something to pay off a high-risk loan 'is not my fault'," Angie said, using finger quotes. "Not to mention," she tacked on in a cold voice, "he's a vindictive son-of-a-pig. Dixie told me that about a year, year and half ago, the cops pressured a guy to testify against Tallon. His wife and daughter were found hanging on their building's fire escape. The son was found tied up, alive, in the bedroom. The guy suddenly got amnesia, charges were dismissed, and he and the boy left town."

I snapped out a string of profanity. The son was left alive as a warning and a reason to recant his testimony.

"So," I said, clinching my glass tightly, "they're coerced into an action by Tallon, either stealing or providing privileged information, left hanging in the wind if caught, and with the additional threat to their family."

"That case you told me about? How is he involved?"

I gave her a brief summary of Mandy's case.

"Damn, Dice. That seems pretty tight. Can you do it?"

I took a sip. "Going to try. I did warn Mandy about the odds of getting a re-trial."

"Even if you do get his murder conviction overturned, it'll still hang over his head. Both their heads," Angie said, frowning. "Unless you can prove that he didn't do it or, even better, who the real murderer is."

"Yeah." I made a face. "Mandy said the same thing."

"I've never really gotten to know Mandy, just sort of chit-chatted in passing or between customers. She seems like a nice person, and I've never heard anything bad about her, either. That asshole has to be stopped," Angie said fiercely. "He rules Hansen's streets like it's his private kingdom and they're his personal serfs."

"If it's that bad, I'm surprised the police haven't gotten involved."

"Oh, they're watching. A cop I know was working undercover in the deli across the street from *Burton's*. But we're back to needing evidence or witnesses willing to talk. It's paranoid city up there, another reason why a lot of my questions got the cold shoulder. Tallon pays for any information that he deems interesting." Angie shrugged. "Then again, maybe we'll get lucky and karma will take him out like it did Cynthia Chandler."

Did she know? Had she guessed my involvement? She's the one who had told me Raynor Silverstone was in town. I hadn't told anyone, keeping the burden of that decision to myself.

Angie snorted. "Don't look so shocked, Dice. I'd do it myself it I thought I could get away with it."

I hid my relief in my glass, taking a long sip. "We'll go after Tallon. Someday." I held up my hand to cut off her reply. "Right now, my focus has to be Aaron Rivas's case."

Her expression turned mulish, but she nodded in agreement.

"For now, you need to go back to your usual haunts before someone reports your interest in him to Tallon. On another subject, I'm interested in anything dealing with drugs. Who's dealing, who's distributing, who's involved, and any rumors about someone providing confidential info. *Specialized* info."

Angie gave me a hard look. "Cops have a traitor?" I nodded. "That's bad news. There's a lot of griping on the street because the local supply is pretty scarce after that big bust last month. Dealers are having to go out of town to make buys. Then, naturally, jack up their prices back here."

She frowned, pulled on her beer. "Not sure, but I may have overheard something the other night. Only caught a bit of it—I was in a bar with the audio turned up overly loud even for Zeros and was wearing earplugs. Something about…the dry spell would be ending soon?"

Frigging great. The SOPs already had a new Omaha distributor? "Are you sure it was about drugs?"

"No. I told you, I couldn't hear much," she said, with an uncharacteristic hint of irritation. "He might have been expecting to get lucky. But considering one of the guys in the booth was a known dealer…."

I nodded. "Ups the odds to drugs instead of sex."

"I'll keep my ears open." She finished her beer in a couple of gulps, then grabbed the jacket lying next to her. "I need to go. Got a six-thirty appointment across town."

"Thought Thursdays were your nights off?" I said, sliding out, too.

"Special case."

Again, I heard that strange undertone. Waiting until we'd exited the bar, I said, "Angie? Everything okay?"

"Just life, Dice," she said as we climbed the stairs. "You know, we can meet elsewhere. It doesn't have to be here."

It took me a second. "Thanks, Angie. I just need to manage it better. But…I'll keep it in mind."

Reaching the alley entrance, my feet came to an involuntary halt. I found myself scanning the sidewalks, the street, the buildings. I could feel eyes on me. Nervously, I scanned again. *Nervously?* Realization of that shocked me almost as much as the thin line of sweat beads popping out between my shoulders.

Stopping with me, Angie waited patiently. And doing her own scan.

Crap, Dice. Get a hold of yourself.

The watcher didn't feel hostile. Still… Licking dry lips, I stepped out.

Angie wove her arm around mine and chattered non-stop about some crazy things she'd witnessed as we walked to my car. She waved good-bye at me through the window as she hurried off to wherever she'd parked. I leaned my forehead against the steering wheel and just breathed.

I thought I had successfully regained control of myself on the drive home. Then a shadow detached itself in my apartment building's entrance and I slammed backward into someone's truck grill.

"Oh. Hi, Lieutenant. Wasn't expecting you," I managed in a semi-normal voice.

"I have an update," Sinclair said.

"So do I. Come on upstairs."

I offered water or a cold soda as we shucked our outerwear. Making coffee had gotten me a hard *no*. I made a mental note to go grocery shopping as I pulled two sodas from the nearly empty refrigerator. Last night's supper had finished off the bounty Grandma had left behind.

"How are things going?" Sinclair asked, eyeing the stack of

files on my kitchen table.

I shrugged. Regretted it. The truck-grill slam hadn't helped my shoulder throb any. "Today has been one frustration after another," I replied as we took seats in the living room. "The one bit I have for you is the exception. A street source overheard a conversational snippet about a 'dry spell' ending soon. A known—to her—dealer was one of them, so drugs was the assumed topic. Said she'd keep her ears open for anything more."

"Damn."

"Yep."

"I'll let Lieutenant Larson know. Sounds as if the cartel has a new distributor lined up and is reopening for business."

"And still no idea how?"

"None."

"What's your news?" I grumped.

Sinclair pulled several sheets of folded paper from an inside coat pocket and handed them to me.

"Lieutenant Larson's report details her unproductive meeting with Agent Sutherland. Sutherland did confirm DEA has an on-going investigation, but refused to provide any details concerning it or the agent replacing Lopez. Or why she wanted two years' worth of files from you."

"Not surprised," I commented, laying them on a side table. I'd do a full read later.

"My report details recent actions Olsen and I have taken to ferret out the informer," Sinclair continued. "Olsen has recruited an Internal Affairs officer he trusts and that survived our vetting. He's now doing a very low-key and off-the-books audit of OPD officers' finances, starting with the narcotics department as that would be the most likely, and will move outward from there."

"What about Detective Macron? My secretary called her 'very haute couture', meaning expensively dressed."

"She gets a stipend from a small trust fund in addition to her paycheck."

"And doesn't mind rubbing it in, evidently." I could tell it bothered him, despite his usual impassive delivery. "By the way, has she made any progress on Duninger's murder?"

"No. There's still no clue as to who or why. The blackmail connection, which his associate did confirm when they apprehended Miss Totusek, is tentative at the most. Macron and her partner have been thorough. I've been reviewing and following up on all their daily reports," he added.

"What about…?"

"Her short stint of unprofessionalism on the Mulligan case was due to personal issues at the time. On review of the files, including her own reports, Detective Macron realizes just how badly she screwed up and is willing to work with you, unofficially, to help set it right."

"I'll think about it," was all I said.

"How about you? Any progress on Agatha Mulligan's murder?" Sinclair asked in turn.

I gave him a summary of my interviews with Warren Decker and the Burnsworths. Hearing about the possible blood stains on the staircase had the lieutenant's jaw tightening. No doubt Detective Macron would be hearing about that tidbit.

"Even if we could get forensics in to check the staircase—which would require the DA reopening the case," Sinclair's words were clipped and harsh, "two-plus years of cleaning products will have made any remaining remnants unusable. Especially in court."

I splayed my hands out in an exasperated "I know" gesture. "I tried to get an appointment with Jadine Decker this morning. She refused, undoubtedly warned about me and the subject by her husband. Louise Burnsworth called around lunchtime to say that Gale Huntington is back but has declined to speak with me. Willing to bet her actual reply was stronger."

Skipped over my Russell/Chandler company frustrations.

"I've started going through my files." I waved my drink in their direction. "I'll keep going but, honestly, I can't think of anything—directly, indirectly, or sneaking in from the back forty—that could have triggered the recent attacks on me. Especially pertaining to drugs."

"Which leaves us the *why* question," Sinclair said. "Does sound like a frustrating day at that." He finished his soda and rose. "I'll brief the others."

"Including Sutherland?" I couldn't help snarking.

"No, but you may hear from her. The surveillance she's assigned to you will inform her of my visit tonight." He picked up his coat. "If she does contact you, that will indicate just how interested DEA is in your activities."

"Felt the eyes earlier. Wondered if it was them or you."

Sinclair paused mid-zip. "Not us. *If* there's another attempt, it won't be so blatant. Everyone's on alert now."

"I'll keep a close eye on my brakes," I joked. His serious reply of "Do that" knocked the cocky grin off my face.

"The weeks and months following a violent assault can be the hardest," Sinclair said nonchalantly as he pulled on his gloves. "Being attacked, injured, isn't new for you. This was different. Emotionally and psychologically different. Let the what-and-how tape of events keep replaying mentally—it'll eventually wind down if you don't suppress it."

"In the meantime?" I asked cautiously.

"Deal with it…work with it. Pretending nothing's changed? That won't work."

Because I had changed. Could feel it down to my bones. I also sensed, instinctively, the lieutenant was speaking from experience.

"Thanks," I replied, walking with him to the door.

I watched him pass the elevator and head toward the stairwell at the hall's end. Just before disappearing through the door and without turning around, he raised a hand in a farewell gesture.

Maybe we did have a budding friendship.

Chapter 24

I added Angie's information about Tallon to a private file I had started on him. Whether or not as part of another case, our paths would be crossing in the future. Then I spent the morning working mostly on background checks.

DEA evidently was very interested in me. At least, Agent Sutherland was. We had a 'brisk' and unsatisfying phone conversation—for her—about files and late-night visits from police lieutenants.

I called Mr. Jetter afterwards. I couldn't tell him everything, but he did need an update on the possible drug connection and DEA's interest in me. I also needed advice on how far I could push the legal boundaries. Could I get Agent Sutherland for stalking?

***

Late afternoon found me sitting in another bar. *Riley's Pub* had been our favorite hangout for years. Originally, Nate and I had been part of a small group, playing pool or darts, drinking, flirting, and just chatting the night away. During my enemy-generated troubles last year, all but Nate had shied away from me. Afterwards, I wasn't sure if it was them from embarrassment or me from resentment, but we'd never drifted back together. Some days I'd been okay with that, other times not. Pulling cautiously on a beer, I realized the tight, slightly depressed feeling about that part of my history was—well, not gone, but mellowed.

Seems more than my shoulder was healing.

The bar had opened a half hour ago and there was only a scattering of others around the room. The bartender had the music on low, which my ears appreciated, as she bustled about, getting ready for the Friday night crowd. I eyed Nate, nursing his own beer across from me. He had asked me to meet him here but hadn't said a word since he'd sat down.

"Okay, Nate. What is it?" My hand flexed around the bottle. "Is it another ER event?"

"No…and yes." He gave me a wan smile. "I've decided to leave Emergency Medicine. Again. Sorta. I can't help it, Dice," his tone apologetic. "I'm on call *only* if they get swamped by a large influx of patients."

Car wrecks. Fires. There'd still be an emotional response, but different. Less personal. "Don't apologize, Nate. This is what you do; what you're meant to do. There's a lot of people, including me, that are thankful for that."

He flashed a grateful smile. "By the way, Bernard wants to give me howling lessons."

I nearly choked on my beer, laughing. "Did you actually do it?"

"Tried to, anyway," Nate said, chuckling. "Ergo the lesson offer. Now he wants to introduce me to his sister."

We both laughed. I felt good, until Nate said he wanted to see me in the clinic on Monday. Scowling, I said, "As long as it's my last frigging X-ray. At least for this." I motioned toward my shoulder.

Nate nodded. "It is. I'm creating a baseline for the new repair cycle, which should be more-or-less complete now. Just do a walk-in whenever you have the time."

"First I'm an anomaly, now I'm a freak," I muttered morosely, saluting him with my bottle.

Nate reached over and lowered my hand back down. "You are Curt Sebastian D'Accio. You are a private investigator with a strong sense of justice that doesn't blind you to all its nuances. You are a damn fine human and an even better friend." He released my wrist and leaned back. "The first shifters of each generation would have felt similar, wondering 'what the hell?' Especially Third Generation and the *monster* epithets they endured. When in truth, each was but the next step on our evolutionary path. As you are now."

I chewed on that for a minute. "Thanks, Nate."

"'That's what friends are for,'" he said, quoting me with a grin. "So, working on anything interesting?"

I was halfway through my explanation of Mandy's case when a fight broke out. It started with two guys loudly cussing at each other, expanded to disparaging family linages, then progressed to pummeling each other. The other patrons scrambled away toward the walls as they knocked over several tables. Unfortunately, the bouncer hadn't come on duty yet. I was debating the wisdom of wading into that melee when the black-haired one let out a human-version roar, grabbed a chair, and slammed it viciously into the blonde's side, sending him crashing to the floor.

Riley's heavy-duty chairs didn't break easily like in the movies.

Nate and I scrambled out of the booth as a second blow connected with a bone-breaking *thump* before we could reach him. I grabbed an arm and yanked him around he as he reared back for a third strike. The chair dropped. Blackie staggered a step to keep his balance and his gaze latched onto me. Then a large fist was headed toward my head. I dodged it and punched him with mine. Hard. He went down like the proverbial rock.

"Ambulance on the way," the bartender called out.

"He's going to need it," Nate said grimly, running his hands over Blondie.

The bouncer and police arrived same time as the ambulance. Belinda, the bartender, related what had happed to them while Nate gave a quick assessment to the medics. It was bad. Damage included broken ribs, broken arm, cracked or broken shoulder, and possible internal bleeding. The medics loaded Blondie up and raced away, siren screaming.

Blackie was starting to come around. Nate recommended that he be examined, too. "Just as a caution as he took a pretty hard punch," he said, not looking at me. Two policemen hauled him to his feet, cuffed him, and half-walked, half-dragged him out to their car.

The remaining policeman took our statements while Belinda and Petey, the bouncer, straightened the room. We'd just sat back down when Petey came over to thank us and plop down free beers in front of us.

"Did you hit him full strength?" Nate asked, soto voice when we were alone again.

I nodded and took a swallow. Beer wasn't scotch.

"Then I hope they do have him checked out. He might have a concussion."

I wasn't about to apologize for fully using my near-Gen strength. "There was no sanity in his eyes, Nate. Blackie would have beaten that guy to death and anyone that got in the way. In fact, Blondie probably would be dead if that second blow had been aimed at his head."

Nate nodded. "I know. At least he kept the pounding to center mass, which will most likely limit his booking to assault charges instead of attempted murder."

I mulled that over for a moment. "So, head injuries can signal a more lethal intent?"

"Uh-huh, but severity counts, too."

Hoping for professional insight, I described Agatha Mulligan's corpse. How the coroner had to piece her skull back together.

Nate shook his head. "That's a nasty level of hate and/or rage. Were there claw or fang signs anywhere on the body?"

I ran the images past my mental viewer. "None that I can remember and, now that you mention it, the coroner's report didn't list any."

"Gens of any level *have* to maintain control," Nate said, tapping the tabletop for emphasis, "due to the level of damage their animal half can inflict. It's why the toddler and teen years are so dangerous. Toddlers are nothing but instinct and teenagers are nothing but hormones. Going clawed in a fit of temper can have severe legal consequences.

"What we witnessed a few minutes ago is a prime example. Psychologists call it a 'killing frenzy' and attribute it to our ancestral fight for survival. The fight didn't start with lethal intentions, but somewhere along the line, 'Blackie' lost it—no sanity you said. He was using his fists and any weapon within reach for maximum damage. If he had been a Gen, his animal half would have taken over and his natural weapons would have left a bloody mess behind. Legal defense in either case is usually a temporary insanity plea. For your murderer, a Gen in that same state would have been more likely to have ripped Mrs. Mulligan to shreds than bludgeon her."

"So, you're saying her murderer was a Zero?" Which none of my suspects were.

Nate shook his head. "It *could* be, as the injuries you described certainly fit a frenzy. However, if it was a Gen, and whether premeditated or spur-of-the-moment, it was a deliberate beat-her-into-pulp act. They never lost control, not even for one or two vicious swipes. Which, by the way, should preclude any future insanity plea," he added.

I heaved a sigh, realizing I should have known that. Time to dig out my old criminology books and have a refresher session if I was going to keep doing murder investigations. "Thanks for the insight, Nate, but—" I flinched as the music level suddenly increased to blaring. The bar had been steadily filling up around us and the end-of-week partying was ramping up.

"Need to buy some earplugs," Nate said, sympathetically. "The *Depot* does suit you better now."

Guilt struck. Our once weeklies at *Riley's* had dropped to only occasionally this past year. Whereas I was at the *Depot* almost weekly, with or without Angie. "You can join me there anytime, Nate. Seriously," I told him. "Just bring a flashlight. Like I do."

"Uh-huh," he replied dryly. He drained the last of his beer. "Let's go."

I paused at the door. As I had when I left my apartment this morning. As I had whenever I left the clinic or any other building today. And like all those other times, I scanned my surroundings. While my pulse did elevate a beat, my heart didn't pound and there were no sweat beads across my back. An improvement. It also helped that I didn't feel any eyes on me, hostile or otherwise.

Nate waited silently beside me. A bit sheepish, I said, "I'm dealing."

His nod was acknowledgement, the clap on my shoulder was approval with maybe a smidgen of encouragement. Guess it was a male thing. We said our good-byes and went our separate ways. I hurried home to give Agatha Mulligan's autopsy report a thorough reading. Maybe another clue or two could be scrounged from it.

There weren't any. Nada. Zilch.

I tossed the autopsy report aside and crossed my arms. Sulked. Besides the massive head and neck damage, there were several premortem bruises on her arm that could have come from the killer, Aaron's scuffle with her, or both. No sign of defensive wounds, which supported the assumption that the first head blow came from behind. At this rate, I'd still be working this case after Mandy was paroled.

My phone rang. I didn't recognize the number.

"Hello?" I said, cautiously.

"Angie's here," said a very distinctive voice.

I gave my phone a disbelieving stare before replying. "Boris?"

"Angie is in a bad way."

Worry sparked. "She needs a doctor?" I asked, reaching for my jacket.

"No. She's drinking Black Mountains." He hung up.

Chapter 25

I grabbed my car keys and bolted for my car. Fridays were one of Angie's most profitable nights of the week. For her to take it off, it had to be serious. Hell. The Black Mountains pushed it way past serious. And getting a phone call from the *Depot*'s don't-get-involved bartender? The wind was howling sideways.

Heavy traffic and two fender-bender jams later, I finally managed to get there. By then, it was fully dark and no moon. I grabbed the small flashlight I kept handy in my glovebox and did a quick survey, wishing for the zillionth time dark vision had been one of my inherited Gen traits. I quick-stepped my way into the pitch-dark alley hiding *Depot's* entrance. Two shifters talking off to the side turned away from my light but otherwise ignored me. A sign of recognition and trust it had taken me months to earn.

Inside, it took a minute to spot Angie. She was sitting in the back corner booth, the heavily shadowed one. I slipped in opposite her. Angie's hands were clasped around a BM bottle, full of its dark namesake. A small pile of bills lay in front of her. She didn't raise her head, didn't move.

A waitress glided up and deposited a glass in front of me.

Tilting her head toward Angie, she said "Fourth" before moving on.

Oh my God. She'd already drunk three? Is she catatonic?

My question was answered when she took a sip, managing to do so without raising her gaze from the tabletop. She still hadn't acknowledged me.

I settled back and waited, as she had for me last year when our moods were reversed. Finding my glass held water explained the waitress's lack of payment request. My worry level went up as the liquid in the bottle went down. Half. Two-thirds. A couple of swallows, maybe?

"My sister is dying."

My hand froze, my glass hanging inches above the tabletop.

"Organs failing. Doc says…doc says three, four months at the most."

"I'm very sorry," I said, setting it down. "Has she been ill?"

"She's been a vegetable."

I sucked in a sharp breath. "What happened?" This was the first time Angie had mentioned any family.

"My mother dreamed of being a dancer," Angie said tonelessly. "As a First-Gen wolf she had the grace and stamina…until an accident shattered her legs. Mom suffered bouts of depression over the years. Dad was twelve years older than Mom and held the family together, especially when Mom was at her worst. I was sixteen, Janet eighteen, when he died of a heart attack at work. Mom managed to do alright for a couple of months, then this…this *damn* documentary," she spat venomously, "was broadcast one night about the *glorious art* of dancing and the various *magnificent styles*."

The hands cupped around her bottle became claws. My heart sank.

"Mom went out our sixth-floor apartment window. Janet tried

to stop her. A Zero, trying to wrestle down a wolf?" Angie's laugh was bitter. "She ended up falling with Mom. Janet lived—if you can call it that—when Mom's body partially cushioned her."

The silence between us was heavy. Heartbreaking.

"When did this happen?" I asked.

Up till now, her speech had been remarkably clear for having downed four BMs. Her reply of "Almost three yearsss ago" was the first to slur.

"Janet'ss…in a long-term health ward. They've been taking good care of her, but Doctor Galloway…last night…ssays her body iss…iss sssh-shutting down."

The bitterness was gone, her voice simply holding a deep weariness. She'd mourned her sister for three years, and now only that last, final step was left. Her hand morphed back to human.

No wonder her mood had been off last night. "Expenses?" I asked quietly.

"Petitioned ssstate. I…" she waved a hand vaguely, "cover resss."

Our health care system had its faults, but it recognized that many families simply did not have the resources for intensive, long-term medical care. If a family's petition for help was accepted, they would only need to cover half to one-fourth of the expenses and the State would absorb the remainder. In extreme cases, they'd pay all of it.

Angie sagged, then leaned sideways against the wall. Probably three-parts weariness and seven-parts potent alcohol.

"Time to go home," I told her. Standing, I caught Boris's eye across the room and held my hand up in the universal 'thank you' sign. I'd mull over the mystery of how he'd gotten my private number later. Thankfully, a nearby patron stepped up to help me wrestle Angie into her coat. I shoved her money into a pocket and got a good grip on her arm. I felt all the eyes on us as we headed for the exit. By the time the door closed behind us, I'd had to slide my arm around her waist to steady her. I flicked my light on.

"Wimp."

Whether or not she intended it as such, Angie's mutter was a bit of comic relief.

Her one-bedroom apartment was only about fifteen minutes away. I was unlocking the door with keys I'd fished out of her pocket when there was a deep growl on my left. Turned my head. *Slooowly*. A large man stared at me from an open doorway across the hall. My inner radar warned me he was a bear of some kind. I didn't need it to tell me he was pissed.

"What did you do to Angie?"

Who was currently slung over my good shoulder. "Nothing," I replied cautiously. "She did this to herself with four Black Mountains."

His eyes widened. "Black—her sister?" he said, his tone shifting from rip-your-face to concerned.

I nodded, pushed the door open. "I'll only be a minute."

Heading for the room I'd studiously avoided during my self-imprisonment, I gently plopped her down on her bed and limited my ministrations to pulling off her coat and shoes. I folded the bed-spread over her.

Stepping back, I couldn't miss the framed picture on the small night table. No question about the two young girls in it being sisters. Angie and Janet had their arms around each other's waist and were giving the photographer broad smiles. Their dad? I glanced at the bed, my heart aching for that lost, happy time. Which was worse, I pondered on my way out. The sudden severance I'd experienced, or the long, drawn-out vigil? If given time to reconcile the loss, would it lessen the pain?

The bear was waiting in the hallway. "Her sister has passed?"

"Not yet, but her organs are failing. They give her about four months," I told him, studying his drawn face. A friend then, if he knew about her sister. "Angie could use someone checking on her in the morning."

He gave a curt nod. "I'll pick up a box of her favorite doughnuts." Held out his hand. "Leroy Whitetail. I moved in last June."

"Curt D'Accio," I returned. At least he didn't do the macho-male grip with our hands.

"Yeah. I recognize you now. Should have kept the beard," he said over his shoulder, before disappearing back into his apartment.

I stared at the door to apartment 217 for a long moment. Finally, I turned away, tired and more than a bit despondent. I couldn't wait for this frigging year to end.

Chapter 26

Saturday, I'd promised myself, would be a mental break along with the physical one. No thinking about any of my cases unless something forced me to. Even the record review got pushed aside. Took care of bills and basic bookkeeping in the morning and then watched a couple of ice hockey games on TV in the afternoon.

When I wasn't on the phone, that is.

Grandparents being early risers, I'd heard from both sets by mid-morning. I assured them I was fine, healing well, and back at work. Grandma must have told Grandpa, because at the end of their call he wanted to know *"about that lynx."* I hem-hawed a bit, then asked if they'd seen the news about OPD investigating a dead guy on a rooftop.

"Yep, watch the Omaha news all the time. Got interesting stuff going on out there."

Nothing more was said on the subject, but I'm sure that was a loud *whoop* I heard as they disconnected.

Then I called and talked with Russell, who was in a good mood. Doctor Bullard had finally agreed to release him next week…after his legal guardian—yep, me—made the arrangements for an on-site aide to assist him. Stifling a sigh, I told him I'd be in touch and called Nate for recommendations.

Angie beat me on calling. I'd planned on doing it sometime early evening, giving her time to get functional. Maybe take her a bottle of aspirin.

Sounding a bit embarrassed, she both apologized and thanked me. I asked how she was. *"Fine, as long as I move slow and don't have to sneeze. I did that once already and it took ten minutes for my eyes to quit watering."* I couldn't help but laugh, then apologized. We talked for a while, and I got a few more details, including the facility where her sister was located. It probably wouldn't make any difference, but I'd ask Nate to check on Janet anyway. Before we hung up, I told Angie I was willing to listen if she needed to talk.

Tom Tall Elk called for an update on me, my case, and the dead sniper on the roof. The police hadn't released any, uh, unnecessary information about the dead guy, like having a rifle pointed at my building. But Tom had his own sources of info, and I could honestly tell him their case had stalled. His voice told me he wasn't satisfied and that he'd probably be hitting those sources for more information.

Merle called in the middle of the hockey game between Nebraska University Huskers and Kansas State Bobcats, a rivalry that went back several decades. I was only half listening as she chatted since the action on the ice was getting wild. The penalty box of both teams seemed to be getting almost as much action as the puck and there'd already been two brawls, one on ice the other off. Fortunately, I managed to get her off the phone right before a Husker forward drove the puck past the Bobcats's goalie. My yell might have temporarily deafened her.

The Huskers won, which put them on track to make the playoffs this year. Whoo-hoo. In the midst of celebrating, I remembered Merle's phone call. A quick mental replay had me realizing I'd agreed to go with her to the mayoral debate tomorrow night. That snuffed out my post-game glow.

****

Sunday's debate at the Hilton Conference Center was the first of three. Melissa Brower almost bounced behind her podium, energetically answering questions and summarizing ideas for city expansion in both size and services. Jerry Louderback was exactly like Merle had described: staid. I'd call him stuffy. His body language consisted of deliberate hand movements and his replies were in an even tone and along traditional lines of improvements within the current infrastructure. Kurt Filbrandt was the best of both, in my opinion. Neither overly exuberant or depressingly stuffy. He smiled. He engaged with the audience. He spoke concisely on issues facing the city and his plans to resolve them, including a few innovative ideas. Yes, I was biased.

With the official question-answer session over, everyone was encouraged to stay for refreshments and to mingle in the adjoining auditorium. The candidates were quickly surrounded as people took the opportunity to speak with them while others bunched up into discussion groups. I headed toward the buffet table along the wall.

Finding an out-of-the-way corner with a plate full of bite-sized sandwiches, I munched while my gaze wandered. Merle had roped me into this, hoping one of us would spot something or someone 'suspicious.' It was highly doubtful that whoever orchestrated Filbrandt's blackmail attempt would be so blatant. I figure most of the scrunched eyebrows and angry expressions scattered around the room probably came from whatever they were discussing. There was a tense undercurrent, though, throughout the room that left me uneasy. One group had a guy at the arm-waving stage and security was already moving toward him.

Scanning for Merle, I found her in the crowd around Jerry Louderback. Hmmm.

"Any particular reason you're scowling at candidate Louderback?"

I sighed as the robbery detective stopped beside me. "Detective Chizek. Fancy meeting you here," I said, flashing a polite smile. "Did you find the debate interesting?"

"Not really," she said, her gaze running over the crowd.

Ah. She was here for the same reason I was.

"Any particular reason?" she repeated, focusing on me again. "Have you learned anything new concerning the Filbrandt case?"

"Why, Detective, I'm shocked. Are you asking if I'm messing around in an active police investigation?"

"Wouldn't be the first time."

Couldn't help grinning at her peevish answer. "Actually, I'm here as Merle Smith's plus one. As for Louderback," I flicked my gaze briefly to him, "I can't but help wonder, knowing what I do."

"You and everyone else in the room," Chizek replied with a candor that left me surprised. "Even without knowing all the details, there's not a single person in this room who doesn't believe the blackmailer's end goal was more about ruining Filbrandt's reputation and election than money. After all, there are bound to be easier targets with actual indiscretions available for blackmail without having to generate it. The question remaining now is who orchestrated it."

"Well, that would explain the tense undercurrent," I murmured.

"Uh-huh. Was it someone on a campaign staff? Or a 'helpful'

constituent? Or one of the candidates themself?"

"With both of his challengers tainted, Kurt Filbrandt could end up winning just on a sympathy and uncertainty vote," I said.

"There have been some suggestions to that effect," the detective replied in a neutral tone.

"That Filbrandt himself tried to skew the election?" Stunned, I stared at her for a moment. Had we all been taken in? I immediately shook my head. "No, no way, Detective. Their emotions when I interviewed them were real. Trust me, I'd have known."

Chizek leaned against the wall. Distance plus noise level would have made it difficult for even a shifter to overhear, but she lowered her voice anyway. "Agreed. Because releasing the faked pictures a month before the election wouldn't give Filbrandt's campaign much time to fight the negative fallout, much less refute them."

"Impossible, I'd say," I replied in the same lower tone. "Woodworkers Security would have done their six-month purge by then, and that night's file, modified or not, would have been gone."

"Do you think the Southside Motel manager—assuming it's still the same one—is going to remember anything that happened six months prior short of a police raid?"

"The motel registration log—"

"Shows Cece Totusek—aka Rosalie Sayer—was there three times total and always in the same room," Chizek said, cutting me off.

I kept my cussing internal. I had missed that, only checking the log for the days Filbrandt's car was missing. "Cece probably requested it," I groused. "Muddles *when* those frigging pictures were taken."

Chizek agreed. "This was a well-thought-out plan, with every-thing timed to completely screw the man and his campaign." She straightened, preparing to leave.

"Detective? A moment?" She'd surprised me by giving me information rather than the usual no-comment-on-open-cases spiel. I'd return the favor. Glanced to make sure no one had wandered close.

"About a certain individual I asked about?" Her eyes went cop flat. "A street source told me he's branched into black market acquisitions. She also spotted your undercover at the deli across the street from his preferred hangout. He needs to be very careful."

Chizek's chin dipped in acknowledgement, then she turned and left.

Scanning the room, I found Merle was now part of Melissa Brower's crowd. Depositing my empty plate in a trashcan, I slouched back and waited. It took another fifteen minutes before she rejoined me. I asked if she'd gotten anything useful.

"No, just the usual tap dance around issues and nothing concrete in either of their plans to fix them. Mr. Louderback did have an interesting idea on revamping the Boondocks."

"That so? Still, I don't think I'd vote for him."

"You live in Papillion."

"So? I'm still entitled to an opinion. What about the Boondocks?"

She waved a hand. "You can read about it in tomorrow's paper."

"Tease."

Merle laughed. "Let's go. I'm hungry and those small squares aren't real food."

An uneasy tingle went down my spine. Glancing around, my gaze locked with Jerry Louderback's. I tilted my head in question; he turned away to speak with someone. Okay, then. Taking Merle's arm, we gathered our coats and made our way to the nearby underground parking.

"Honestly, Merle," I said, as the car warmed up, "I can't see why someone would have gone to all the trouble of generating a whole set of fictious pictures, just to win a mayoral race."

"Seriously? You don't know about the power that flows through the mayor's office? The city council?" she asked, her tone surprised. "Permits, Dice, issued or withheld. Zoning that can mean millions for a developer, not to mention the awarding of contracts for it. Committee appointments. Funding—city, state, or federal—redirected to specific city projects or departments. Favors exchanged, here and there, along with backroom agreements. And, if they have long-term political goals, it's a stepping-stone."

I simply sat and stared at her for a long moment. Like most people, those things were abstract concepts in the background of our everyday world. But, putting it together like that? "Well, damn," I finally said. "Call me naive."

Chapter 27

Tuesday morning, I huddled over that wonderful first cup of coffee. Bleary-eyed, aching, and wishing for a few more hours of sleep. I'd spent most of Monday coordinating with the medical services company Nate had recommended, getting Russell discharged and ensconced at home, arranging for a grocery delivery—he must eat out a lot—and dealing with a number of odds-and-ends that included brushing off a couple of inquisitive reporters.

Nolan Baranski, the nurse aide, had arrived shortly before three o'clock with his duffle bag. A Second-Gen bear, he'd be able to handle Russell and his wolf. That barely gave me time to change into my gym clothes and make my appointment on time to be mauled by Maisy. She definitely pushed the boundary between therapist and drill sergeant. After a long, hot shower and a quick supper, I had spent way too many hours going over police documents, trial transcripts, and my notes.

My revised suspect list had moved Warren Decker down to join the Bristols due to alcohol impairment and my gut. Terrance Decker was still hovering midway. While I didn't want to believe a fifteen-year-old was capable of such a brutal murder, it was possible. That had narrowed the most likely killer to one of the Huntington twins or Jadine Decker.

Pouring myself a second cup of coffee, I pondered my next step. Face-to-face meetings with my main suspects were definitely in order. Their responses to questions, both verbally and bodily, could reveal more than they realized. Question was, how? Corwin Huntington was still out of the country and both women had brushed me off. I'd figure something out. Just as soon as I finished up the Vogel background check.

I heaved a sigh. And I still owed Nate an X-ray visit.

* * *

"…so, yes, everything points to him being a level-headed young man, not a fortune hunter." It was midafternoon and I'd found enough to provide Mrs. Vogel with an oral report. Her daughter had come bouncing home from college last Friday with a surprise fiancé in tow. The family was rightfully concerned. A single child, Miss Vogel stood to inherit a fairly large estate.

I had spent hours talking with everyone from school counselors to the local sheriff and newspaper editor. Other than one teenaged beer-party bust, I'd heard nothing but good about David Ulrich and his entire family. After a moment's internal debate, I said, "Mrs. Vogel, have you asked your daughter if she's going to be happy, long term, with a farrier's rural lifestyle?"

There was a sharp inhale on the other end of the line.

"I've been so worried about him, I hadn't even thought about her," she admitted. "Rachel's social life is quite active and she does love shopping, especially with her friends." There was a very audible sigh. "Do you think two people with such different back-grounds can be happy, long term?"

My brief time with Tabitha flashed before me. Our lives had

been so different. "Ultimately, it's up to them," I told her gently. "If they're each willing to recognize what's important to the other and compromise, it's possible."

Another sigh. "Then I need to make sure they've started that conversation. Thank you, Mr. D'Accio, for everything."

"You're welcome, Mrs. Vogel. I'll get a written report and final bill out to you tomorrow at the latest."

Hanging up, I gave a sigh of my own. It was nice to be able to provide a favorable report. I'd started building that report when Diana came in.

"A message from Louise Burnsworth came in while you were on the phone," she said, handing a paper slip to me. "Miss Huntington can meet with you this evening at the Raven Country Club, nine-thirty, in the European Room."

Yay, was immediately followed by a stab of annoyance. I'd have preferred our conversation in a less public environment. I scowled and resumed typing. If she expected that to temper my questions, she was in for a surprise.

The report wasn't quite finished when Diana rang in.

"Caller on the office line demands to speak with you and he won't give a name."

Hmm. I picked up. "Curt D'Accio. What can—"

"I know who's trying to kill you and why," a cold, hard voice interrupted. "It'll cost you five thousand."

"Is that so?" I drawled. My level tone belied a sudden increase in pulse rate. "Got something more for me to go on? Otherwise, you're the fourth would-be scammer I've had to deal with," I lied. Silence told me he hadn't expected that.

"The electrical fire at your warehouse was engineered. Thomas Besset took out an undercover cop and her DEA contact. The agent's body is buried just north of Glenwood along the Loess Hills Trail. That good enough?" came the brusque reply.

My hold tightened around the phone. If that last was true, it should make Agent Sutherland happy. "For now. Five grand will get proof positive of my problems?"

"Physically, no. But I'll give you enough details on the who, what, and where to get everything you need to take them down. Meet me at the old Elmwood Brewery at F and Eighty-Seventh Street. Enter through the loading dock. Six o'clock."

My eyes flashed to the wall clock. 4:38.

"How do I know this isn't a trap?" I snapped out before he could hang up.

"You don't," the voice admitted. "Bring a backup if it'll make you feel safer. If you're late, or bring more than one other, all you'll see is my taillights. I'm leaving town as soon as we're done." He disconnected.

I wasted a few seconds swearing, then had Diana cancel my evening appointment with Maisy while I called Tom. Found he was out of town on a case. We chatted for a moment then told him to 'look me up' when he got back. Not wanting to worry him, I hung up without letting on the real reason for my call. After a moment's indecision, I dialed another number. It was answered on the third ring.

***

The Elmwood Brewery Company sat near the center of an area filled primarily with industrial and commercial service businesses, which began emptying out at five o'clock. Now, at a quarter to six, the area was pretty well deserted. A vehicle hadn't driven past in the five minutes we'd been sitting here. Security lighting illuminated several parking lots around us, empty except for various company trucks and vans parked for the night. Normal city noises were a distant background hum.

Except for the grimy windows, the long, single story building looming in front of us resembled my cousin's poultry barns. Elmwood's parking lot was mostly dark, with a single weak security light at its front entrance. The realty company listed on the For Sale sign kept it cleared of snow, probably for access by would-be buyers. The rear, where the loading dock was, lay in deep shadow. Naturally, I thought, sourly.

"I don't like this," Lieutenant Sinclair said flatly.

"I'm not happy either," I grumbled as we studied our surroundings through the windshield of his unmarked police car. The lieutenant had insisted on taking it instead of my very noticeable sports car.

I'd made the call for an assist to Sinclair instead of Lieutenant Larson. She would probably have overridden my agreement, surrounded the area with cops, and expected to wring every bit of information out of him in interrogation. That cold, *experienced* voice told me he'd be watching for that very thing and we'd end up with nothing. Sinclair had unhappily agreed to accept the arrangement as a 'confidant informant' exchange—albeit an expensive one—as letting one lesser fish slide to get the big shark.

"He's here…watching," I muttered, running my gaze around the area. Searching for the eyes I could feel.

"*Some*one's watching," Sinclair retorted. "Doesn't mean it's your informant."

True. Twisting to face him, I watched his head swivel as he took in everything. "I'm willing to call it off if you think we should," I told him. As much as I wanted to hear the caller's information, I trusted Sinclair's instincts, both natural and experience-honed.

I was still waiting for his answer when lights flicked on inside of Elmwood, drawing a grunt from the lieutenant. "We go in," he finally said. "Cautiously."

The lights made it a little less ominous, although it was hard to see much through the dirty windows. Having them cleaned might increase the odds for a sale. Exiting, I walked around the front of the car. When Sinclair didn't immediately join me, I turned to find him tossing his coat back into it. His suit jacket followed. Next, he removed his belt and all its accruements. Lastly, his shoulder holster joined the pile after tucking his gun into his waistband.

Eying him warily as he locked the car, it was obvious Sinclair was prepared for a quick shift if things went bad. While I would finally learn what his Gen form was, it'd also mean the situation had turned nasty. I had made my own preparations, too. My weapon was still holstered, but loosely, and my coat hung open for quick access. Drawing speed still wasn't up to my pre-shot level, but at least my weird genetics had me healed enough to do it.

The lieutenant's head lifted and swung in several directions as we approached the loading dock. "Too many overlapping scents," he warned in a low voice.

I nodded in understanding. We were going in blind.

We aimed for the human-sized door set to the left of the large cargo ones. We took up positions on each side of it, then I pushed it open. No shots. Sinclair flowed through the opening and immediately crouched off to one side, weapon out. I quickly followed, mirroring him on the opposite side. No shots again. I released the breath I'd been holding. So far, so good. Although, if an ambush was planned, this large open space full of hiding spots would be perfect.

On the left were beer vats—tanks, actually, since they were

taller than me and as big around as a herd's water trough. Set two to a row, I could see at least a dozen more pairs running the length of the room. A path separated them from a mishmash of piles of furniture, cardboard boxes, wooden pallets, and raw lumber. Bare metal shelving lined the wall behind them.

"What? Don't you trust me?"

I recognized the sarcastic male voice as my mysterious caller. "No. Show yourself or we're leaving," I returned coldly.

A man stepped out from a hallway on the opposite side of the room. That would be the office area. Warily, he held his hands out to either side. "I'm armed, but it's holstered. Appreciate it if you did the same."

I kept both gun and attention centered on the man, knowing the lieutenant was using all his senses to determine if it was indeed safe. When he straightened and slowly tucked his weapon away, I did the same. Leaving the door open, we started toward our 'host.' He also began moving forward and, by mutual consent, we all halted center of the room and a bit more than an arm's length apart.

Silence lingered as we studied each other. The informer was a bit more than six feet with a stocky build. Shaggy blond hair swept his collar and eyes of icy blueness dominated a narrow face. I wasn't insulted when he seemed to dismiss me in favor of focusing his attention on Lieutenant Sinclair. Smart Zero. He knew which of us was the most dangerous.

"You're letting us see you?" It was almost as good as giving us his name.

"I'm leaving, and the night patrol would have stopped to check on seeing your vehicle in the parking lot and no lights. Burke Realty is known to stop in—do a bit of cleanup or check for transients. Got the five thousand?"

I pulled a wad of bills from a coat pocket and held it out. Taking a wary step forward, he plucked it from my fingers and stepped back. "That's half," I said, briefly displaying another wad of bills. "You get the other half if what you say is worth it."

His eyes narrowed, but any attempt of hard-nosed posturing was forestalled by a sudden low rumble from my left.

"Who and *why*," Sinclair snarled impatiently.

I kept my attention focused forward as the guy took a reflexive step back. Despite the tense situation, I couldn't help a smug feeling. That didn't sound feline. *So, bear of some sort*, I thought, despite my Gen-dar still refusing to cooperate.

"Drugs." The guy's gaze skittered between me and Sinclair. "Omaha Midwest Port is the trailhead of the Mashazan Cartel's American supply chain. From here, it's separated and shipped out to distribution points across the country."

My brain reeled at the sheer volume that implied. "How?" was all I managed to get out.

"Product comes in by cargo ship, mixed in with legit items for specific vendors under Chandler Import's inventory. The individual crates, sealed at their originating ports, are then signed for and handed off to the companies as-is after arrival."

A light bulb went off. "The new customs inspections." His head gave a single jerk in confirmation. "You're trying to stop it."

"Delay it and not me—I'm just security. Word has come down about a number of changes being implemented, including new routes and distribution points. None of which will happen before the next shipment arrives."

"It's under sail now?" Sinclair asked sharply and without growly undertones.

"Left port this morning."

"Who's the boss and where's his center of operation?"

"He's—" His attention shot past us.

Sinclair yanked me between two vat rows a split second before gunfire rang out and the guy's face exploded. More bullets *pinged* around us. Handguns, no rifles, my brain automatically cataloged. Multiple ones.

We crouched behind our metal protection, weapons drawn. I took a peek around the side. The door we'd left open for a quick exit had also provided a quick and silent entrance for the shooters and— *crap*.

"Three humans, one tiger, and one frigging large mastiff," I said, assessing the figures scattering through the junk.

I ducked as more bullets whizzed by. Five assailants. The drug boss wanted to make sure—I rotated on my heels. Scuttling forward a bit, I risked a glance toward the front of the building. The man sneaking toward us from that direction dove behind a dilapidated desk when he saw me.

Six, probably more outside. The drug boss had sent a small army.

"Pincher move," I snapped out, alerting Sinclair. I jerked back, a bullet searing its way across my arm. Whipping around, I fired at the first target I saw—the tiger. An angry squall said I had at least nicked him before he made cover.

This was bad. We were pinned down in a vulnerable spot while they could work their way to a better angle, shielded by all that debris. Sinclair squeezed around me in the confined space, taking point.

"Keep them pinned down—I'm calling backup," I said, fumbling my phone from my pocket.

"Not soon enough" came in a deep growl. My head jerked up.

Sinclair's jaw was thinner, longer; his eyes coal black. "Smell gasoline."

My stomach pitched in horror. Burning the building would eliminate us as well as any DNA traces of our attackers.

Standing, Sinclair shoved his gun at me and kicked off his shoes. I gaped as his shirt was split apart by enormous fur-covered shoulders. Incisors longer than my middle finger erupted from the elongating muzzle of a large ursine-shaped head. *Bbbbear*? my brain stuttered.

Sinclair snarled out a challenge that rattled a nearby window and nearly had me peeing in my pants. *Not bear*, I corrected, dazed, my brain catching up with my eyes as he bolted out of our shelter. *Wolverine*. A Third Generation wereform Wolverine. *Holy frigging hell.*

Screams and gun fire. Vicious snarling-hiss. Then everything went quiet.

How long was I frozen? Seconds? A minute? Two?

Pocketing my phone and stuffing Sinclair's gun in my waistband, I stepped out into dead silence. Except for a low rumble that didn't come from machinery. The lieutenant was looking around at his, uh, handiwork. I counted four heads and torsos, none connected. There wasn't a lot still attached to the torsos. The fifth torso still had his head attached, but was impaled on a metal rod and appeared to be minus its spine. His nude state said he'd been one of the shifters.

I swallowed hard. No getting information from them.

Suddenly, the man behind the desk lunged out and raced back toward the front and an exit. I surged forward but had only gone a few steps when an object came sailing past me. It hit the runner square in the back and sent him flying forward. I winced at the sound of his head hitting the floor. He didn't move, but there was a moan. *Yay, a live one.* Winced again when I got to him and saw what Sinclair had thrown. Well, it had proved useful, and the head's original owner didn't need it anymore. I walked back to Sinclair.

Who was still rumbling.

I stared in awe at the towering powerhouse. His wereform stood a good foot taller than his human's six-seven. Unlike the long hairs of his full animal, the dark fur covering him was a fine, downy layer that only enhanced the muscular torso you could probably break a brick against. Sinclair's huge, powerful arms ended in long, wicked-looking claws with a matching set poking through his overly stressed socks. Thank God, his pants had stayed on. The leg seams were split open to accommodate thick thighs and they were a might short on his hairy legs, but the rest had stretched enough to keep the essentials covered.

He hadn't gone unscathed, as there was bleeding on his left shoulder and arm. I was relieved to see his muzzle and fangs did not bear the same, uh, testimony as his claws. When those black eyes fixed on me, a factoid from a college social science class popped into my head. *Wolverines and badgers, the only two Mustelidae species, are the least stable of the shifters as they merge more deeply with their animal half. Especially wolverines,*" my professor had stressed. *"Approach with caution if one is agitated.* I swallowed. Sinclair was well past agitated.

Licking dry lips, I said in my calmest, smoothest voice, "Well, Lieutenant, what do we do now?"

The rumbling got louder. An incisor peeked out from a curled lip.

I had the sudden, insane image of me smacking him on the nose like a misbehaving dog. Uh-huh. Right. *Good way to lose the whole arm, Dice.*

"Impressive."

The voice had my gun snapping up as we whipped around. A woman stood in the doorway, her gaze roaming the room. Her weapon was out but pointed down toward the floor. The rumbling beside me dropped deeper and I could almost feel his muscles bunching.

"Very impressive," she said.

Gutsy. "Who are you?"

"DEA." The gun disappeared into a jacket pocket and she began walking toward us, seemingly unfazed by the slaughter around us.

Gutsy and experienced. I lowered my weapon as Sinclair's rumbling trailed off. She appeared about my height with brown hair currently worn in a braid over her shoulder. By the time she stopped just outside of arm's length—the lieutenant's—I'd noted light brown eyes, a band of freckles across her nose, and my Gen-dar's feline ping. I wasn't the least bit insulted when her gaze skipped over me and stopped on him. Scanned him from head to paw and back.

"Agent Leona Barlow," she identified herself.

"Well, Agent Barlow, what are you doing here?" I asked, suspicious as she hadn't produced a badge.

"Saving your butts."

Sinclair snorted; I glared. "I believe the lieutenant took care of that."

"Not the two arsonists outside with gasoline cans," she said, her tone hard. "I've called for backup. And an ambulance."

That would be the sirens I could now hear in the distance. "And you just happened to be in the neighborhood?" I pivoted, keeping her in view as she nonchalantly walked past us.

"Did he manage to give you any useful info before becoming brainless?" she asked, ignoring me in favor of rifling through the dead informer's pockets.

Something in the manner she asked that had me hesitating. "He was getting to it when *bam*. A couple of more seconds and we'd have had a name." Truth.

She pocketed a set of car keys as she stood. Eyed me suspiciously. I expected her to press me, but my irritation was real. *Just a frigging few more seconds...*

Evidently satisfied, Barlow turned to Sinclair. "I recommend you shift back before they get here, Lieutenant," she said. "The medics might be a bit hesitant about treating your wounds. And you might want to put that weapon away, too," she added, flicking a glance my way.

I holstered my gun as Sinclair began the reverse shift. With the same speed exhibited earlier, he was human again in an impressively short time. Most large shifters needed a full minute or more to change. I hadn't consciously clocked him, but I'd bet Sinclair had done it in half that time. I didn't know enough about Third-Gens— *did anyone?*—to know if that was a common trait for all wereforms or if this was unique to him.

His wounds were easier to assess now. The shoulder one was a gunshot but those on his arms were from the tiger's claws which— I narrowed my eyes—appeared to be partially healed. It was as if he'd gone through rapid repair, but without the unconsciousness. Had his incredible Gen-form made the difference? Given him an edge? Not like I was in any position to point out anomalies.

"How's yours, Mr. D'Accio?" she asked, eyeing me.

I glanced down. "Surface graze only. Our prisoner probably has a concussion."

Her eyes lit up. "One's alive?"

The sound of squealing tires and baring sirens announced the cavalry's arrival.

"Down but breathing," I confirmed.

"Excellent. I'll take him with me."

"No, you won't," Sinclair snarled.

Oops, the Gen half was still a bit dominant.

"DEA has—"

"No standing in this," Sinclair interrupted, though the brusque tone was human. "An organized attack was made on a police officer. Me. OPD has jurisdiction." His upper lip did a Gen-curl. "I'll forward any information I learn that may be of interest to the DEA."

The pouring of cops through the door and ordering 'hands on heads' forestalled any further argument. Recognizing Lieutenant Sinclair eliminated the handcuffs, and he vouched for me. Agent Leona Barlow was forced to produce her badge for identification. Giving us both a glare, she turned on her heel and headed for the exit. She was pulling her phone out as she went through the door.

The lieutenant and I exchanged a glance as I handed over his weapon. It wasn't hard to guess who she was calling and about what, since she'd be busy with the informant's car. It was bound to be parked somewhere close. Sinclair borrowed my phone and called Lieutenant Larson. He briefed her on events and that DEA would probably try and yank our prisoner away. From the sounds I could overhear, Larson was hauling butt out of the precinct even before he finished. He called Detective Brinkman next.

By now, more ambulances had arrived. Several medics were filling up body bags. The parts would need to be DNA matched at the morgue. A medic came forward, nonchalantly dangling the head Sinclair had tossed by its hair. It was the last straw for one young newbie Zero officer who bolted outside.

Sinclair ordered two officers to accompany our now semi-groggy prisoner to the hospital and to not relinquish custody to anyone other than himself or Lt. Larson. He refused to leave with the medics until Brinkman and his partner arrived to take over the crime scene. I was almost sorry to miss the coming confrontation in the ER, but I'd had enough of hospitals. A medic's cleaning and bandaging was all my wound had required. If I was lucky, it wouldn't even scar.

Due to the shear amount of work needing processed at the crime scene, I was allowed to leave with the promise of filing my statement at OPD tomorrow. *First thing,* Brinkman growled.

Excellent. I had a nine-thirty engagement with a possible murderer.

<u>Chapter 28</u>

The European Room turned out to be a plush lounge. A combination of seating areas and tables dotted the room, most of them currently occupied. A huge fireplace dominated one wall while a softly lit bar took up its opposite. A third wall had a series of recessed alcoves that would provide more private seating. The overall lighting was dim, with individual lights strategically placed around the room to create what I assumed was a cozy experience. Soft music played beneath the low buzz of conversation.

My guide headed toward one of those privacy alcoves. My ears caught the low audio hum generated by a sound suppression system as we reached it. Okay, maybe this wouldn't be so bad. As I settled into the seat across from the brown-eyed blond, Gail Huntington directed my guide to bring another scotch. *MacEverson*, she specified, as I shucked my coat.

She tilted her glass slightly. "This is your favorite brand, isn't it?" she said, her tone coy.

Flirting? Possibly. An attempt to redirect the meeting? Maybe. Letting me know she'd researched me? Definitely. It's a good thing I'd parked my bad mood with the car. So, I merely smiled and acknowledged it.

"Thank you for taking time to speak with me," I said, pulling out my notebook.

Her attention flicked to it then back. "Louise was a bit vague about what you wanted. Said you were asking questions about Grandmother's murder. I was curious, then surprised when I discovered you were connected to the Chandler family. Now, seeing you, I'm…intrigued," she said, leaning forward.

That lazy smile was probably supposed to be sexy, as was that open invitation to look down the low-cut blouse at her cleavage. According to Merle's notes, Gail liked to aim those 42-Ds toward any guy that struck her fancy, leaving a lot of broken relationships and marriages in her wake.

I pulled my wallet out as a server arrived with my drink. "I was a PI before I became associated with the Chandlers," I told her, handing him my credit card. "I saw no reason to discontinue or change my lifestyle. I like my work."

"You like digging up people's secrets?"

She certainly did. Merle had labeled her a "vindictive rattle-snake," ruining reputations and businesses alike.

"There are some unethical practitioners of my profession," I responded, keeping my polite tone in place. "Those who will do anything for equally unethical others as long as the price is right. I believe you know Alex Griffin personally and, indirectly, Allread and Gledhill Consulting."

Her eyes narrowed, the flirting attitude snuffed like a candle flame as she leaned back in her seat.

"*My* inquiries are kept within the bounds of my client's needs and my own ethical standards. I don't dig up dirt," my gaze caught and held hers, "so that someone can sling mud—publicly or privately."

I stopped whatever she was about to say with a raised finger. She fumed while I added a tip to the credit slip, signed it, and sent the server on his way. "With the polite necessities over, let's get down to business," I said with a bland smile. "As you've acknowledged, I've been hired to look into the murder of your grandmother, Agatha Mulligan."

"Why?" She sipped on her scotch. "The guy's in prison."

"Someone feels the case needs to be re-examined."

She snorted. "Family trying to get their 'dear innocent boy' set free?"

I had debated how to approach the questioning on the drive over. That sneering countenance tilted me to the hard-nosed rattle-her-cage method. "Louise screamed. You ran downstairs to the den. What did you see?"

"A lot of blood. Grandma on the floor," she replied.

No hesitation or emotion. Simply making a statement, I wrote down. "The injuries were excessive; how did you know it was her?"

"I recognized her housecoat and hair." she answered, showing a bit of irritation this time.

"Your bedroom is one floor up and you're a Gen. You expect me to believe you—and your brother—heard nothing while someone pounded away on your grandmother?"

"I don't give a damn what you believe," she snapped. "*I* heard nothing. *Corwin* heard nothing. Our mousy cousin probably didn't either as he was at the other end of the hallway. You always this crass?"

Are you always this heartless? "Who got there before you?"

"The two servants, obviously, and Uncle Warren." She snickered. "He looked a bit green."

Probably from a combination of booze and blood. So far, her story was matching the servants'. "And the others?"

She shrugged, took a sip while appearing to think. "Cousin Terry showed up slightly ahead of his mom. Corwin was behind them. By then *everyone* knew what had happened, what with Uncle Warren yelling for the police and cussing. Aunt Jadine grabbed Terry and hustled him away quick-like before he got to the den. Straightening her spine and pitching her voice higher, Gail parroted, 'No, you do not need to see that,' then spit out an epithet.

Had she ever liked anyone other than her brother? Assuming she did.

"They treated him like he was something special," Gail's tirade continued. "Still do. Sure, he's smart. So what? He's a mongrel spawned from the low-class marriage my aunt defamed the family with. No matter how much he or his father posture and pretend, they'll never be one of us."

I kept my disgust off my face. "You had a screaming match the night before and practically assaulted your grandmother with a water glass."

"So?"

I kept my gaze on her over the rim as I took several swallows from my glass. She finally got the implication.

Her lips pressed together tight. "What the hell are you after?"

"Agatha Mulligan's killer," I replied brusquely. "The one sitting in prison isn't it."

"I get it," she bit out angrily. "You're trying to spring him by making one of us appear guilty. That reasonable doubt thing."

"You hated your grandmother. Agatha Mulligan dominated your lives, controlling you and your brother with financial threats. Her murder ended that and you're both burning through the fruits of your ancestors' labors."

Gail's eyes turned into golden orbs. "Go public with that insinuation," her words reverberating with a coyote's growl, "and my lawyer will slap you with a defamation lawsuit big enough to bankroll a medium-sized nation."

I angled forward. My cold gaze met her hot one squarely, showing I was unafraid and unimpressed. "I've studied the crime scene photographs. I've reviewed the reports. Aaron Rivas did not murder Agatha Mulligan. Someone else in that house did."

Something flashed across her face too fast to be deciphered. The gold disappeared, leaving her human eyes completely expressionless. It was her silence I found most telling. Figuring I wouldn't get anything else from her, I matched her silence and finished off my drink. Then pocketed my notebook, grabbed my coat, and walked away.

Gail Huntington was a disgusting elitist as well as a bona fide sociopath. No, she wouldn't have had any trouble whacking her grandmother if the opportunity arose. Like taking advantage of a thwarted home intruder. Did she? Or...*could it have been her brother?* Had the self-contained twin finally erupted? That might account for her sudden silence.

Chapter 29

I stopped in to check on Russell the next morning and gave him the bad news. To say Russell was unhappy about Chandler Import being used to move drugs was a gross understatement. At least we now know the motive behind both of our attacks and several months of bad luck, excluding the weather incident. His wolf dominated the last fifteen minutes of our conversation. Nolan was keeping a close eye on him as I left for the office.

I was updating my Rivas case file with my observations and notes from last night's meeting when Diana rang in on the office line.

"There's an Alex Griffin on the business line wanting to speak with you."

That was sooner than expected. "Tell him to make an appointment, preferably Thursday or Friday." I wanted time to do research. I knew Alex Griffin only by reputation and intended to remedy that.

"Mr. Griffin says his schedule is committed and strongly recommends today," Diana relayed a couple of seconds later in a prim tone.

"He does, does he?" *Strongly?* Gail Huntington had landed on him, claws out. I debated and settled on being annoying. "Tell him no and that next week suits me just fine."

Recommends, I grumbled, reaching for my cup. It was empty. Diana was hanging up as I crossed the office to the coffee bar. "Did he make one?" I asked, filling my cup.

"No. Said he would be in touch."

I bet. I turned and leaned back against the counter. "Alex Griffin is a disreputable lawyer," I warned her. "If I can prove my client's brother is innocent of murder, or at least show reasonable doubt, his clients would fall under the resulting cloud of suspicion. He's planning to either buy me off or threaten me in some manner to ensure I don't."

Her lips pursed. "I take it that's not an unusual service for him?"

"His office slogan is probably 'By hook, crook, or cash.' If he calls back, don't give him anything before next week."

Her phone rang almost before I finished speaking. Nope, wasn't Griffin. It was one of the next-door lawyers requesting two more background checks. I huffed out a breath. This was not normal; they must have cases stacked on cases. I really couldn't complain, as it was profitable work. Giving Diana a nod of acceptance, I headed for my desk. I'd start on them as soon as I finished transcribing my Huntington notes. Researching Alex Griffin couldn't wait for long. The man was too used to getting his way, of being in charge. I wouldn't be surprised if our paths crossed before Monday. And then there was the on-going issue with the DEA and Lieutenant Sinclair's prisoner. He had promised to let me know what they learned, if anything.

I took several fortifying swallows of coffee and started pounding the keyboard.

***

I was relaxing on a bench at the gym, wiping off sweat and cooling down after finishing my last set of exercises.

"How's the shoulder?" Maisy asked, sitting beside me.

I raised it, did a few arm rotations. "Doing good," I told her, grinning. It faded at the calculated look in her eyes. Uh-oh.

"Too good," she said matter-of-factly. "I checked the newspapers. Your shooting was three weeks ago. Why did you lie about the extent of your injury?"

"I didn't," I replied, resigned to the inevitable.

"There's no way for your shoulder to have healed this fast," she snapped in a disgusted tone.

"Maisy…" I glanced around at the half-dozen or so working with various pieces of equipment. "Somewhere private?"

Two minutes later, we were sitting in the office she shared with another PT instructor. Her expression went from surprised at my Zero-Plus status to astonished at my bone repair as I gave up my secrets.

"Wow," she finally said, kneading the back of her neck. "That's …incredible. And your doctor can verify?"

I nodded. "Another doctor who assisted in my surgery is also aware. She's planning on publishing a paper on an anonymous Zero patient with Gen traits as evidence of our continuing evolution." I paused; cleared my throat. "She's only aware of the normal rapid repair. My bone repair is, uh, new."

"It's going to be kind of impossible to hide that," she replied, not unkindly.

"Eventually, I'll be outed," I agreed. "My Zero-Plus status slowly is. But, as long as possible, I'd like to keep my simple, quiet life."

"Otherwise, you'd be under a medical and journalistic

microscope."

"Yeah. Maybe other family members, too."

She laced her fingers together on her desktop. "Friday is your last scheduled workout. There's no sense in continuing Physical Therapy with me."

I shook my head. "I'd like to continue for at least another two weeks."

"I understand why. But most won't give it a second thought, figuring you've decided to do the rest on your own. I'd wait a bit, though, before engaging a trainer. Don't worry, I'll keep your secret."

"I want to continue with you, Maisy, because it's working. Truly," I told her. "Yes, my collarbone is healing faster than usual— maybe the rest of my shoulder, too. Those 'associated pieces' you spoke of." Nate couldn't verify that as soft tissue didn't show up in X-rays, but I hadn't had any twinges pulling my weapon last night. "You're not only ensuring everything heals correctly, you're honing them into a working whole. We need to finish it. I don't want *good*, Maisy, I want *great*."

She flashed me a brilliant smile.

"But we can drop back to the original three days a week," I added.

Chapter 30

Thursday went about as fast as slogging through knee-high mud. I hung around the office, taking care of odds and ends and things that had been pushed aside. Waiting for Lieutenant Sinclair's call. Or visit. Which never came. Frustrated, out-of-sorts, I headed straight for the *Depot* as soon as we locked the door at five o'clock. I really needed that promised freebie.

I could also check on Angie. Assuming she showed up.

The *Depot* and half a glass of slow-sipped scotch worked its magic, and I had mellowed by the time Angie and a White Top beer slid in across from me. We gave each other a hello nod and sat in companionable silence. I didn't need to ask how she felt; I could see the resignation in her slumped shoulders. She had accepted the inevitable and now simply waited for the call. We would talk later when she was ready and it wasn't so raw. For now, I would give her the comfort of a friend.

My mind drifted to the days and weeks after Tabitha's murder. The grief. The pain. I had hidden from it at first in dreams and unconsciousness, until a sharp-tongued Diana had made me face it.

"It hurts, Diana," I had whispered from my hospital bed.

"She's gone."

"I know, Curt, I know. Treasure the time you had and the memories you made," she had replied. *"And live,"* she then said in a hard voice. *"Live to spite them, live to look the bastards in the eyes when they're sent to rot in jail."*

I found the killer. It took over a year of me obsessively searching, while the killer just as obsessively tried to stop me. In the end, neither of us truly won. She might be rotting in hell, but I had lost friends, my spirit-sister, and a piece of my soul.

"You're somewhere far off."

I blinked a couple of times before focusing on Angie. "Memories," I replied.

"How's your brother-in-law doing?"

"His balance is still a bit off and he has a few gaps in his memory, but his overall retention has improved. Russell's home now, having agreed to a two-week home rest with on-site medical aide to get the doctor to release him. The aide is a Second-Gen bear who is keeping him there. Russell's wolf was ready to run out and rip throats when—did you see Channel Three's news report yesterday about Elmwood Brewery?"

"Uh-huh. It was a bit vague, though. A battle between police and a Boondock gang and involved drugs. The single survivor is being held for questioning."

I filled Angie in on our meeting-turned-ambush. Flabbergasted was her best facial description on learning that Chandler Import had been—unknowingly—running drugs for the whole country. I glossed over the resulting 'brawl' and shoot-out, omitting Lieutenant Sinclair's Gen form. That, I instinctively knew, was not for common dissemination.

"I'm still waiting to hear from the lieutenant," I said, my

annoyance showing in my tone. "I hadn't even heard they were members of the Locques gang until Channel Three reported it."

Angie finished off the last of her beer. "Well, if the DEA is involved, they've probably slapped a none-of-your-business restraint on everything. They're worse than the cops in hoarding information."

Had to agree with her there. "Fortunately," I smirked, "Sinclair told Agent Barlow that OPD had jurisdiction due to the circumstances. She was not pleased. Senior Agent Sutherland probably had a conniption fit."

She snickered. The waitress stopped beside our booth. I declined a refill, but Angie handed over her empty bottle and a ten.

"How's Mandy's case coming?" Angie asked.

"Hers or her brother's?" I asked dryly.

"She's in trouble?"

"She's in jail. That statue she stole got her eighteen months. Pleading guilty up front got her a lighter sentence. Told the judge she was sorry, wanted it over and done. As for Aaron? Not good," I said, shaking my head. "Someone in that house killed Agatha Mulligan but…how do I prove it? The evidence, what there is of it, is so…so…so *neutral*." I blew out an exasperated breath. "There's nothing that weighs more in one direction or another."

"Meaning it could be any one of them," Angie said.

"Well, no," I said. Then summarized what I had found so far, including my reasoning for eliminating the Bristols and Warren Decker. I paused briefly to let Angie accept her fresh beer. "And," I finished, "unless something definitive comes up pointing directly at Terrance Decker, I refuse to believe it's him."

I held up a hand to stop her protest. "Yes, I know, there are undoubtedly teenage killers out there—you've probably met a few.

What I'm factoring into my current opinion is the sheer insane level of violence the crime was committed with."

"How do you know he's not insane?" Angie said, playing devil's advocate. "You haven't interviewed him—got a feel for him yet, right?"

I scowled at her. "No. But everything I've found out indicates he's a stable and highly intelligent young man."

Angie shrugged and took a swig of beer. "You know what they say about smart people and the crazies. That they're the two sides of a very thin blade which can cut either way. Makes me wonder about you sometimes."

I stared, nonplussed, until I caught the twinkle in her eyes. "Ha, ha," I said, rolling mine. "I will interview him if I get a chance, as well as his mother and Corwin Huntington. The first is dodging me and the second is still out of town."

"So, the best you can probably do will be a retrial and him freed due to reasonable doubt."

"And that's not going to happen unless I can get enough to force it. I hate politics," I finished, downing most of my remaining scotch.

Angie was quiet for a moment. "What odds do you give the Omaha Threshers for going to the playoffs next year?"

The sudden change in subject caught me off-guard. "About fifty-fifty," I said, "if they keep the same lineup they had this year. That new pitcher has a fastball that would make a shifter's eyes twitch."

"Uh-huh. That new coach they hired last spring…"

We spent the next several hours discussing baseball, soccer, the new mall under construction at 144th and Dodge, several business ideas Angie was batting around, and a number of other various light-hearted subjects that avoided the darker ones we didn't want to talk about.

***

I was surprised to find the person knocking on my door at O-dark-thirty the next morning was Lieutenant Sinclair. My Gen-dar practically stood on its head and screamed *Wolverine* as I let him in. *Naturally, now that you know what he is*, I told it. Maybe that had been the problem all along, I mused as he settled into a chair at my kitchen table. I had never met a Mustelidae before. Or a Third-Gen, as far as I knew. With the lieutenant tipping the rarity scales on both, my confused radar had apparently defaulted to waving a danger flag and called it good.

"Morning, Lieutenant. How's the shoulder?"

"Healing, thanks," he replied, pulling out a notebook.

"How's your prisoner?"

"Busy making deals."

"No doubt." Murder. Two counts of attempted murder, one being of a police officer. He was facing the death penalty. I hit the start button on the coffeemaker which, fortunately, I'd prepped last night.

"Coffee will be ready shortly," I teased, then held in a grin at his grimace. I took a seat across from him. Yawned, then focused on my visitor. He wore his serious face and it was important enough this couldn't wait till later and in my office. "I'm listening."

"Your dead informer is Joseph Cartile. He was a security floater, meaning he picked up temporary jobs as needed by whoever needed the extra. His bank account, though, showed regular cash deposits. He was on someone's payroll.

"The man in custody is Charles Staker. He and all the other dead are members of the Locques gang out of the Boondocks. According to him, their boss—one Alvin Murré—took a twenty-thousand-dollar contract to eliminate an informer and the PI he was meeting. I was an unexpected third body," he said, glancing up. His lips actually turned upward in a brief smile.

Unexpected in more ways than one, I thought, visualizing again that towering wereform.

"Staker and the others were given the location and time of your meeting at approximately five o'clock," Sinclair continued. "Since you didn't receive the same information yourself until shortly before five, Cartile was either already under suspicion and being monitored in some manner or…"

I frowned, not liking either the pause or the level gaze I was getting. "Or?"

"Or your office is bugged."

"Not possible," I said stiffly.

"I consider the latter to be the more accurate assessment. Given the proactive paranoid nature of the group, they'd have taken him out before now if they considered him a threat."

"If true, then they would have known I was bringing you," I countered.

"Doesn't mean they passed it on," Sinclair said, an eyebrow rising. "It would have made it harder to get the Locques, or any other gang, to take the contract if a policeman was involved."

After staring at him for a moment, I slumped back in my chair. He was right, especially with that suspicious timing. "I've not had a recent break-in and deliveries are made to the outer office. I've used the same cleaning company for years—I'll see if they've had any recent hires. I'll also get a bug sweep from a security service."

I ran a hand through my hair. "Frigging hell, Lieutenant. If it was in place last week—"

"Our and the DEA's investigations are compromised," Sinclair finished, nodding.

I got up and snuck a quick cup of coffee. Took a badly needed large gulp. My office. Bugged. "It's a good thing, then, we were still in the dark on most things," I said sourly.

"They were undoubtedly already aware of our investigations through the informers," Sinclair replied, sounding unperturbed. "The most telling would be the specifics of my involvement and our recognition of internal leaks. And your growing involvement. You said you'd been under surveillance?"

"Yeah," I said, sitting back down. "For a couple of weeks now I've felt eyes on me. I've been a bit more…sensitive since my shooting," I added lamely when his head tilted slightly. "Yes, I know, another Gen trait."

The lieutenant was aware of my Zero-Plus status. Well, the old one. At this rate, I thought sourly, I'd be a Gen in everything but shifting. Hell, maybe even that would show up in another year or four. I gulped coffee.

"The Locques are a dead end as far as Mashazan is concerned. They were a short-notice hire because they needed someone fast and their regular enforcer—the rooftop sniper—had been taken out. The gang's usual business was low-end drug pushing with the occasional enforcement gig. They had been getting their products through Victor Gleeson's distribution channel and were more than happy to beef up their sagging profit line."

"Means they also have no clue about anything higher. What about the phone call to the gang boss?"

"A CC number, since disconnected. As it stands now, the entire gang is under arrest on charges ranging from conspiracy to murder to illegal drug distribution, with the addition of several federal weapons violations. One idiot had a case of dynamite stored under his bed.”

We fell silent. Sinclair got up, poured a cup half full of coffee then finished filling it with hot water. *Wimp*, I thought, grinning into my cup. A powerful Third-Gen wolverine should be able to handle a strong cup of coffee. Not that I was about to tell that to the spine-ripper sipping watered-down caffeine across from me.

“Well,” I finally said, “at least we know how and where the drugs are coming in now. That’s one shipment that’s not going to hit the streets. Is Senior Agent Sutherland putting together a tactical team?”

“No,” Sinclair said calmly, “because I’ve only informed her of the gang’s anonymous hiring and the location of her dead agent’s body. Why did you lie to Agent Barlow?”

“I don’t know…something in her voice that felt wrong?” I said, scowling at the wall behind him.”

“Same here. I’ve kept all mention of it from my report. The information about Chandler Import needs to remain—for the time being—strictly between us.”

“Uh, I told Russell. I did tell him to keep quiet about it for now.” It was more about figuring out future PR and liability issues than anything else. The lieutenant appeared a bit annoyed, so I didn’t mention Angie. Besides, the booths were soundproofed and she wouldn’t tell anyone. Probably.

“So, what are your plans? Swarm the ship when it docks?” I asked.

“That’s one option, and if the ship makes it here.” I gave him a questioning look. “Not knowing how much Cartile told us before he died, Mashazan’s paranoid boss is between a rock and a hard place. He doesn’t want to lose several millions of dollars-worth of product, but he doesn’t want to risk us getting our hands on it either. The affected packing crates' information might very well break the organization on this end."

"You think they'll intercept it before it gets here?"

"More likely they'll redirect it. No telling how many of the crew are cartel members."

"Can we intercept it before it gets here?"

He nodded. "It would take federal authority."

Meaning DEA. "What can we do?"

"First thing is to identify which cargo ship the drugs are coming in on. I can arrange tracking its progress through a Coast Guard contact I trust. Then we'll tackle the Fed problem."

"If I remember right," I drawled, thinking furiously, "Chandler Import has two—three maybe—ships scheduled. I'll give Miss Heiser a call—no?" I said, seeing Sinclair's head shaking.

"There has to be several people involved with the cartel at Chander Import," he said. "They'll be on the watch for issues that might affect their operation."

"Like passing info about Russell's plan to implement customs inspections," I said. Should have realized that myself. "His wolf was attacked to stop it and then me to further delay it." Not to mention, burning down our warehouse.

Sinclair nodded. "If the informer learns we've identified not only the how, but which ship specifically, they'll move faster. As unscrupulous as this group has proven, I wouldn't put it past them to just sink the ship rather than let DEA get their hands on it."

The word *evil* came to mind. "Okay. I'll head to CI's office first thing. I'm sure Miss Heiser has documents I need to sign. While there, I'll *inquire* about any inbound ships and if warehouse arrangements have been made for the shipments. I'll call you from... somewhere with the info."

Sinclair left a few minutes later. I left a voice mail on the office machine, letting Diana know I'd be stopping at Chandler Import this morning and asked her to arrange for an electronic bug sweep of the entire office. I left another voice mail for Angie, asking her to keep mum on what I'd told her last night. Soaping up under the showerhead minutes later, I couldn't help wondering how far and deep we'd find Mashazan's tentacles. I also figured Miss Heiser would be surprised to see me unsummoned.

Surprised? Marlee Heiser nearly fell out of her chair when I voluntarily presented myself at the office. Her astonishment was exceeded only by her efficiency in producing a stack of reports and other paperwork. Guilt hit me, not realizing some functions, acquisitions, and even two promotions, had been held up for lack of authorization, i.e. my signature. Russell had trusted his company to me and I'd let him—them, down.

It took three hours of due diligence to make up for my neglect. Miss Heiser scraped the bottom of her to-do drawer to take advantage of my presence. In the process, I learned that, yes, we had acquired a lease on a suitably sized warehouse. Under the guise of curiosity, I asked about any incoming shipments. There were two: one from Asia and the other from South America.

In return, I provided the staff with an update on Russell's condition, assuring them that he should be able to resume the helm of this ship in another week or two. I didn't miss the relief that crossed several faces. Matched the one I was wearing.

Exiting Chandler Import's offices, I rode the elevator down to the first floor. There, I took a corner table in *Woodman's Café* and ordered an early lunch. I pulled out my phone and called Sinclair. While there were only a few other customers and they weren't close by, I still kept my voice low.

"The *Tongo Bird* is inbound from South America. It's scheduled to arrive at the Omaha Midwest Port next Thursday," I told him.

"Which means it'll start navigating up the Mississippi late Monday or early Tuesday. I'll alert my Coast Guard contact." He hung up.

"You're welcome," I told my phone. Since there was no sign of my Rueben and fries, I called my office for an update.

"Alliance Storage Service recommended Swenson Security for the electronic sweep," Diana told me. "They finished about an hour ago and found one listening device in your office. It's been 'neutralized' and they left it for you to see."

"Where was it?"

"Underside of a client chair in front of your desk. I've checked with Roxy's Cleaning Service. The crew working our office has been stable for over a year. Mrs. Roxy has promised to check into it."

"Call Swenson Security back, have them meet me in the parking lot in, say, an hour to sweep a paranoid's car."

***

Swenson Security didn't find an audio bug. They found a tracker.

"This is similar to the other one?" I asked, scowling at the black rectangle in my hand.

"No, sir," the tech introduced as Jamie said. "The one in your office was a basic listening device. You can get them in a number of places. That?" he nodded at my hand, "It's military grade."

Frigging DEA. Had to be.

"Um, sir?" The tech cleared his throat. "Considering, would you like us to sweep your home too?"

"Might as well," I said sourly. "I seem to be underestimating everything." That got me a sideways glance from the tech's assistant. I gave them my address and said I'd meet them there. Then I stomped into my office.

"Diana, please call my afternoon appointment. Extend my apology and ask him to reschedule. Where's the bug?"

"On your desk. Car bugged?"

"No. Yes. A tracker," I said over my shoulder, heading toward my desk. Picked up the innocent-looking disk, studied it for a moment, then switched my gaze to the chair. According to the technician, it would have picked up a conversation anywhere in the room, not just at my desk. How long had it been there? Wouldn't know that until I figured the who and how.

"Won't be back today," I told Diana, stalking past her desk. "Weather looks to turn nasty, so close up when you're ready." My "Have a good weekend" sounded surly, even to me.

"Have yourself one, too," Diana called out as I pulled the door closed behind me

Not at this frigging rate.

The two Swenson Security techs were waiting for me in the parking lot. I took them upstairs and let them into my apartment. "Go ahead," I told them. "I need to make a phone call." Tossing my coat on a chair, I stepped back out in the hall. Dialed the lieutenant's number.

"You were right," I grumped when he answered. "My office was bugged. Swenson Security also found a tracker on my car. I have them checking my apartment now. While it's not likely to have been compromised, I'm a bit paranoid at the moment."

"Can't blame you," Sinclair replied. "I had my office swept this morning as a secondary caution. It's clean."

"As soon as the techs are done, I'll bring both devices to you.

Is there a way to trace electronic bugs?"

"They don't come with serial numbers," Sinclair said dryly. "But our electronic guys might be able to narrow it down somewhat."

"Alright. See you shortly." Disconnecting, I walked back inside to see Jamie exiting my kitchen area. I gathered he was the senior of the two.

"The main area is clear, Mr. D'Accio. Alan is checking the rest of your apartment."

"If there'd been one, I think it would have been out here."

He flashed a grin. "You'd be surprised at some of the places we've found them."

The second tech walked out of the hallway. "All clear back—"

We all froze when the gray metal box in his hand beeped. At the second beep, Alan began sweeping the instrument around.

I sent Jamie a narrow-eyed look. "You said this area was clean."

"It was," he responded, confused. "What are you showing?" he asked, joining Alan.

The guy rotated right, left, then faced me. He glanced up, down at his machine, back to me, then gave Jamie a questioning look. Then they both eyed me.

"*I'm* bugged?" I said in disbelief.

"Unless it was placed very recently, it's not in your clothes— they get washed. Do you wear those boots all the time?" Shook my head. "Then...your wallet."

I pulled it out of my pants and tossed it to him. Their machine let out a constant string of beeps when Jamie held it up to it. He moved to the kitchen and began emptying my wallet. Cash, credit cards, driver license, gun license, receipts were piled on the table.

Then he began pulling open and eyeing each section.

"Found it," he declared, pulling out what looked like a small penny. "It was lodged at the bottom of an unused card slot." He ran his thumb over it. "A bit sticky on the back to keep it in place."

"That's a bug?" I said, dumbfounded.

"Tracker," Jamie corrected, examining it at eye level.

"I've never seen one that small," Alan marveled.

"This came from a very advanced lab," Jamie said, handing it to me. "Anything else we can do for you, Mr. D'Accio?" he asked in a neutral tone.

"No. You've done a great job, thanks. Send your bill to my office."

From the sideways glances I was getting while they packed up, I was going to be a hot topic at their office. I politely saw them out. Since both were shifters, I waited several seconds to ensure they were several feet from the door before I let the cussing out.

***

My escort deposited me in front of Lieutenant Sinclair's desk where I waited silently until he finished his phone call. Sounded like the DA's office from his end of the conversation.

"Hope your day has gone better than mine," I groused as he hung up.

"Doubtful," he replied. "You brought them?"

I pulled them from my coat pocket. Laid the first one down. "Electronic listening device found stuck on the underside of a client chair that's situated in front of my desk. Common everyday variety according to Swenson Security's specialists."

I laid the second one down. "Electronic tracking device located under the front wheel well of my car. Military grade, according to same expert."

Sinclair's eyes narrowed and he picked it up. "Figure DEA?"

"Who else? But whose Feds, ours or Mashazan's?" Sinclair frowned, nodded in understanding. "Last but not least, this is how I'm pretty sure Agent Leona Barlow joined our party at Elmwood Brewery." I laid the last item down. "A mini-tracker hidden in my wallet."

Surprise flashed across his face. "That's a tracker?"

"Uh-huh. The two technicians were quite impressed. They're probably wondering what government office is interested in me and why," I said wryly as Sinclair picked it up.

"Impressive," he finally said, examining it closely. "And a bit worrisome."

"Yeah. Makes me wonder what else they have tucked up their sleeves," I said. "Anyway, Agent Barlow had to have inserted it when I was in the hospital. Patient belongings aren't usually kept under lock and key." Easily assessable for anyone wearing scrubs. "We've only recently learned exactly *why* I was targeted, although we've known it somehow involved the drug trade after the ballistics were run on the sniper's rifle.

"Normally, I'm only peripheral to Chandler Import. This conservatorship is temporary and recent. So *why*," I leaned forward and tapped the mini-tracker, "did Barlow tag me weeks ago? What did she and/or her boss know that involved me and that we didn't? Does this have anything to do with that two-year request of files? Having Joseph Cartile contact me and offer up information on Mashazan was an unpredictable wild card, and way after my shooting."

Sinclair leaned back in his chair and stared thoughtfully off into space. I could almost see his brain cells churning.

"Let's assume," he said slowly, "there's an office, in another department or even inside DEA itself, that's aware of—or at least suspects—they have a high-level leak. That could be why Agents Sutherland and Barlow are keeping things even closer to the chest than usual. Let's also assume something alerted them to Omaha as a pivotal position in the Mashazan Cartel's operations."

"Like an experienced DEA agent being taken out?" I suggested.

His attention focused back on me. "Then…when they started sniffing around, you popped up on DEA's radar due to a number of past cases that have resulted in the apprehension and breakup of several drug operations."

"All low-level, like the Locques gang," I lied, keeping my voice level. My secret tie to Victor Gleeson's very major bust being the exception.

"And the recent attacks give weight to the you-know-something scenario."

"Except we now know that wasn't the reason."

"Agent Sutherland doesn't." Sinclair's voice was flat. "For all we know, both reasons are valid. There could be some fact sleeping in your brain that is giving the cartel's boss indigestion. You found nothing in your case files?"

"No, and I've gone through them twice. What now?"

"Now?" Sinclair's tone hardened. "We get with Lieutenant Larson—update and plan. Then arrange a meeting with our local DEA agents so we can call them on their bullshit."

I made a fast call to Maisy, cancelling yet another session since there was no telling how long our evening session would last.

None of us were surprised that Senior Agent Sutherland wasn't interested in a meeting. That is, until Lieutenant Larson informed her that we had new information about Mashazan's operations. The she made the expected demand of 'hand it over.' We agreed to…at three PM Saturday in my office. And we insisted Agent Barlow accompany her. None of us had her contact information.

We could hear loud yells of 'obstruction' and 'withholding information' threats along with other unprofessional verbiage coming across Larson's phone. She gave us a wide grin and a minute to enjoy it, then hit the disconnect button.

Chapter 31

It was 3:02 and neither DEA agent had shown up.

We were lounging in the outer office. Lieutenant Larson was sitting in Diana's chair and Lieutenant Sinclair was propped against her desk.

"Think they'll brush us off?" I asked from the visitor's chair I was warming. The other two were positioned in my office.

"They're trying to throw us off-balance by being late—will they, or won't they? Personally, I'm hoping they won't," Larson said, her eyes glittering angrily.

Lieutenant Larson really, really, *really*, did not like Senior Agent Sutherland. Something more than the usual territorial antagonism between law enforcement agencies. Had to wonder what happened in their meeting.

When we'd told the lieutenant about the shipment, she'd argued that we didn't need Federal authority to intercept the *Tongo Bird* once it passed New Orleans and was in the Mississippi River proper. *"The Coast Guard would be more than happy to assist a drug bust,"* Larson had insisted. While she wasn't wrong, and it was tempting, we ultimately convinced her that we wanted answers and this was the only bribe, uh, bait we had to get it.

"They'll show," Sinclair said, crossing his arms confidently. "Sutherland wants what we have. They'll give it fifteen, twenty minutes then stride in and try to take charge."

Sinclair was dead on. At 3: 18, the bell above my office door jingled and the two DEA agents marched in. Well, Sutherland marched. Agent Barlow did the usual shifter glide. Watching, I idly wondered which cat her other half was.

"Alright, we're here," Agent Sutherland said in the arrogant tone we expected. "We going to do this meeting standing or what?"

"Or not," Lieutenant Larson said bluntly. "The meeting was scheduled for three o'clock and you evidently didn't consider the subject important enough to be on time. We have other things to do and you've wasted twenty minutes of our time. I vote to postpone this until a more *convenient* time. How about you, Lieutenant?" she asked, addressing Sinclair.

"I'd just as soon get this over with," he replied and straightened up. Giving Sutherland a cold look, he added, "And I'm tired of DEA jerking us around."

A flush had crept slowly up Sutherland's neck. Agent Barlow's only reaction was to cock an eyebrow.

We all traipsed into my office. I pointed the agents to the two chairs facing my desk and took my seat behind it. The lieutenants took the chairs positioned on either side of me. We faced each other, the lines of mistrust firmly drawn.

I studied the two agents.

The lieutenants' byplay had succeeded in establishing that we were in charge of this meeting. Senior Agent Sutherland was fairly oozing with her usual disdain and arrogance, with an added undercurrent of anger she was having difficulty hiding. Agent Barlow was relaxed but alert. And, if I wasn't mistaken, amused. At us, or seeing her superior thwarted?

"I'm beginning to wish we'd taken your suggestion," Larson said aside to me. "I could use a drink."

"Me too. We could always reconvene there," I offered. I'd been half-serious when recommending *Jojo's* conference room.

"I also have things to do," Sutherland snapped. "What's this new information you have about the Mashazan Cartel?"

"We not only know how they're bringing the product in, but where and when the next shipment is due to arrive."

I didn't fault Lieutenant Larson for her smugly satisfied tone. We'd earned a bit of gloating. We had agreed to let Larson take point where Mashazan was concerned. After all, they did fall squarely in her department.

Both agents straightened. "Tell me," Sutherland demanded.

Larson crossed her arms. "That depends."

"On what?" Sutherland said, anger replacing arrogance.

"On the answers we get to questions we have. You have intel we don't and it's time to share. Our two people might even still be alive if you had."

"I am under no obligation to—"

"Ask," Agent Barlow interrupted, her first words since arriving. Sutherland whipped around. "A little cooperation won't hurt," Barlow added, unfazed by the glare she was receiving.

Oooo, boy. I didn't bother to hide my grin.

"What do you want to know?" Sutherland snapped, turning back to us.

"When and why did you initiate your investigation here in Omaha?" Larson said.

"Two years ago," Sutherland said coldly. "My office made the decision to address the cartel aggressively. Using the interstate system to move their product was a given, so we drew up a list of cities that could function as hubs. Omaha is on the I-80 east-west corridor, and is, essentially, in the middle of the country. It was considered logically, and logistically, a prime distribution point. We sent in one of our best agents, Damian Lopez, to investigate."

She shifted her gaze to me. "The information you provided was accurate. We've recovered Agent Lopez's body."

I gave her a nod, glad for his family's sake.

"Did Agent Lopez manage to find any leads?" Lieutenant Larson asked next.

"Yes. Shortly before you contacted me for resource assistance, we'd established Victor Gleeson as Mashazan's local distributor."

That long? "How many lives have been ruined by the drugs you *allowed* through for months?" I spat out, furious at the very thought.

"Our focus is the elimination of the Mashazan Cartel and the influx of their products. We can't stop people from indulging in bad habits. If they chose to do so, then it's on them."

Silence. The arrogance. The complete indifference. The only ounce of goodness was the anger I saw simmering in Agent Barlow's eyes. At least until she caught me watching her. Then it vanished behind an emotionless mask. Good to know she hadn't been chiseled from the same stone as Sutherland.

"And you didn't think to inform OPD? My department?" Larson said, her tone withering.

"No need to." Sutherland waved a hand dismissively.

I thought the lieutenant was going to come out of her chair.

"After Lopez's loss, we managed to acquire an informer in Victor Gleeson's crew," Sutherland continued. "Gleeson was receiving his supply per the cartel's usual anonymous method, but we were hoping to build a pattern that would alert us to the next shipment. Then we'd flood the area with agents and watch all avenues of transport. Same as what we'd initially planned with Lopez and Plummer. We had our first concrete shot at this group and it was ruined by a frigging tipster," she said, her tone disgusted.

That made my part in it even better, I though smugly.

"Did your informant learn anything?" Larson asked in a tightly controlled voice.

"Bits and pieces—nothing of any real value. Until a certain private investigator's name popped up in a conversation."

I blinked. "Me? In what way?"

"He only overheard snippets of the conversation. That you could be a problem for something they had in the works," she said matter-of-factly.

"Gleeson's operation was taken down over a month ago. When did you learn this?" Sinclair asked.

"Roughly two weeks prior to it."

Voice dripping with contempt, I said, "I was shot two weeks after it." Then added a couple of things I probably shouldn't have but didn't care.

"You knew Curt D'Accio was in danger for a *month* and did nothing?" Sinclair's words were frigid.

"Agent Barlow was assigned as surveillance and to keep track of him."

"I wasn't warned because you hoped to nab whoever made an attempt." A flat statement, not a question.

Sutherland shrugged. "Attempted or actual murder charges would have given us leverage to get the person to turn on his employer."

She hadn't cared whether I died or not. "I knew another woman with the same disregard for human life as you," I said coldly. "Fortunately, she's dead."

"Is that a threat, Mr. D'Accio?"

"No, because you're not worth the effort. You tagged my wallet when I was in the hospital?" I said, switching my attention to Barlow.

"No. About three weeks earlier when you were working out at a gym. A male agent slipped in and accessed your locker. I'm good," she said without a hint of ego, "but so are you. Exceptionally so, I will add, for a Zero. You would have eventually realized someone was tailing you."

I tipped my head at her compliment. "Actually, I did get an on-and-off uneasy feeling for a while. Nothing specific, though."

"That would have been entirely unnecessary if you'd informed us of the situation and the agent involved," Larson said. "We would have been happy to cooperate."

"If you had provided a reason as to why you wanted my case files, instead of storming in and trying to strongarm me, that might have gone differently, too."

"You would have turned them over?"

"Not without a warrant. However, knowing why you wanted them, I would have reviewed them closely and let you know what I did or did not find." Paused for a beat. "As I've done for the lieutenants. Why two years-worth?"

"Several reasons," Sutherland provided grudgingly. "You've had a disproportionate number of events—attacks and office intrusions—for your profession during that period. Plus, you were responsible for several dealers now currently residing in prison. We didn't know if your problem status was due to knowledge of or from being a thorn in their operations."

I shook my head. "All of those events, Agent Sutherland, were related to one case or another that I was hired to look into."

"How about the attack in Kansas City slightly over two years ago? That's never been explained," Sutherland said shrewdly. "The one where you were almost killed and your wife was."

A gray Honda creeping down the inside lane…the glint of blue steel…her body jerking backward with each impact…

"A drug angle was explored and dismissed during that investigation." Sinclair's angry rumble pulled me back from the past.

"She spent five years floating around the Caribbean and the South American coasts," Sutherland accused hotly. "The perfect setup."

I took a steadying breath and locked my emotions down. "Happenstance, Agent Sutherland," which was all the explanation she was going to get. "And has nothing to do with why the cartel targeted me."

Sutherland pounced. "Then why did they? I've answered your questions, now answer mine," she added when I hesitated.

I glanced right, then left, got head nods from both lieutenants. Okay, all cards on table.

"The reason ties in to how Mashazan is bringing in their product. Joseph Cartile managed to tell us that much before he was killed." Agent Barlow's eyes narrowed. Yes, I lied. "What comes into Omaha isn't just for local consumption. Omaha is *the* hub. Everyone of Mashazan's American regional distributors receives their product quotas from here."

Shock registered on both agents' faces.

"We're supplying the entire country?" Barlow said in a did-I-really-hear-that-right voice.

An animated Sutherland's eyes lit up. "Mashazan is *here*. We can cut off their entire supply, its head—the entire organization."

"At least the US side," Barlow corrected. She tapped her leg. "Assuming the same MO for other countries, and with enough backtrails, it's possible the cartel could be rooted out entirely." She shrugged. "Which will simply be replaced by another one."

"A never-winning battle," I said, sympathizing.

"Job security," she replied with a wry grin.

"Details. Now."

Sutherland was back to her scowling DEA persona. They got the details. Russell's changes to departments. The implementation of customs inspections. The attacks on both of us. The warehouse fire. All designed to hinder and delay, as Joseph Cartile had said.

"Lieutenant Sinclair has a Coast Guard contact tracking the *Tongo Bird*," I finished, rubbing the back of my neck tiredly. "Due to the mess and uncertainty here, we're worried Mashazan's goons will redirect the ship and take off all the pallets and containers that could point to them. Maybe even hijack it, depending on how many of the crew are on their payroll. There are several good spots for it once the ship clears New Orleans."

"They'll have to get the cargo manifests, too," Barlow contributed. "Else it will identify what's missing and who it was going to."

"We'll have to put together a task force," Sutherland's fingers tap-tapped on her leg, "have them track parallel to the ship. Move in wherever they strike."

"You'll hijack the hijackers, huh?" I said, amused.

"Intercept, not hijack," Agent Sutherland replied, sounding a bit annoyed.

"Putting a task force together will also alert the informer that's embedded somewhere in your chain," Lieutenant Larson said.

Sutherland stiffened. Barlow didn't. Interesting.

"DEA does not have a leak," Sutherland snapped.

"Sure, it does," Larson said, her voice all sugary. "The Mashazan Cartel has operated for a decade under your nose. Ghosts moving millions of dollars' worth of drugs undetected. You said Omaha and Victor Gleeson were your 'first concrete' shot at them. Have you truly not had *any* other leads? Or did they all go *pfft* and disappear?"

Agent Barlow looked sideways at her boss.

"Mashazan polices itself ruthlessly by removing any hints of weakness or compromise before it can become an issue," Agent Sutherland snapped. "If you're searching for a leak, I suggest you check your own backyard. Agent Lopez went eight months undetected. He teams up with OPD and ends up dead."

"Strange," Larson drawled. "Officer Erin Plummer was successfully undercover for a *year*. Then she ends up dead two weeks after partnering with your agent. Either way," she continued, her voice hardening, "we recognize the timing is suspicious and are investigating the possibility of an informer within OPD. You need to do the same."

"Agreed," Barlow said swiftly, giving Sutherland an indecipherable look.

Why did I suddenly get the feeling Agent Barlow's status was a bit more than current appearances?

"If it makes you feel any better, the cartel also has tentacles inside Chandler Import," I told them. "They probably started making their plans as soon as Russell began drafting his changes. Which explains the 'in work' comment your informer heard."

Sutherland agreed. "Who would take over the company if you

and Russell both are conveniently gone?"

"That would be Darrell Chandler, Russell's uncle. And no, I don't see him in Mashazan's pocket if that's what you're implying. His son though, Trace Chandler?" I frowned, "He's a conniving, vicious viper. Him I could see."

"We'll be looking at everyone, including the board members. When does the *Tongo Bird* dock?" Sutherland said.

"Next Thursday evening."

"I have a suggestion," Larson said. "If you can bring yourself to *cooperate*, that is."

"What do you have in mind?" Barlow asked.

Uh-huh. Definitely something there, I thought, looking askance at her.

"First, no actions that even hints we're onto them. Odds are, they'll let the ship come into port as that's less risky than a hijacking." Sutherland scowled but nodded. "Do you have a number of local agents that you fully trust? Good. We put together a team..."

By the time my office emptied, we'd hammered out a plan. Monday, I'd announce that the customs inspections would start with the next ship, which just happened to be the *Tongo Bird*. An assault team comprised of trusted DEA and OPD personnel—to be notified personally—would lay in wait. The FBI would not be notified in advance, per Agent Sutherland's insistence, which was sure to generate plenty of pissed off complaints to her superiors.

I leaned back in my chair and closed my eyes. Waited. She moved cat-silent with no sound, no whiff of perfume, but I knew when she retook her seat. "What can I do for you, Agent Barlow?" I asked without opening them. *Jaguar.* I was suddenly sure of it.

"You knew I hadn't left with the others?" she asked after a brief pause.

"Uh-huh."

"I wanted to apologize for Agent Sutherland's remark."

"Which one?"

"She can be a bit..."

"Caustic?" I offered. Heard a low chuckle.

"True. So, I suppose all of them. But specifically," she said in a quiet voice, "the one about your wife. I've read the newspaper spread that was done on her life. I'm sorry you didn't have more time with such a wonderful sounding person."

"Thank you," I said, eyes still closed.

"I disagreed with Agent Sutherland's decision to not give you some kind of warning."

It hung in the silence. Part of me recognized she couldn't have gone against her superior. The rest childishly asked, *why not?* Then the tinkle of the bell above the door told me she was gone. After a bit, I returned the chairs to their places, locked up the office, and headed home to my empty apartment.

***

I was expecting dinner from *Cho's Chow* when I opened my door later that evening. Instead, I got a wolf on the prowl.

"Mr. D'Accio? My name is Alex Griffin and I'd like to speak with you."

"You were told to make an appointment."

"I thought holding a friendly conversation in a private venue would be more conducive to reaching an understanding," he replied with a smile I found patronizing.

I was in no mood to put up with him. On top of everything else, the Kansas attack and Tabitha's death hadn't hit me this hard in months. Probably due to the way Agent Sutherland had tried to club me with it.

"You thought wrong. Make an appointment." I stepped back.

The smile disappeared; his tone turned curt. "I don't think you're aware of the situation."

"Make an appointment," I repeated and closed the door just short of a slam.

<u>Chapter 32</u>

I survived Sunday and my memories without a drop of scotch. Balanced my checkbook and took care of a few chores. Paid Russell a visit to brief him on where things stood and picked up groceries on my way home. Then spent the afternoon rooting for my favorite sport teams. Sutherland called about suppertime with news about an important addition to our group. She had worked with Sofia Mason, a now retired inspector, early in her career. When contacted, Miss Mason had agreed to join the takedown. I couldn't wait to meet the person that Senior Agent Sutherland would willingly vouch the trustworthiness of. Then turned in early as I hadn't slept well the previous night.

***

"Miss Heiser, good news," I said by way of greeting Monday morning as I walked into her office. "I talked to Sofia Mason, an old family acquaintance in St. Louis who's a retired customs inspector. She's volunteered to fill in until we can get a permanent hire."

Her brows drew down. "Authorization hasn't come in yet."

Waving a hand, I said, "It will be, I'm sure. In the meantime, we're covered. Sofia should arrive in town sometime today."

"No, we're not," Miss Heiser said firmly. "That authorization has to be in place, along with copies for our files so as to cover any legal questions and/or issues that may arise."

I studied the woman for a minute and made a decision. Closing her office door, I asked, "Can you keep a secret?"

"Depends on the secret," she replied, eyes narrowing.

Making myself comfortable in her visitor chair, I provided a quick summation of what, why, and who all was involved. Her initial reaction of surprise was replaced with intense concentration. Then she went all legal on me.

"Mr. Chandler is aware of all this?" I nodded. "Will the various federal agencies hold Chandler Import accountable?"

"Nope. It's quite obvious that while some employees have to be involved, the company itself is being used without our knowledge. Russell is more worried about a hit to Chandler Import's reputation and business aspects once this becomes public knowledge."

"The Chandler family, too. Especially now, with it coming to light during your conservatorship," she said. "Doubly so as you've implied there is high-level involvement."

My deer-in-headlight look met her level one. Mentally, I said a few choice words. Verbally, "Russell isn't—he was attacked, nearly killed!"

She nodded. "Which we'll be sure to highlight. Hopefully, they'll be able to ferret out all those who are involved. In the meantime, I'll work with Mr. Chandler on crafting our initial public release."

"Russell still has a live-in aide. This has to be kept *secret*," I cautioned.

"Understood. We'll be discreet. In fact, the announcement will appear more legitimate if it comes from my office. I'll have the notice sent out internally by lunch and submit a snippet to the Herald's business section as I normally would."

Relief hit. I rose. "Thank you for handling this."

"Thank *you*, Mr. D'Accio," she said, coming around her desk, "for trusting me."

As we walked out into the main office area, she continued. "Please have Miss Mason come in as soon as possible, preferably today as I'll need a copy of her certifications for our files and to get her company paperwork started. Since she'll be working out of the warehouse, I'll alert the manager there to prep an office for her. If there are no issues, the customs office should be active by the end of the week."

Boy. Was she good. "Excellent. I'll let her know."

"You're welcome," she replied before returning to her office.

This did indeed feel more natural than me doing the grandstand announcement, which might have made the cartel boss suspicious enough to move immediately. Miss Heiser deserved a raise. I noted the curiosity on several faces as I made my way out. The gossip train was fired up.

Step two accomplished.

I arrived at my office to find appointments with Alex Griffin at eleven o'clock and a potential client at two-thirty. That gave me time to review the file I'd started on him. Fortified with a cup of my brew, I started going over my notes and the prodigious amount of article printouts Diana had stacked and waiting. The man certainly enjoyed the limelight.

Alex Griffin was in his late fifties and a First-Gen wolf. Got his law degree from Creighton, passed the Nebraska bar on first try, and immediately opened Griffin Legal Services. He was also licensed in Iowa, Kansas, Missouri, and Colorado. In other words, I mused, all the nearby states where he might need to bail his clients out of trouble. Married twice. Divorced twice. No kids on record. He lived in the ritzy Regency conclave and attended ritzy events, a different young woman on his arm each time from the photos. Articles about him or his court cases were, on the whole, remarkably bland. Those few that were negative were carefully worded. Finding articles where Griffin had won a number of libel lawsuits over the past twenty years explained both.

A quick pass on Janson Allread and Rufus Gledhill hadn't improved their odor any. Their two-man consulting office had racked up several pages of complaints and six lawsuits, none of which went anywhere. The lawsuits were either withdrawn or beaten by Griffin in court.

I watched Gertie swimming in her tank as I mulled it all over. Alex Griffin liked publicity, liked throwing his legal weight around, liked being considered important, and most definitely liked being in charge. He wasn't used to being brushed off as I had done last week. And after Saturday night, whatever tactic he had originally planned got tossed.

***

Alex Griffin declined coffee and barely waited for Diana to close the door before making his opening salvo. "I trust you are in a better mood than on Saturday."

"So far," I replied. Yep, a 'friendly conversation' had been superseded with 'claws out.'

"My clients and I would like for you to close out this so-called investigation you're on. It does no one any good," he said.

"I believe Aaron Rivas and his sister would disagree with that," I commented.

"They're a couple of low-class thieves hoping you can throw

enough doubt to get one of them out of prison."

I bristled at both his disdainful tone and the 'low-class' depiction. "Aaron was railroaded into prison. The police investigation wasn't just botched, it was basically non-existent. Which I'm sure your clients encouraged."

"My clients had nothing to do with the police investigation."

"That's certainly true," I shot back, "as they weren't even questioned. In fact, no one in the house was, nor was there even a cursory search of the house performed which might have found evidence contrary to the obvious."

His wolf was suddenly watching from behind his eyes. "What evidence?"

"Who knows?" I said, not about to throw the Burnsworths to the wolf. "It's a moot point now, isn't it." I kept my expression neutral under his suspicious stare.

"Raking up the old case is useless," he sneered. "The DA isn't about to reopen what was an open-and-shut case on the flimsy word of a rented investigator."

I'd just been relegated to the same low class as my clients.

"We'll see," was my reply. "If your clients are innocent, then they shouldn't be worried if it does happen."

"On the contrary. *If* the case is reheard, and *if* Mr. Rivas's conviction is overturned, everyone in that household would fall under the redirected cloud of suspicion. My clients would also face the social and financial stigma that would create."

My, my, does that mean fewer invites to parties? "Unfortunately, that can't be avoided."

"Yes, it can," he said.

Here it comes.

"Normally, I'd offer to make it beneficial for someone to drop an investigation or close it as inconclusive. For you," his lips peeled back in a wolfish grin, "I'll make you regret it if you don't."

My gaze never left his face as I calmly swiveled my chair. Left, right. Left, right. Stopped when the first hint of unease flittered across his face.

"If you have researched me, as I have you," his eyes flashed briefly, "then you knew I've faced threats before and didn't back down."

His expression turned malicious. "My resources might be a bit…different."

"You mean your pet PIs? Your warping of the judicial system? I have resources of my own, Mr. Griffin. I'm not your usual prey, and things may not go well for either of you."

"Are you threating me?" he said, definitely wary now.

I let out a derisive snort. "You're the one making threats. I've expressed a warning."

"Then I guess there's nothing left to discuss," he said, rising stiffly.

"Nope." Standing, I couldn't help adding, "May the best resource win."

His eyes cut sharply to me but remained silent as I escorted him out of the office. All the way out. "Well, Diana," I huffed, "that was interesting."

***

My afternoon appointment cancelled, leaving me free to catch up on things until Sofia Mason arrived midafternoon. The woman introducing herself to Diana matched the picture Sutherland had emailed me. Brown-gray hair, brown eyes, bronze skin, and the vibe of a bear. The DEA agent had neglected to add that last tidbit. Sutherland had insisted we keep our charade from everyone, including my secretary. I had raised a very hot protest but was forced to back down when, surprisingly, both lieutenants agreed with Sutherland.

Sofia," I said with a grin. "How've you been? Long time no see." No lie there.

Playing her part, Sofia gave me, *yep*, a bear hug. "I'm good. How are Lloyd and Eva?" she said, surprising me with my grand-parents' names.

"Ornery as ever," I replied, inhaling air after she released me. Sutherland must have briefed her on my family.

"Wouldn't expect less from a D'Accio."

"Diana, Sofia Mason is an ol—*uh*, a long-time friend of the family." A sharp elbow in the ribs had me reclarifying the relation-ship.

"Welcome to Omaha," Diana said, her eyebrows arched in amusement.

"Sofia is a retired customs inspector and has graciously agreed to assist us until we get a permanent one."

"Gracious my foot. I was bored stiff. You saved me from volunteering janitorial services at the local arena," she added with a mischievous wink.

I laughed, liking this affable woman. "Miss Heiser wants to start your paperwork as soon as possible. I'll take you over and introduce you. Then we can get you checked in. I've reserved a nice long-term stay suite for you. Give me minute to alert Miss Heiser we're on our way."

"So, you would know all of Curt's teenage antics?" I heard Diana ask as I headed into my office.

I stumbled to stop. Crap. Didn't think about that.

"Oh, yes," came Sofia's reply in a pseudo whisper, "tons of them, and they'd be amusing to tell. Unfortunately, I'm sworn to secrecy on most of them."

Me and Miss Mason were going to get along just fine.

Chapter 33

"You look chipper this morning," Diana remarked as I entered the office. "Spent the evening reminiscing with Miss Mason?"

"It was great. The evening practically flew," I said truthfully, peeling off my coat before heading for the coffee bar.

I'd taken her out for a late supper, primarily to continue our facade. It turned into several hours of banter and laughter. I shared a few family details, since she'd only gotten a high-level brief from Sutherland. I even related a few of those 'younger antics' to help maintain her cover. She reciprocated with tales from her life and work.

By the time I dropped Sofia off at her hotel, I was ready to make her an honorary aunt.

"Sofia is at the warehouse today, getting settled in. Miss Heiser will call if she needs anything else. How's my day shaping up?" I asked.

I sipped as she rattled off appointments at ten, one, two-thirty, and four. Wow. Didn't usually have that many in one day. Business was definitely booming. I pulled a folder out of the safe Diana said Detective Brinkman had dropped off late yesterday. I eyed Mandy's file, but left it behind. Mashazan's takedown was my current focus. Besides, stepping back from her case, rather her brother's case, for a couple of days would give my subconscious time to churn through all the pieces. I could wake up the end of this week with the killer's name prominent in my brain.

Right. As if a good-luck fairy was out there listening.

Settling at my desk, I found two reports in the folder. The first was a summary of Brinkman's investigation on the rooftop sniper, which was an interesting change from no-comment-on-open-cases. Lieutenant Sinclair undoubtedly ordered it due to circumstances.

Thomas Besset's case was as cold as the snow that still hid the bullet that killed him. I gave low odds it would ever be found, considering it could be anywhere between his head and my building. While the who-do—I had to snicker—mixture of scents had successfully masked the killer's personal scent, it in itself was easily traced by police shifters. He'd entered the building through a side door, gone straight up the stairwell, then straight back down, which successfully avoided the building's security cameras. However, a security camera two buildings down recorded someone moving swiftly along the sidewalk in the right timeframe. If it was him, Brinkman wrote, there was no way to ID the heavily bundled figure.

Which was a good thing, considering who was the most likely culprit. It kept the thoughtful looks I was currently getting from turning into uncomfortable questions.

Deposits to Besset's healthy bank account came in from a different offshore bank, which was closed two hours after the 'mystery death' had hit the news. The only other sign of his sideline profession was a cash-and-carry phone kept in a bedside drawer. No stored phone numbers and its partner on the other end was most likely dumped at the same time as the bank account.

The second item was a joint report from both lieutenants. They had narrowed down the personnel for the takedown, choosing only those from their Southeast precinct they personally knew and trusted. The list of names comprised detectives from several departments, patrol officers, and a few retirees. While confident none of their choices had been compromised, they asked me to contact them if I knew of any rumors or innuendo about anyone on the list. They would personally contact the participants on Friday. Short notice, yes, but I doubted anyone would complain once they knew what was at stake and with a traitor somewhere.

No word from either DEA agent yet. Not surprising, as they would be quietly and unofficially pulling in people they trusted. They and the lieutenants would need to coordinate soon, which now included the Coast Guard. Sinclair indicated he'd be contacting his contact's commander. He would brief the man on the situation and request cutters to be staged above and below the port to intercept any watery escapees.

I stared off into the distance. How were we going to sneak a large number of people into position? The others were no doubt working on that, still…if I was the cartel boss, I'd have lookouts posted around the port perimeter and along the two main access roads. Lookouts with shifter senses. Kinda, sorta hard to sneak up on or past them. *Hmmm.*

By the end of the day, I had three new cases and an idea. I had politely declined the guy that wanted me to find something, anything, that he could use to sue his detested neighbor. Or better yet, get her arrested and jailed. If things were that bad, one of them needed to move.

As I made my way to my car, I felt eyes on me. *Now who?* They hadn't been there this morning. I pondered as my car warmed up.

Another attack? God, I hoped not, and taking me out now served no purpose. Well, I suppose there's always revenge if I had pissed them off enough. The cartel's spies should be monitoring DEA and OPD, especially as that tidbit in the morning paper's business section should have made them aware Chandler Import now has a customs inspector.

That same tidbit had Diana fielding calls from several CI board members. After a rather arrogant one from Russell's obnoxious uncle, I'd contacted Miss Heiser and told her to schedule a board meeting for Wednesday night. Which, I thought wryly, would play into our plans, especially if one of them was, indeed, on Mashazan's payroll.

I pulled out my phone, made a couple of calls, then headed for *Riley's*.

***

Riley's Pub was primarily a hangout for Zeros. Shifters were welcome, but they usually needed earplugs to protect their hearing during the party hours. As did a certain Zero-Plus. Fortunately, this being a Tuesday, the light scattering of patrons around the room were more interested in after-work relaxing than carousing. The music and noise levels were bearable to those of us with sensitive ears.

I'd been slow-sipping a beer in a corner booth I'd selected for privacy for about twenty minutes when Lieutenant Sinclair slid into the seat opposite me.

"I'm assuming this is a pretense of camaraderie in case someone is watching?" he said, signaling a waitress for a beer.

"Pretense?" I said, teasing. "You mean we're not friends?"

"I find friendships…difficult," he replied with a candor that stopped me.

I knew nothing of his personal life. His professional persona was stiff. Distant and unemotional. I'd equated him to a marble statue. But then, as a homicide lieutenant, wouldn't he need to build up a shield against what he saw and experienced on a daily basis? Could I handle scenes like Agatha Mulligan's murder over and over? *Hell, no,* I answered myself honestly. Then there was his Gen form. Intimidating, frightening to most people. It would be hard to relax around people you know are walking on eggshells, afraid they'll trigger your shift.

All that flashed through my mind in seconds. As soon as the waitress stepped away, I locked my gaze with his. "I got no problem with your job or your Gen form," I said, using my most serious voice. "As for you personally," I paused, then gave him a wide grin and a wink, "you do need to lighten up a bit."

"At least when off duty," Nate tacked on, sliding in beside me with a beer in hand. Tossing his coat on top of mine, he added, "So, are we bonding?"

Sinclair blinked; I laughed. "Maybe a little. I called Nate to join us to make this appear more like a friendly get-together than what it really is," I explained to the lieutenant.

"And what's that?" Nate asked, curious.

My reply of "War council" halted the bottle halfway to his lips.

"Then maybe I should sit in, too," Agent Barlow said, scooching in beside Sinclair. "Move over big guy."

I held up a hand at the look on Sinclair's face. "I did not call her. What are you doing here?" I said, scowling.

"Following you," she said, peeling off her coat. "Things seem to happen around you." She waved off the waitress heading in our direction.

"It was your gaze I felt when leaving work?" If not, I'm going to have my car scanned again.

Her head tilted as she studied me. "You sensed it?"

"I've grown a bit sensitized to watchers over the last few years," I replied nonchalantly.

"Due to all the wounds I've bandaged," Nate added in a droll tone.

"Yes, your dossier makes for an interesting read. Do you really plan to discuss…things…here?" she said.

Dossier? My brow scrunched. Okay, we'd address that later.

"As long as no one takes the booth behind us we have privacy," I replied. "Everyone in this room—except you two—are Zeros. And since this is supposed to be a social outing, you and the lieutenant need to flirt a bit." The look on both their faces was worth a chuckle.

"You can't be sure they're all Zeros," she snapped.

I shrugged. "You can go around and sniff them if you'd like to verify it."

Nate choked on his beer. "Dice can usually tell who's a Gen and who isn't," he finally wheezed out. "Gen-dar he calls it."

Her eyes narrowed. "How accurate?" she asked, suspicious.

"It's only failed me once," I answered, flicking a glance at Sinclair.

"Are you really a Zero?"

"Can't shift a hair," I told her truthfully. "Are you really with the DEA?"

"Of course."

Too bland, too quick. "I'll rephrase," I said, acting on a hunch. "What federal agency signs your paycheck, Agent Barlow?"

Silence. The three of us stared at her, waiting. She shifted her gaze to Nate.

"Oh. I'll just…"

I halted Nate's rise with a hand on his arm. "Dr. Nathanial Gordon is trustworthy and one of the top ER doctors in the country," I told her coldly. "You might want to consider having his expertise on standby when things go down. Do you really believe they'll just roll over and show their belly?"

Nate stiffened under my hand, and I saw his sharp look on the edge of my vision. I would have to fully brief him later.

The agent ran her gaze around the room, then over the three of us. "National Security Agency," she finally said in a low voice. "Currently attached to the Drug Enforcement Agency for the mutual goal of bringing down the Mashazan Cartel."

"You were neither surprised or affronted, like Agent Sutherland, when the possibility of an in-house traitor was brought up," Sinclair said. "Which means you were already aware of it. Is that why you were attached?"

Good. He'd seen it too.

"Yes, and that information doesn't go past this table. DEA leadership and its operatives—including Agent Sutherland—believe I'm here only to help to dismantle the cartel."

Nate let out a low whistle. "The DEA higher-ups are in the dark?"

"Which means you believe the leak to be high in the chain," Sinclair said.

Her lips compressed, as if she'd realized she'd said something she shouldn't have. "Agent Sutherland's level at minimum," she finally conceded.

"I take it your main objective is to sniff out the weasel. You're here by your lonesome—no backup support? Thought so," I added when she nodded. "Then consider us your ad-hoc team, helping you to take down Mashazan and all its tentacles."

"The three of us have worked together before," Sinclair said brusquely. "We know how to keep confidences. Even from each other."

My wince stayed internal, even as Nate and I nodded.

"Whatever you share," he continued, "I personally vouch that it will not be disclosed unless there's no other choice."

She hesitated for a moment, then blew out a breath. "Screw protocol. Seven months ago, a DEA-NSA joint raid—three months of planning—went sideways. Our target had to have known we were coming to set up the ambush. Three agents were killed and several wounded, including a friend of mine that's now in a wheelchair for life." Her jaw flexed.

"Three weeks later, my boss received a late-night call from a DEA contact. Asked him to meet at an all-night diner. Said it was imperative they meet; he had critical information about Omaha and a leak. The man never showed up. His body was found in his car the next day, in a park clear across town with a, quote, 'self-inflicted', unquote, gunshot wound in the temple. Lopez and Plummer were hit the next week."

Our booth was quiet while we processed that. Getting the waitress's attention, I held up four fingers and my bottle.

"Wouldn't your sudden attachment to DEA have raised suspicions?" Nate asked.

She shook her head. "My boss contacted his DEA counterpart *after* hearing about the two Omaha deaths and offered our agency's assistance in taking down the cartel."

Our beers arrived. As the waitress collected our empties, I told her to put all four on my tab.

"What? No chips? You can afford it," Barlow mock-complained.

I pursed my lips, then told the waitress, "Two orders of chips and salsa. Medium." Barlow batted her eyelashes at me after the waitress left. I rolled my eyes.

"You two quit flirting. Why am I here?" Sinclair asked me.

"I have an idea of how to get that shipment with minimum casualties."

"I'm all for that," Nate pipped up.

We all were. "I had planned to go over it and let you pass it on to Sutherland. Seeing as how Agent Barlow is here, this works out better. She's less likely to get brushed off." Sinclair's grunt was probably agreement. "So, have there been any changes? The plan is still to watch, follow, and then take everyone down at wherever they take their haul?"

"No changes," Barlow confirmed. "We're hoping some of the upper leadership will be on-site coordinating their midnight supply run and we'll bag them along with impounding the product."

"The way I see it…" I paused, waited until the waitress deposited our order and left, "…that has a lot of potential problems."

Barlow scowled. "We're experienced agents, well-versed in raids of this type. We know what we're doing."

"Meaning the *inexperienced* and *bumbling* OPD amateurs," I scooped up salsa, "will be relegated to perimeter and backup support?" Popped the chip in my mouth. *Ummm, good.*

Barlow's silent scooping of salsa was all the affirmative response we needed. Sinclair shot a glare sideways and asked about my idea.

"Doing it the DEA's way is risky. Paranoid cartel boss is bound to saturate the area with lookouts—the port, the access roads, everywhere. All it will take is spotting any of our team, watching or following, and the alarm will go out. Then it becomes a claws-out, free-for-all rout. There's no telling how many civilians will be impacted or how badly. My idea minimizes that risk by reducing the footprint we have to watch and control."

They listened and munched as I outlined a better plan than the current one. After I finished, Barlow and Sinclair exchanged a look and an eyebrow question. Their nods were nearly simultaneous.

"You know, Dice," Agent Barlow saluted me with both her beer bottle and my nickname, "that just might work. Assuming, we can get the cartel's head to believe it," she added.

****

I was in the Chandler Import office early the next morning, talking with Miss Heiser when Sofia Mason came bustling in.

"Mr. D'Accio, Miss Heiser, did I hear right? My credentials are invalid?" she said.

"Miss Heiser?" I said, pretending to be surprised.

"It's true, and I planned on briefing you about it this morning," Miss Heiser replied. "There appears to have been a miscommunication when Miss Mason retired, resulting in her credentials being deleted instead of marked as inactive."

"What idiot did that?" Sofia demanded, hands fisted on hips. "It was Althea Bennington, wasn't it. The woman has hated me ever since I got her reprimanded for drinking on the job."

I stared. Her act was completely believable.

"I don't know the particulars, I'm afraid," Miss Heiser said. "Mr. Jameson, your old boss, has extended his apologies and is working on getting you new ones. He says it may be late Friday or Saturday before they're ready and in the system. Unfortunately, that means I won't be able to file them with the port's office until Monday."

Her tone one of aggravation, Sofia said, "Fine. I have a ship coming in a couple of days. Can we have them unload like usual, except store everything in the Chandler warehouse without disbursement?" she asked me.

I nodded. "We can and we will. It won't hurt the businesses to wait a couple of days to get their shipments."

"Excellent. You'll keep me informed?"

"Of course," Miss Heiser said.

With a wave of her hand, Sofia exited with the same bustle she blew in with. I went with Miss Heiser to her office, as she actually did have a document for me to sign. I gave her a discreet thumbs up as I sat down since we'd left the door open.

Both she and Sofia deserved Oscars for their performances. That whole scene was aimed at our unknown informers. If their boss was convinced they had the weekend, then it would be less risky—and a whole lot easier—to steal their stuff from our warehouse than to breach the ship and its cargo hold. This also reduced our risk of premature discovery. We'd establish a safely hidden watchpoint and have the team members staged nearby, ready to move in at the first sign of intrusion.

Our plans were moving forward. The next play was mine.

To say that evening's board meeting was raucous was an understatement. Everyone clamoring to know every move I'd taken, demanding to know why Russell hadn't resumed leadership, and irritated they hadn't been consulted before hiring Sofia Mason. I gritted my teeth through the session, managing a whole forty-five minutes. I walked out after restating that everything should be running smoothly by Monday, despite the wrinkle with Sofia's certifications.

Riding the elevator down to underground parking, I ran everything through my head. Had we missed anything? Had our performances been believable? Would the cartel still opt to go with their original plans? Would our plans go as intended? Or would everything go horribly sideways?

I trudged slowly toward my car, pensive, lost in all the what-ifs and maybes.

Chapter 34

Mid-morning Friday, I stepped out onto the Chandler warehouse's loading dock, the last leg of Sofia's tour of the huge, not-quite-squarish, fifty-two-year-old building. Sitting on the corner of Vernon and Tenth Streets, it was further from the airport but closer to the Omaha Port than the old one. The offices were tucked into the northwest corner, along with a small adjacent eating area. Human-sized entrances and a few windows were located on the east and west walls, while the north wall was solid. The south one was also solid, except where the wide loading dock doors opened. The dock itself was large enough to handle four or five trucks at a time.

Sofia had been busy the past few days, getting the warehouse arranged for her customs work. It had been effectively divided in two. The main area of the building now held all the current inventory. The southeast area was the new Customs section. Every-thing off the *Tongo Bird* and all future international cargo would be stored there until inspected. For now, the two areas were simply separated by a wide gap. There hadn't been time to install a permanent divider of some kind, Sofia explained.

We stood under the protective overhang, carefully keeping out of the way of employees rapidly unloading *Tongo Bird* cargo from a sixteen-foot box van. A second one was pulling in, the dock area having its own direct access from the street. Another nice feature and convenient for our plans, I thought, watching as the truck slowly began backing into place.

I scanned the dark-gray cloud ceiling that had been slowly lowering for the past hour, promising an abundance of snow even I could smell. "The storm wasn't supposed to hit until this evening," I complained.

Sofia raised her head, her nostrils expanding a couple of times as she sampled the air. "Well, wouldn't be the first time the weathermen guessed wrong. To be fair, those Canadian Clippers were named after those old maritime ships for a reason."

True. They'd been the fastest things on water for half a century.

"This could complicate things," I said, worried. "We can't delay the unloading—everything *has* to be here." All our plans centered on this building.

"It'll work out," Sofia replied, unruffled. "Everything is ready."

Anna Drayan, the recently promoted warehouse manager, hurried over to us right as the first snowflakes began to fall. *Crap, crap, crappity.*

"Miss Mason, Mr. D'Accio. The weather is moving in, as you can tell."

"Do you think you'll be able to get the *Bird* unloaded before it gets worse?" I asked.

"Not at our current rate." She gestured toward the trucks. "Those two were the only ones saved from the fire. Bulky pallets, containers, and crates fill them up pretty fast. However, my husband and his buddy—I vouch for both—have a fifty-foot trailer rig and will help if I ask them."

"Do it," I immediately responded. "Have them send a bill to the office for their time and gas. Once everything is in, lock the place down and send everyone home."

Anna nodded, pulling out her cell phone as she rushed off.

"You need to go home, too," Sofia told me. "Do you or Mr. Chandler normally hang around and oversee unloading?"

"No, and you're right. I'm…edgy, I guess." I rubbed my neck.

"I understand." Sofia laid a hand on my arm. "I'll be here until lockup and give you a call when it's done. Besides," she said with a grin, "you need to get that little blue thing safely parked some-where."

"My Crossfire can handle all sorts of rough weather," I mock-scowled.

"Including snow up past its bumpers?" she asked, her amuse-ment plain.

I conceded the point with a laugh. "Like most prudent people, I wait for the roads to be cleared by our industrious city employees."

Waving goodbye, I walked around to the main parking area where I'd parked my sports car. As the engine warmed, I debated the idea of buying a second car. Something older, heavier, able to handle Nebraska's changeable weather and could also be used for stakeouts. I currently rented something if my sports car wouldn't blend in with whatever neighborhood I was surveilling.

When I pulled out of the warehouse parking lot, the snow was coming down thick and fast. By the time I reached my apartment, almost an hour later than it should have taken, a four-wheel drive vehicle was on my to-do list. At least I had made it home. I had crept pass numerous vehicles in ditches.

Sofia's call came less than three hours later. Anna's husband and buddy-in-law's rig had vastly speeded things along.

"The warehouse is secured physically and electronically," she told me. "According to Anna, the *Bird's* captain also unloaded cargo destined for Sioux City."

"Can he do that?" Sioux City was the next large city north of us and had the distinction of straddling three borders: Nebraska, Iowa, and the Dakota Territory.

"He didn't ask," Sofia said dryly. "Evidently getting word the Clipper is generating ice floes upriver spooked him."

"Really? A sea captain spooked by a little ice?"

"If your normal route covers the Gulf and the Caribbean, yeah."

We laughed, said our goodbyes, and hung up. I called Russell with an update and a recommendation for a semi-rig added as one of the warehouse's vehicle replacements. Afterwards, I stared out a snow-crusted window. The pieces were in place, the bait set. All we could do now was wait for the trap to be sprung.

***

Saturday dawned with crisp blue skies and a balmy minus twelve degrees. The arctic blast had deposited just under nine inches of new snow in the Omaha metro area. Areas to the south and southeast had received twice that. Snowplows rumbled in the distance, clearing the main thoroughfares. Residential streets, like mine, should be open by this afternoon.

I sipped coffee and stared out at the blinding white blanket, an uneasy mood settling over me. The warehouse district should be navigable by this evening, our trap waiting. A gut feeling told me Mashazan would be moving tonight, as we had counted on. The cold and snow were an unexpected boon for both our plans, keeping most people indoors. Fewer witnesses for them, fewer collateral casualties for us. *Casualties*.

The view outside my window wavered. It was no longer

pristine; it was covered with bright red splotches. I double-blinked and the red was gone. I didn't believe in premonitions or visions, but, *wow*, that had been so *real*.

The more I thought about it, the more my disquiet grew. I took a long draw from my cup. Decision made, I reached for my phone. It was answered on the third ring.

"Tom? Got a minute?"

<u>Chapter 35</u>

At nine-thirty that evening, five of us were crammed into a *Depot* booth. When I had explained this evening's adventure, not only had Tom declared he was in, but he'd recruited a couple of others.

Darlene Stark, a slender Second-Gen cougar, was tucked between me and Tom. I didn't know her very well, having been hired after I left the agency. But Tom wouldn't have brought her if not confident in her abilities. Max Anderson, a Second-Gen tiger, and Mike Halligan, a muscled Zero, filled out the bench seat across from us. Mike might not have claws, but those two large knives sheathed on his thighs and prior Marine Special-Ops experience made him just as deadly as his employees. Armed with a Ruger .357 tucked in my belt and my questionable wits, I was the least dangerous person sitting there.

Max gazed out into the *Depot's* perpetual twilight. "Come here often?" he said, his tone both dry and curious.

"Several times a month, usually," I replied.

Would I get the 'not welcome' vibe now? I'd felt the entire room's attention when I escorted them in; my guests certainly would have. The waitress had flicked an unreadable glance at me as she returned with our beer orders. Was Boris's suggestion of 'don't come back' in my near future? But the *Depot* was the perfect place as we awaited news, out of the weather and far enough from any watchers the cartel might have positioned around the area. By happenstance, the new Chandler warehouse was five blocks due east, straight down Vernon Street.

"I've heard about this place," Tom said, glancing around, "but never stopped in. It's a bit…low key."

"I like it," Darlene said, taking a sip. "Y'all sure it'll happen tonight?" she added, her southern heritage slipping out.

"Pretty sure," I admitted.

"Tonight is the perfect night for an OPs mission," Mike said in my support. "Streets are empty and potential witnesses are tucked in somewhere warm. Waiting until Sunday leaves open the possibility of anything happening to screw up their plans. From more bad weather to Miss Mason deciding to start her customs inspection early."

Mike should know. "If we're lucky," I said, "the Mashazan Cartel will cease to function after tonight, at least here in the States."

"I can't believe it," Max said, shaking his head. "Their drugs are all coming through here? Do you know how much that has to be?"

"Uh-huh. Multi-million dollars' worth," I said. "No telling how long they've been using Chandler Import."

"It's the perfect setup, what with Omaha in the middle of the country," Tom said grimly. "Law enforcement—Feds and local— are watching all the usual coastal entry points, both sea and air. The product comes in here via the river, gets broken down into distribution packets, and then shipped in every direction via the interstate system. Add in highly placed informants," his voice acquiring a growl, "and it's no wonder law enforcement was blind."

More low growls reverberated around me; Mike's eyes turned to hardened steel. Several interesting comments were made about what should be done to those traitors. Very medieval-minded, my booth companions. We spent the next couple of hours slow sipping beer and relating tales of our various cases, with Max winning the oddest. He spent a week guarding a pasture because the owner's cows kept getting out. Turned out, it was the owner's brother assisting them.

Max shook his head when I asked why. "Didn't ask. I reported it to the owner and cleared out fast. Family feuds are the worst. Haven't heard about a death, so they must have kept it to fists."

"For now," Mike commented, chuckling.

I brought up Who-do and asked if they'd heard about it. They hadn't, and I described what it was.

"Well, that explains a few things," Darlene said, disgust lacing her words. "I've been investigating a theft thought to have been perpetrated by a whole gang, but couldn't figure out how the larger members I scented had squeezed in through the opening. If it was only one or two yahoos, wearing this Who-do confusion…"

Tapering off into a growl expressed her opinion quite plainly. Her voice had also morphed into a pissed-off Carolina twang.

"I'll warn all my people about it," Mike said, brows pulled down in concern. "You say it's expensive? Then, hopefully, we'll only encounter it on the high-cost cases."

Unfortunately, that would include murder as well as theft.

Tom asked, "Will they really tell you when it goes down, Dice? They probably consider you a handicap in the claws-out brawl it's bound to turn into. Even with a gun."

"I might *only* be a Zero, but that doesn't mean I'm helpless," I countered, sharing a smile and a nod with Mike. "Trust DEA, no. I do trust Lieutenant Sinclair, who promised to pass the alert on as soon as he got it, along with wherever they're rendezvousing. I don't know how many we'll end up with. Both DEA and OPD are limited by who to trust and staying under the traitors' radars. I'm willing to bet that with what's planned tonight, those will be on high alert. Too many agents or officers pulled away from their assignments or weaponing up in the armory would probably trip several flags. They're going to need all the help they can get."

I had a gut feeling it wouldn't be enough, which is why I did my own recruiting.

"That's why DEA didn't contact the FBI for assistance, even unofficially?" Tom said.

"Worry of another traitor, yes, although I think territorial attitude might have also been a factor."

Mike snorted out a "Count on it."

"We're counting heavily on surprise and—" I broke off as my phone rang. "Go ahead," I said, putting it on speaker.

"Trucks entering dock area. Meet at Twelfth and Bland, Hot-Sub Deli."

I could hear the tension in Sinclair's voice. "Understood. We'll be in an HIS company van," I replied and hung up.

I met each of my friends' gazes. The relaxed atmosphere of the past hours was gone, replaced with hard-eyed determination. *Soldiers* was the word that came to mind. An apt description, I thought, as we slid out of the booth. A battle loomed before us, and I couldn't help remembering those bright red splotches.

Chapter 36

Mike pulled in beside the other vehicles in the deli's dark parking lot, which put us about two blocks southwest of the warehouse. The deli's back door was open, the lights off, figures lounged along the back wall. Agent Barlow and a couple of others were gathered around their own non-descript van. Mike and I went inside while the rest of our group opted to help prop up the building. More shadowy figures were scattered around what was the kitchen area. A couple of glow sticks, carefully held low by their owners, provided a bit of light. A dim light leaking from the manager's office had me peeking in around the half-open door. The lieutenants and Sutherland were talking over a map spread across a desk.

Nope, they were arguing.

Agent Sutherland's slashing arm cut off Lieutenant Sinclair. "I don't care—let the small rats run. We'll need everyone for the raid. I want the drugs. I want the one in charge because the boss isn't going to risk tonight's heist with anyone less than a senior lieutenant. We can't risk them being alerted."

Larson's response was lost because I was backing away fast enough to tread on Mike's toes. "Sorry," I whispered. Counting what heads I could see, my heart dropped at the low number. I recognized Lieutenant Olsen and Detective Montgomery from Robbery, who stood with Detectives Brinkman and Addison. Detective Swanson was introduced as the other gray-haired retiree.

"Is everyone in here OPD?" I asked, leaning against a stainless-steel sink.

"Yep. DEA doesn't mingle," Olsen said.

"Don't want to be sullied by our presence," Brinkman snarked.

"Or our incompetence," someone muttered.

Wow. The antagonism between local and federal authorities ran deeper than I realized.

The office light went out and its door slammed open. Larson stalked outside while Sinclair joined us. The weak light didn't hide his angry expression as he watched Sutherland's arrogant exit out the back door.

"The Feds have asserted operational jurisdiction and control." Lieutenant Olsen made it a statement, not a question.

"They have. DEA is hoping to nab a high-ranking lieutenant tonight," Sinclair said as an engine fired up.

I fumed silently, agreeing with the mutterings around me. OPD was being shut out, relegated to foot soldiers. It was obvious Agent Sutherland intended to convert this into a career-enhancing promotion. Sinclair let out a low whistle, drawing everyone into a compact group. A couple of more bodies popped in from the front dining area and identified themselves as Levi and Franks in last-name-only terse tones. The one cramming in with our people from outside didn't bother.

"That everyone?" Sinclair asked Larson. "Then listen up. Our spotters have verified three large cargo trucks, two men each. Two smaller vans disgorged a total of ten more. Those already in shifter form appear to be perimeter guards, the rest went inside. They shut down the alarm system in seconds."

"Meaning they have the code from an insider," I interjected angrily.

"DEA will come in from the north and will breach the building through the east and west entrances. We're to move in from the south, taking control of the dock, the trucks, and detain everyone we find or that DEA flushes out of the building."

"How many for our side?" I asked. "Counting us five, which includes three Gen and one former Special Ops Marine." There was a muttered *thank God* from the back.

"Twenty then, counting DEA's five."

"*Twenty?* That's all?" I said in dismay. Mike's expression said he didn't like that either. Our opponents might have less at sixteen, which was lower than I was expecting, but a battle's outcome could turn on that small of an edge. At least most of us were Gens of some sort, according to my Gen-dar.

"A couple of agents Sutherland had called in were sidelined by the snowstorm. We couldn't afford any unusual activity tipping off the enemy, which is sure to be in paranoid hyper-alertness," Sinclair said matter-of-factly, then glanced around. "All Second-Gen who plan to shift do so now. We'll apply a yellow spray dye. Yellow tape for everyone else."

The method to easily distinguish shifter friend from foe had first been used during the Great European War. Law Enforcement and militaries world-wide still used it. The tape addition was utilized when needed, such as in this instance when we didn't all know each other.

Darlene, Max, and Brinkman slipped outside with Swanson, Levi and the unknown guy. Lieutenant Sinclair, I noted, did not.

Unless Lieutenant Larson took charge, he'd need to stay human. Tom, Olsen, Montgomery, and Addison were our First-Gens, leaving us with four Zeros: me, Mike, Larson, and Franks. We assisted each other, taping strips down the back and front of our coats. Underneath them, we all wore security vests; Mike had thoughtfully brought one for me. I don't know about the others, but I was wishing we had some of the European ones. Expensive, theirs contained a layer of chain mail that gave both bullet and claw protection.

By the time we were ready, so were our shifters.

The no-name guy had worked the spray can with a sense of humor. I wasn't the only one choking down laughter as we walked out to the parking lot. Even Lieutenant Sinclair gave a grunty-huff. While they all had a dot on the forehead between their ears, the lines going down their sides differed. Max, already tiger-striped, had vertical lines. Brinkman's broad bear sides had wavy lines, as did one of the wolves. The other wolf—bet it was Levi—sported a fancy curlicue across her sides and back. Darlene, the only cougar, had polka dots and batted her lashes playfully at me.

The moment of levity broke the too-tight tension swirling around us—something I faulted the DEA for. If that had been his intent, it worked. Plus, their laughing comments identified him for me: O'Boyle was the IA officer doing the audits for Olsen. When Sinclair motioned to gather around OPD's unmarked van, all I sensed from my fellows was professional readiness.

O'Boyle, a First-Gen, was taped as Lieutenant Larson handed out one-size-fits-all tie straps and tranq guns, whispering they were set for mid-range. The four-cylinder handguns operated the same as my Ruger. We were all popping open the one we'd received and verifying its state by glow-stick. It was a safety move since one could have been loaded incorrectly. Yep, my color-coded cartridges were green. Wise choice, considering our current situation.

Blue cartridges only affected Zeros, while Red was for Gens—they'd kill a Zero. Green was in the middle, safest for use against Zeros and Gens alike. Most Zeros were knocked out immediately while a First-Gen could take up to a minute, depending on size. A Second-Gen was usually only rendered sluggish. I couldn't help peeking sideways where Sinclair was giving out instructions, wondering if there was another color specifically for a Third-Gen's metabolism.

When all was ready, we moved out as silently as we could, keeping to the plowed and, thankfully, empty street as long as possible. Sneaking up on shifters was difficult in the best of times, which this wasn't. Cold air carried sound well and half-frozen snow crunched when stepped on. At least the lack of a breeze meant our scents shouldn't betray us.

Arriving at the intersection with Tenth Street, we pressed up against buildings while Sinclair took a cautious peek around the corner. The warehouse was directly across the street from us. "Loading underway" was a whisper we passed down the line. The lieutenants huddled over Sinclair's phone. Waiting.

Seconds ticked into a minute. Two minutes. Three. Where was the DEA? They should have been in position by now. At this rate, those trucks would be—

Sinclair's phone vibrated. He tossed it into a pocket, growled, and bolted toward the warehouse. Tom and the other Gens swarmed behind him, leaving us Zeros to catch up to them. The air was filled with snarls, growls, and yells by the time we got there. Two low *booms* announced DEA's entry and battle sounds from inside the building now joined those outside.

An unmarked wolf staggered to its feet. Mike tackled it to the ground and Larson began tie-strapping its feet. I slipped around them, heading for the dock. The trucks faced outward, their rear cargo doors wide open against the dock for loading. I tranqued a coyote Darlene had trapped on top a truck cab. Several humans bolted out through the dock doors. I dove for the warehouse trucks that had been parked off to the side as several bullets whizzed past me.

Hearing only a few shouts from my fellow raiders among several furry lumps told me we'd met our first goal. The guards were down and we controlled the dock area. Mostly, I mentally corrected, as shots rang out from behind two of the open truck doors, scattering my companions. We were pinned down, unable to go help the agents inside. But they were doubly so, from the sound of gunfire still going on inside.

I caught sight of Max slinking forward under the closest truck. I dropped the tranq-gun and pulled my Ruger from my waistband. Didn't know what he had planned, but I put a bullet through the truck's open door to give him coverage.

"Surrender now," Sinclair called out. "You've nowhere to go."

This time I put the bullet through the cargo body to emphasize that. Max was crouched under its tailgate. Did the other two trucks have others waiting under them? We heard Agent Sutherland yelling the same message inside as Sinclair had.

Would they give up? Decide to fight it out?

Two guns came flying out this side of the trailer, followed by "Don't shoot" and two guys with hands on their heads. I stepped out and motioned with my gun barrel for them to jump off the dock. They did; it sounded like the scene was being repeated around another truck.

"Prisoners to the front of trucks," Sinclair called out.

My two had a tiger escort. We'd secured the exterior. I glanced at the warehouse. Gunfire was still ongoing, so they could probably use some help. I'd taken two steps in that direction when the situation didn't just go sideways—it somersaulted off a frigging cliff.

Two large utility vans careened in from the street and screeched to a halt. I dived back behind my protection, then stared in shock and dismay as at least a dozen of mostly Second-Gen shifters vaulted out of each one. My team got off several shots before they were swarmed. Snarls, growls, and screams filled the air.

I saw Larson go down under two shifters even as I leveled my Ruger and fired. I'm sure I hit one. The two drivers had taken up positions behind their vans with rifles. Positioned off to the side and half hidden by a warehouse truck, I had an excellent firing angle and took full advantage of it. My next shot took out the closest shooter. Two more shifters went down before they realized where I was and bullets slammed into the engine block from the second sniper. I ducked back, swearing profusely and out of bullets.

Huddled, I flipped the cylinder open while yanking the speed-loader from my coat pocket. I'd no sooner snapped the refilled cylinder closed when a snarling mastiff charged around the bumper. I couldn't halt his momentum, but a quick trigger pull stopped the mauling he'd intended. Pushing the massive body off of me, I rose to a crouch and peeked out.

Tom had ripped off a truck door and was using it to batter shifters aside…until two large wolves launched off the truck cab onto his shoulders and he disappeared beneath them. *Dammit!* Max was a whirlwind, twisting and slashing at the shifters surrounding him. Several forms lay unmoving on the icy ground—one wore yellow—but flashes of yellow amidst the battling groups told me not all of our team was down. Then a snarly-hissing midnight-black wolverine barreled into the fray. Sinclair.

The shooter fired. If the bullet hit the lieutenant, it didn't stop him. My jaw clenched; he had to go. *Wrong angle from here.*

I dashed to the first van, its bulk protecting me from bullets but not shifters. I shot the panther before the wolf slammed into me, knocking my gun away. He went for my throat even as we fell. I blocked his jaws with my forearm, wedging it as far back in his throat as I could. Pain seared my arm, but those jaws couldn't close farther. More pain as the wolf's claws slashed as he fought me. Teeth gritted, I forced his head back and groped for my gun. *Too far!*

There came a blood-curdling scream that even gave the wolf pause. Then he was ripped away from me by two First-Gen felines. They eviscerated him with a single stroke, flung his body aside, and bolted away. *What the hell?* Rolling to my feet, I got my second shock of the night.

Shifters. Pouring in from the street. I didn't even try counting.

Howls. Snarls. Roars. The parking area had become a claws-out war zone—a horrifyingly savagery straight out of European War video clips. Clumps of three to five Gens fighting, ripping into each other...into our foes. I saw Max's tiger stagger and collapse, the ones that'd been attacking him now buried in a roiling, snarling pile of teeth and claws. There—Levi's wolf, staggering, being gently nosed aside by a cougar. More shifters flowed over the dock and inside, where gunfire stopped and screams commenced. Then... silence.

Utter quiet. In the building. Outside the building.

Sirens sounded in the distance.

Shifters flowed back out of the warehouse. The tsunami of fur began receding back toward the street. A First-Gen feline approached, his right coat sleeve ripped off and bloody gashes down both pants legs. His features morphed back to human. I stared, flabbergasted, recognizing the face as that of a fellow *Despo* regular.

"Olaf? What—how?"

"I read lips," he simply said. "Will you be alright?"

Cradling my arm against my chest, I leaned heavily against the van and managed a wan smile. "I will be now. Thanks to you and your friends." My smile melted. "Did you lose anyone?"

"No. I'm sorry we didn't get here sooner."

I swallowed, averting my eyes from what was left of the other shooter. Took in the bodies strewn across the open lot. Saw Tom staggering to his feet, his vest hanging in shreds. "You came. That's what counts."

Sirens were a lot closer now. A whole gaggle of them from the sound. Well, can't hold a noisy war without getting reported. By now, Olaf was the only one of our rescuers remaining.

"Better go," I told him. "I owe all of you a round or two of drinks."

His reply was a crooked grin and a wave.

A jaguar limped toward me as Olaf loped out into the night. Got a *huff* when I asked "Agent Barlow?" She swatted a piece of intestine toward its owner and my gun toward me, then laid down on top of it. "Thanks," I murmured as police cars and ambulances came to a sliding halt at the lot's entrance. At the same time, movement on the dock was Agent Sutherland and a couple of her people coming out.

Once again there was total silence as we all stared out across the carnage.

There was no other word for it.

Then things went into hyper-driven chaos. Shouting, all sorts of vehicles and people showing up. Even the Police Commissioner showed up, demanding to know—*RIGHT NOW!*—what the hell had happened. Pretty sure I laughed when the Lieutenant roared back, literally, that he didn't have time and would file a report later.

Things were becoming a bit dreamlike.

Shifters had morphed back to human forms. I stared in awe at a nude Sinclair, talking/issuing orders, ignoring the lacerations down his arms and crisscrossing his torso. A nasty bullet graze still oozed blood across his back. Someone had thoughtfully provided him with a coat that was tied around his waist. Would they want it back?

I watched, numb, as medical personnel sorted through the bodies, at the small number that they gathered up and raced away with. Max. Levi. A blood-coated body that I was sure was Mike. A couple of others I couldn't readily recognize, though one had gray hair. Agent Barlow's shoulder lacerations didn't appear deep or bothering her, so I had waved off the medics coming toward us. I was hurt, my arm and leg throbbing, but nowhere near as much as the others. That plus the obvious fact I was standing made me a low priority.

A deep rumble from Barlow drew my attention, then glanced in the direction she was glaring. Well, crap. Agent Sutherland and her pissed off expression were marching straight for us.

Didn't that just top off this wonderful escapade.

"D'Accio! I want a full explanation!" she demanded, halting several feet away.

I blinked. Looked down at Barlow. "Any idea about what?" I asked her, pressing harder against the truck when it tried to shimmy away. A fresh wave of pain jabbed where my side pressed against the grill. Flimsy vests. The wolf's claws had gotten through it. Need to buy one of those European ones.

The jaguar shook her head. Then gave a low growl when Sutherland took a threatening step closer.

"Now, now," I admonished. "Mustn't growl at your superior. Oh, right. She's not. Growl away, my dear." Waved my good hand, then grabbed the hood thingy for balance. *Whoa.*

Barlow rumbled, drawing my attention again and drew a claw through…it took a couple of blinks before I could see clearly. It appeared I'd acquired a red puddle around my boot. And, yeah, my coat sleeve was pretty wet, too. Well, hell. That wolf had done more damage than I thought. Golden eyes stared up at me.

"You're right. Pressing my luck, Agent Barlow." Telling Sutherland, "We'll talk later," I let go of the thingy and fell into darkness.

Chapter 37

I awoke three days later, once again under Dr. Patel's care at Saint Benedictine Hospital. She gave me a quick inventory of my injuries, which included the expected bite wound on my right arm and lacerations down my left side and leg. Unexpectedly, I also had a bullet wound through the fleshy part of my left shin. The shooter must have clipped me as I reached the truck, although I hadn't felt it at the time. Wasn't adrenaline great?

Dr. Patel assured me everything was healing normally—my normal—and I should be able to go home in a few more days. She refused to tell me anything else, saying that my brother-in-law had asked to be notified when I was awake.

A nurse was removing the IV from my good arm when Russell came in. He stood by silently. No "How you doing?" or "Glad to see you awake" or any of the usual hospital banter. That was a bad omen. He pulled up the visitor chair after she left the room, his expression somber.

I fisted a hand, took a deep breath, and said, "Alright, Russ, give it to me. My friends?"

"Tom Tall Elk and Max Anderson survived with mostly

lacerations and bites. They've completed rapid repair and will be sent home today or tomorrow. Darlene Stark didn't make it. I'm sorry."

That hurt.

"Mike Halligan is in ICU. He has a concussion, broken ribs, and lost an eye. There are lacerations and bites over seventy percent of his body."

"But he'll live?" I said, holding back a curse.

"Yes. It was touch-and-go there at first—massive blood loss— but thanks to Dr. Gordon, he'll pull through. I understand his fiancée has been visiting him daily."

That rocked me. Fiancée? No one had mentioned Mike was engaged. I swallowed. "OPD?"

Russell looked away for a moment. "Their losses include Lieutenants Larson and Olsen, Detectives Addison, Montgomery, and Swanson. Officer Franks will be confined to a wheelchair due to a severed spine. The rest sustained mostly lacerations."

I stared unseeing at the blanket across my legs while a storm raged inside. I finally met Russell's gaze. "Tell me it was worth it," I demanded hoarsely.

A tired smile lit up his face. "You broke the Mashazan Cartel."

"Completely?"

"That second round of shifters—you'll be hearing about that— decimated your opponents, including the ski-masked man in charge with no ID."

Yeah, that would have pissed off Agent Sutherland.

"Luckily," Russell continued, "one of the first responders recognized the body. Peter Alcot?" He cocked his head questioningly.

"No clue," I told him.

"Alcot was Head of Security for Stanford Dawson."

It took a second. "The Chandler Import board member? *That* Stanford Dawson? He's on the cartel's payroll?"

"No, he writes the checks. He *is* Mashazan," Russell added at my shocked look. "Dawson figured things had gone wrong when time passed and he didn't get any word from Alcot. Thanks to the quick identification, DEA caught him and his daughter as they were boarding a private jet with a flight plan to Brazil."

No surprise there. Only two of the South American countries had extradition agreements, and Brazil wasn't one of them.

"DEA and other authorities have been quietly ripping the cartel apart. Following email and financial trails, Dawson's accounts, and those of the companies whose containers held drugs. Stanford Dawson's inner circle is almost rounded up—there's one still in the wind. Digging out their 'affiliates' is ongoing, such as the rumor they've arrested several OPD personnel linked to the cartel. They are getting a *lot* of information which, I'm told, is being passed to authorities in the appropriate countries—names, lab locations, and such—and that they've started their own housecleaning.

"Mashazan is dead, Curt. Congratulations."

My smile faded. "But the cost was high," I said somberly.

"It usually is," he agreed just as quietly.

We sat, each thinking our own thoughts. After several minutes, Russell stirred.

"You haven't asked about the DEA team."

I snorted. "Don't need to. I saw them walking, *walking,* out of the warehouse. Didn't any of them appear hurt," I added with a derisive snort.

"Alcot had mostly Zeros and First-Gens inside with him for lifting and carrying. Two agents did sustain bullet wounds, one seriously, but no deaths thanks to that second influx of shifters. Agent Sutherland…let's just say her subsequent conduct has not endeared DEA to the local authorities."

"Taking control? Locking everyone else out?"

"Sounds like you know her. The local attitudes toward Agent Barlow, who is not DEA, is more positive."

"She's NSA."

"You know? Well, thank goodness NSA has higher standards. As soon as she heard that first batch of shifters and realized what was happening, she abandoned the fight inside for the one outside. According to a report I've heard, she kept the assholes at bay so Lieutenant Sinclair could complete his shift. Wolverine." Russell shook his head. Smirked. "Bet that gave them a nasty jolt."

Been even more so if he'd used his wereform.

"She asked me to marry her."

What? Who? "Barlow?" Russell's out-of-left-field statement had me confused.

"Marissa Dawson. She'd been hinting at it for several months. I wasn't ready for that level of commitment. At least, not with Marissa. I didn't feel…" he paused, as if groping for the right words. Looked me straight in the eye when he found them. "I didn't feel what you did, what I saw in your eyes and heard in your voice, when you spoke of Tabitha. That's why I finally broke things off."

Loss reared its head, but, surprisingly, it didn't cut as sharp or as deep as before. I realized Russell was giving me this mournful, miserable look.

"I can't help but wonder…" he trailed off.

"Was it you, or was it Chandler Import she wanted," I finished when he didn't.

He nodded. "The company's resources would have been…

advantageous to them."

Especially to expand their drug empire. The widow, with her father's support and husband's shares, would have taken over CI after Russell's tragic and unexpected demise. Bet *that* scenario had crossed Russell's mind, too.

He heaved out a huge up-from-toe sigh and I immediately felt contrite. "How are things with you, Russ?"

"Better," he said and added a lopsided grin. "Still a few small holes in my memories. Short-term is much improved, though things do occasionally slip away. I've taken to making notes, keeping lists to counter that. I've released the aide back to the agency with Doctor Bullard's blessing. My secretary will be getting a few new duties and an upgrade in title and pay."

"Then you're ready to retake the helm?" If it wasn't for my leg, I'd have danced a jig when he nodded.

"I'll call Mr. Thoreen and Miss Heiser. Get things in motion. We'll address the board together after you're out of the hospital."

We fell quiet again, and this time I felt the tug of sleep. Russell didn't miss my yawn.

"You need your rest," he said, rising. "I'll leave word with the nurses to keep visitors away until tomorrow. Judging from the number of inquiries, you'll have plenty. I'll call and update your grandparents. By the way, if it hadn't been for a two-day blizzard out west, your Grandma D'Accio would've been sitting here."

I groaned. "Tell her/them I'll be on my feet in a couple of days. It's nothing like last time."

Russell laughed and waved goodbye. Staring at the door slowly closing behind him, I realized the stilted relationship that had existed between us was gone. Did that mean he no longer held his mother's death against me?

Nate, by virtue of his medical degree, didn't count as a visitor. He arrived around suppertime, bringing me a tasty and filling meal from *Cho's Chow*. We chatted, he did his own exam, and left behind copies of the previous days' newspapers.

The Omaha-Herald Sunday edition's blazing 'WAR ZONE IN EAST OMAHA' heading was just the start of its brutal depiction. They even had a picture of the dock's "war zone" that someone had taken before the police sealed the entire area off. Interviews with several emergency responders were graphic. Russell and his uncle-in-law had issued a joint statement—did the editor fall out of his chair?—expressing their shock and dismay that a 'trusted board member' was a drug kingpin and had secretly utilized Chandler Import's resources for his illegal empire.

Other than the Dawsons' arrests, there was nothing at all about the cartel's people, living or dead. Nothing about the drugs found, type or quantity. Nothing about the cartel dismantling, here or elsewhere. Nada. Zilch. DEA wasn't just withholding information, they were throttling it. I'd gotten more info from Russell, which posed the question of who he'd been talking to.

I switched to yesterday's paper.

Police Commissioner Franklin and Chief Constantine had held a joint press conference Sunday evening. Merle Smith's article did a recap of their information, which turned out to be little more than the basics. *"...sting operation...ambushed by large cartel force... unknown group took out the cartel members...DEA-OPD task force assisted by the heroic employees of Halligan Investigative Services and D'Accio Investigations."*

Some task force, I grumped. My friend's frustration was evident in the rest of the article.

"The authorities continue to remain silent, citing their usual

'on-going investigation' clause. But this, my readers, wasn't just the usual 'drug raid' as they obliquely refer to it. This was a major, major event with a battle unlike Omaha has witnessed before, culminating in the arrest of high-level cartel leadership and seizure of an unprecedented amount of drugs. And that is ALL we're being told when so many questions remain.

"What exactly transpired last Saturday night, what has been learned, and what is being done with the information? Why was the cartel willing to field such a large force in a deliberate attack on law authorities? And who ambushed the ambushers, leaving their bodies scattered like concert litter? Hopefully, those answers will be coming soon."

Merle then provided a formal listing and a condensed bio of our dead. I read those slowly, absorbing the information of their lives in honorary acknowledgement of their deaths. She then closed her article with her own personal message, followed by a quote from the Commissioner's Sunday press dance: *"We extend our condolences to the families of those who died taking down this ruthless drug cartel."*

My mood wasn't so good by the time I finished reading.

<h1 style="text-align:center"><u>Chapter 38</u></h1>

Wednesday started on ranch time. I'd fielded calls from both sets of grandparents before the hospital served breakfast. Such as it was. I left a voice mail on Angie's phone, letting her know I was okay, healing, and going home soon. Then I called Diana. It was socially rude to call before eight o'clock, but I wanted to catch her while still at home. After several minutes of chit-chat, I told her to leave the office closed for the rest of the week. The weather and me recuperating were valid excuses, plus I could now focus my attention on Aaron's case.

I spent the morning mentally reviewing my Rivas notes, which also helped to keep away the recent, unwanted images. A nurse popped in mid-morning to check on me and deliver a wheelchair. I'd asked for a set of crutches. They were undoubtedly concerned about me falling and reopening wounds, but I only needed something to take the weight off my leg. After repeated requests, a disgruntled ward nurse finally brought me a pair.

Shortly before lunch, Tom Tall Elk walked in. There was a bandage on his left cheek and another one on his neck. The street clothes would be hiding more.

"Tom, am I glad to see you," I said, giving him a broad smile. "Although, it looks like you're leaving. How's Max?"

"Doctor is with him now and should be releasing him, too. I was cleared a little bit ago." He ran his gaze over all my bandages. "How bad?"

"Bite," I raised my arm, "claw marks, and a flesh wound through the leg. Nothing like what you and the others sustained. I've heard about Mike and Darlene," I said, my tone shifting into somber.

Tom nodded. I clenched my blanket.

"I didn't expect...I wouldn't have involved—" Tom's scowl stopped me.

"Don't you blame yourself or feel responsible," he snapped. "The decision to help you take out a malignant blight on society was ours. Personally, I was glad that you asked me and none of them, *none of them*," he repeated with a pointed finger, "hesitated when I explained the situation. What went down Saturday was not only unexpected, but frigging *unreasonable*." He was back to scowling. "There had to have been more at stake than a few crates of drugs, especially as clam-mouthed as the authorities are being."

I checked the closed door, then leaned forward and whispered conspiratorially, "A little birdy visited me yesterday." Tom wore a grimly satisfied expression by the time I finished relating Nate's information about the cartel's dismantling. "I'm sure they'll announce everything once its back is broken," I concluded, "but they're trying to net all the rats before they jump ship or burn it down."

"Understood. Okay to pass the info on? Thanks," he added when I nodded.

A dark-haired woman with Ameri-Tribe features entered. The additional *badger aler*t I was getting told me who she had to be before Tom introduced her.

"Curt, this is Sally Swift Hawk, my wife's cousin. Sally, this is Curt D'Accio. You've heard me talk about him."

"Don't believe everything he's said," I joked.

"I don't," she replied, studying me.

"Mike?" Tom asked Sally, a questioning lilt in his voice.

Her face broke into a smile. "He's awake. Doctor Ambrose is with him now."

I understand his fiancée has been visiting him daily. "You're Mike's fiancée?" I reached over and grabbed one of the crutches leaning against my bed and held it out to her.

Puzzled, Sally looked from it to me to Tom and back to me as she took it.

"So you can properly chastise me for getting your menfolk nearly killed," I told her. Tom snorted and took a step back.

"Thank you," she said. Lips twitching, she placed it back with its mate. "But I believe you've beat yourself up enough over that."

A broadly grinning Max pushed the door open, his street clothes signifying he was headed home, too. "Curt, what have you been up to?" he said. "I asked for your room number at the nurse's station and got three scowls."

"Oh, well, I had a bit of disagreement with the staff and kept pressing the 'call' button until it got resolved."

That produced chuckles from the guys and a head shake from Sally. She excused herself to go see about Mike and we talked quietly for about fifteen minutes or so. Mostly about Saturday's near-fiasco and remembering our teammates.

Tom rubbed his chin. "Curt? Those shifters? The ones that saved our butts? Did you arrange…"

I was shaking my head. "No. I was as surprised as everyone

else. A local must have seen what was happening and called their friends and neighbors together." Olaf was a local.

Tom's eyebrows arched slightly while Max's went the opposite direction. Yep, they knew I was holding back info, but neither called me on it. The door swung open and a nurse brought in my lunch tray. She gave me a grumpy look and departed without saying anything. I eyed the offerings: fried chicken, potato salad, green beans, two rolls, a fruit salad, and a chocolate pudding cup.

Max chuckled. "Think they might've put something 'extra' in as retribution?"

"Naw," I replied. "They're too professional." I hope.

Sally returned at that point with upbeat news. Mike had passed his cognitive tests and was showing signs of improvement in all other areas. Time and rest were what was needed now, same as for the rest of us. With that, Tom and Max said their goodbyes and left with Sally, their chauffeur home.

I ate my lunch while watching the noon news. Nothing new there, including the commentators' gripes about the silence on anything pertaining to the Mashazan Cartel or the Tenth Street Battle, as they were calling it. At least that 'raid' misnomer had been upgraded, I mused darkly, clicking the television off. It stopped being that when we were ambushed.

I spent the first part of the afternoon fielding phone calls from friends, business acquaintances, and reporters—even news media from as far as New York. Breaking up a major drug cartel was major news.

Then two OPD Narcotic detectives arrived and I spent the rest of the afternoon being interviewed about pretty much everything for the last two months. Then questioned. And re-questioned. Finally, losing both patience and temper, I scowled at the lead detective. I had crossed paths with more detectives in the last couple of months than in the last couple of years and I was just. Flat. *Tired*. Of their attitudes.

"Listen, Detective Calderoni, I've answered that question twice already—rewording it again isn't going to change my answer. Or any other. Not to mention, the very nature of some of them only make sense if you're looking for—and maybe expecting—collusion between the Chandler family and the Mashazan Cartel."

"We have to examine all aspects of what had been, evidently, a long-term…situation," Calderoni said blandly.

Uh-huh. Score another one for Miss Heiser. "Are you trying to save face from having something this massive going on under your noses?" I said in my coldest voice. Leaning forward, I continued with, "I'm going to terminate this interrogation with an observation that you seem too dense to consider." Both detectives stiffened. "If Russell Chandler had been complicit, he would have delayed adding customs inspections until after the cartel redirected their shipping or, better yet, not instituted it at all. Get out."

Lo and behold, they'd barely stomped out the door than Lieutenant Sinclair pushed it open.

"I see your reputation for pissing off the police remains intact," he observed as he walked in.

"Is OPD trying to salvage their reputation by smearing that of others?" I snapped.

"No," he replied calmly. "Besides all the internal turmoil we're currently experiencing, there's a number of individuals upset that they weren't brought in on our investigation."

"You mean pissed. I would think they'd understand the reason *why* we kept our numbers limited."

"They do." The lieutenant glanced at the closed door.

"However, Detective Calderoni is one of those that wonder why a couple of low-level officers—like Franks and Levi—made the trustworthy-cut and they didn't."

"Well…fine. I can see that," I conceded, "but can't they leave the attitude at the office?" After a moment, I belatedly added, "My condolences on OPD's losses. How are you and the others doing?"

"Healing. Dealing." Sinclair's toneless reply said plenty more.

"Shouldn't you be on medical leave?" I asked, studying him as he lowered himself into the visitor chair. Even a powerful wolverine would need time to heal from the damage he'd taken.

"I refused. OPD could not afford to lose two department heads at this time. I'm on medical restriction and threatened with suspension if I don't follow Chief Constantine's long don't-even-think-about-it list," he said, his tone a bit rueful.

"I'm sure the Chief would have found someone to run Homicide in your plac;e," I teased, grinning at Sinclair's narrow-eyed response. He'd loosened up from the marble statue of our initial acquaintance. Sobering, I asked who was running Narcotics in Larson's place.

"Detective Daniel Calderoni. He's also leading the follow-up of the cartel investigation and raid. I can't be part of it as I was involved."

I glared at the closed door. That made the detective's insinuations even worse. "How is that going?"

"A lot of documenting, interviewing, and tying up loose ends. That unknown second swarm of shifters?" he said, half questioning.

"I had nothing to do with that. I'm still as dumbfounded as everyone else that a group of locals came to our rescue and wiped out the cartel's people." Since that was nothing but the truth, I had no problem meeting and holding Sinclair's gaze. I took his grunt as acceptance.

"There was one cartel survivor. A tranqued Zero perimeter guard," Sinclair corrected.

"Ah. He was down and they left him alone."

"Yes. When the rescue force swarmed in, the other guards made the mistake of trying to fight, even those that were a bit woozy from our darts. Once they slung a claw…" He shrugged.

I swallowed, remembering the torn and bloody forms. Remembered a wounded Sinclair directing the chaos. Remembered an unwounded Sutherland stomping toward me. Which reminded me… "Do you know what happened to my Ruger?"

"You'll have to ask Agent Barlow about it," Sinclair said, his lips twitching. "Last I saw, the jaguar was trotting away with it in her jaws. Nobody tried to stop her."

"You wouldn't happen to know her phone number, would you?" She'd probably return it eventually, but I'd prefer sooner rather than later.

"No, but I do know why Stanford Dawson was willing to amass such a force to keep that shipment." He paused, then said, "Desperation."

"Because…?" I said, willing to bite.

"Those crates and containers were stuffed with drugs. Cocaine and masha mostly. DEA is hesitant to even try and put a value on them."

I was flabbergasted by the thought of how much that could be.

"Their usual method was to rotate drug shipments between companies in their 'network,' which kept things unpredictable. The drugs would be inserted among the legitimate cargo. This time, knowing there wouldn't be another shipment until they had established new operations, they solidly packed every one of 'their' containers with drugs—not a single legit item among them. The plan was to gradually release their stockpile through their current channels while they reorganized, thereby keeping the money rolling in and their customers happy.

"I'm told that, between confiscated documents and prisoner interviews, DEA has provided authorities in several South American countries sufficient intel that they are now happily raiding warehouses and dismantling labs right and left. Mashazan Cartel's South American head and upper management are in jail, under heavy guard and no bond."

"That's great. I'm sure everyone else would like to know that, too," I said a bit tartly.

"There is a press conference being planned for Friday evening. DEA will be providing a high-level outline of what's been found and what's been occurring, here and elsewhere."

"Uh-huh," I said, warned by the lieutenant's flat tone. "What's OPD's participation? You've had a large hand in accomplishing this."

"I understand Commissioner Franklin and Chief Constantine get to show their support by standing behind Agent Sutherland and bobbing their heads in agreement."

"That's it?" I said, outraged. "Agent Sutherland and DEA will be taking primary credit?"

"For now," Sinclair said. "We struck a deal with them, agreeing to keep everything shared in-house until after their PR show, as long as they provided any and all information pertaining to us locally. Names, bank and business accounts, etcetera, which they have.

"However, a memorial and recognition ceremony for the task force members and families is being planned—two weeks from now to give us time to heal. Representatives of both local and national newspapers will be invited. Franklin, Constantine, the mayor and maybe a few others will speak. They will be providing any details DEA will have *inadvertently* overlooked," he said with just a hint of smugness. "You and your friends, of course, are expected to be there."

"Looking forward to it," I told him, feeling a lot more cheerful. Especially if I could get in a few verbal punches toward a certain obnoxious agent. "How has the information you've gained played out?"

"A number of retail businesses have remained closed since Sunday as we filter out who knew about the 'extra' merchandise in their shipments."

"The salespeople probably didn't have a clue," I said, thinking it over.

"None that we've found, so far. Nor most of the managers, either. The affected containers were signed for by special 'handlers,' and taken to Dillman Brother's Depository on Harmon Street— which is now under DEA control. Drug packages were removed and the real orders delivered to the appropriate businesses. The drugs were then repackaged in plain boxes to be sent out to their regional distributors. Anonymously, like to Victor Gleeson, who was the local one."

I nodded, remembering the description of Gleeson's operation. "Rumor has it that you've arrested your traitor."

Sinclair nodded. "Several, in fact. Commissioner Franklin's executive secretary's gambling addiction was being funded by the cartel."

I grimaced. "That's not going to help his reelection."

"A civilian tech admin in IT was being blackmailed with proof that he'd beaten a street prostitute to death in Iowa—which he'll be facing once we've finished with him. Officer Alreca Simmons, a narcotic detective-in-training, was a secret cartel member they were trying to insert. The fact that she passed through the lower ranks undetected has Internal Affairs re-evaluating policies and eyeballing the rest of us. Four ex-Chandler employees have either been arrested or have arrest warrants out for them. One of them was the previous Chandler warehouse manager."

No wonder he was foot-dragging to find a new one.

The lieutenant imparted a few more interesting tidbits before leaving. The remaining afternoon was boring, but my evening sure wasn't. I had a veritable parade of visitors and well-wishers. Nate, Diana, Angie, Sofia, and Merle I had expected. But the Filbrandts? Phyllis Gustin? They were just some of my past clients that popped in or called to check on me. Even my lawyer, Mr. Jetter, stopped in, and Mandy Rivas called from prison. The hospital staff had to finally shoo the last ones out.

I went to sleep surprised, bemused, and gratified.

<h1 style="text-align:center"><u>Chapter 39</u></h1>

Shortly after eleven o'clock Friday morning, I was hobbling my way across the hospital lobby. Between my insistence and the enthusiastic recommendation from the staff, Dr. Patel had, grudgingly, released me. I'm sure she would have liked to observe me longer and for other than actual medical needs, which mainly amounted to stitch and bandage maintenance at this point. Something I had become quite good at.

I had popped in to say goodbye and wish good luck to Mike, so Russell's car was ready and waiting for me at the main entrance. Despite the portico being clear of snow and ice, a sharp-eyed orderly insisted on escorting me out and helping me into the car. I thanked him as he tucked my crutches into the back seat and breathed a sigh of relief as we pulled away.

"I know the feeling," Russell said, shooting me a crooked grin.

I made it home without gaining any new injuries. Russell saw me to my apartment and checked to see if I needed anything. Nope. I had a large bag of bandages from the hospital, plenty of coffee, and could call in food if needed. He updated me about the upcoming meetings on Monday with his lawyer and the Chandler Import board as I prepped the coffee maker. Then Russell floored me by asking me to take Stanford Dawson's vacant board seat.

"I don't want it," I told him, hitting the start button. I desperately needed my high-octane caffeine after two days of the hospital's version. Yet, some thirty minutes later, Russell left with my reluctant agreement to do just that. His calmly laid out argument, which included my part ownership, was underscored by what I'd realized myself these last couple of weeks working with Miss Heiser. Darn it.

I transferred the coffee pot to the table for convenience and sat, carefully stretching my wounded leg out underneath it. Filled my cup and pulled my notebooks to me, determined to spend the rest of the day reviewing my case notes on Agatha Mulligan's murder. Wished I also had the pictures, but they were locked up in my office safe with Macron's useless report.

It had been over a week since I'd actively thought about Aaron's case, so reexamining everything with fresh eyes might—maybe, hopefully—spot something missed previously. Like a solid clue that pointed toward Mulligan's killer. Gail Huntington was still at the top of my list, with her brother a close second. Still…proof. I needed proof. Lieutenant Sinclair and his whole chain of command needed proof.

I flipped my first notebook open, Mandy's confident statement reverberating through my brain. *"My brother may be a thief, but he's not a murderer."*

Hours later, I took a break to watch the DEA's press conference. Yep, Franklin, Constantine, Sinclair, and even Calderoni stood behind Agent Sutherland, their faces wearing a uniform blankness. She introduced herself and ignored everyone else. Sutherland's opening statement was her only concession to them. Barely.

Ripples And Repercussions

"Last Saturday, a task force comprised of federal agents, local law enforcement, and local citizens successfully raided an Omaha warehouse. Numerous cartel soldiers were eliminated in the ensuing fight and a large amount of illegal drugs was confiscated. Information gained from this operation has resulted in the total and complete eradication of the Mashazan Cartel."

I was infuriated on their behalf. Especially as she proceeded to list those results.

The identification and arrests of cartel members, here and overseas.

The impoundment of half a dozen bank accounts, here and overseas.

The shutdown of American distribution points and supply lines.

The destruction of overseas drug labs.

Nothing about DEA's ten years of frustrating ignorance until *locals* became involved. No mention that the raid was primarily planned and executed by *locals*. No recognition that the whole frigging thing would have failed if not for the intervention of *locals*.

I managed to sit through the whole DEA-glorifying production with minimal swearing. Our turn was coming. I couldn't wait for the reporters' questions when… A grin grew slowly as a delightfully perverse idea came to me. Merle Smith had kept her visit to my hospital room as a friend, tamping her reporter side down. That restraint deserved an exclusive.

***

My interview with Merle was aired Sunday evening. It was in the "fireside chat" mode, according to her. We started off with how I had become involved and my teaming up with law enforcement personnel. She asked very specific, pointed questions. I answered in a relaxed, non-aggressive manner but pulled no punches. The problems we ran into, from the lack of cooperation to worrying about informers, local and federal, learning about our plans.

"That's the real reason the task force was so small?" Merle asked. *"What about backup?"*

"Yes, and there wasn't any. We weren't expecting a gang war and I'm sure Agent Sutherland had her reasons to not call them in."

That's what they'd been arguing about in the deli manager's office.

"What about the backup that did arrive? The shifters that came to the rescue?"

"That was a totally unexpected but extremely welcome surprise. However they determined we needed help, I doubt few, if any, of us would have survived if they hadn't shown up."

"DEA hasn't issued any statement about them or those who died," Merle commented.

She'd kept her words neutral. I didn't.

"Considering their opinion of locals, I'm not surprised. Admitting their entire operation was saved by a bunch of locals would require swallowing their arrogant egos first."

<u>Chapter 40</u>

Needless to say, Monday was busy.

Most of the phone calls and emails I received were complimentary, if not downright jovial, and I shrugged off the few that weren't. Like the one that came from Agent Sutherland's office. The guy didn't bother identifying himself, but he had the same level of hostile arrogance. He opened with a "violation of agreement," which I countered with "that was with OPD and only until after your PR farce." That was followed by a rude tirade that contained several not-so-veiled threats.

I let him finish. Then told him, in very clear terms, that I would be filing a stolen weapon report with OPD against Agent Barlow if she didn't return my Ruger. Their office would be listed as the point of liability since she had been working under their aegis when she absconded with it. He hung up before I could mention having witnesses to her appropriation of it.

Hah! That tweaked his nose, not that I'd actually do it. Agent Barlow had been the single positive factor in the whole DEA fiasco. She had fought alongside us and… *"I'm sorry you didn't have more time with such a wonderful sounding person."* Her voice and the compassion it held drifted through my thoughts. We could use more Feds like her.

My conservatorship was legally terminated and I took Diana out to lunch to celebrate. I finished out the day by meeting with Chandler Import's board and I officially became a member. The welcoming smiles and 'about time' comments surprised me. In-between, I made numerous calls myself, trying to find someone, anyone, who knew how to get ahold of Agent Barlow.

Tuesday, I accepted a slew of work from next door. Most were background checks that had accumulated while I was out. But one hesitant request was to verify an alibi. It would require me calling a taxi and hobbling out to talk with the defendant's co-workers. I assured the concerned lawyer I could handle it.

Diana drove me and Agatha Mulligan's case file home that evening. I had accepted her offer to chauffer me to and from work for the remainder of the week, mentally making a note to include a bonus in her next check.

Nate showed up with takeout from *Chicago House*. We dined on spaghetti and calzones before tackling my bandages.

"The woman seems to have just disappeared," I complained as he worked on my side.

"I'm assuming you mean Agent Barlow," he said absently, taping a fresh bandage in place.

"Who else?" I groused. "I'm still waiting for her to return my Ruger. Not sure why she even took it."

"Keep the police from confiscating it, maybe?" Nate offered, examining his handiwork.

"Wouldn't be the first time," I said. "Since I only use it in self-defense, I always get it back. This time was no different."

He shot me a disbelieving look. "Are you serious? It was a

frigging war with numerous casualties, Dice, and your gun was part of it. You *might* have eventually gotten it back, but not any time soon."

I frowned down at the back of Nate's head as he crouched beside me. Was that possible? Had she realized that and protected it for me? OPD had my gun's ballistics on file. Would there be a request to turn it in once everything was processed?

"As for Agent Barlow, she could have decided to keep it as a souvenir," Nate added, starting to peel the bandage off my leg.

"I hope not. And—" I winced, surprised that spot still had hairs left. "I haven't had the chance to thank her for helping me—us at the warehouse."

Nate's gaze shifted to me for a second then returned to my leg. "Hmmm. You using your crutches to walk?"

"When I go out." I shrugged. "Mostly I just limp around the office and the apartment."

"Well, you need to use them more. The wound is a bit puffy and reddish." He poked at it gently. "Don't see any sign of infection… yet. But it needs more care, less weight."

"Fine. But they're awkward to manage."

Nate opened his bag. He pulled out a tube of ointment and began spreading it on my wound. "I'll bring a cane with me tomorrow," he glanced up, "if you agree to use it *all* the time."

"Deal," I grumbled.

❋ ❋ ❋

Thursday evening, Nate drove me to the *Depot*. My first stop was the counter, where I politely requested Boris to open a tab. That got crossed arms and a look of utter disbelief. Then I told him that everyone's drinks were on me until midnight. Considering he'd watched his bar empty out that night, he would know why. He stared at me for a moment longer before nodding and crooking a finger at a waitress. Nate knew why because I'd told him.

Taking two beers with me, I joined Nate in a booth, my cane on the seat beside me. We watched the waitresses move from one table to another, telling patrons the good news and taking orders.

The occasional person came up, thanking me for the drinks, asking how I was doing. Chuckled over my interview, which apparently had been a big hit among the *Despo* crowd. I spotted Olaf at a nearby table, partially hidden in the shadows. I mouthed *thank you*; he raised his glass. Angie didn't show until almost nine o'clock.

"Didn't know if you'd be here," she said, sliding in next to me.

"Brought my own doctor." I nodded toward Nate, who rolled his eyes.

"By the way," she said casually, "I ordered a pitcher of White Top and three glasses. Frank said everything was on the house till midnight. Thanks."

Angie, being a fellow *Despo* and a street denizen, would know the why and probably most of who had participated.

"Frank?" Nate asked, sounding confused. "I though the bartender's name was Boris."

"He's a mystery man," I said. "No one knows what his real name is. We all just call him what feels right. To me, he's Boris the bear. Marge had called him Hugh for his size."

Nate looked toward the bar, then back. His "I'll go with Boris" had both Angie and me laughing.

Sonja, according to her nametag, deposited the beer and left. I poured us all a glass and Angie asked how Aaron's case was coming.

"Not well," I admitted. "I've been going over my notes and the police file in the evenings." And sometimes way into the night. "I still can't find any definitive clue that says 'aha, you're it'."

"But you have narrowed it down," Nate said, being supportive.

"More or less," I agreed. "But 'most likely' and 'could have' won't get Aaron Rivas a new trial."

We sipped beer, laughed, and bantered as the clock slowly ticked toward midnight.

***

My Friday started off with a good mood. I hadn't realized just how badly I'd needed that simple, relaxing time with friends. I had gone straight to bed last night, no reviewing of notes, nothing dealing with a case. It didn't take long to finish the last background report, then I hit Aaron's case with fresh energy.

Diana walked in with a sheaf of papers. "Detective Macron popped in, left these for you. Said she hoped it would help."

Really? "She still haute couture?"

"Yes, but her attitude was boutique," Diana commented before returning to her desk.

I had to puzzle that one out, not well versed in female nomenclature, then focused on the papers. Didn't take but a minute to let out a low whistle. I was holding a detailed, in-depth background review of everyone attached to Agatha Mulligan's murder case, including both full and part-time staff. Information accessible to police that I'd be hard-pressed to dig out, if at all, like stuff from expensive private schools. Lieutenant Sinclair had said Detective Macron wanted to make amends and, boy, had she.

I did a quick scan on my least-likely suspects: the Bristols, Warren Decker and his son, Terrance. Found nothing surprising or that would make me move them higher on the list. I settled back and focused on the others.

Gail Huntington's penchant for screaming and throwing was fully developed by seventh grade, as evidenced by the number of high school incidents that had gotten her 'excused' for several days. Guess 'suspension' wouldn't look good on future resumes or society pages. There were an abundance of teachers' notes where words like "undisciplined, uncooperative, and spiteful" figured prominently. Nope, she hadn't changed a bit.

Reading between the lines, Corwin Huntington had been an asshole, but evidently no more so than their average privileged students. Until the tenth grade. He went claws-out in the middle of gym class on another male student. Corwin spent the last five weeks of the school year on 'home study.' Another face saver. Also, according to Macron's notes, his grandmother paid the other boy's medical bills and wrote a large check to his parents to keep the incident out of the courts and news media.

Hmmm. Louise Burnsworth had described Corwin as controlled and self-contained. That type tended to explode spectacularly when they lost it. So…maybe I shouldn't focus so much on his sister?

Those last two thoughts were reinforced by the time I finished reading the report on Jadine Decker. Merle had mentioned fights during Jadine's high school years, though nothing serious or that had gotten her 'excused.' However, during her second year at Kansas State, she was involved in two really nasty ones—one per semester—that had required large keep-it-out-of-court payments. She had transferred to Kearny University during the following summer where she got her historical linguistics degree and a husband—Warren's finance diploma was from there. Was the transfer her decision or the Dean's? Nothing violent on record since.

I tossed Jadine's report on my desktop. My thoughts were doing the same circling as Gertie was doing in her tank. Gail…Corwin… Jadine…Gail…Corwin…Jadine. My gut said it had to be one of them.

I went to feed Gertie. While dashing fish food, I resolved to interview my other two suspects next week. I needed face-to-face impressions. Corwin should be back by then, if not already, and would probably talk to me, if only out of curiosity.

Jadine? That might take some finagling.

Chapter 41

I fidgeted in my seat beside Max Anderson. I'd expected to be down in the main seating, perhaps even in the front row. But here I was, on the stage with others from my 'team.' I hadn't expected to be in the Hilton Conference Center, either. Dismay was a mild description of my feelings when Russell pulled into the parking lot.

Next to Max was Lieutenant Sinclair, then Detectives Brinkman and O'Boyle, with Officer Franks in a wheelchair on the end.

I leaned forward on my cane to speak around Max. "Lieutenant? You said this was for friends and family."

"Originally, yes," he replied dryly. "Plans were upgraded after the Public Relations office was buried under the number of requests."

Levi was the next to arrive, taking the seat beside me.

"Officer Levi, good to see you. Everything going well?"

"I'm doing fine," she replied. "And after the night we had," she patted my leg, "you can call me Lisa."

"Lisa," I acknowledged, ignoring Max's snort. Yes, that phrase usually implied something else. "Means you can call me Curt," I said and added a wide smile.

Tom Tall Elk came out on stage, followed by Sally Swift Hawk wheeling Mike Halligan. Tom sat next to Lisa while Sally parked Mike's chair and took the end seat next to him.

"Hey Boss, when you losing the wheels?" Max asked.

"Next week," Mike replied.

"We'll see what the doctor says," Sally said.

"Next week," Mike repeated, eyeing her resolutely out of his good eye. "Regardless of what he does say."

We laughed when Sally teased him back with "*aarrgh*." With the black eyepatch he was sporting, he'd been getting a fair amount of that. Fortunately, Mike was taking our pirate teasing in the same good-natured vein they were delivered.

Finally, the dignitaries came out from the other side of the stage and lined up behind the podium. Besides Commissioner Franklin and Chief Constantine, there was Governor MacIntosh and Mayor Giard. No wonder they had to move the venue.

After the usual introductions and why-we're-here speeches, they began the award presentations. I learned later that there'd been such a row over who got the honors, they had to split it among them.

Commissioner Franklin gave law enforcement's highest honor, the Medal of Valor, to the OPD survivors. A solemn Chief Constantine awarded the same posthumously to OPD's fallen, which were accepted by family members.

Governor MacIntosh awarded the civilian equivalent to the rest of us. I nearly fell off the seat I had just retaken when Dorothy Stark came out to accept her sister's. No one had mentioned that Darlene had an identical twin. From the exprecessions on my companions' faces, only Mike had known. Wow. Way to keep a secret.

Then Mayor Giard stepped forward.

"I and my entire office wish to thank all the unknown civilians who raced to help on that chaotic night." He stared straight into the reporters' cameras. "You didn't have to. It certainly wasn't your fight. Yet you did, and without expecting—or wanting—recognition. You not only saved them, but the countless lives that would have been ruined if you hadn't. You honor all Nebraskans and make your fellow Omahans proud." Then he gestured to the audience. "Will all those who agree, please stand."

The entire audience didn't just stand, they clapped and whistled. Those of us on the stage joined in as best we could. It lasted almost five minutes, with the cameras panning the room the whole time. Pride filled me. The *Despos* were getting the recognition they deserved, albeit anonymously. At the conclusion, everyone was encouraged to step into the auditorium for refreshments.

The original idea to include a press conference had been scrapped, mainly due to my tell-all interview with Merle. The memorial stayed as it should be: dignified and no politics.

I worked my way through the throng toward the buffet tables. Like with any large gathering, the usual small conversational groups had formed. Friends gossiping, businessmen having an informal meeting, politicians giving impromptu PR statements.

I eyed the group around Jerry Louderback as I passed. One of the tidbits Sinclair had shared was that Stanford Dawson had donated a large sum to his mayoral campaign back in June. While that in itself wasn't condemning—he'd also donated sums to several charities—it could explain the drive behind the blackmail attempt against Kurt Filbrandt. I had spent an entire evening dreaming up a conspiracy where the Mashazan Cartel would be the behind-the-throne power in Omaha through the mayor's office as well as exploiting Chandler Import to its fullest.

I chuckled quietly to myself as I picked up a cup of fruit punch, thinking of the frustrated nights and well-deserved heartburn the Dawsons and their inner circle must have experienced when their plans began unravelling. Russell had broken up with Marissa in July and announced the customs inspections in August. Then I had taken over the company instead of Russell's uncle, whom Stanford Dawson had been stroking in anticipation of him succeeding Russell—one way or another. Last, to top it off, the blackmail scheme fell apart.

I took a sip, turned, and found myself face-to-face with Jadine Decker.

"Mr. D'Accio," she acknowledged formally.

"Mrs. Decker," I returned. "I appreciate you coming. Is your husband here, too?"

"Yes, somewhere in this crowd. May I speak with you for a moment?"

Surprised, wary, I followed her out into the hallway. Apparently, I was about to get my interview. We ended up in an empty room around the corner from the auditorium.

"I'd like to start by offering my congratulations, Mr. D'Accio. You and your friends have done a major service to our city."

"Thank you."

"That said," annoyance crept into her voice, "your insistence on digging into my aunt's murder is doing a disservice to my family."

I took a sip. Waited.

"Warren has told me about your theory. Even if true, I see no way you could prove which of the twins murdered her."

I cocked my head. "Interesting, in that you specified them, when there were seven people in the house. Including, of course, you and your family."

"The twins are hot-tempered, uncouth, narcissist *brats*," she spat out. "Especially Gail. She has been nothing but an embarrass-ment to the family. Both she and her brother hated their grand-mother and the rules she forced them to live by."

I nodded as if in agreement. Then said, "From what I've learned, there was plenty of hate to go around. Agatha Mulligan hated your husband because he was from the Boondocks and, by extension, you and your son."

Her jaw tightened, so I poked some more.

"She ruined Warren's partnership with Matlock and tried to keep Terrance from joining an elite collage fraternity."

"Agatha was determined to be rid of us," Jadine said coldly, her eyes now the gold of her wolf. "She intended to ruin Warren's career, destroying any and all opportunities with his company and any future ones. She sneered—*sneered*—at Terrance's suitability to her socially snobbish friends. She had notified the charities I supported that she would refuse to endorse or donate to them any further unless I was removed from their boards."

I'd have to add those last two items to my notes.

"By making things so miserable for us we'd move out of state, my bitch of an aunt could then pretend we didn't exist. So, yes, we hated her. My cousins hated her," Jadine said in a voice so cold it almost burned. "The killer should be praised, not prosecuted. Her death was a boon to this world."

To your family. "None of that gave anyone the right to beat her to death or frame an innocent man for it," I told her, aware I was alone with an aggressive, possibly murderous, wolf.

"Regardless, *my* family comes first for me. Suspicion will hang over all of us professionally and socially if you succeed in freeing him. You will stop this investigation," she took a step forward, "or I will ensure *your* professional and social life are ruined." She brushed past me and out the door.

Such a civilized wolf. Claws and fangs kept tucked, all the while… I frowned. Something dangled, tantalizingly just out of reach. I mulled it over, *click-clicking* my way back to the auditorium.

Inside, I scanned the crowd for Russell. There he was, talking with Mayor Giard. Jadine was ensconced in a group of well-heeled friends. Her husband was headed in her direction, two cups of fruit punch in his hands. Yes, Jadine was all about family. If she had known—I froze. My eyes tracked Warren, watched him hand a cup to his smiling wife.

"She intended to ruin Warren, destroying any and all opportunities with his company and any future ones."

"I've never told them."

She knew. She had known about Agatha's appointment with Warren's boss. My gaze flicked to Jadine, immediately dropped when I saw her watching me.

"She has excellent control over her wolf…"

…never lost control, not even for one or two vicious swipes.

"No, you do not need to see that."

The scene of how it probably went down coalesced in my mental window. Dropping my cup into a trash bin, I looked around again for Russell, more than ready to leave.

***

I spent all day Sunday typing up a neat, concise report. First, I summarized Agatha Mulligan's antagonistic household. Then I presented my interpretation of the crime scene versus Detective Macron's, included the various bits and pieces I'd uncovered, and why Aaron Rivas couldn't be the killer. I closed with an outline of each family member and their possible motives, if any, without specifically pointing at any one of them.

Would it be enough?

Chapter 42

No, it wasn't frigging enough.

I took it to Lieutenant Sinclair on Monday. He gave it to Chief Constantine, who deferred the decision up the chain to Commissioner Franklin's Office. You would think OPD's leadership would attempt to save face by owning up to a mistake by one of theirs. Nope.

On Wednesday, I got a terse phone call from the head of Franklin's PR office. *"While the police evidence could possibly be considered subpar, it was sufficient for the jury to render their verdict. The Commissioner's office sees no reason to pursue this matter further."* I was also told in no uncertain terms to *"desist in my smear campaign against one of Omaha's upstanding families."*

I had my regular meeting with Angie the next night. She had a booth, a pitcher of beer, and glasses ready by the time I arrived.

"Justice. Where's the justice?" I morosely asked my glass. "The Commissioner is averse to anything that might swamp his re-election boat and Chief Constantine won't go against him and risk his cushy appointment."

Angie licked her lips. "Hang onto it and resubmit again after the election.”

“How’s that going to appear? Deliberately withholding embarrassing evidence until *after* elections?”

“They’ll just say they were looking into it, taking time to reevaluate everything so as to get all the facts straight. Use the extra time searching for more clues yourself, maybe pinpoint the real killer. If you can do that, OPD and the DA will jump on it for sure. Beat their chests about how they stand for that justice you mentioned.”

I already knew the killer’s identity but had no way to prove it.

Use Wolfbane crept into my thoughts.

With no proof of Tabitha’s killer’s crimes to take to the authorities, I had loaded and aimed the professional assassin at Cynthia Chandler like any other weapon. *“I didn’t think you’d appreciate your daughter being murdered any more than your brother.”*

“You knew what coming to me could entail.”

“I want justice.”

Use Wolfbane. As you did before.

No! I beat that insidious temptation down with extreme prejudice. Once had been enough. Gulping a mouthful of beer, I made a decision.

“It’s not fair to Aaron, making him sit another six months or more in prison,” I told Angie. “I’m going to turn over what I have to my lawyer, Mr. Jetter. Have him file, petition, whatever, with the DA’s office.”

Her glass *thunked* hard on the tabletop. “No. Wait until after the election.”

I shook my head and remained silent.

“Don’t do it, Dice,” she urged. “Maybe it’s not fair to Aaron, but he'll survive. You dump this chamber pot now, you'll not just piss off a lot of people, you'll make enemies. Powerful enemies that can—*will*, cause you problems and not just the Mulligan family."

I sipped my beer. Angie's obvious worry for me warmed the cold spot I'd borne all day. She was a good friend. "Possibly," I told her. "But it's the right thing to do."

"Dice," she said, exasperation leaking into her voice, "you—"

She broke off when a guy stopped beside our booth. The cold air coming off his leather jacket indicated he'd just come in.

"You drive a blue Crossfire, right?" he said.

"Yes," I replied warily.

"There's a snowplow beating it into the junkyard," he informed me before giving a nod and moving on.

I grabbed my coat and bolted, Angie hard on my heels. My car was parked one block down from the *Depot's* warehouse. We hit the street in time to see large taillights disappearing around the corner. I slid to a stop in front of a crumpled blue metal mass. The top was smashed down into the seats, the driver's side ripped open. The front wheels were splayed out and the undercarriage was flat on the ground.

"This is a warning," Angie said quietly. "You could have been in it."

"No, it's an entitled brat's hissy-fit," I snarled, my hands curled into fists. My report had undoubtedly been leaked to the Huntington twins, and one of them—probably Gail—had ordered Alex Griffin to do something about me. My car had made for an easy target and he'd tasked one of his sewer rats with it.

***

As soon as the 4-wheel drive Jeep Diana had leased was delivered to the parking lot, I headed out. First up was the police department.

I'd given my statement last night, but was asked to 'stop in' for any further questions. The snowplow had been easy to find: blue paint chips on the blade and a skunked cab. It was void of any fingerprints, including those of the last known operator. City officials were investigating how the keys had been removed from a locked and alarmed building. The witness that alerted me could only attest to a shadowy figure in the darkened cab.

"Do I have any enemies?" I repeated, staring at the young detective who had asked me that. After a moment, he cleared his throat and rephrased to "who was at the top of my list?" Told him I'd have to get back with him.

I left with a copy of the officer's report for my next stop: my insurance agent. Since I was keeping the official police photo, I told her where to find the remains if she needed pictures for the claim. My appointment with Mr. Jetter wasn't until this afternoon, which gave me time to do a few things in the office.

I had Diana make two copies of everything in my Aaron Rivas case folder. One would go into the safe as a spare, as I didn't trust something happening to my primary one. The other was for Mr. Jetter. Amelia Roxy called to personally apologize for my office being bugged by a now unemployed individual who had no problem in taking money for something that appeared innocuous. *"Nothing really important happens in a PI's office"* had been her shrugged justification, according to Mrs. Roxy.

Would she consider death unimportant?

According to the date Mrs. Roxy gave, the bug had been placed the Friday after my appointment as Russell's conservator. Stanford Dawson had moved quickly after the board meeting ended, obviously wanting to monitor me and my activities. He would have gotten an earful from my phone conversations on Monday, the day after my encounter with Cece. He would have learned I knew the photographer's name as I called all those organizations. He would have learned about Filbrandt's hiring of me and his willingness to go to the police. Learned of the blackmail attempt.

Alfred Duninger was dead by midnight.

On Wednesday, he'd have learned how much I had uncovered in my investigation during my interview with Detective Chizek. That had to have contributed to my shooting that same evening. Then there was our meeting concerning the Mashazan Cartel and our plans—past, current, and future.

No, nothing important. I fumed about it all the way up to my appointment with Mr. Jetter.

I started off by giving him a high-level summary of the police case. How Aaron acknowledged the theft attempt but disavowed the accusation of murder. Jetter's reading of the dismal police report produced a two-minute-long disgusted tirade. Then I presented my viewpoint and expertise verbally as well as my written report. By the time I finished detailing all the additional information I'd gathered, he was fully on board.

Mr. Jetter said he'd alert the prison warden he was Aaron Rivas's new lawyer and would arrange to talk with his client as soon as possible. He would have to verify and get official statements of my interviewees' information. The Burnsworths' and possible blood spots on the stairs especially interested him. He also liked my many notes of personal opinion and/or observation, saying it gave him insight into the family dynamics.

As the meeting was closing, I told him I'd been threatened with several defamation lawsuits by the family. I didn't mention my car or the other threats I'd received.

Mr. Jetter snorted. "You didn't create the circumstances—

someone in that house did. You've merely researched and reported *facts*. When the case is reopened, any resulting suspicions or bad vibes are on them as it should have been from the first. However, going forward, I do recommend you refrain from saying anything remotely pertaining to this case. Or toward the family," he added sternly when I started to say something. "Not only could that be construed as defamation by the family, but as prejudicial in this or any ensuing court cases."

Well, that ruined my fun.

"It'll take me about a week or so to pull everything together. I'm not surprised by Commissioner Franklin and Captain Constantine's disinclination to reopen the case. The system does hate to admit to a mistake, especially one as egregious as this one. I'll be filing my amicus brief with the District Attorney," he said with a shark grin.

I left Mr. Jetter's office with the promise of an advance notice before filing his brief. He probably thought it was to prepare for the official fallout, not to mention the media frenzy once this leaked to the press. I could handle those. What I needed to prep for was exposing a killer. And now that I'd pulled the trigger, so to speak, the whole family would be gunning for me.

Speaking of guns, I fumed, where the hell was Agent Barlow and my Ruger?

Turns out, they were waiting for me in my office.

I strode through the door. "Diana, I need to—" Everything screeched to a halt when I spotted Agent Barlow. Watched her rise with liquid grace from a visitor's chair.

"Mr. D'Accio. I hear you've been trying to get in touch with me."

I blinked. "Yes. Yes, I have. You, um, have my gun?"

She walked over to Diana's desk and laid a small gun case on it. Opening it, she drew out my Ruger. Ran her hand along its barrel. "Excellent weapon, Mr. D'Accio; I compliment you." She held it out. "I took the liberty of cleaning it. I hope you don't mind."

"Not at all," I said, accepting it. Flashed a smile. "Thank you for returning it. And for your help at the warehouse."

She inclined her head slightly and closed the case. Zipped her coat and pulled a pair of gloves out of her pocket. "I'm glad to see you've recovered from your injuries," she said, sliding the first one on.

"You too," I replied, watching her work the second one on. "Are you heading back to, to wherever?" I asked. Was there someone waiting?

"Yes. My plane leaves tonight." She picked up the case. Met my gaze for a second. Or three.

I stepped back and opened the door for her. "Then, Agent Barlow, I'll wish you good luck on your next case."

"Same to you, Mr. D'Accio."

I closed the door behind her. Turning, my forehead scrunched at the look of amusement on Diana's face. "What?"

"Nothing, nothing," she replied blandly. "You were saying before being sidetracked?"

I was? "Never mind," I told her crossly and stomped into my office. Sitting at my desk, I examined my gun. Not only had it been cleaned, but she'd oiled and buffed it, too. Popping the cylinder open, I found it prefilled with ammo. Huh.

Retrieving my holster from a drawer, I studied the Ruger for a moment before sliding it in. It was interesting, intriguing even, that Agent Barlow had returned it ready for immediate use. Was it in recognition of my recent escapades? Or anticipation of new ones?

***

Exactly one week later, I got Mr. Jetter's call at 9:27. He would be ruining DA Peterson's weekend later this morning.

"Think they might try to weasel around it?" I asked.

"They can't. We have a witness."

I straightened. "What?"

"I acquired a list of the residents of Aaron's apartment complex at the time of the murder from Coldstream Reality Management. Then sent two interns to interview any of his neighbors that were still there. They found Hiram Walker.

"Mr. Walker, a resident in a first-floor apartment, was staring out his living room window, waiting for a ride, when Aaron Rivas returned home the night of the murder. Mr. Walker noticed his disheveled appearance, which included a ripped shirt. It was obvious the young man had been in a recent fight, but he didn't think anything about it. Nothing new, especially for young males."

"He saw that through the window?"

"The building has entry-way lighting, plus Mr. Walker is a Second-Gen wolf with excellent night vision. To continue, when Mr. Walker's ride to work arrived approximately fifteen minutes later, he left his apartment and exited the building through the same hallway-slash-entrance Aaron used coming in. The only fresh scent in said hallway—it was approximately three-thirty in the morning— he recognized as Aaron Rivas's tiger." Jetter paused. "It was the *only* scent."

I understood immediately. "No blood."

"None, for a man that was supposed to be dripping in it. Nor had he noted any stains on that otherwise ruined shirt."

"Why the hell didn't he come forward?" I said, shocked.

"Mr. Walker and his driving partner are long-haul truckers. By six AM they were on the road to Chicago. From there to St. Louis, then Kansas City, Denver, and finally back to Omaha. It's a regular route for them, taking five to seven days as a rule."

"He was gone when the police interviewed his neighbors." Of all the frigging bad luck.

"Assuming they bothered." I hear his snort. "They certainly didn't follow up with anyone missed on the first pass. Mr. Walker learned Aaron Rivas had been booked for murdering Agatha Mulligan when he returned home. By request of the family, the news media did not describe the crime scene, simply saying she'd fought him before being killed. Mr. Walker assumed that accounted for Aaron's disheveled state and was unaware of the blood discrepancy.

"Mr. Walker was quite appalled to learn he could have prevented Aaron's prison stay. We have a signed affidavit to the aforementioned. He is also more than willing to testify to same on the stand."

"That's…that's…*wow*." I ran a hand through my hair. For want of a little effort, Aaron's life had been turned upside down.

"I know," Mr. Jetter agreed. "Anything further on the real killer?"

"Nothing that I can prove," I hedged.

"Understood. Watch your back." He hung up.

***

The following Thursday, I was about to leave for a couple of interviews when Mr. Jetter and Aaron Rivas walked into my office.

"If there's anything I can do for you—within reason—ask," Aaron said, my hand being pumped more than shook. "I owe you."

"How about no more midnight requisitions," I replied, grinning.

"Hah! Count on it."

Turning to Mr. Jetter, I said, "This was fast. I hadn't seen anything in the news about his case."

"Once the DA's office confirmed everything in my brief, especially Mr. Walker's statement, they couldn't get Mr. Rivas released fast enough. As to the silence," he grinned, "they're trying to figure out the least embarrassing spin on it."

"What now?" I asked.

"Mr. Rivas will be staying in a hotel for the foreseeable future. There's still a number of details that need clearing up concerning his situation, one of which is the breaking and entering charge. It wasn't used at his trial but it's still on record. I'm confident it will be resolved by using his undeserved incarceration as its time-served. In the meantime, the appropriate response—from both of you—is 'no comment' to any question pertaining to anything on, about, or anywhere near the Mulligan case."

"Not a problem," I chuckled. "In fact, I'd prefer my name stay out of it entirely."

Jetter shook his head. "That's not possible, since your investigation is the documented reason that led to this."

I exhaled a wistful sigh. So much for that hope. "I'll tell Diana to batten down the hatches. Aaron? Have you talked with your sister? Does Mandy know you've been cleared?"

A wide grin nearly split Aaron's face. "Yes. She's ecstatic and sends her thanks as well." His expression shifted into somber. "Mandy is in prison because she tried to help me. If I hadn't..." He took a deep breath, released it. "As soon as things get straightened out and find a job, I'll start paying down your bill, which I understand includes Mr. Jetter's services. Mandy said you'd take payments."

"Which means there's no rush," I told him, ignoring Mr. Jetter's knowing smile. He'd probably guessed I had no intention of passing that cost on. "Getting yourself settled and back into the world has priority."

We had a few more minutes of chit-chat, then shook hands and they left. As I began the bundle-up process required for a minus twenty-two windchill, I couldn't help thinking about Aaron and Mandy. About things we had to live with. If one was lucky, they would all be minor.

I wasn't and mine weren't.

***

The news broke on Monday, New Year's Day, courteous of an anonymous tip to the Omaha-Herald. Which wasn't from me, as I informed several irate callers. DA Peterson gave a short, terse press conference the next afternoon. I couldn't help but notice his usual backdrop of OPD personnel was missing. Peterson confirmed Aaron Rivas had been released and his conviction overturned due to new evidence. Agatha Mulligan's murder case was being reopened. He added that the original detective in charge of the investigation had been suspended pending an internal review. Following an abrupt finish, he stalked away from the podium without taking any questions from the clamoring reporters.

I couldn't think of a better way to start the year.

Chapter 43

It was late and I was putting the finishing touches on a report when I heard the bell above the office entrance jingle. Paused for a moment before calling out through the open door, "Sorry, the office is closed."

The lights in the outer office went out.

Seconds later, a heavily bundled up Jadine Decker appeared in the doorway. A thick coat with hood covered most of her, with jeans and heavy boots completing her ensemble. A person would be hard pressed to tell if a man or woman was under that, much less provide any identification. Undoubtedly her intent.

"What can I do for you, Mrs. Decker?"

She pulled her hood back with one gloved hand and a gun from her coat pocket with the other. "I'd say you've already done enough," she said coldly, closing my office door.

I eyed the 22-caliber weapon warily. Small in size, but the damage would be massive as the bullet ricocheted inside my skull.

"Arms on the desk, lean forward," she ordered, her gun pointed unwavering at me.

I complied, saying nothing as she came around the desk and

carefully pulled my gun from its holster. Backing back around, she dropped it onto a client chair. "You knew it was me. I saw it in your eyes, there at the Conference Center. How?"

I crossed my arms and leaned back in my chair. "Agatha Mulligan's appointment with Mr. Monjaraz. You knew about it despite Warren not having told anyone."

Her cheek twitched. "I'll have to remember that."

"You also didn't want your son to 'see that' when you hadn't, supposedly, seen Mrs. Mulligan's remains yet." Got another cheek twitch. "So," I said, stalling for time, "how long have you been planning this?" It'd been almost a month since the bombshell news had dropped. "Nondescript, loose clothing for any street cameras. A common weapon anyone can get. And it's Friday, so any scents will be faded, too old to be useful by the time my body is found on Monday."

She smirked. "Especially if there's an open window." Her expression and voice both hardened. "I warned you. Told you to stop investigating."

"I did what the police should have done back at the beginning, regardless of the inconvenience," I said, keeping my tone nonconfrontational.

"Inconvenience?" Her jaw flexed. "An account that Warren was supposed to take on was suddenly switched to another," she spat out. "Terrance came home with a black eye—he won't tell me what the fight was about but we can surmise, can't we. My name has been removed from the Omaha Children's Charity website and I've been asked, discreetly of course, by several members to step down from the board. Although they're more than happy for my continuing, but silent, patronage and funding," she snarked.

I shrugged. "How are things for the twins? A few less party

invites?"

"Don't know, don't care," she snapped. "My family has become social pariahs and it's all your fault."

"No, it isn't," I said, my regret unfeigned. "You could have easily moved to any city in any state that had the jobs, charities, and social scene that suited you. You could have built your lives away from Agatha Mulligan and her bitter manipulation. Now Warren and Terrance will always be known as whose wife-slash-mother committed a brutal murder."

"No, they won't. Rumors and suspicions can be overlooked. Redirected."

"Throwing Cousin Gail in front of the train?" I said, amused.

"That disgusting brat is as much an embarrassment as her mother was," Jadine sneered. "Saving my family is the only fitting use for her. Agatha's whole side of the family is a waste and have more than earned their demise."

"Earned their demise?" I echoed, rocked by a sudden suspicion. The overdose. The hit-and-run. "Why?" I carefully asked.

"Why?" Her wolf glared out at me. "Because her son was a bully who enjoyed forcing himself on young females. Her daughter was a rutting pig, even going after men who had the integrity to tell her *no*."

Jadine had been assaulted and her husband targeted by a nymphomaniac. Her and her wolf's aggressive instincts had melded together into a protective killer. To anyone who threatened her family, like Agatha Mulligan. Like me.

I slowly shook my head. "Out of curiosity, when did you learn about Agatha's appointment with Mr. Monjaraz? Even Warren didn't know about it until after her death."

Silence. Would she admit it?

"That night, after the thief escaped out the window," Jadine finally said. "She was raving. About how she was going to ruin Warren. About how she'd make sure he would never get another job in Nebraska. About how she'd see him charged for the theft since Warren had obviously given the house security code to a fellow *Boondock scum*. I couldn't take any more. I picked up the statue and beat that miserable excuse for a human out of existence."

"Then proceeded to frame an innocent man."

"Innocent?" she snorted. "He's a thief. A nobody that would've ended up in prison for something."

"That makes you as arrogant and elitist as your aunt was." Her lips compressed into a tight line. "Pulling that trigger won't solve your problems."

"No," she snapped, pointing the gun barrel at my head. "But it will be satisfying."

I'd run out of time. I braced myself—then the bell jangled.

Her eyes flashed toward the front office, then back toward me. I didn't move, simply said, "Put the gun down, Jadine."

The door flew open, the doorway prudently empty for several seconds. When no shots were fired, two men materialized in the opening. It was Olaf and Jeremy, a Second-Gen grizzly bear.

I had set my trap weeks ago, having anticipated Jadine's retaliation. I had rented a portable alert kit from Swenson Security and hired several of my fellow *Despos*. The PAK's transmitter was in my desk's top drawer; the receiver was in a small office I had leased where the shifters waited. None of us had been happy that the closest one available was two blocks down the street. Then I had worked late almost every night, partially due to increased business, partially waiting for the inevitable. The office lights going out had told me it wasn't another late-working lawyer stopping in.

Jadine backed away, her gun wavering between me and the men giving her cold stares.

"Right now, you're looking at life imprisonment," I said, my voice flat, expressionless, "because your lawyer will call Mrs. Mulligan's murder a crime of 'overwhelming passion.' Premediated murder will get you the death penalty." I suppose they could try for a temporary insanity plea, despite no evidence of a killing frenzy. Highly doubtful, though, with two witnesses. That pistol wouldn't be more than an irritant to them, especially Jeremy.

Emotions flashed across her face: anger, frustration, disbelief, and, finally, defeat. Her arm dropped. Jeremy walked over and took her gun from her. Laying it on my desktop, he handed me mine.

I used my office phone to call the police, then turned off the recorder hidden in my in-basket. I had turned it on with my right hand while my left pressed the alert button. Worst case? They'd know who killed me. No way could a defense lawyer argue the tape was biased, like they'd probably try with my shifter friends.

Studying the woman sitting ramrod stiff in a chair, hands clenched, her face void of any emotion, I felt sympathy for her family. For me, it was over. Case closed and a murderer caught. For Warren and Terrance Decker, it never would be.

***

Hours later, I sat in my living room, an undercounter kitchen light providing the only illumination. A soul-deep weariness filled me as I stared into the darkness, replaying the events of the past few months. From my hiring by Mandy Rivas to the complete desolation on Warren Decker's face as he listened to the taped proof of his wife's crimes at the police station.

Thought of the lives irreparably changed by one man's decision.

Steal a painting? No problem.

Two years in prison for Aaron. Grand-theft and prison for Mandy. Agatha Mulligan dead. The Decker family torn apart: one incarcerated, the others devastated.

Events shaped by choices; choices shaped by events. Lives shaped by both.

My birth as a Zero-Plus was a natural culmination from generations of DNA blending. Yet, the advantages it provides has been the framework around which my life has entwined. If I had died with my parents, I wouldn't have become a private investigator, which led me to tracking down and falling in love with a wandering heiress. If I had died with Tabitha, her killer would have remained unpunished, and I would not have become a vigilante.

Cynthia Chandler's choice to hide her daughter's true parentage impacted an untold number of lives. The repercussions from that single, decades-old decision are still rippling through lives today. Mine. Russell's. Ray's, and even Merle's. How many more lives will be affected before they peter out? How long before the pond's surface once again smooths out?

Aaarg. I scrubbed my face with both hands. Too much thinking. Pushing up out of my chair, I headed for a hot shower and a lonely bed.

<u>Epilogue</u>

The clouds hung low, still fat with rain despite having filled the ditches over the past two days. For now, it wasn't much more than a mist that tried to soak my coat. It was having more success with my hair as I wound my way slowly through the cemetery's paths. Reaching my destination, I saw that, once again, I was the last one. Two bouquets of flowers leaned against her headstone. Ray and Russell.

Adding mine to the grouping, I briefly wondered which of them had left flowers on Marge's grave. I'd gone down to Plattsmouth back in June and found a small but gorgeous bouquet slowly wilting. Russell hadn't mentioned it and I rarely saw Ray. It was a nice gesture toward my spirit-sister. I should ask so I could thank them.

I ran my hand across the marble top, felt the familiar pain settle in my chest. "Hello, Tabitha. It's been another year without you. This year has been…interesting." To say the least.

"Russell has made some great changes to the company and it's growing, both in visibility and value. And, surprise, I've been a board member for months now. Unfortunately, that means there are social functions I can't duck out of." My new status had also put me on several ambitious females' dartboards, all hoping to hit the bullseye. "But I'm dealing, and Russell and I are getting along pretty well now. He's been dating off and on since—oh, I haven't told you about the Dawsons."

I kept the telling short and simple. How the Dawsons were crooks and wanted to take over Chandler Import to further their drug empire. How their tentacles had reached as high as a DEA Deputy Director. How they were finally taken down. "That flood of local shifters saving our butts has become a local legend. They're calling them the Fang Brigade." It had also become a point of pride for many of my fellow *Despos*, as well as their secret. I had sensed a change in the bar's atmosphere since. A little less despondent; a little more…charged?

Which reminded me…

"A nasty loan-shark with a theft-ring sideline got taken off the streets. Ran across Clayton Tallon in one of my investigations. Angie, along with a couple of other *Despos,* worked a combination trap-con on him that finally gave the police the evidence needed to arrest him."

Detective Chizek, to be precise. I made sure of that after learning she held herself responsible for the deaths of a man's wife and daughter. She was the one that had pressured him to testify against Tallon. Even better, both Mandy Rivas and Dave Smithers had their sentences commuted to time served in return for their additional testimony against Tallon.

"Besides playing spy, Angie is busy getting her new business up and running. She finally decided on a combination of retail and ice cream shop. She's calling it *Happy Memories*. The retail side will sell gift and special event items: cards, balloons, stuffed animals—things that can make happy memories. And it's a rare person who doesn't love ice cream.

"It's in honor of her sister. Especially the stuffed animals. Her sister loved them and her favorites were buried with her. Janet, her sister, had been in a long-term home for several years, brain-dead from a fall. She passed away earlier this year."

It had been a nice funeral. Many of the home's staff had attended, along with Angie's friends and neighbors. Nate and, surprising me, Russell had attended. Russell had simply said he was there to support me as I supported my friend. My brother-in-law had changed over the past year. His near-death experience was partially to blame, but I believed the on-going conflict with the Chandlers has more to do with it. Darrell and Trace had faded into the background after last year's turmoil, but we both knew they were watching, waiting for any chance to strike.

What else?

"My business has also been growing and I'm going to ask Thomas Tall Elk to partner with me. He likes working for Mike, so…that's a maybe. Omaha's election this past May was kind of dramatic. Police Commissioner Franklin won his re-election by only a double handful of votes. Literally. They recounted *five* times before it was conceded. The new mayor, Kurt Filbrandt, won in a landslide. I couldn't vote, of course, but I was rooting for him. No, not because of the name," I chuckled, "but because he is a really honorable guy. He refused to back down when one of his opponents tried to smear him."

Documentation buried in Dawson's financial records had finally linked Jerry Louderback to Alfred Duninger. He had withdrawn from both the mayoral race and the state. He'd not only fled in disgrace, but under a cloud of suspicion about his connection to Alfred Duninger's murder. I had a sneaky feeling that off-the-wall conspiracy I'd concocted had been fairly close to truth.

The soft lights along the walkways glowed brighter. Darkness was falling fast under these clouds. As if in an effort to hurry me along, the mist was turning into a steady drizzle.

"I'm changing, Tabitha," I quietly told the name chiseled into marble. "Becoming more Gen-like. Perhaps…more." My senses, my awareness, had all sharpened, and that bone repair, permanent or not, lurked in the background. "But I'm still me."

I ran my hand across her headstone in a final caress. "And I still remember you," I whispered, before walking away into the dark.

<u>*Acknowledgements*</u>

I would like to thank the many members of my extended family that have provided advice and/or answered questions on everything from the intricate workings of city government to weapons to medical procedures. A special *Thank You* to proofreaders, Jack and Tara.

Titles by R. D. Chapman

Blurring Reality Series
Shattered Reality

Blurring Reality

Tangled Reality

Reality Kicked

D'Accio Investigations Series
At Any Cost

Ripples And Repercussions

Nature's Daughter Adventure Series
Nature's Daughter

About the Author

R. D. Chapman has been an avid reader all her life. A retired empty-nester living quietly in Nebraska with her husband, she draws on a lifetime of experience ranging from cook to software developer to craft characters and stories. She writes in a blend of SF&F, urban fantasy, and mystery with a smidgen of humor and romance. When not writing, she loves spending time with the three Rs: Reading, cRocheting, and Relaxing.

* * * * *

Thank you for reading *Ripples And Repercussions*. If you have enjoyed this book, please consider leaving a review, as they are essential to expanding my sales and readership. Even a few simple lines will help. Thanks!